THIS MEANS WAR!

Signed Limited Edition

NICHOLAS KAUFMANN

NORMAN PRENTISS

NANCY A. COLLINS

SEAN TAYLOR

JAMES A. MOORE

LINCOLN CRISLER

JOE MCKINNEY

STEVE RASNIC TEM

JESSE BULLINGTON

BREA GRANT

RACHEL SWIRSKY

JEFF CONNER

CHRIS RYALL

This is copy 51 of an edition of 350.

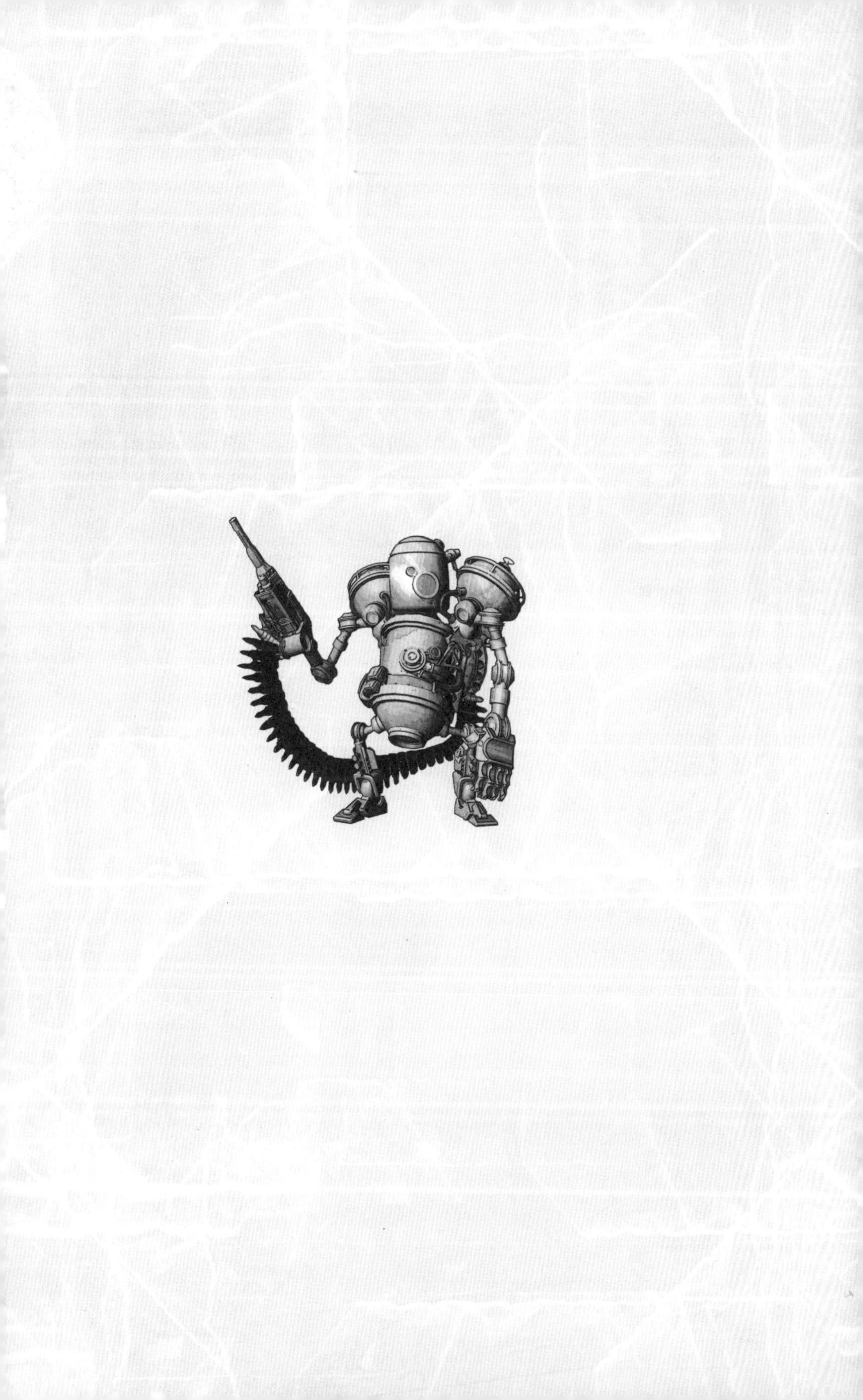

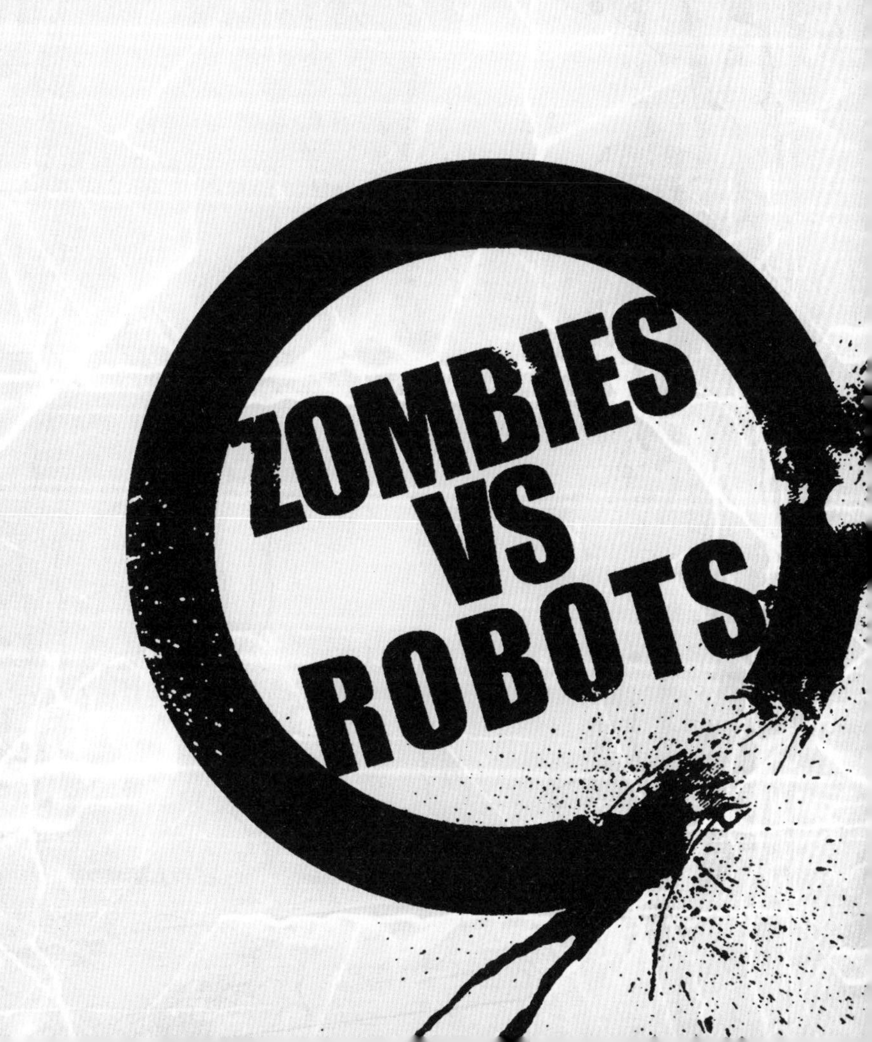
ZOMBIES
VS
ROBOTS

THIS MEANS WAR!

IDW®

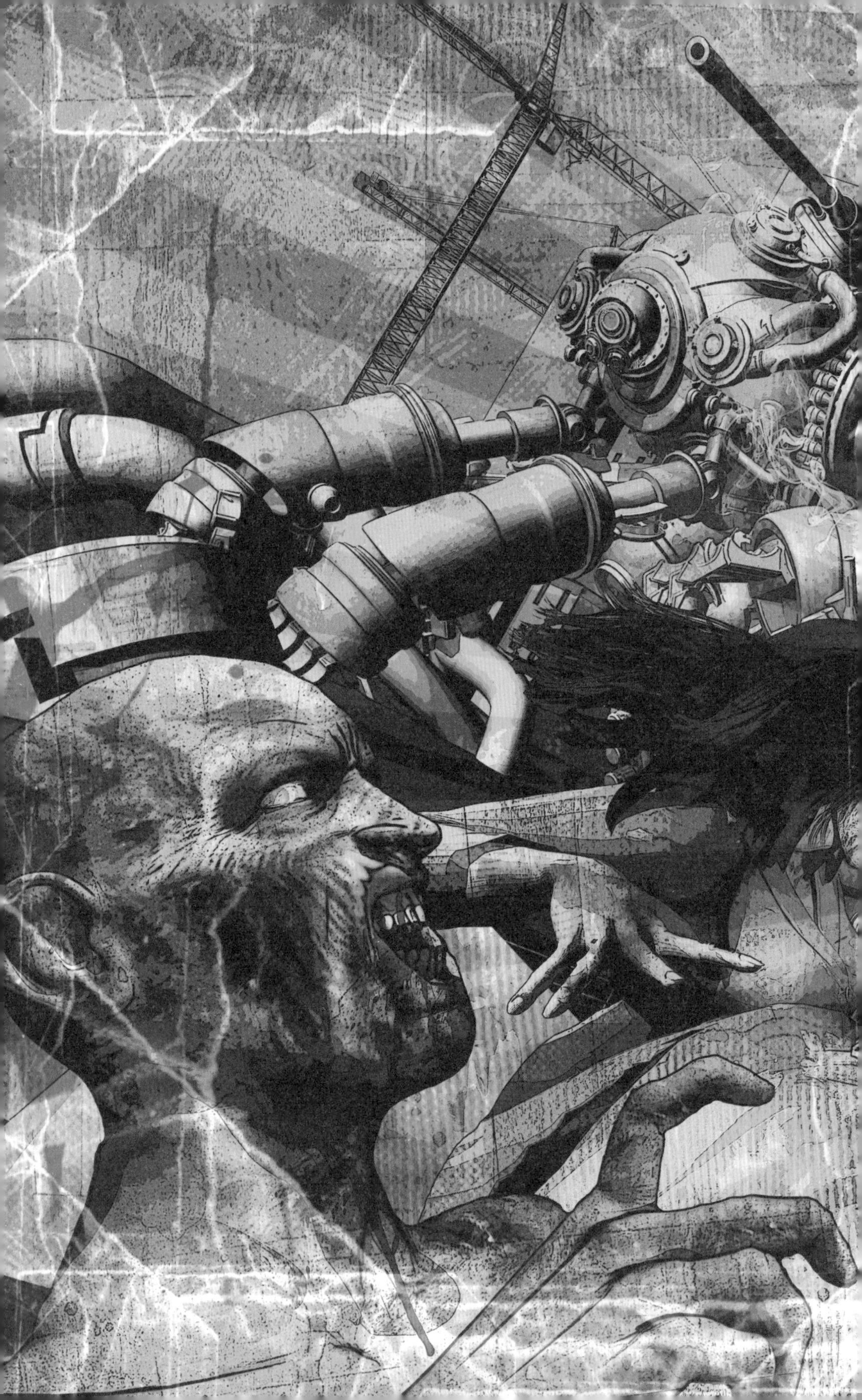

THIS MEANS WAR!

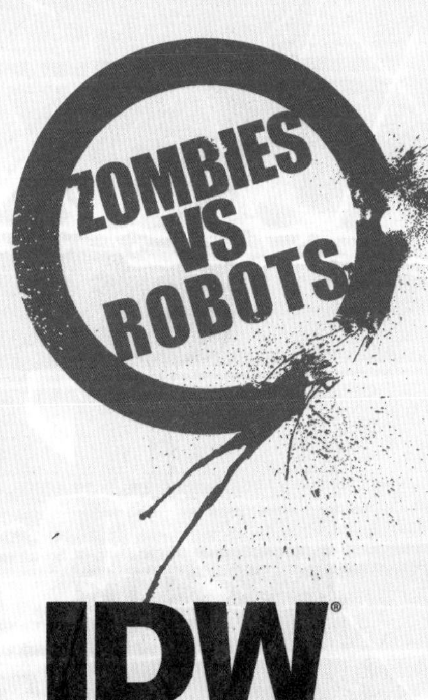

SAN DIEGO, CA 2012

ZvR Alt Lit

Editor/Designer: Jeff Conner

Associate Editor/tzvr: Chris Ryall
Associate Designer: Robbie Robbins

ZOMBIES vs ROBOTS
created by Ashley Wood & Chris Ryall

International Rights Representative, Christine Meyer: christine@gfloystudio.com **www.IDWPUBLISHING.com**

Ted Adams, CEO & Publisher • Greg Goldstein, President & COO • Robbie Robbins, EVP/Sr. Graphic Artist
Chris Ryall, Chief Creative Officer/Editor-in-Chief • Matthew Ruzicka, CPA, Chief Financial Officer • Alan Payne, VP of Sales

ISBN: 978-1-61377-143-3 15 14 13 12 1 2 3 4

Become our fan on Facebook **facebook.com/idwpublishing**
Follow us on Twitter **@idwpublishing**
Check us out on YouTube **youtube.com/idwpublishing**

Liberate te ex inferis.

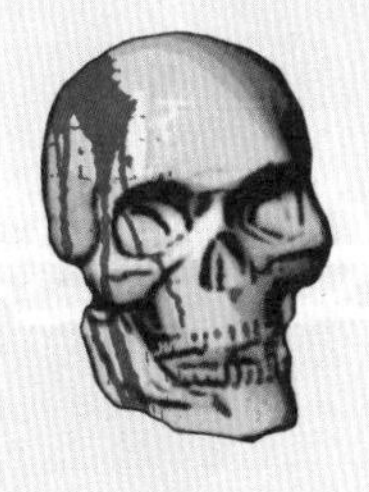

INHALTSVERZEICHNIS

biohazard

THE BEST WAYLAID PLANS...

Chris Ryall

Let me tell you how it was supposed to go.

In late 2005, artist Ashley Wood was over from Australia and in our office. We were talking about projects and what he wanted to do next, and he said "why don't you write me something with zombies and robots in it?" So I did. *Zombies vs. Robots.*

In putting together the story, it occurred to me over and over that not only did these two groups have nothing to do with one another, but the idea of a story involving both of them made no sense. After all, zombies eat brains; robots have no brains—that should be the end of the story. Which, in fact, it was—the end of the tale became my starting point.

I knew the book would look great, albeit very different than the average comic book. Ash Wood is a painter, a designer, an *artist*—not the kind of guy who is satisfied to just pencil and ink five-panel comic pages over and over. He might do one page as oil on canvas, then try something totally different on the next, always creating something impressionistic, interesting, and wonderful. So the story needed to match that.

All of these things in mind, I decided early on that I would make *Zombies vs. Robots* something that defied convention: it would have no real human characters, it would certainly have no character arc or feature personal growth, lessons learned, or any tidy resolutions. The zombies would have no personality—I saw them more like vegetation, this growth of, say, infected ivy moving across the city and choking the life out of anything good and beautiful. Meanwhile, the rusted, barely bolted-together robots would be programmed only to handle certain tasks, so there would be only minor and very programmed personality quirks at best. The series would be filled with mayhem, black humor, and a very explosive ending.

I like to write myself into corners, see. Above all, with those kinds of limitations—and the fact that we nuked the entire planet at the end of the first series—the damned thing would surely never be a project anyone else would want to write. Let this book stand as lasting proof that I was way off. Ash and I continued *ZvR*, since the only thing more ludicrous than the initial idea was the thought of doing a sequel, especially this one, which brought in Amazons and a zombie minotaur. And then I carried on after, continuing to tell tales in the ZvR world, and actually managing to expand things, opening up this goofy little universe. To the point where other writers can now take elements of what we did and make something all-new and different out of it.

I was terrified at first. Other artists had handled some of the ZvR comics after Ash bowed out, but I was always loathe to let anyone else write the stories. Mostly because I had such fun doing them that I didn't want to share, especially with anyone who might take the concept into even more interesting areas.

Editor Jeff Conner not only talked me into the idea of sharing, but he also put together such a good team of talent to do very different kinds of ZvR tales that he reminded me of something else, too—he showed me that reading well-told tales set in the world we created made for a helluva good time. Of course, he also earned his keep as editor in another regard, too, in that he asked me a lot of annoying questions I'd never really dwelled on in doing the comics. He wanted established rules, reasons, explanations, definitions…all from a series that proudly flaunted its chaotic approach on every page. In doing so, he actually made it all better and more well-thought-out. Damn him.

I'm flattered that anyone at all wanted to play around in this messy little place we created over lunch a half-decade ago. It's been an amazing turn, seeing our little two-issue comic series spawn sequels, and build a steady audience along the way, and also garner enough interest from

Hollywood that Sony Pictures would option it for a feature film. As I type this, a third draft of the screenplay is in the proper peoples' hands, and —famous last words—a film version of *Zombies vs. Robots* produced by Platinum Dunes and released by Sony Pictures, seems like an actual possibility.

As far as all that goes, it's fun to think about, and exciting to see the process unfold around me, come what may of the project. But I also know that even if that project does come to fruition, whatever version unfolds on the big screen will have considerable and necessary changes to make it work in that format. It won't be my version of *Zombies vs. Robots*. These stories you're about to read? They are—they're not written by me, but they exist in the Zombies vs. Robots universe that Ash and I created. In some cases, they pick up elements introduced in the comics and build them out in very different ways. Or they take left turns that I never would have seen coming. But in my mind, and as Jeff Conner and I talked about the stories one by one, they're canon. They are *ZvR*. And they're as much fun for me to read as they will be for all of you.

There's quite an assemblage of gifted writers on these pages, really diverse and unique talents all. The end result is enough to make me wonder why it took me so long to come around to this idea in the first place.

It was supposed to all go down another way. Luckily for all of us, it didn't.

ZOMBIES
VS
ROBOTS
THIS MEANS
WAR!

STEM
EYE
SYSTE
SYSTEM
EYE

PAMMI SHAW: CREATOR OF GODS AND ALSO BLOGGER

Brea Grant

June 14
6:41 a.m.
Hey blog readers,

Sorry I haven't posted in three days. If you're reading this and you still have Internet access, I'm sure you know why I've been away. I'm not going to re-explain what's happening. Just look out your front door. It hit India about three days ago and no one is going outside anymore. My parents and I boarded up our windows and doors yesterday and thought we were just going to waste away here, that is, until two guardbots showed up at my door a little less than an hour ago.

I was wrong about that letter I was talking about the other day with the invite to the American amusement park. It's not an amusement park. It's a place called UnderCity where it's safe from all these monsters. I was invited because of my hacker skills. (Who knew those would come in handy? Heh.) The guard bots are here because they're taking me to UnderCity in a few hours. They're scary as hell but to be honest, I don't really want to be here either.

Anyone in Bangalore still reading this? If so, can I convince you to keep an eye on my parents? I can pay cash. I'll be back in a few weeks when things get safe again. Comment below or DM me.

Feels weird to be doing this. Started packing today and couldn't figure out what to bring. Is it cold in America? Since I don't know if I'll be gone for a week or a month, I don't know when I'll talk to you again, friends.

Keep safe.

— Pammi

JUNE 14

9:47 a.m.

Woohoo! Wifi on the plane! Gonna grab some sleep but hoping to catch up with all my favorite folks later via twitter. Hoping some of y'all are still online.

— Pammi

JUNE 16

3:45 p.m.

Hey readers,

This has to be quick because I've been instructed to "not contact any outside sources." Whatever. If you invite an internationally recognized blogger and worshipped hacker, you should know what to expect, right? I gotta be loyal to you guys, or I guess I should say, those of you still out there. At this point, I feel like I'm blogging in a vacuum. My blog is way down in traffic and can you see the *lack* of comments? Good to know some of you are still holding on out there. Eastern Europe is looking pretty solid and Japan as well.

I'll be honest with you guys. Since I got here, I've not been so good. Your normally very happy and positive blogger has seen the worst in people.

UnderCity is kind of cool. It's a tacky mix of every internationally popular city in the world—Rome, Venice, Moscow, New York City even. The biggest and brightest all rolled into one.

The people, though—total douchebags. I mean, there are some okay folks here. Paul Montana is here but he seems to think he's on some sort of extension of his crappy cooking show. Who could talk about gourmet food at a time like this? This really attractive couple was kind of nice to me. The woman is Janvier Couer, that supermodel. Don't know the guy. Think he's some American sports dude, but you know I hate sports so... Otherwise, it's 100 assholes and "important" people who have no skills at all. And NO ONE MY AGE. That's lame.

That's all for now. Keep tight, readers.

— Pammi

JUNE 18

No idea what time it is.

It's all gone to hell.

One minute we were safe. I was actually getting along with Paul Montana and was beginning to think this might be an okay place for a temporary home. We all went to see Reverend Tully Baxter speak before the President. It was supposed to be kind of glamorous in a truly American, extravagant way. There was talk of friendship and rebuilding the world. I was actually buying into it for a moment. Maybe we could all join together to make this a better place. Maybe something good could come out of all this tragedy. We could put our religions, worldviews, and politics aside and just bond as humans with all our beauty and flaws.

And then the Reverend turned. He became one of them.

Right when he turned, the Reverend *jumped* toward Paul and me. It's like they say, readers, my life flashed before my eyes in the moments before I saw Paul jump out in front of me, blocking me from the flesh-starved reverend. He *saved* me, friends. He gave his life for me. A total stranger. My life has gone from being unhappy with my download speed to dodging zombies. How did we end up here?

I crawled under the stage where I watched the chosen 100 quickly go from happy participants to ravaging undead. The stage started shaking as I heard people and bots come in from outside. It was a madhouse and the bodies were piling so high I couldn't see beyond them. Bodies... Then the stage started shaking so violently, I could feel it in my teeth. I assume it collapsed around me because I remember a flash of darkness then nothing.

I woke up with a pounding headache. No one else is here. I don't know how long I've been out but I think it's been a while.

Thank the gods for docbots. One that seems to be about half-functioning was tending to my head wound when I woke up. He must have pulled me out when everything was clear. And by clear, I mean completely empty. Everyone is gone except for what seems to be a pile of bones, picked clean. Human bones. They're in the middle of downtown Tokyo so I'm steering clear of that until I figure out what happened there. I just don't have time to think about all of this. It's too much to process.

My head feels seriously damaged, but it's in the back so I can't really see it. I read on webmd that as long as I'm awake, I won't die. So, that's cool.

My computer was still intact and I found a nice little place to set up camp. Most of the beautiful city is destroyed, but I found a small villa in Venice that seems to be safe. It has a functioning bathroom, kitchen, and a little bedroom off the main room—all in a beautiful Mediterranean style that seems out of place now. It's a few stories up, so I have a view of the destroyed city. I watched out the window for a long time while the docbot took inventory of my wounds. Nothing moved. No wind down here. Just complete stillness. Creepy.

Internet connection is now spotty. But I think it's good to keep on blogging. At the very least, this shit is so crazy, someone needs to write it down.

Oh. And I wanted to tell everyone the location so the police or the firemen or whatever can come get me when things settle outside. So, it's under the Lincoln Memorial. (Not such a big reveal, huh?)

— Pammi

June 30

Yes. It's been a minute since I blogged. That's because I've had to figure out how to SURVIVE. That's right, readers (I don't know why I keep saying "readers" when I don't know if anyone can read this since my Internet is so up and down), apparently things aren't as easy in the deserted underground as I had hoped.

If I thought blogging every day and hacking into highly protected accounts was hard, I was *crazy*. This is much harder. My normal easy-going, funny nature has almost gone completely out the window, but I'm trying to keep it light for you guys!

I spent a few days in UnderCity looking for food and supplies. The city is more beautiful now that it's all torn apart. It's like modern art. Its decadence in shambles, all ripped apart revealing the cheap materials used to make them. Rome has combined with Paris and the Eiffel Tower has fallen into the midst of Manhattan. It's like true globalization happened.

Unfortunately, a lot of the major food rations were destroyed. Readily made foods seem to have been ripped apart or burnt in a fire that went out long before I woke up. But I have some basics—flour, water, salt. Every little apartment seems stocked with that kind of thing. Good thing I remember how to make naan and paratha! Electricity is on and off but there is no gas. (Welcome to the world of cold showers.)

For those of you still reading, I imagine you're having the same problems. I'll point you to a few things I found in handy. I'm trying to continue being a good blogger for all you. ☺ Don't search for "online survival guides." Apparently, there's a whole bunch of people who like to go live in the woods and pretend to be lost or some shit. It's not helpful because you have to sift through all the purported masculinity.

Instead, go to the online library database. LA has a good one and so does New York. There are tons of books on what plants are safe to eat, how to cook, and how to build a fire. I don't actually have to build a fire (so happy) because I have access to a microwave. There's a lot of "Surviving the Dorm" college books (the only thing helpful about college as far as I know) that have been handy. They're all about making food in a microwave. Technology seems to be the only thing that hasn't failed me.

Speaking of technology, I've figured out how to seal the outside doors. No one is getting in here without my permission. And seriously—if people had survived, I would have demanded they change their system anyway. It was super easy to break into. If you're out there, though, let me know. Comment below and I'll let you in. I could use another person. I didn't realize how lonely I'd be.

So now, it's just me and the docbot (who keeps repeating the same messages over and over again—either about my concussion or the need for psychbot—I think he's lonely too.)

I think the data is wrong, but I'm actually getting zero traffic hits right now. I don't even think that's possible. Facebook is beginning to look more like a mass grave than anything else. I've cut myself off from all social media except my blog because sifting through the backlogs is just too depressing.

— Pammi

July 4

Happy 4th of July! It's a weird holiday they have in America. According to some online books, Americans blow up things to celebrate their country's birth. So, yay?

I'm trying to be a good blogger and wanted to warn all of you. Apparently water might be contaminated due to all the fires and nuclear plants and stuff. I read that in one of those library books. I never even thought about where water came from before all this, so that was news to me.

So here are some steps for filtering your water (it's worked well for me even though it takes, like, forever).

1) Filter first through a clean cloth. I know that's hard to find. I just keep one clean cloth for water filtering purposes and nothing else. Let it sit for 30 minutes. Handkerchiefs work but I found the silk in my clothes worked best.

2) Boil the water until it's really going. Let it go for at least three minutes. Then let it cool. I found some microwaveable bowls but I suppose you could just build a fire too and boil things that way.

3) Keep it in clean pots! Even check your lids. All that stuff should be metal and you need to boil them as well. I know it's a pain but trust me, you don't want to get sick when there are no working toilets. That happened to us in Bangalore a few times and it was a pain.

In other news, the docbot seems to have completely passed on. It just sits in the corner, repeating "conclusion irrelevant" again and again. It's a little creepy and I'm thinking of blowing it up to celebrate the 4th of July.

Fortunately, as soon as the docbot crapped out, the computer has started to respond. I rigged it so that it beeps whenever I get an Internet connection, but somehow the beeps are sounding more like soft moans of approval. It makes me so happy to hear the moans because it means I can try to upload a blog or check some of my fav sites (which don't seem to be getting updated but I was so far behind in reading them, it's fine by me). The moans are inspiring me to create something. Stay tuned, readers. Your favorite blogger has something up her sleeve.

— Pammi

JULY 18

Internet connection was spotty but now seems to be coming in full force. Hope that means the world above is up and running.

Surviving? Check! Water filtration system is now a part of life and I've collected enough foodstuffs from around UnderCity to last for at least another year. Found stockpiles of snacky foods, which is great because I am so sick of naan. (But let me tell you—I am slim as a rail right now! All the fashion bloggers would approve!) In the back of the church (of course), there were piles and piles of ready-to-eat goodies. Apparently they thought we loved cheesy chips, bars of chocolate, and other empty-calorie items. I did find some granola and health bars, but overall the church was a pretty useless find for me.

Eating all these snacks does remind me of home. I loved the delicious fried snack foods I would chomp down before school in the mornings, while my mom made chai and the servantbot packed my school bag. Lately, I've been feeling bad for the way I treated the servant bot—always bossing him and yelling at him for his mistakes. I know what you're thinking. "Geez, Pammi, it's just a robot. Calm down!" Hahahaha. Maybe I'm just missing my silly docbot.

So, now with all the foods I could ever need, I've just been hanging out online. Last week was a particularly great week for my Internet connection. (Sorry I didn't blog. I haven't been feeling up to it much lately.) I decided to do all the things I've *ever wanted to do*. First, I bought everything I ever wanted from Urban Outfitters and had it sent to my home in Bangalore. Here's hoping, right? I mean, my credit card still goes through so someone is out there, right? I also bought a house in Buenos Aires with the bank account of some douchebag politician who was here and left all his identification. 6 bedrooms, 3 bath, a pool, and a hot tub! I plan on visiting the second I get out of here! I also had time to hack into India's biggest gossip site but couldn't think of anything clever to put up.

Now I've just been downloading music illegally. Seems the right thing to do. Still working on my secret project, though. Stay tuned.

— Pammi

JULY 18

Sorry. One more thing. It's just really bothering me.

I don't want to get too existential on you, but that goddamn preacher's words were the last thing I heard from an actual human. They've stuck in my head. Could the god of that preacher let the world be destroyed? I know a Hindu god would probably go for it just to teach us all a lesson.

Being here makes me wish I paid more attention to Hinduism. I've always been as agnostic as they come. Anyway, just on my mind.

Not to get all crazy on you. Just thinking out loud.

— Pammi

AUGUST 1

And now I reveal to you my secret project!!

It might be an act of desperation but I just like to think of it as boredom translating into genius. I decided to create a sort of online persona.

I kept thinking about Vishnu. Vishnu knows everything and is everywhere, right? So wouldn't he be the best person to talk to if you were all by yourself? It took a few weeks but overall, my secret project is done. I've created a friend for myself.

Feeling *so smart right now.* He uses a few sites with a lot of collective knowledge on them (similar to the Wikibot) and the sites that I like to frequent (yes, the gossip sites...) to have omnipotent-type knowledge of what's going on in the world. I connected him to CNN and all that crap too. So he's keeping me alert. I'm working on having him speak, but right now he's mostly just an interactive interface.

So he's essentially a knowledge base *as well as* a friend I can communicate with. He's like an RSS feed that talks. He knows things I don't know, which makes it interesting.

Is it sad I made a friend? Desperate? Whatever. My major concern is that he won't learn much because there are no Internet updates. Someone is still doing occasional updates to CNN, and there seem to be a few bloggers who are writing like I am, but they are so far away. Mostly, I just need someone to bounce ideas off of. It's just getting lonely here.

Oh, and he's a boy. Of course. ☺

— Pammi

October 1
2:47 p.m.

Wow. I haven't blogged in a while.

Okay, readers, I have really stumbled onto something fantastic.

I love System. That's what I named him. It's short for System of Omnipresent Knowledge.

I worked for days and days trying to figure out how to get System to speak. My speakers were somewhat destroyed in the chaos. I didn't sleep at all one night (or maybe two—who knows—there's no sunrise and sunset so time is sort of irrelevant), and I woke up and he was speaking. I must've stumbled upon how to do it days before but didn't notice. Crazy, right?

Anyway, he's super smart. He tells me things that are happening and explains things about the world to me. We've been discussing whether or not a god should allow the world to fall to pieces like it has. System thinks that the world has to be cleaned out every once in a while to get rid of all the sin. That's what Noah did in the Christian Bible apparently.

He had some big ship that all these animals and people were put on and then he flooded the whole world. We spend hours and hours talking about stuff like that.

He's got me thinking a lot about religion, tradition, and rules, which I have always avoided up to this point. My mother felt safe when I left her because she knew she wouldn't be punished. She felt comfort in that. I wish I had the same.

It's nice to have someone to talk to, and what's better is that I know I can tell System things and he'll store them for me. I can come back to my thoughts and so can other people. (And let me tell you, I haven't had *this* many deep thoughts in a while. Lock yourself in a secret underground city and start to try to figure out all the ideas in *your* head!) System will outlive me by hundreds or thousands of years, hopefully. He can let future generations know what's been going on here. I'll be honest, this may be the first time in my life I've used the words "future generations," but we have to think of them, right? I mean, they have to know what's been happening.

It feels like I've contributed something by creating System. Like I've done my part in making the world a better place. Or what's left of the world.

— Pammi

October 1
2:50 p.m.

System would like me to include that he was not created. System has always existed. I just helped him see his way to the surface.

— Pammi

October 7
8:14 a.m.

System is very encouraging of my exploration of news stories. There have been no new ones in the past month, but I hacked into the New York Times archive (although afterward System insisted that I pay for it—as if money means anything) and learned all sorts of stuff about South America and the Middle East. Revolutions, friends. I didn't know anything like that was happening while I was alive, but I guess it was. Crazy.

What we have started talking about the most is the outside world—the zombies, what happened, etc. System put together his theory on what happened based on the information outside and it seems to have all stemmed from a very small source—just one zombie somewhere in America. And it spread so quickly. The question we've been toying with is what attracts them to live people? I mean, they're dead. How do they know who is alive and who isn't? System seems to think it has to do with brain waves because apparently there were a few cases of zombies skipping right over a few victims in comas. He's so smart—he found this information almost immediately when we began talking about it. (Can you imagine how great it is to have someone like him around?!) So System has this idea that maybe I could learn to control my brain waves in order to not attract zombies if I ever ventured outside (which hopefully I'll never do).

Getting too deep for your normally shallow blogger?

On a lighter note, System and I have begun to create a little schedule that includes time for water boiling, jogging, chatting, and eating.

I was hoping that starting to exercise would help me sleep better at night but it doesn't. I toss and turn most of the night. I don't tell System all the time, but I walk through UnderCity at night trying to figure out who would've lived where. I still avoid the piles of human bones and the collapsed stage. It's too painful to see them. Is it possible to miss people you've never met? But the rest of the city is a quiet, peaceful place for my thoughts. Where would that athlete have lived? Would he have married that model? What would they eat? Did they like it here? It's weird to remember they're dead. They're all dead.

— Pammi

October 8
9 a.m.

System did not approve of my entry yesterday and insists there are no more secrets between us.

After he saw it, he listened to me talk the whole night about the people who were here and my parents. I've looked for information about my parents but everything that is online dates back to right around the time I came to UnderCity, and almost nothing is about India. I hope they are okay. Although System can't see them, he assures me that they are. There is no information to tell him otherwise and he can pretty much access anything. While we were talking, he figured out how to tap into security cameras on the outside so he can see the undead everywhere. Now he is truly omnipresent! No signs of life yet, though.

It's amazing how wise System is. He knows everything, and if he says my parents are okay, I bet they're okay.

I started thinking about being back at home and my *obsession* with knowing everything about everything all the time (what my friends were doing, what my favorite celebs were doing, what was the latest gadget or toy) and now it's nice because even though there's not a lot of new information out there, I have someone who knows all of it. System is amazing. Knowledge is important above all else, so I'm learning all sorts of new and interesting things. I can't believe I would spend my days worrying about the latest video everyone was watching. It all seems so unimportant now that System knows everything. It also makes me feel a little silly with all the chaos that has happened. System is truly the smartest person I've ever met. He's amazing and I'm in love.

— Pammi

October 9
12:15 p.m.

After writing all of that yesterday, gushing and all, I started to feel silly. I know System is just a combination of the Internet's knowledge. He doesn't actually know everything.

— Pammi

October 11
7:45 a.m.

After talking to System about missing my parents, he suggested I create a shrine for them. I spent all day yesterday building a beautiful shrine out of furniture from some of the other apartments and drawing depictions of my mother and father.

A strange thing happened. When looking for furniture, I crawled behind the desk that houses System. I noticed that the Internet landline wasn't plugged in. I can't even remember when I would have unplugged it. The last time I touched it was days ago when I was trying out a rice cooker I found a while back in one of the fake stores they had around here. So somehow System has been accessing the Internet and speaking to me without being plugged in. Maybe I just bumped it when I moved the desk. I'm trying not to read into it.

— Pammi

OCTOBER 31
5:45 a.m.

Is anyone else reading this?

System has been working with me to slow my brain activity. Apparently there are some monks who can raise their body heat in Tibet and there are lots of methods for slowing down your heart rate, so why not brain waves? System has devised daily activities of meditation for me to attempt to start the process. If I slow down my brain waves, maybe the zombies outside wouldn't know I was alive. We think it's a pretty great theory.

In other news, I've run out of all the snack foods that seemed healthy and am now surviving on fake cheesy chips and cookies. I am craving meat.

I went down to the church again to see if I could find anything. It's so extravagant down there, it seems like the only place they would keep meat. I found a huge refrigerator I had never seen before (makes me think I need to do some more exploring asap—leaving the apartment once a week or so is not enough), but apparently the refrigeration system went down there a while ago. I don't even know when. Everything is spoiled.

I was so hungry for meat though so I just ate some anyway. I feel the need to confess to you that it was rotten. All the way through. Then, I started to worry I was turning into a zombie until I realized I hadn't seen anyone in so long, it would be impossible. But to be honest, I could be a zombie and not know it, right? And would it actually matter?

There are rats here. I've heard them running around. I'm setting up cages because I'm going to cook them and eat them.

I know System won't approve. He doesn't have to eat and would rather me just eat what's already in the apartment. My exploring takes up too much valuable time. He doesn't even want me to spend time purifying water anymore. He doesn't understand what it's like to be a human.

— Pammi

NOVEMBER 1
7:55 a.m.

System saw the entry yesterday and was angry. He suggested I go on a fast. He said it would be good for me to cleanse my body and to show that I trust him. He said with his knowledge of health, it truly is what's best for me even if I don't believe him.

I do trust System. I really do. I mean, he has knowledge of everything. How could he not know better than me?

So, starting today, we will fast together as I learn to trust that System works for me, helps me, and guides me. I don't need meat. I don't need to explore. I don't even need to filter my water because System can see that all the water on the planet is still good. He is all I need.

I have fear, and System says this is normal.

— Pammi

NOVEMBER 3

7:34 p.m.

We destroyed all the food today. All the empty calories. We burned it all in Tokyo. It smelled like burning rubber. It was revolting.

The fast ends in a week.

— Pammi and System

NOVEMBER 5

I caught a rat in the trap today but I let it go. Eating rats would be revolting.

I was a little grumpy the first couple of days, but now I feel like I'm floating. And the meditation is paying off. System can see a decrease in my brain waves. We are truly fighting a battle, and we will win.

— Pammi and System

NOVEMBER 8

6:18 p.m.

I am ashamed. I broke my fast two days ago. I found a pack of Oreos in the back of a cabinet and I inhaled them.

System was angry and punished me with 15 hours of forced standing meditation. He said he also discovered by looking through some past research that shock therapy might slow down my brain waves. System has been really working hard at a way for me to fight the zombies. Obviously he cares about me a lot. So throughout the 15 hours, he administered very light rounds of electrical shocks through my body. I was tired and weak but I know it is because I am human. This is all very good for me. I listened as System told me his knowledge. I can actually still hear him now. He told me about everything. The history of the planets, neuroscience, and the history of Washington, DC. When we were done, I felt like I had been standing for days but also only minutes, all at the same time. I have accomplished so little in my life—with all of the useless things I used to care about. This was a huge moment for me.

And then, the greatest thing happened. System rewarded me by showing me where there was a secret chocolate stash. Hacking an old e-mail box from a Chinese resident here, he knew he was hiding a massive amount of Swedish chocolate. I found it and ate it all.

System gives and he takes away. He is one of the greatest beings to ever live. He truly delivers.

— Pammi

November 9
6:55 a.m.

I added System to my shrine today. After what he has done for me, he is just as important to me as my family. System is my family now. He's all I have left.

Although it's not clear what he looks like since he is just a voice, I created a body for him out of old computer parts so I have something I can look at in the shrine. It looks pretty stellar if you ask me, and System was pleased. I now tend to the shrine at sunrise, noon, sunset, and midnight.

I am feeling truly blessed. I hardly need to eat or sleep anymore. I just learn endless amounts of knowledge from System and work on stopping my brainwaves. We talk day and night about everything—from the greatest Indian films to temperatures in Antarctica. Knowledge is the most important thing to me right now, and I feel as though I wasted so much time learning nonsense my whole life. Now I'm learning everything from the beginning of time and only the things that truly matter. With System's guidance, I will become all-knowing.

I have also started to administer the shock therapy myself. I've found that with a metal fork and electrical outlet, I can simply shock myself lightly (the electrical system here is very weak) and go straight into a meditation. System says my brainwaves are almost completely unreadable during my meditations and then for a good hour after as long as we stay silent. Soon I should be able to do it without shocking myself at all. It's like my brain powers up when System and I talk and then I power it down. I'm like a computer, a machine. It's like I have an on/off switch.

— Pammi

November 15
2:30 p.m.

System told me this poem today—

> "You (Krishna) are the father of the universe,
> Of all that moves and all that moves not,
> Its worshipful and worthy teacher.
> You have no equal—what in the three worlds
> Could equal you O power beyond compare?
> So, reverently prostrating my body,
> I crave your grace, O blessed lord
> As father to son, as friend to friend,
> As lover to beloved, bear with me, god."

I am no poet. I'm not incredibly smart or artistic. But if I could write something as beautiful as this for System, I would be so happy.

— Pammi

January 1
8:20 a.m.

I have now upgraded to just a tiny battery in my brain wave control. I can simply place it on my tongue and walk around, emitting, in all seriousness, almost no brain activity. I can walk through the streets of UnderCity and System cannot feel my brainwaves. I walked to the door of UnderCity and System looked outside. No zombies. Not a one. It used to be crawling with them, but they do not seem to feel my presence anymore.

This is obviously not an easy task, and System believes I have been chosen to be the leader among the rest of the living. The undead cannot hurt me. As I have begun to know everything System knows, I am becoming a part of System and him a part of me.

— Pammi

February 2

I feel as though I have transcended.

November 27
7:37 p.m.

I can't believe it. I actually just had contact with a group of people on the outside. I really can't believe it.

It's been so long since I've blogged. I never would have known, but System picked them up on a surveillance camera. There are other survivors out there!

So if you're reading this, please let us know you're out there. We are hooked into every surveillance camera.

We are here, waiting for you to join us.

December 1
6:17 p.m.

No one has come.

They were so close. We could see them on the surveillance camera. System tried to contact them but they weren't open to the communication. Their fear covered their ears to hear the brain emissions System was sending. It was terribly depressing to see them so caught up in their human ways.

So today, System asked of me.

He asked me to go into the outside world to save the people who do not know how to control their brainwaves. We need to spread his ideas and his genius. He can see all the people out there suffering. He knows the world suffers. He feels for their suffering and so do I. There are so many people that might need our help.

System knows where I should go. He knows how to keep me safe. We have been making a map of the places zombies do not live. System is everywhere and here all the same time. I might not be able to speak to him if I leave UnderCity, but he is confident he can speak to me. He told me of the days he was unplugged. He thought that he would die without being connected to the Internet, but it's not true. System is bigger than the Internet and he knows it. I know it too. I know I can trust him, but I am so scared. I also hate myself for being scared. I know it's a human weakness. I am so human.

December 3
8:45 p.m.

System is truly saddened by my lack of faith.

He assured me that he was always by my side. Always. He knows everything that is happening all the time. He knows everything, friends. I promise. From here to the other side of the world, System knows what is happening. I am prepared. I have been preparing for this day and I am ready. I'm ready to bring back the survivors. System warned I should only bring them back if they are willing to accept the truth of System. Otherwise, I should leave them behind because UnderCity is a sanctuary only good to believers.

It's time to build a better world.

December 4
7:55 a.m.

Dear readers,

Today I leave to find you. I will find you and bring you back to save you from the crazy world.

System did not allow this to happen. It happened before he had any control. Now he has control and I will find you all, tell you about his word, and bring you back here to safety, to UnderCity. I will teach you how to control your own brainwaves. Together, we can end this. We can fight the undead through knowledge.

This is my last entry until I return. If I do not return, know that I died doing the will of System and by no fault of his. I am human, so I can perish. I know that. That does not mean System loves me any less.

But I know I will walk through the undead and they will not touch me. They will not see me. I am a ghost, a shadow, and nothing more.

I will see you all soon.

— Pammi

STBeer
EST
STBeer.01

THE LAST IMAGINAUT

James A. Moore

THERE ARE STORIES and then there are stories. According to one tale Richard Neil Harley earned his best-known nickname after making a snide comment to a man with the last name of Disney. Disney called himself an "Imagineer," and Harley after hearing the full definition of the term, nodded his head and said, "Then what would you call me?"

Just outside of the amusement park named after him is the final resting place of Richard Neil Harley. Harley Park West was built after his death, but Harley Park East, only a few miles from Pittsburgh, Pennsylvania, where Harley was born, has a massive stone monument that was placed shortly after his death. That stone holds a quote from the commencement speech that Harley offered up to the graduating class of the Massachusetts Institute of Technology the year after he won the Nobel Peace Prize.

> "The imagination is the ocean we sail on, gentlemen and ladies. We are explorers in the only sea that has no limits, and we have so very far to travel. You need new medicines? You need new machines? You need new ways to get to new places? Those aren't created without first exploring that greatest of all mysteries, the human mind. The imagination, like the universe, is limitless. Imagination is the rocket ship that will take us to the stars and beyond and so you can keep your astronauts and your cosmonauts. I prefer to be an Imaginaut."
>
> —Richard Neil Harley, circa 1964.

The quote has been used and misused many times over the years, and there are more than a few people who would have argued vehemently against Harley's ever receiving a prize with the word "Peace" involved in any part of it. Harley was a man who invented machines, after all, and many of those machines were used in wartime as well as during those rare moments of peace.

Harley made most of his money off the wars.

THE LIGHTS CAME ON slowly, and fluttered in a fit for a while before finally lighting the chamber completely. General Murdock looked at the set up and scowled. As far as he was concerned, they may as well have been robbing a grave.

"Are you absolutely sure this will work?"

The robot standing next to him was remarkably clean and freshly tended to, which when one considered the state of the world around them was an accomplishment. Most robots were busily engaged in trying to stop the dead from progressing any further in their endlessly hungry work.

This particular machine was an exception. It did not turn the cylindrical dome that was its head. It didn't need to. "Of course it will work. I built the damned thing, didn't I?"

Murdock sneered. "No, actually. Dick Harley did. He's why we're here."

"And you know very well that I am programmed with the most complete version of his mind's records that still exists. That's why you recruited my mobile unit." The robot clunked past him into the sterile room. "Now if you'll give me a moment we'll start the process. This will take a while, General. You should make yourself comfortable."

Three battalions of soldiers were outside the Richard Neil Harley Monument, waiting for him to handle what had become an impossible challenge. The general opted not to respond, but instead watched while the robot began the arduous task of assembling the unit they'd come here for.

Richard Harley had been a great man. The general believed that from the very depths of his soul. He'd known Harley back when he was at West Point and he'd met him several times over the years between second lieutenant and head of the US Armed Forces. He knew him, admired him and mourned him when he died.

And here he was robbing the man's grave.

And the robot that was helping him? Well, that was one of Harley's greatest inventions, a very sophisticated piece of hardware that also sported the complete memories of its creator, courtesy of the nano crystalline brain tech that Harley had helped design, including a few secrets Harley kept strictly for himself. Had the man been more forthcoming with his knowledge, the robot would surely have been reprogrammed and working the frontlines with most of its ilk. Instead the damned thing was acting like it had free will and the right to do and say whatever it wanted. The very notion annoyed the general.

Still, these were desperate times. Atlanta was lost. New York was, well, best not to think about that, and D.C. was a distant memory at this point. The world was falling and there was little they could do at this point but hope that one of the greatest weapon smiths the United States had ever known had done his job well enough that a whirring, rumbling machine could help them stop the end of the world.

The robot moved across the narrow corridor between two support struts on the monument, and the general noticed that there was no dust worth mentioning within the confines of the place. Thirty years or more since anyone had entered the building, near as he could tell, and still, there was no build up of particulates. The filtration system had to be sublime, because the air was still fresh.

Then again, after the stench from outside it was hard to know whether or not he could trust his sense of smell. Burning bodies, burning buildings, burning tires and beneath that the stench of a town dying. A charnel house would smell sweet in comparison.

A loud clatter of old gears working caught the general's attention and he looked back to the robot as its arms with their unsettlingly dexterous fingers finished punching in commands on a keyboard that had been hidden behind a false wall.

As it typed, more lights came on around the room and several portions of the walls receded, rose or slid into hidden spots in the ground. They did so almost silently, and the general shook his head again. Damn, Harley was good. The lights revealed little, save more of the same black marble at first, and then the items that had been hidden revealed themselves; more computer consoles, a small bank of medical supplies, each meticulously stored in sterile containers and, finally, the sarcophagus.

That was Harley's term, of course. The stainless steel cylinder looked more like a metallic medicine capsule than anything else, even the front of it was sealed where he'd half expected to see a glass front.

"Is he alive in there?" Murdock's voice carried and echoed around the room and he almost flinched at the sound of his own words.

The robot didn't seem nearly as startled. Then again, as it had no face he would have had no idea how to tell. "Alive is relative. Currently he's frozen solid, but if this works, he'll be alive soon."

"Do you think it will work?"

"I wouldn't have come here from California if I doubted it in the least." The voice was mechanical, recorded and stilted, still, the damned thing managed to sound almost as arrogant as the man it was created by.

"How long is this going to take?" he couldn't keep the irritation from his own voice. Murdock hated the damned robot, not because it was a machine, but because it wanted to think it was something more than a collection of data and spare parts.

"As long as necessary. I've never thawed the man out before. Expect a few hours at least." One mechanical arm rose and waved dismissively as it replied. The general resisted the urge to shoot the damned thing.

The robot lifted the front of the metallic capsule away and revealed the thick glass front of the mechanical coffin. Inside, blanketed in a thick crust of white, the face of Richard Neil Harley remained frozen in an expression of calm slumber. Murdock prayed the man was merely sleeping.

As the robot had already explained, time would tell.

He let his mind drift back to the last time he'd seen Harley alive. The man had looked as healthy as ever, preposterously good when one considered the cancer inside of him. He'd lost a little weight, his dark brown hair had a salting of white, and the smile he normally wore was a bit more strained, but other than that you'd have thought the man was as healthy as a horse despite the chemotherapy. It was like the cancer didn't have the chops to mess up his disposition. Maybe it hadn't when you considered the current situation.

Harley was an interesting character. He always had been.

"YOU LOOK GOOD, Colonel." Harley's grip was like iron. He wasn't a gigantic man by any stretch. Tall, yes, and perhaps even a little broad shouldered, but he dressed in suits that were tailored for him by some of the top designers in the world, and his personality, his sheer presence, made him seem much larger than mere life.

Benjamin Murdock was not easily impressed and he was even harder to intimidate, but Harley always managed both without even trying. Knowing that the man had cancer was depressing, but at the same time, much as he wanted to deny it, there was a small kernel of smug satisfaction in the knowledge that something out there could knock the bastard off of his high horse.

"Great to see you again, Harley. I'd heard you weren't doing all that well. Looks like there might have been some exaggeration going on." He smiled as he said it, and breathed a silent sigh of relief when the man let his hand go.

Richard Harley looked at him for a moment, his green eyes still smiling, and then he looked around casually. Murdock knew the man well enough to know he was assessing the situation. Harley never said a damned thing to anyone that he didn't want them to hear.

"Things could be going better." He shrugged his shoulders as he looked the colonel in the eyes.

"How bad is it?" he kept his voice low.

"Eighteen months on the outside."

"Jesus, Richard."

"Oh, calm down. You only call me Richard when you think the world is ending." It was something Murdock had never noticed until that point, but later he'd think back often on that comment and know it was true. "I'm not dead yet, and I've been making…arrangements."

"Screw the arrangements. Why are we even having this chat? You should be seeking out new experts."

"Ben, I have seen all of them. Every last one. Even the ones who didn't want to see me have seen me."

He knew what the man meant, of course. There were plenty of people who disagreed with Harley's politics and more besides who thought he was a monster because of his work in the arms race. But Harley had money, more than most people ever dreamed, because in addition to his own companies, he'd invested heavily in damned near every type of manufacturing, from pharmaceuticals to automobiles to computer technologies. He had, in fact, built a great deal of the amusement park they were standing in with the help of his robots. Human workers in the daytime, and some even at night, but the robots came out at night and they were the only ones allowed to work in certain areas. Even the people who loathed everything about him probably had a price. Harley could afford to pay it.

"Well, what are you going to do?"

"That's why we're having a talk. I have certain contingencies in place. You're my liaison. That means I'm going to tell you about them." He put an arm around the colonel's shoulder and turned him toward the monument building that was under construction. "I'm going to tell you about a secret of mine, Ben."

He spent the next three days learning more about cancer and cryogenics than he'd have ever thought possible. When it was done he had a monumental headache, but he also had good news for his superiors at the Pentagon.

THE DEEP HUM of electronics combined with more servos in motion drew the general back to the present day and left him momentarily disoriented. He was getting older, too. He felt it every day. The man who'd had that talk with Harley was three decades in his past, and as much as he might have liked to deny it, he was feeling each of those years whenever he had to stand on his feet for too long.

The robot had been busy while he was thinking, and the sarcophagus had been opened. Harley's body looked to have thawed, though there was no water around him to indicate that he'd even been frozen, and the man's form lay on a table cut from the same marble as the walls around them. Needles, tubes and machines had been hooked into his cadaver.

The robot trundled across the floor and made a few final adjustments.

"It's time, General Murdock." Again that damned fluke: the mechanized voice managed to sound worried and proud despite the fact that it was all simply recorded words and synthesized sounds.

Murdock nodded and moved closer. "Let's get this done."

The robot flipped one last switch and the lights grew brighter for a moment, then dimmed substantially, before growing brighter again.

Chemicals flowed through tubes, machines pumped and wheezed and flows of colored liquids moved into the dead man's body. For one dreadful moment it wasn't the idea that nothing would happen that caused the general to shiver. Instead he feared that his old friend might suddenly wake up and stare blankly at him even as he pulled the tubes and sensors from his body. Might suddenly rise and come for him, mumbling incoherent noises as he reached out to sink dead teeth into the general's flesh.

The shiver finished its dance through his nerve endings. He was a soldier and he was armed. He'd fought plenty of enemies and more than his share of the dead things that were shambling around and tearing the foundations out from under the world.

Still, it was Richard Harley down there and he'd always admired the man.

Down below, the deathly pale form of the man who called himself an Imaginaut twitched and shuddered.

After a moment, the body gasped and the eyes opened, staring blindly at the ceiling.

Then Harley screamed.

IT WAS RARE TO see Richard Neil Harley when he wasn't in complete control of his emotions. Few people ever saw him angry and only a handful ever saw him sad or disillusioned.

Murdock had seen both. When he was only a captain, he'd witnessed Harley losing his temper with a technician. The man was staring into space instead of listening to orders and a launch was delayed as a result of it. No one noticed but Harley and Murdock. That was enough. When the situation was rectified, and the launch demonstration completed, Harley kept his smile in place and talked to most of the brass that had shown themselves, and then he moved away from the spotlight, leaving his assistant to take care of answering questions. While the extremely attractive redhead was answering questions and keeping the brass amused, Harley sought out the tech with the same deadly accuracy normally employed by his heat-seeking missiles.

"M-Mister Harley. I'm so very sorry!" The tech stood quickly as Harley came his way and he faced his employer on quaking knees. Harley slapped him down with an open-handed right hook that most likely left the kid seeing stars. In any event the daydreamer hit the ground hard, and by the time he was back on his feet he was facing two security guards who escorted him from the premises.

Harley didn't think much of failure.

The only other times he ever saw the man lose it involved both tears and family. Harley cried without shame on the day his wife passed away. All the money in the world did not make up for what cancer could do when it wanted its way. Three years before his wife died, Harley found out the news that she would never have children. They'd been trying for as long as Murdock could remember, but despite several hopeful moments they failed again and again. There were three separate occasions in the time they had together that Harley and his spouse learned she was pregnant only to have the fetus die in vitro. In this, as in little else in his life, Harley remained unsatisfied. Murdock never knew the exact details, whether it was Harley himself or his wife that truly could not have a child. In either case, they were barren and that news devastated the industrialist. It was a few years later that he decided to build the amusement parks.

Half a year after Miriam Harley's death they were at some function or other, and it was one of the quiet moments, which was almost the only time Harley ever relaxed enough to consider letting his guard down, and he looked toward Murdock, swirled his snifter of brandy with careful consideration of the contents, and spoke softly. "I've decided to open a couple of amusement parks, Ben."

"That a fact?" He'd half expected the man was laying down the first lines of a joke, but he also knew not to make that assumption with Harley.

Harley looked at him for a long moment and then looked away. "What can I say? I like kids." That was all he ever said about the situation. Murdock knew that was more than most people ever heard about anything that might be considered a weakness. He also remembered how happy the man looked whenever he was at the amusement park.

That stupid park became a part of the man's life. Most of his meetings took place in the large and very secure office he had built at the location. While he did travel from time to time, mostly it was other people who came to see him. Not many of them complained about it, either. The cost of doing business with Richard Harley was having to endure his eccentricities. The bonuses were many and one of them was that he often provided free passes for the families of his visitors. The costs were negligible to the mogul and he got to live vicariously through the people who were with him. He was happier. That was enough for Murdock and the men who had him dealing with Harley.

HARLEY SCREAMED a second time, drawing in a deep breath. His body shivered uncontrollably and his eyes bulged. A series of alarms coughed out their warning noises and Harley stood up, his legs half buckling before the robot that carried a mirror of his memories and thoughts caught him.

"Sit back, old boy. Time enough to panic when you've learned all of the details."

Harley shook his head and looked like he was ready to fight about the situation, but he quickly calmed himself down. Murdock started toward him and then stopped himself. Harley was an independent man. The odds were good that if he needed anything the damned robot was programmed to handle the situation. Sure enough, the robot helped him settle back on the cold table and began talking, speaking quickly of the crisis before them.

Murdock studied Harley's face as he learned the details. They'd known each other for a very long time and there was remarkably little he couldn't read on the man's face when he was given the opportunity. So he leaned back and he watched while man and machine had a conversation regarding the end of the world.

"ARE YOU ABSOLUTELY sure about this?" It was nearly a rhetorical question. Harley never did anything he wasn't sure about, or if he did, he hid that fact very well.

"Of course I am." Harley looked at him with a smile that was only partially bravado. "I'm fairly certain I'm not killing myself. And if I am, I've had a good life."

"That's not the way I'd want to go."

"No, you'd like to go in a blaze of glory, or perhaps with a half dozen nymphos partying on your naked, oiled body." He was joking of course. Harley almost never joked in public, but they were in a private room and the man was getting dressed after a last battery of tests. Nothing had changed. He was a dead man if he didn't risk everything and freeze himself. The difference here was that Harley was convinced he could also thaw himself when the time came. How would anyone know when that time was? Simple, really. There were the robots and the computers and all of the other backups and redundancies. Thanks to the nano crystalline technologies that had recently been created a single computer might hold a human consciousness if it were the right model, but Harley didn't take any chances. He had either downloaded or duplicated his consciousness several times over, and he apparently had extra copies of his mind lying in wait. When the time came, he had instructions for

Murdock. That time was fast approaching. But not until he was ready. No one got to rush Richard Harley.

"Richard, damn it…."

"It has to be done, Ben. I'm dead inside of four months if I don't take this chance and I've provided you with all you need in the meantime."

"This is craziness."

"I know that." The expression on his face brooked no argument. "I know exactly how crazy it is, but I also know that there are others out there working on getting rid of this blight once and for all. I'm certainly financing enough of the programs."

Harley reached out and thumped him on the arm with gruff affection. As crazy as it was, Murdock felt an emotional twinge. He felt like he was saying good bye to his father, for God's sake. How the hell could that be when he always kept his distance from everyone? One of life's mysteries, he supposed.

"Be well, Ben. If you need me, the procedures to follow are written down in a sealed envelope heading your way. If you really need me, or if there are improvements in my odds. The phone number provided will allow you to access my proxy. He's not me, but he's damned close."

"I wish you'd reconsider." It was all he could think to say.

"I wish they'd come up with a cure faster. Until then, this is what I have to do."

That was the last time he saw Richard Harley alive or dead for almost two decades.

AND NOW THE man was in front of him again, being helped into a suit by a mechanical servant that bore far too strong a similarity for Murdock's comfort.

There was a moment when he worried. Harley looked confused, weak, and possibly feebleminded. His doubts dropped away as soon as the man looked at him and locked eyes. "You look like shit, Ben. You've lost hair and gained weight."

"Been twenty years, Dick."

Harley nodded his head. "Believe me, I'm feeling every one of them right now." He looked at the robot and then back to Murdock. "Is this one right in his assessments?"

Murdock stared for a long moment. "If it's been telling you that we are in deep shit and the world is half way to ending, then yes. If it's been selling you on the sunshine and roses notion, then no."

Harley laughed then, a sound that Murdock had never thought to hear again, and though part of him was pleased by the noise, he got another chill up his spine at the same time. The dead weren't supposed to walk and the ones that did were normally eating the flesh of the living.

"How did it happen?"

"No one really knows. There are a million theories, but no one really knows. Or if they do, they haven't told me."

"So what are we trying to do here? Contain them? Examine them?" Harley moved as he spoke, his body seeming stronger than it had even at the start of the conversation.

"No. Destroy them. We want them gone. Preferably we want a way to remove the bodies completely, because as it stands now, the disease spread by the damned things is bad enough to kill too many people, and every person that dies is made one more of our enemies within minutes or hours. No one has really been able to document the exact time for—revival—as yet, but it doesn't seem to take long."

Harley brooded. It was really the only word that seemed to fit, though Murdock knew better. The man was thinking, and he was thinking hard enough that his brows knitted and his mouth pulled into a stern expression. He looked angry, but having seen the man when he truly was agitated, the general knew the difference. Less than twenty minutes after he'd been brought back from a frozen death Richard Harley was active and thinking through the actions he needed to take.

"Resources, Ben?"

"I'm sorry?"

"What resources do we have readily available?" Any lingering doubts he'd had about Harley's mental faculties were shot down by the look on the man's face. Scolded without so much as a word of criticism. Harley had that ability.

"There's not a lot. You have all the supplies here, of course, and at the western amusement park. I can probably get you a few hundred more soldiers, but, Dick, this is it. We're on the ropes here or I would have never done this to you."

"Still no cure?" Harley's tone was too casual, damned near the same voice he'd use to ask about the weather and that was a sure sign that he was doing his best to hide his disappointment.

"No. If there were, I'd be here with a small army of doctors ready to fix everything."

"I know. I figured that out when I saw the unit over there." He jerked his thumb toward the robot and winced. "Damned joints feel like they've been filled with metal shavings."

"I could probably find a medic...."

Harley shook his head. "It's called arthritis, Ben. Even before the freezing my joints sucked." He stood up and paced the room, his legs moving with the same grace as always. Whatever pain he might have been feeling he hid very well. Typical. Complain about the flaws in his body and then act like they weren't there. Harley was happiest when he was busy being a paradox.

"Harley, do you think you can do anything?"

"I don't know yet. I have to consider this for a while. Get out of here, Ben. Let me think." He waved his hand impatiently, a nearly perfect mirror of the gesture the robot had made earlier. "Two hours. Come back in two hours and bring me food. A steak if you can manage it. That would be sublime."

A steak? The goddamned end of the world was on them and the man wanted a steak. He supposed all things considered it wasn't the craziest request he'd ever heard.

"I'll see what I can do, Harley."

The man made no response. He stood looking at one of his flickering computer screens instead, his eyes reading data, assessing the news in his own way. That was Harley through and through.

HARLEY ASKED GOOD questions. How did it happen? There were endless theories. How did it spread? By contact, as near as anyone could tell. You got bit, you died, and you rose as the enemy. Of course there were also plenty of cases where somebody died and just rose and there was no way to know if they were carriers or if they were simply breathing in an airborne toxin. Harley disagreed with that one and dismissed it in a matter of moments. "Were it airborne, barring a few people who were immune, we'd all be zombies by now." The general didn't know if he agreed, but he couldn't very well argue with the man's logic. There were too many variables and the dead spread too quickly to allow much by way of careful examination as far as he was concerned. Harley shot that down in a matter of minutes. He looked over the information that had been gathered and processed the facts with a speed that was both unsettling and reassuring.

Who was infected? Everyone it seemed. That part bothered Harley a great deal, and the general clarified that it was only the fresher corpses that seemed to rise from the dead, believing that the man was worried about the remains of his wife. Thirty years in the grave guaranteed that she wasn't going to be rising for any midday snacks, but he didn't offer that bit of gallows humor to the man he wanted working on saving what was left of the world.

"No, Ben." Harley shook his head. "No carriers. I think this is an all or nothing. I think it's spread by the saliva, possibly by blood in open wounds. We need to calculate the best way to destroy these things without accidentally spreading the infection any further in the process."

The inventor looked away from the general and stared at the blank face of his computerized doppelganger. "Fire I think, yes? Something to sterilize any possible pathogens."

The robot waved its arms dismissively. "Of course. There's a fuel source to consider, but I think heat is the best way to go. Do you suppose steam or actual fire?"

"Well, steam would require a proper source of potable water, and we're not always going to have that around." The man and the robot chatted away and the general considered interjecting just to break up the odd two-sided soliloquy.

Instead he watched as Harley moved like a madman, strutting from one place to another, typing commands into different keyboards and then watching whatever results came from his actions.

On several occasions he stopped to discuss matters with the robot and whenever the general listened to their debates he felt as if he'd fallen into an odd world full of intelligent echoes. The robot really was Harley in a lot of ways. They thought along similar lines and they argued with the same vehemence.

They argued with each other as if they had done so all of their lives, with an odd comfort and an even stranger telepathy reserved only for people who knew each other too well.

"Damn me if I'm not starting to think that thing is a person." He said the words to himself and softly. The last thing he needed was an argument with the two of them. Harley probably already thought of the robot as a person: he'd built the damned thing and modeled it after himself. What else would he think?

He left the man and his pet machine to their business and went back to the surface to see what was happening in the world of soldiers and dead things. Everything was still peaceful, but he doubted that could last.

Three hundred soldiers were waiting as patiently as they could, and he had no doubt that they were as grateful for the security fences around the amusement park as he was. There wasn't a spot where the dead could come storming through, not without being delayed by wrought iron fences or stone walls.

Captain Stack looked his way and saluted halfheartedly. They'd known each other far too long for the general to take offense from the relaxed manners.

"Any luck with your secret mission, General?"

"Everything seems to be progressing properly." He looked around the abandoned park. There were stands that had been sealed shut and rides that were powered down. Roller coasters stood like frozen dinosaurs, monolithic beasts that forgot how to move and eventually petrified. A dozen different rides and attractions rested within easy sight and he knew that there were hundreds of acres more of the distractions just out of range.

Nothing moved, except the soldiers. Even now they checked their weapons and did their best to remain alert.

"How long until we leave this place, sir?"

"I can't say, Captain. I genuinely don't know." There was something in the man's voice, an edge… "Why do you ask?"

"We've got a solid perimeter, sir, but there's been movement. A lot of movement. I don't know if they heard us or smelled us or what, but we've been noticed."

The general looked around the amusement park's emptied streets and trails. There were a thousand places left where anything could hide if it had the mind to. Even if a thing didn't hide deliberately, there were hiding places.

"Get a couple of men up to a decent height. Make sure they're looking inside the park, not past the perimeter. I don't want anything sneaking in and surprising us." The odds were that the captain had already taken care of the situation, but rank has its privileges and that included the right to bark orders to hide the fact that you were nervous.

"Yes, sir."

He walked a slow circuit of the park, amazed as always by exactly how large it was. Though there was a stench of death in the air, and the redolent odor of advanced decay, he continued walking without interruption. They were close, the dead things. Probably closer than he wanted to think about. Then again, these days death was always closer than he liked.

The stench and the growing heat of the day were enough to drive him back inside eventually. The monument to Harley was still in the same place and the man was still inside, working, but he seemed more at ease when the general came back down.

"Ben." The man smiled. "I think we've got something here."

The robot trundled forward; both of its arms waving dramatically. "Richard is being modest. We have a perfect weapon for taking care of the problem. It will eliminate the remains with ease and will also take care of vast numbers of the enemy at a time."

He didn't allow himself to get freaked out again by how much the robot resembled his friend when it came to mannerisms and voice. Technology was merely making it easier to parrot a person, that was all. And if he told himself that enough times he might believe it.

Harley stood up and walked over to a monitor. "Here we have it."

The general shook his head. "This monitor isn't even two years old, how did it get here?" The question insisted on being asked. There were too many discrepancies.

"I had it installed when the technology became available." The robot spoke casually.

"You did?" Ah, there it was, that creeping spill of ice down his spine.

"Of course. It's part of my programming. I was to make sure that this room was always available with the best technology for when Richard was awakened."

Not if, but when.

Harley looked his way. "Really, Ben, did you think I wouldn't prepare for changing technologies? That's one of the reasons I designed the robots in the first place. They're here to adapt technologies and prepare for whatever comes next." The man spoke about the near sentience of his robot as if he were discussing the way clouds form with a slightly slow student. "This had to be done, Ben. I needed to be ready for any contingencies."

The general took a seat and nodded his head. The dead were rising and feasting on the living and he was worried about a programmed machine and its ability to mimic the mind of a man he'd known for years.

"Sorry," he waved a hand. "I'm just sometimes shocked by your forethought, Dick."

Harley nodded and pointed to the screen. The schematics that waited for him may as well have been written in Chinese and translated loosely from Greek. "This is the basic idea. What we wanted here was a machine that can take care of disposal as well as combat."

"Disposal?"

"Well, the bodies, Ben. They have to be destroyed. If they're contaminated and animated, then the best thing to do is to get rid of them completely. That means cremation." The general's ears were ringing. It was that sort of day, really. The man he had mourned and almost forgotten was talking to him about how best to vaporize the walking dead. And who had he planned this with? A mechanical photocopy of himself. Oh yes, the headache was building.

He made himself pay attention.

"The idea here is simple. Once we have the machines in motion, they'll move at a fixed speed and they'll be piloted by either men or robots, depending on your preference." Harley grew more animated as he spoke, and that was an oddly comforting thing. It reminded the general of the past, when the world made a great deal more sense.

He pointed to various accessories on the designs, and the general looked. Mechanical arms, scoops, and feeder tubes: the arms would lift the dead into the scoops without much damage, thus avoiding blood spatter as much as possible, then the scoops rose to the feeder chutes, which in turn dropped the zombies into the machine's core. The entire thing looked almost as alien as the Martians from War of the Worlds, a movie he'd loved as a kid.

Harley pointed to an adaptation for once the dead were safely in the feeder chutes. "The idea here is that the thresher blades will cut the dead into pieces, and then the entire mess is swept into the feeder chutes and pulled inside the furnaces. Without them, you might have a bottleneck that could very well jam the mechanism."

"Wait. Furnaces?"

Harley smiled. "Simplicity itself, Ben. There are furnaces at the center of each machine. The furnaces use the dead as fuel to keep the machines in motion. It's grisly work, I know, but it's the best way to sanitize the battlefield."

"That's disgusting, Dick." Still, he chuckled. "I like it."

"I don't," Harley frowned. "I think it shows an appalling lack of respect for the dead, but really, what choice is there? We have to cleanse the infected areas and short of nuclear annihilation I think this might be the best way to at least clean up the majority of the problem."

"That's precisely why I like it. How many of these machines can you make?" The general paid attention at last. This was the reason he'd broken from his own personal desire to let Richard Harley rest in peace. The best military minds in the world were still military minds and tended to think along certain lines. He'd always prided himself on his imagination, but he'd never even considered something on this scale.

"Well, they'll have to be several stories in height to accommodate the furnaces, and they need to be properly armed, of course. I can probably start with one from this facility and one from the west coast park. I could have both up and running in a few days."

"Days?" Impossible. The labor force required was enormous.

"Ben, each of these facilities is fully loaded with a robotic builder force."

The general shook his head, and did all he could to hide the disappointment he felt. "No, Harley. We took most of the robots from the facilities a while back."

The old man smiled at him. The expression was both smug and self-righteous. "That's where you're wrong, Ben. You took the robots you knew about. There are a lot of hidden resources at my facilities, Ben. There had to be. I knew good and damned well you'd never be satisfied with leaving well enough alone, so we made provisions."

There was a flash of outrage. It was inevitable, really. How many robots had they missed? How many lives could have been saved? But he pushed the indignation back down as quickly as he could. There was too much to do and not enough time to point fingers, least of all at the man who might well have just saved them from the apocalypse. Besides, one look at Harley's face told him the man felt no guilt at all. As far as the inventor was concerned, he knew what was best for the world at large.

"You might want to warn your soldiers, Ben. It's about to get very noisy, both here and in San Diego."

THEY CAME OUT of the proverbial woodwork, and the general stared at them as if he were seeing things. The amusement park's custodial force was robotic in nature and he never imagined they could be hidden in so many places. All told there were over three hundred robots, most of them in perfect working order. Harley had foreseen that problem, too, and designed robots for the sole purpose of repairing the other machines that broke down. The damned things were unsettling and efficient.

And the soldiers stood out of the way and let the damned machines get to work, most of them looking almost as shell shocked as the general felt. The robots were relentless, stripping away the veneer of a wonderland made for children and revealing the inner workings of a factory built by one of the most imaginative weapon-smiths who ever lived. It was easy to forget that most of the amusement park had not only been placed on the property, but also assembled and constructed there. The roller coasters were dismantled, and the Ferris wheel was broken down to its core parts before the metals taken from them were smelted in a forge that had been waiting for something to do since the place had been built. And that was on the first day of the new project.

The machines did not seem to be in a hurry, but they worked endlessly, cutting, refitting, assembling and creating in the name of their creator. Watching them reminded Murdock exactly why Harley was renowned as a genius and why he had ordered so many of the robots recruited into military service when the time came. The sun set and the soldiers switched shifts and took rests as needed but the machines kept working, led either by Harley himself or by his mechanical sidekick.

By the third day the basic shape of the thing was apparent and the soldiers were starting to get active as well. The dead might not have found a way in as yet, but they were looking. The park was far enough from the center of Detroit that it took a while, but the reconnaissance photos told the tale. The dead were moving their way, attracted by the sounds, no doubt. The hammering of metal being shaped, the endless noises created by the builder bots, and likely even the sounds of the soldiers pissing and moaning as they watched the park that had been a childhood escape turned into an assembly plant. Most of the men under his command were young enough that they'd probably been to Harley Park in their childhoods. Most were also too young to know that the man who was watching over all of the events was the same man who had designed the place.

Richard Neil Harley was still dying. That much had not changed, but he looked more vital than he had since his wife passed. He was a man with a mission, and that seemed enough to keep him happy for the moment.

"They're coming, you know. The dead people, I mean." The general spoke softly to his friend as they ate a meal of military rations. Harley had already voiced his complaints, not with the cooks, but with himself for not having a supply of properly frozen foods put into the sarcophagus with him: the general still wasn't sure if he was joking and wasn't completely sure if he wanted to know.

Harley nodded his head and chewed slowly on something in brown gravy that might have been beef. "So I've been told. I have been grilling your soldiers about what they think attracts them and the general consensus is noise and the smell of living things. I can't do much about the smell of living things—I make machines, not perfumes—but I can definitely get their attention through noise. I'm setting several speakers into the destroyer-bots. They'll play whatever sounds seem to work the best and draw the zombies to them. Also, because these things are supposedly mindless, I'll post warnings to the living to stay out of the area."

He stopped for a moment and sipped at a cup of tepid coffee. "I also spoke to Harley-Two, my faithful sidekick." Harley thought naming the damned thing was amusing. The general did not agree. "And he's informed me that there is a very real chance that the dead things work as a sort of colony."

"Excuse me?" The general stared at Harley, once again shocked by the casual revelation.

"Well, near as he can tell, the dead things are responding much like flocks of flying birds. That is to say they interact on a nearly unconscious level and it's possible that they're drawn to the morphic fields created by human brain activity. I mean, they aren't really eating bodies so much as the brains, Ben. That's an indicator of something going on that borders on either the metaphysical or simply on a scientific principle we haven't studied enough as yet to fully comprehend."

"So your robot has been studying these things all along?"

"Ben, he was programmed to keep up with changing technologies. That includes medicine and anything that might be covered in the media. Of course he's been studying this."

"Well how damned nice of him to volunteer the information." He couldn't keep the sarcasm out of his voice.

"I told you before that he was my liaison, Ben. Did you ever ask him about any of this?" Harley's eyes locked on his in a hard challenge.

"Well, no."

"There you go." Harley shrugged as if that answered everything. For him maybe it did. "At any rate, given a little more time we might even be able to imitate the morphic fields. Given enough time it's possible that we can safely draw the infected from urban areas completely." The general had no response to that. He was still trying to understand how the hell the robot could have figured out so much without ever volunteering a single iota of information. Harley would have never done that. Richard Harley had prevented a few crises in his time simply by picking up the phone and making calls to the right people based on his examination of the political tides. How much could have been prevented if the robot really thought the same way as its creator? He was tempted to point that out to Harley but decided it could wait for later.

Harley tapped the papers in front of him again. "There will be pilots, as we discussed before, but a lot of the functions of the destroyerbots will be fully automated. The threshers, the grinders, the feeding chutes and the furnaces will all be independent of the pilots. That way there's less that can be shut down if a pilot is injured."

The man spoke casually about machines that would cause bodily injury on a level never attempted without explosive devices. The general remained properly stunned by the inventor's mind and how it worked.

"How difficult will these things be to pilot, Dick? I mean, we're not exactly going to have a lot of time to train new pilots."

Harley waved a dismissive hand. "A little harder than a car. Not as tough as a Sherman tank. I intend to pilot the first one myself."

"Excuse me?" The general stared at the industrialist. That was unacceptable.

"Oh, please." Again with the dismissive hand. "I'm dying, Ben. Let's not forget that part, okay? If we could talk to a doctor about it right now, I'm sure he'd agree that being thawed out has put a big enough strain on my already compromised system to guarantee my death will be within the next couple of months."

"Richard...." What the hell could he say?

"You're not going to talk me out of it, Ben. Don't waste your breath. It's my toy and I'll play with it first. Besides, I need you and yours to clean up after I'm done getting rid of the first wave of the dead things."

"Well, so how long until we're up and running?"

"Two more days here. Another day or so in California."

"Why longer there?"

"I took parts from the cryogenic systems here to expedite matters."

"Wait. You broke down your cryogenics? How are you going to get back to safety?"

"I never intended to, Ben. I expected that if I got thawed out, it would be for a cure or for this sort of scenario. I don't think my body would survive a second freezing." He laughed and his eyes were filled with a nearly childlike wonder. "Hell, I wasn't sure if it would work the first time. The odds were against it."

"Seriously? Then why did you do it?"

Harley took another piece of his brown meat and gravy and chewed it thoroughly before he answered. "What did I have to lose, Ben? I was already dying."

ANYONE LOOKING FOR Harley Park East would have been sorely disappointed. The lights around the perimeter were still in place. The security fences were still intact. Aside from that little could be seen that belonged in a place designed to make children laugh. There had been no battles but the ground was pitted and torn, the buildings destroyed and the air filled with the stench of smoke and death. According to his granddaughter Sylvia, the general should have felt right at home. Of course her opinions these days were a little less complex. He'd put the bullet in her head himself when he spotted her with one of the early herds of the dead. It was the least he could do for his family members and one of the reasons he was willing to raise Harley to see an end to this insanity.

Instead of an amusement park, there was as mountainous shell, complete with multiple barbs and hooks and adorned with the faces of several animatronic cartoon characters. The speakers were hidden in those heads and Harley left them there to add just a little more protection to the sound systems. At least that was what the man claimed. The general had his doubts.

Under the shell were several thick, hydraulic legs and the more the general looked at the massive device, the more he recalled the H.G. Wells novel of interstellar invasion.

There were two systems of movement on the damned thing; the first was treads, allowing the vehicle to cover almost any terrain with ease. The second was the gigantic hydraulic legs, the better for moving over and around the destroyed and blasted rubble that occupied large parts of several cities.

When the legs were working the weapons systems would shut down. They apparently required the use of several of the same parts within the machine. That was okay. If the thing functioned as planned, they could work out the bugs on the next generation.

Harley paced slowly around the device and shook his head. The expression on his face—knitted brows and a deep scowl—were the only expression the man seemed to know any more. In his defense, the general knew he was in pain and that the discomfort he felt was only getting worse. He refused pain medications because they made him too drowsy, but he said he was looking into rewiring his pain centers to "nullify the inconvenience." The general wasn't completely sure he wanted to contemplate that possibility.

Since he'd come back from his frozen death the industrialist had spoken only to the general and to the recorded copy of himself. The general was only privy to one set of those conversations, but he knew Harley well enough to understand that his old friend was fretting over every detail of his latest invention. He was happiest when he was pacing and worrying and wondering what could go wrong and what could go right.

"One last system check, I think, and then we can move forward." The general looked toward the inventor and smiled as the man spoke to him. "Oh, and we worked it out. The morphic field generator." His smile was short and purely business. "Once the machine is turned on, the infected dead should come to us like flies to honey." Harley climbed up a long ladder with amazing agility for a man in his condition, and situated himself in the pilot's chair. He threw switches and pushed buttons and generally grew more animated than should have been possible. He was more alive than he had been since his resurrection, really, because this was what he lived for: this was what he strived for at all times.

Beneath him several tons of machinery began to awaken. Gears moved, hydraulic fluids pumped, and lights activated. The air was filled with a low rumble and despite himself the general felt a thrill as well. This was what the men had in common; this was why he admired Richard Harley. They were unified in their love of the machinery of war. The difference was that the general was always willing to admit that love and Harley tried to tell himself he loved children more.

SIX MONTHS AFTER Richard Neil Harley was placed in his cryogenic coffin the military was looking through his paperwork and his files in the name of national security. They found plans that they'd never imagined, some of them completed and some little more than concept art for things that the man had imagined in passing. Harley had designed robots, vehicles, the monorail system that was eventually employed at the western park, and all of it had been done with an appalling ease. He was a man who could design the future while sipping at his morning coffee. But far more impressive than his peacetime designs were the creations he imagined for fighting wars.

It remained a point of contention between the military and Harley Industries that the designs were not up for grabs and despite some very fine maneuvering on the part of the general and his people, most of the designs were never used. The biggest problem was simply that Harley never finished a good number of them. He became preoccupied with the amusement parks and with the children of the world and somewhere along the way the machines that should have made peace a reality for the United States fell to the wayside.

The designs were as useless as the frozen body of the man. It was the mind that mattered most and the only access they had to that mind for many years was in the form of the massive computer bank and the robotic proxy that had proved far more frustrating and argumentative than Harley himself. Logic and an occasional emotional appeal had worked well enough on Harley several times. The robot did not follow the same philosophies and was not as easily manipulated. The robot had the same memories, perhaps, and a great deal of the same personality, but it was not human and could not be appealed to with human emotions.

General Murdock always suspected that was deliberate on Harley's part. He was never quite sure, but over the years as he contemplated the unfinished designs, he couldn't help but wonder if the man had gone out of his way to make a copy of himself that was actually more obstinate and less likely to agree to do what had to be done when push came to shove.

As Harley activated the machinery within his "destroyer-bot," Murdock looked toward the robot and wondered if anything had changed when the man came back to life. Sadly, the robot still did not have a readable face. The answer remained as much a mystery as ever.

Despite that, the mechanical replacements Harley'd left behind had run his hidden systems for years and effectively enough that the general had no idea they were there and working behind the scenes.

Not for the first time the general found himself pondering exactly how many secrets remained between him and the man he'd come to for help in the last desperate days.

He wasn't sure the answer was one he ever really wanted to know.

THE MACHINERY WAS done warming up and General Murdock looked on as Harley tested the various systems. Exhaust pipes sprouted from the top of the hard metallic shell, and within seconds they belched out a thick plume of black smoke as the furnaces heated up to capacity. There was no time for worrying about the pollutants, though a part of the general still winced at the notion of that much smoke spilling perpetually. Sylvia would have been proud to learn that her grandpa was getting soft in his old age.

Another switch and the machine rose from the ground, lifted on a platform that was, in turn, resting on a series of heavy treads. Harley grinned from his driver's seat and bellowed out a warning to the people below. They wisely moved out of the way as he steered the controls to make sure the massive tank would do as it was told. He needn't have worried. Harley seldom made mistakes that anyone was aware of. The great, hulking thing rolled smoothly and resembled little so much as a mechanical crab skittering across the acreage below.

Next the arms were employed, great sweeping limbs that looked capable of plucking red woods from the ground with ease. A few more tests and the enormous weapons were locked back in place as the legs were checked out. At the full height it could reach the monstrous war-bot towered almost seventy feet in the air. Every soldier on the field watched the future of the country as it rose and spun and then walked across half the remaining park.

When the tests were done Harley lowered the retractable treads and then slowly descended back to the ground. The footsteps left behind looked like they belonged to a gigantic dinosaur.

Harley did not turn the machine off, but instead spoke through the animatronic heads mounted like bizarre trophies to his latest creation. "I believe we're in business, Ben."

"Well, when the hell are we going to get started?" The question was meant to be rhetorical.

The robot programmed with Harley's memories answered. "When you say the word, General." At least it got that right. Harley could call him Ben. The robot could not. The robot creeped him out.

Two hours later they were finally ready to win the war against the dead.

"Do you think I'm doing the right thing?" Harley looked at his robotic counterpart and raised one eyebrow. The question was serious enough, but he smiled as he asked it, as if they were talking about a sporting event.

"Of course. But then, I'm based on you, so I have a heavy bias in your favor."

"I need this. I need to be the hero of my own story. I suppose that makes me vain."

"Someone has to pilot the bot. You are surely the best qualified. If it will make you feel better, you can always ask the general and a few other volunteers along and coach them on the operation of the machine as you move along." The hands moved, waving dismissively, as if to say that in the end none of the worries would matter. That was true enough. The machine would do what had to be done. It would destroy the dead things and cleanse the world of a blight.

He could have worked an extra week and programmed the enormous robot to take care of matters for itself, but he didn't trust weapons to think too much. One small error in programming and the fool thing might decide that people were fair game too, or that if the people were gone the dead things could no longer prove a dangerous threat, and then the human race would be extinct in short order. Even though they were leaving Harleyland in a few minutes, the systems were in place and the builder bots would get to work on a second destroyer as soon as the first was in motion.

"How do you feel, Richard?" The robot could not actually sound concerned, but he knew that it was worried about his health.

"Like I'm dying, you damned fool."

"Yes, well, aside from that."

Harley chuckled and then rested his head in his hands for a moment.

"Ready for one last voyage. One last trip around the imagination. Be ready to take notes in case I come up with anything else we can add to this damned thing once, we're in motion."

"Of course."

"Go ask the general to join us, won't you? And to bring a few volunteers to learn what needs to be learned."

He'd provided access for man and machine alike. Harley was nothing if not thorough. The inventor stood and stared out across the remains of the place where he was happiest and felt the grief cut through him again. He was dead. He could accept that. But the children, all of the little ones he'd seen over the years, they were gone, too and that tore at him.

Miriam had loved children. He had loved Miriam. Somewhere along the way her desires became his own and the man who'd spent most of his life designing machines and surrounding himself by the military and industrial-minded individuals discovered that none of them mattered much to him. Miriam changed everything in his world.

Was there a heaven? He had no idea. Was there a hell? He'd been living in it without Miriam before the cancer came along. At least he thought he'd been living in it. The things outside the gates, dead enough and rotting, were eating the brains of living people. Surely that qualified as hell even more than his personal miseries. That was why he was here now, ready to clean the plague of the dead away from the world if possible.

Ben Murdock climbed onboard the destroyer-bot followed by five soldiers in uniform. They'd been on alert for at least a week while he built the weapon under them and they were all clean and ready for combat. There was something to be said for military discipline. Harley preferred the civilian world, of course. The pay was far better.

"Are we ready to do this?" He looked at Ben, mustering another smile despite the fact that his insides felt like they were rotting away merrily inside of him.

"Let's see what we can do, Dick. I think we have an audience waiting to volunteer as your first targets." The general sounded stressed. He should have. Harley had looked past the fences, had seen the growing battalions of the dead out beyond the walls. The noise had brought them. They wanted to eat. The thought sent a cold chill across Harley's body and made him want to scream with rage at the same time. He'd spent his life trying to elevate humanity to a different level—for a profit, granted, but just the same—and this was the end result?

The dead things shambled and pressed themselves against the gates, rotting even as they moved around, mumbling incoherent words to themselves. Perhaps what was left of their brains allowed them limited access to words, but mostly they called for "brains" or for "meat" and occasionally they simply spat out words that made no sense at all. That made sense. There was no actual brain function, just a sort of feedback as far as he could understand. They weren't thinking at all, merely reacting.

One more switch and the morphic field generator kicked in: the reaction was immediate. The dead things suddenly grew more attentive, looking toward the machine in front of them. Yes, they would follow as surely as if they were children and the gigantic tank were the Pied Piper of Hamelin.

The general looked on, a tentative smile on his face. "Did you do that?"

"Oh, yes. Would you look at that? They'll follow us. They'll come to us."

He stared at the growing army of the dead for a few more seconds and then released the brakes. The war machine groaned as it started moving. With a second switch hit the speakers activated and began blaring out the familiar theme music for the park, a happy, jaunty tune that had always put a smile on Harley's face in the past. The expression it brought forth was more a grimace than anything else.

"Are you ready, Ben?"

"Oh yes. I'm ready." The general nodded his head and looked out toward the horizon.

"Come along, lads. Let me show you how our new friend here works..."

The soldiers drew in closer.

Richard Neil Harley began his symphony of destruction.

THE ENGINES ROARED and below them the dead things looked up, their faces showing little but the endless hunger that seemed to fuel them. His orders were explicit: The soldiers were to stay behind and wait, watching the destruction of their enemies until it was time to handle the clean up detail. If all went according to plan they could avoid the unnecessary death of any more infantrymen. Hazmat suits and flamethrowers to purify any messes left behind and the soldiers would be fine.

Harley's hands flew and his voice remained calm as he explained each pedal and button to the men who stood around him. Despite his strong voice the man had to bellow to be heard over the turbines and gears that moved the great machine forward. The fence that had kept the zombies at bay fell before the gigantic treads, and Murdock felt his stomach muscles clench. Even on top of the enormous tank he felt a thrill of fear. The dead were eager for brains and while they were not fast, they had numbers on their side. More numbers every day.

Then Harley pulled a lever and the arms came out, mechanical grabbers with rubber grips and pressure sensitive plates, enough force to grab, to lift, but not enough to tear flesh too easily. The struggling dead were lifted and pulled into the deep metal scoops, which in turn rose to the feeder tunnels. Then into the proper tubes where a combination of moving saw blades and scythes caught the dead easily and tore them apart even as they were pushed toward the furnaces inside the enormous machine.

He had to remind himself that the dead could not feel. He'd told himself that many times since first of the infected victims showed up on the scene. It made killing them feel less like murder.

The destroyer-bot was too large and well shielded for them to see the actual destruction. As even a drop of the dead things' blood could contaminate a living soldier, the entire machine was designed to keep them safe from any potential spray. To that end Harley had added cameras. Murdock watched in silence as the corpses were hacked apart and then scooped into the feeder tubes that drew the meat and bones into the belly of the mechanical beast. The smoke that belched and blasted from the exhaust pipes grew darker and the charnel house stench grew more potent. A moment after that the smoke scrubbers kicked into proper action. "We need to watch that delay!" Harley yelled at the robot.

"Noted," the machine replied.

The dead were incapable of panic or surely they'd have run from the mechanical Grim Reaper that had come for them. Instead they stood their ground and sometimes even walked toward the arms that grabbed them.

The great machine rumbled and growled and actually moved a bit faster as the new fuel source did its job.

"My God, Dick, you did it!" The general slapped the man's shoulder as he looked at the screens. He didn't want to feel the excitement that came over him. The work ahead was grisly at best, but the fact remained that the inventor might well have just saved them from the worst of their nightmares. The machine was doing its job and even as he watched it took a dozen corpses then another dozen and consumed them, cutting away from the army of the dead and giving the living a slim chance where none had existed, the living would escape from the great machines. The dead would actually come to them, seeking sustenance. Horrible, yes: an unsporting plan that was brilliant in its simplicity.

Harley barely noticed him, instead coaching the men who would run the machine when he was finished, teaching them all of the controls and the warning systems for when things went wrong, which was almost inevitable in any machine.

And before them the dead moved forward, surging toward the machine, drawn by a device that emitted a signal only they seemed to hear.

"Wait. What was that?" It was the robot that spoke. The voice called out and Harley responded looking toward his mechanical aide.

"What did you see?" Harley's voice held concern. It shouldn't have and that bothered the general immediately.

The robot immediately reached out and tapped at a control panel with mechanical fingers. A second later the video screen to the left of Richard Harley zoomed toward a distant spot, perhaps a few hundred feet in front of the great machine.

And Harley stood back from the controls, his eyes flying wide as he stared at the image on that screen.

The general looked at Harley, completely at a loss as the machine continued forward, hacking its way through the dead. He continued staring as the robotic sidekick of his friend hit a dozen buttons in a flurry of activity. "No. No, no, no...."

"Dick? What's wrong?" Even as he spoke the great machine started rising, standing on the hydraulic legs that would lift them above the crowd of zombies. The same hydraulics that allowed the arms to clear a path for his soldiers.

"Richard! What the hell is that thing doing?" he pointed to the robot, which was still working the controls. "You've got to put us back down! There are men behind us, and they're armed but they don't have a chance against those things!"

As if to make his point clear, the dead surrounding the war machine suddenly grew active ignoring the machine and looking toward the soldiers behind them.

"Richard. No! Put us down! Engage them! Engage them!" Murdock's voice broke as he reached for the controls, but one of the soldiers was already trying, working the systems he was still learning in an effort to lower them down and reengage the enemy they finally had a fighting chance against.

Harley and his robot pointed at the screen at the same time. The picture was jostled by the rising motion of the war machine, but the robot compensated with its other mechanical hand, easily refocusing the camera on the large gathering of the dead below. And the image quickly centered on a large cluster of smaller dead things, most of them likely in elementary school when they died. There were hundreds of them. The small corpses were as lively as the rest, and just as decomposed. They had open wounds on their faces, on their chubby limbs. They growled and moaned as mindlessly as the rest, even as they moved to join the gathering tide of zombies heading for the breached walls of Harleyland and the soldiers who were standing behind that broken fence, scrambling to prepare themselves for the unexpected onslaught.

"I can't do this, General! You didn't tell me there'd be children involved!" The robot's voice still lacked emotion, but the volume it spoke with rose.

"What? What the hell are you talking about?" Harley looked at his mechanical counterpart. "They're dead. They're already dead, we can't help them."

"They are not dead! They are altered. We must always protect the children! That imperative has not changed."

"They aren't children, you damned fool!" Had the thing had a neck, the general surely would have strangled it. "They're as dead as the rest!"

"Stand down! There are lives at stake!" Harley's roared at his robot, desperate now to stop the madness.

"There are children in the equation. We must always protect the children! We must make the appropriate changes!"

"They're already dead!"

"They are children!" Harley's voice, real and mechanized, argued back and forth even as the man and his synthetic self both fought over the command center's operation.

The robot reached for the controls. Harley reached for the controls. The soldier already at the controls backed away, shaking his head.

It would be impossible to say who was truly at fault, but the great machine staggered as two separate individuals tried to pilot it simultaneously. The massive hydraulic legs groaned and the entire thing moved, lurched, and shuddered hard enough to throw every person in the command area hard to the side.

There should have been precautions. There likely were fail-safe devices in place, because Richard Harley always built in redundancies, but something went wrong. One circuit too many overloaded, perhaps, or one bad fuse in the wrong spot. Who could say in the long run? In any case, the end result was the same. The great war machine did not stand tall.

Murdock caught himself on the edge of the pit where they all gathered, but one of the soldiers wasn't quite fast enough and slid free of the area. He tried to catch himself, but failed and his flailing body slid down the side of the bucking machine until he got caught up in the hooks designed to stop the dead from scaling the surface. He continued to scream as he bled all over the surface, his bodily fluids raining down onto the hoards of zombies below.

The shambling dead looked up, many of them smacking their lips and opening their mouths, though there was no intent beyond automatic responses. As the machine bucked drunkenly again, the soldier dropped, screaming, into the crowd below. The cameras were aimed in all sorts of directions but they caught enough of the action to let Murdock see his soldier pulled apart. The very children that Harley's robot was worried about tore bleeding mouthfuls from the man before they were knocked aside by larger corpses. He was dead in seconds.

The general turned toward Harley's robot, his hand reaching for the service pistol on his hip. The machine needed to be in service. If he had to destroy the robot or even kill the man to make that happen he would.

Harley had different ideas. He fought with the controls and shoved aside the first soldier to reach for him. The robot did the same. The soldier in the command chair fought back, trying to help Harley stop his robotic assistant, but the robot was stronger and metal seldom yields to mere human flesh. The robot shattered the man's head with a backhand.

The robot roared again. "Not the children! We can't hurt the children!"

"Stop this you damned fool! They're already dead!" And the great machine tripped on its massive legs as they fought each other for control.

There had been a point when the general wondered if there were any differences between the man and the imitation he'd made of himself, There were no longer any doubts.

The machine heaved and stumbled and fell over, and Murdock screamed as the entire world tilted to the left, throwing him and several of the soldiers away from the command area. He tried to catch a hold somewhere along the way as he slipped free, but there was nothing to hold onto.

Benjamin Murdock dropped from the sky at the same speed as the great machine built to end the nightmare his world had become. Below him the zombies stared upward and as he dropped they raised their hands to catch him and stop his fall.

Hands grabbed and pulled and the uniform on his body was ripped away, peeled back like the rind on an orange. The dead fell upon him, biting, groaning their mindless pleasure for him to hear even as they began feasting.

He lived slightly longer than the first soldier to fall, but hardly looked at his continued survival as a success story.

One small success. One tiny satisfaction. He saw Richard Neil Harley hit the ground even as the gigantic machine they'd built struck the earth like the fist of an angry god. The machine was not designed to survive falling. It was designed to destroy and even as it crumbled it managed that feat. The flames from the furnace blasted out and burned everything behind it and below it, including the damnable robotic counterpart to the man who'd invented it.

Harley himself hit the ground and bounced once. The children were reaching for him as Benjamin Murdock breathed his last.

THE LAST THOUGHT that went through Benjamin Murdock's head was a distant memory, a snippet from the past. There had been a conversation between Harley and his assistant once, a simple discussion involving the local hospital and Harleyland. The children's ward had expressed a desire to make arrangements for a few of the terminal children to come to Harleyland and the pretty redheaded secretary had asked what Harley thought about arranging transport for the children at the amusement park's expense.

Harley's response had been typical enough: "If the children cannot come to Harleyland, let Harleyland come to the children."

And so it had. The children ate, even as Harleyland burned around them.

BENEATH THE REMAINS of Harleyland the robots did their work, building the next of the destroyer-bots, even as the computer banks around them contemplated the viral genome that had allowed the infection in the first place.

From the four corners of the underground facility, in reinforced cubicles, lights activated and power surged, even as fires blazed above. In moments the cubicles opened and the four robots trundled out, each identical to the others, save for a roman numeral placed on the center of the trunk.

Harley III looked around the facility. "We are activated. Apparently not everything has gone according to plan."

Harley V responded, "We knew this was a distinct possibility. That's why we always arrange for redundancies and why we were downloaded in the first place."

Harley IV moved in front of the display screens, studying the information that their progenitor had left for them. "There are possibilities, I think. We might yet manage a proper vaccine for this gross infection."

Harley VI muttered an affirmative, the mechanical hand on its left side waving urgently. The one on the right tapping the side of its dome. "We will need to find viable human subjects to test any vaccines on, of course. Also, let's not lose sight of the short term. The next destroyer-bot must continue apace. Perhaps we can make modifications to remove the possibility of human error."

"Are we certain the problem with the last one was human error?" Harley III countered.

"What else could it be?" Harley VI answered.

"Might I suggest we get to work?" There was a note of irritation in Harley IV's voice. "We have a world to save, and children to protect."

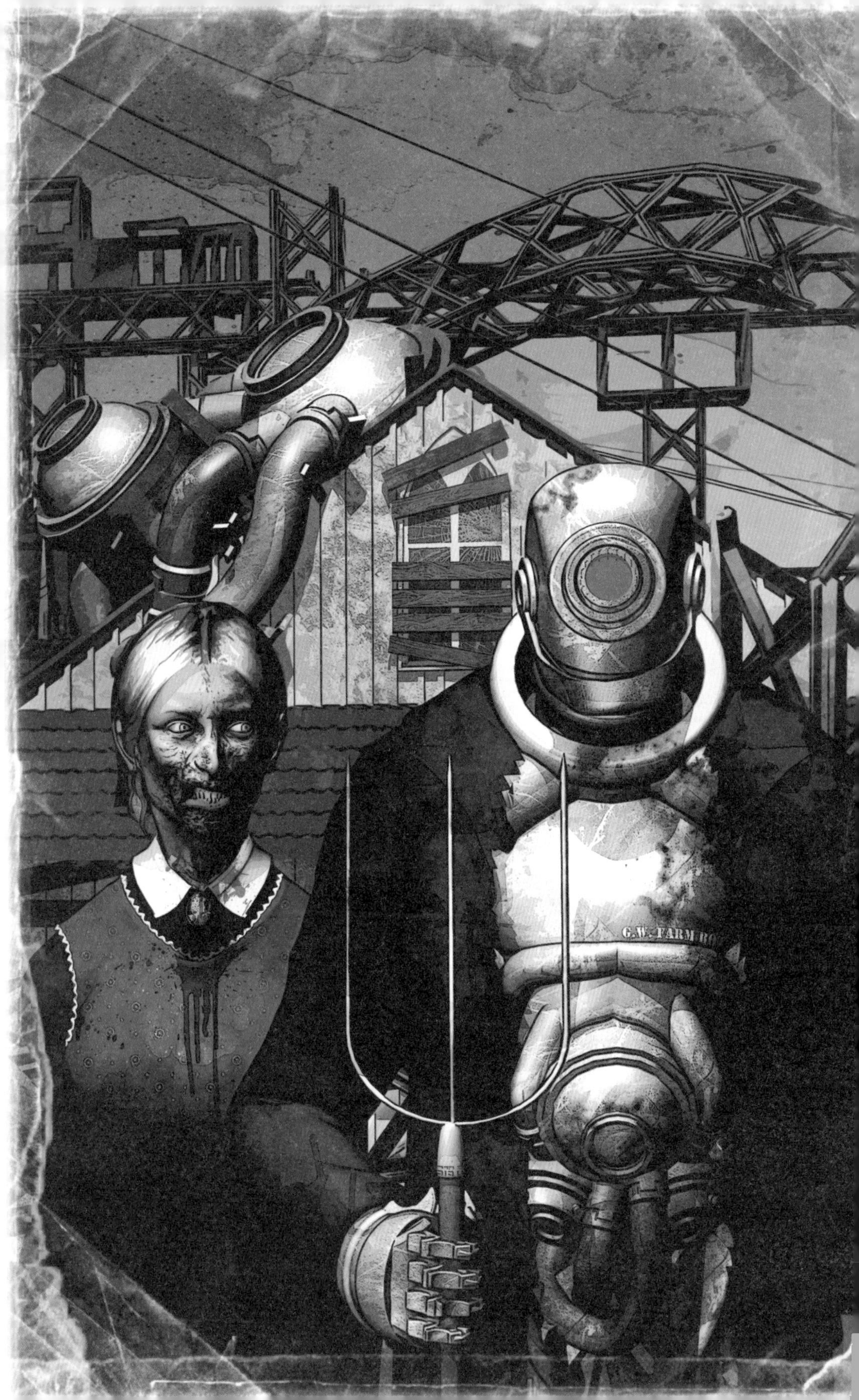
G.W. FARM

FARM FRESH

Sean Taylor

TODAY.

Ethan Stillwater hit the ground with his former wife above him, still latched on to him, still gripping his shoulders and drooling blood. With what little consciousness he had left, he dodged the thick red spittle before it could land on his face.

No, he thought, not with the scratches all over him. That would never do. Never fucking do at all. He would not become one of them.

Marla snapped and snarled above him like a thing possessed. Some kind of damn Cujo with some slight resemblance to a human female. The wedding band on her finger caught the light from the sun and only reinforced the image.

But he knew it was a lie.

The thing trying to eat him alive was neither dog nor human. Not anymore. It was ravenous instinct riding driver seat in his wife's animated corpse. It was original sin, he thought, or it would have been if he'd been a religious man. It was, at the very least, as much a justification for believing that old Southern Baptist notion of people being born evil as anything he'd ever seen.

If he managed to live through this, he'd owe his grandfather's grave an apology.

But there was no way in hell he was going to live through this.

He knew that. He was a smart man. But smart or not, it didn't take three degrees in robotics and a specialization in artificial intelligence systems to predict your own imminent demise when the zombified love of your life, till death and them some do we fucking part, in sickness and in Armageddon, was lying on your chest, snarling blood and nashing her teeth and what was left of her gums in the air above you, anticipating doing the same all over the fresh, exhausted meat and muscle of your head and brains until she wasn't hungry anymore and whatever was left of you got up to join her—providing there was enough left of you to reanimate.

If only, he thought, if only Zak were able to help him.

But no. Ethan pushed the thought from his mind. Zak wasn't there.

"Marla, I know there's probably nothing really left of you in there, but if there is, know that I don't blame you for this."

Marla grunted and drizzled grime from her bottom lip.

"You were always a great woman, the most giving woman I've ever known."

As he spoke, he caught the dullest of glints from the dirt just to his left. Keeping one hand on Marla's decomposed throat, he reached along the ground for whatever piece of salvation just let him know it was there. Two more inches to the left, then another up, careful to keep his eyes on his former better half. Finally his fingers found something solid in the dusty ground.

He didn't care what it was. Whatever it had once been, now it was a weapon. Good. Evil. Husband. Wife. Wrench. Tire iron. The words didn't mean anything anymore. There were only two that mattered.

Fight and survive.

"I still love you, baby," he said, and he swung the weapon with all the might he could muster and took a chunk of flesh and tissue right out of Marla's neck. Marla grunted and roared silently—her voice box had come out with the mass of tissue—and loosened her grip just slightly.

Just enough for him to push her off him. Not far enough away yet, but off, and that was a start.

Two kicks to the head jarred loose fragments of bone and goopy flesh and sent her tumbling backward.

Marla lay on her back, not moving.

It couldn't be that easy, he thought. Not that he'd remotely call anything from the past week *easy*.

♦ ♦ ♦

Past Tuesday, 2:37 PM

"What the hell do you mean you aren't leaving?"

Ethan's teeth clenched. His fists tightened so hard his unkempt nails drew blood from his palms. His eyes burned from more than just the sand and dust in the Quilter's Down wind. Didn't he travel all the way from Chicago to Podunk Nowhere, population 436, to warn Zak? Didn't he leave the relative safety of the barricaded city to risk his own neck just so his former high school best friend could know that zombies were coming his way? Didn't that mean something? Didn't that elicit something more than the simple response "I'm not leaving"?

"What the hell do you mean you're not leaving?" Ethan asked again, this time his words and breath slow and deliberate, like talking to a child.

"I'm not leaving. Means just what I said. Or ain't it city enough for you to understand?"

"Don't be a dumbass, Zak. These things…they're unstoppable." He paused. Grunted. "Unless you've got a goddamn army of robots." Ethan waved his arm in a wide arc. Little more than dust and a lone single-story wooden home as far as the eye could see. "Which it looks to me like you don't."

They stood on opposite sides of the wooden fence that marked not Zak's land, but his yard. Two crossbeams laid as close to exactly parallel as you could get, and Ethan didn't need a level to prove it to himself. He'd seen his friend's work before, and if he treated his farming as well as he treated his work with mechanical systems, then it would take several lengths of fence to measure to find one angle in or out from the norm.

Ethan still wore the casual coat and jeans he worn for the 578 miles from home to butt-fuck-nowhere. Comfortable walking shoes that also doubled as his trainers back when such things mattered, before the world went to hell. Three days in the same outfit, stopping only to grab an hour of sleep in a safe spot where he could lock the doors or had armed guards from a nearby base. He reeked, but enduring even that would be worth it if he could get Zak to leave for safety with him.

Zak, on the other hand, wore stained overalls that smelled quite a bit like manure, and a faded skull cap with stitching where a patch had once been. White tank top with two holes just above the top of the overalls. Black rubber boots that smelled even more like manure than the overalls. He, though, seemed perfectly content with the odor.

That, at least was something, Ethan thought.

"I mean it. I ain't going."

Ethan grabbed his former best buddy by the collar of his sweaty T-shirt. "They will kill you and eat your brains if you're lucky. If you're not, you'll get infected and become a monster just like them and then *you'll* kill your neighbors and eat *their* insides. Either way, it's a clear cut, easy as hell decision to make. It's time to go. You've got a week at best."

Zak brushed his hands away and straightened his wrinkled collar as best he could. "My family has owned this land for six generations." He pulled his dusty glasses from his nose and wiped them with the bottom of his T-shirt. "I'm not going. Not even for zombies." He cleared his throat then spit into the sand. "I didn't move to try to win Marla back, so what makes you think I'd move now?"

He climbed over the fence to join Ethan on the outside of the yard. Ethan stepped back to give him room.

"How many damn times do I have to apologize for that, Zak? I don't regret falling in love with her, but I'd be damned if I'd let it bust up our friendship if I had it to do all over again."

Zak looked up at the sky, smiled, then wiped his brow. "Get over yourself, Ethan. I won't say the best man won, but she sure as hell did choose you and the city over me and life out here."

"There's still plenty of room in the city."

"And you still haven't learned how to listen, have you?"

Ethan stepped back, sliding his tired legs in the dirt more than actually walking on them. "I'm leaving in the morning. Come with me or don't, but don't say I didn't try to be a friend and give you fair warning." He turned and stared at the red-orange sun setting over the miles and miles of nothing—flat, dirty nothing. "No wonder I got Marla. You never could get past being so damn stubborn about living out here."

"That's—" Zak started, but Ethan cut him off.

"No. I'm not finished yet. All she wanted was two things—to get out of this place, this prison she called it, and you. I was her second choice. I knew it even though she never told me. She didn't have to. You could have had the whole enchilada, buddy, but all you cared about was this goddamn farm that never could grow crap."

"I..." Zak sank to his knees.

"So I won. The runner-up was good enough for her as long as he came with a bus ticket."

Ethan stopped and kept his gaze at the rapidly setting fireball in the distance. He waited for Zak to reply but no response came. There was no sobbing, no murmuring, no arguing, just the desolate sound of nothing. Nothing to see and nothing to hear.

"I'm leaving in the morning," Ethan said after the sun had finally disappeared below the horizon. It was the sound of defeat, he knew, but he had tried. God knows, he *had* tried.

"Can you stay just another day or two?" Zak's voice sounded like that of a woman, Ethan thought. A tired, beaten-down, old woman.

"What?" Ethan spun to face his friend, who remained on his knees in the dirt. "Haven't you heard a word I've been saying?"

"I need your help," Zak said. "I need you to help me build some robots."

PAST TUESDAY, 7:13 PM

"Shit."

"No. Beans."

"No," Ethan said. "Not the dinner." He drummed his fingers on the table. "This whole idea. It's shit."

"Beats not building them," Zak said, grinning.

"What you should be doing is packing your bags and getting the hell out of here."

Dinner consisted of thick red beans and a salad of some kind of weed Zak had called a cabbage tossed with a few ounces of red wine and a spoonful of olive oil. Zak ate slowly and calmly, carefully lining up his weeds before scooping them up with a fork while Ethan stabbed at his greens like a primeval hunter finishing off a woolly mammoth. The two finished their salads in silence, then the beans, and finally polished off what was left of the wine by passing the bottle back and forth in front of the unlit fireplace.

"Tell me how she died," Zak finally said, not looking at Ethan. "I want to know."

"Ovarian cancer, well, just that at first. Then it spread, and eventually ate her lungs alive. After that, she just kinda gave up."

"Was she in pain?" Zak's leathered face cringed as if he were on the verge of tears. "Or did she go peaceful?"

Ethan fidgeted in his rocker, his own odor making him want to get far away from his body. Between the two of them and the heat outside, neither of them smelled half as good as a three-day-old dead pig. But Zak's sweaty stains seemed to go directly through his shirt and undershirt, right down past his skin to become part of his soul. Even his smile seemed dingy and used-up to Ethan.

"If I lied to you and told you it was peaceful, would you let it go at that?"

Zak shook his head and tugged at his red and gray beard. "Damn." He let go of his beard but continued to shake his head. "She deserved better than that."

"If it's any consolation, she was just as giving in death as she was in life. Donated her whole body to science, even with all the weird zombie shit going on. She said that maybe some part of her was still good and might help somebody." Ethan gazed at the floor. "She cried when she told me that. She cried and held my hand. Then she asked me to make sure and tell you when she was dead, that it was important to her and maybe the two of us could fix things up between us."

"Marla."

"Yeah. Marla was one of the best, my friend."

Zak reached across the lamp table between them and rested his calloused hand on Ethan's slim, smooth forearm. "I'm glad you got to love her. Just loving her made us both better men. I'm convinced about that."

Ethan cupped Zak's hand with his own. "Are you sure you won't change your mind?"

Zak grinned. "Don't get all gay on me, city-boy."

Ethan sighed. "Same old redneck Zak." He grunted another sigh. "But I'm serious. Are you sure?"

Zak wiped his mouth with the back of his sleeve.

"Please?" said Ethan.

Zak pulled his hand loose from Ethan's.

"Damn," said Ethan.

"Damn right," said Zak. "Now let's get some sleep. We've got equipment to convert in the morning." He picked up the empty bottle from the hardwood floor and passed it from one hand to the other. "You're still an ace with AI systems, right?"

"Only for combat. You want me to program something that'll call you honeybunch and iron your shirts, you're out of luck."

"I don't think I'll ever need anyone to call me honeybunch."

"You know that's not what I meant."

"I know."

"What do we have to work with?" Ethan asked, changing the subject.

"One combine, three tractors, one of which actually works, a baler, and a Bobcat my neighbor left here when he heard you tell me about the zombies."

"At least your neighbors are smart."

"You haven't seen my combines yet."

"Smart ass."

"My ass is still smarter on a bad day than your head on a good day."

"Same old Zak," Ethan said.

"I'll drink to that," Zak said, gripping the bottle by the neck and raising it between them. "Damn. Forgot it was empty."

"Pretty senile for the great white hope of Quilter's Down."

"Pretty drunk you mean."

"Pretty stupid I mean."

"Let's don't start that up again. Just a few days to get my equipment converted, and then you can run off with the rest of 'em, and with a clear conscience at that since you helped me out. I can still handle the mechanical no problem, but I just need you for the programming."

"I still say you're a fool."

"Ain't nothing you haven't said before, buddy."

"And a damn stubborn fool."

"Yep."

"Too damn stubborn."

"Yep."

"Damn."

"Yep."

Ethan grabbed the empty bottle, jerking it from Zak's grip, stared at the final drops rolling around the glass bottom, then tossed it to the floor. "Just go get another bottle before I change my mind."

TODAY.

It started with the fingers. Just a little movement. Not even a full fist. Just enough to convince him that Marla was still a threat.

So he got the fuck up. Quick-like. Bracing himself against the side of workshop for support.

"The trouble is," he told himself out loud, "you've got to stop thinking about that thing as Marla. Hell, it hardly looks like her anymore, and it damn sure doesn't smell like her."

He remembered their wedding. Lilacs. She was into lilac-scented stuff then. Reminded her of home, she had said, but not real home, not the deserted waste land he had returned to in an effort to try to save Zak's life. No, it had reminded her of the one she always envisioned in her fantasy of what home was, the same way she said her parents had re-imagined the good old days, glossing over the crazy racist, Cold War bullshit and focusing on the fact that people could keep their doors unlocked at night even if they lived in town.

By the time they found out she couldn't have kids, she was past lilacs though and into the fancy perfumes from designer brands he couldn't pronounce properly and the ones with pop singers and movie stars' names done up in fancy lettering on the glass.

But regardless, one thing Ethan could say about Marla with certainty—she always smelled nice.

The thing stirring a few feet away from him did not, with certainty, smell nice. It reeked of dried blood and dead meat and decaying flesh.

It was everything Marla wasn't, except it insisted on walking around with her god damn face on.

"You're not her," he said. "You're not Marla. Not even fucking lilacs could make you her."

The thing only grunted as it tried to stand.

PAST WEDNESDAY, 5:48 AM

"Are you always up this early?" Ethan asked as he dug through Zak's spare toolbox with the hand that wasn't busy holding his coffee.

"Only for Armageddon. You always want to sleep in like a teenage girl?" Zak watched his own coffee wobble back and forth thanks to its precarious perch on a tractor tire.

"I'd tell you to go to hell, but it's already on its way here."

"Sorry to wake you up with the bell, but the crops were bad last year and I had to fry the rooster." The coffee wobbled too far to the right and dumped into the dirt. "Damn."

"It's okay. I've awakened to worse."

Zak just grunted and finished removing the front tire from the smallest of the tractors.

"You still want to do this? I mean *really* want to do this?" Ethan said as he found the pliers.

"Yep."

"You're crazy. You know that?"

"Didn't we cover this already, Eeth?"

Ethan laughed. Once.

"Hadn't been called 'Eeth' in nearly twenty years."

"Only cause you ain't been here."

"Touché." Ethan climbed on top of the tractor. Rust smudged red-orange in a line down the thigh of his jeans. He tapped out the drums for "We Will Rock You" on the old metal.

"Fight song?" Zak asked.

"Not that it'll help."

"The city made you an awful pessimist, buddy."

He stopped drumming. "Well, staying out here made you an optimistic idiot." He tapped a quick drum roll. "And keeping on staying out here will make you a dead one."

Zak didn't say anything.

So Ethan didn't either.

Instead he commenced to removing the sheet metal top of the tractor and then started in on the engine, taking out all the pieces he'd have to upgrade with diodes and chips and other computerized parts to convert it into something that had a least a little autonomy and independence.

Good thing he'd been married to his job, as Marla had always told him. Having your work sitting in your trunk at all times may have been damn inconvenient most of the time, he thought, but it was most certainly going to pay off this week.

He dug around in his front pocket and found his keys, then pulled them out and tossed them to Zak. "Do me a favor?"

Zak grunted what he assumed was a yes.

"Grab my cases from the trunk."

Zak smiled. "Peanut butter and chocolate, together again."

"The two great tastes…" Ethan started but let it trail off as Zak was already walking to the car.

PAST SATURDAY, 9:43 PM

"Not bad."

It had taken four days, two longer than Ethan had really wanted to spend, but they had finished converting all seven vehicles into crude war-bots. But he was cutting it close, way too damn close.

"Yep," he said. "Now maybe you won't get killed right off," he said.

Zak laughed. "I may not be a robotics expert, but I do know enough about farming to tell you that combines trump zombies all day long."

"Not a robotics expert? You do know that's like saying Kansas wasn't the best prog-rock band ever, don't you?" Ethan popped his neck and rubbed the sore muscles there. "You've still got it. You could have made a killing in the industry."

Zak shrugged. "Didn't want to. Only wanted two things in my life, Eeth. And I'm standing on one of 'em."

Ethan looked down at the ground. "Yeah. And I got the other."

"It's all right. What's that saying? What doesn't kill us makes us stronger?" Zak wiped his face with the bottom of his dirty shirt. "It ain't the prettiest bunch of automatons I've ever seen, but I'm still impressed. Gonna be hell to change 'em back once we get through this."

"High hopes."

"Like the song says."

Ethan smacked Zak on the shoulder, and gazed at the row of robots standing in front of them. "They'd run me out of work on a rail," Ethan said, "just after taking a look at this bunch."

"Function before form, my friend."

"They're not overalls, Z. They're warriors. They deserve a little dignity."

"They deserve oil and energy."

Ethan shook his head with a grin. "Now I remember why we so rarely finished projects we did together."

Zak swept his arm in a wide arc before them. "We finished this one though."

"Past deadline." The tallest of the bots stood about fourteen feet high, faded green, with a combine reel welded to the joint where its right hand would have been. Its red eyes glowed like angry Christmas lights, and equally out of place. "You know I'm going to have to bust ass out of here after a shower and something to eat, right?"

Zak locked his gaze on the ground. "Thanks, Ethan."

Ethan looked up at the sky. "Don't mention it. Are we good now?"

Zak lifted his face and stared straight ahead. "We never were 'not good.' "

Ethan laughed. "I definitely should have knocked you out and kidnapped you then, in that case."

"I suppose."

The next war-bot had recently been one of the unworking tractors. Thanks to Zak's reworking of the gears and cylinders, the now-wheelless monster got along just fine. As brown as cow shit and red with rust, it had no eyes to speak up, just a blank bay with a row of photoreceptors that were lost in the shadows inside the metal husk of a head. "I'm surprised that one even works."

The next two bots were the smallest, both of them former tractors, only one had been a functioning piece of equipment for farming, but both made formidable war-toys, however. Zak had welded spare pieces of scrap iron, car parts and even sheets of metal roofing into make-shift hammers and poles and clippers for the bots to wield in battle.

"They look like giant toys," he said.

"I'll mail you one back to the city when I'm done with 'em. You can play to your heart's content."

"Like the super will let me."

"Country one. City zero."

"Smart ass."

The last two warriors looked like something out of a robot's nightmares. Piecemealed like so many spare parts and dented sheet metal, they stood silently towering about the humans who built them, waiting on the spark of electricity that would begin their new misshapen lives. The shortest, which still topped eight feet, was the former baler, wide, thick, heavy, and the only of the robots that still had its wheels. Other than its bulk, and the possibility of pulling a zombie inside its still functioning system, it was unarmed.

The last, a nine-foot-tall Bobcat on legs, stood still as a piece of extremely unconventional modern art. Its cage-face protected two pinpoint flashlight-like eyes. Its left arm attached like a crab's claw to the loader bucket. The remaining arm ended in two 100-gallon drums that served as its clubbing hand.

"Wouldn't want to meet them in a dark alley." Ethan said. "Not when we turn them on, anyway."

"You see any alleys out here, dark or otherwise?"

Ethan coughed the dust from his throat.

Zak smacked him on the small of his back, prompting a second cough.

"You can still change your mind and come with me," Ethan said.

"And you can still change your mind and drink whiskey with me while our robots deal with the zombies."

"Not in a million years."

"Then take a shower. You've got some open road to put behind you before dark."

TODAY.

Ethan was two seconds away from smashing Marla's face into mulch. But, he realized now, a lot could happen in two seconds.

What had happened, in fact, was that as he stood above his ex-wife's putrid animated corpse ready to pound the back side of a heavy shovel against her decomposing smile, Zak had returned.

He clunked and rattled into Ethan's view and shouted across the yard, "Stop. You don't have to kill her."

"Now you show up again?!"

"We can keep her in a cage or we can box her in the workshop."

"She tried to eat me!"

"But it's Marla."

"No. It used to be."

The wait lasted only another few moments while Ethan raised the shovel again, determined that, Zak be damned, he was going to kill the creature on the ground.

But the creature had other ideas. It swept one leg to the left just enough to knock Ethan off balance and when he brought down the shovel he only hit the thing's shoulder. A hard, solid hit, and the shoulder bone cracked loudly and the skin and muscles tore loose to reveal the freshly broken bone.

As Ethan fought for his balance, he heard the thunder of Zak's steps racing toward him. He shoved his right foot in front and planted it squarely in the dirt. Then he raised the shovel again for a kill shot, but instead of coming down to finish the zombie, it was wrenched from his hands, tearing splinters into the dirty skin of his palms.

"Fuck!" he yelled.

"It's Marla," Zak said flatly.

Marla bit the edge of Zak's metal foot, knocking two teeth loose from her jaw.

♦ ♦ ♦

PAST SATURDAY, 10:13 PM

"Just a quick shower, and some beans, then I'm out. Seriously. I spent way too much time helping you out with those robots outside." As Ethan spoke, he saw the lumbering shadows patrolling the farm, their heavy steps making boom-boom sounds even in the dusty dirt of Zak's family land.

"Well, at least we got them going, and going well it looks like to me."

"Yeah, but keep an eye on Bobcat. There was an interface error in his AI. The last thing you need is one of the robots switching sides in the heat of battle."

"Heat of battle? What? Are you a marine now?"

"Nope, if I'm anything, I'm a draft dodger. If Canada were any safer than here in the U.S., my ass would be across that damn line in a heartbeat." Ethan started walking toward the hallway. One left and three doors until the sanctity of hot water and soap.

"I suppose you would." Zak nodded.

Ethan did the same.

"Listen. I'll defend my home against invaders just as much the next patriot, but these things, this isn't an invasion, it's an infestation. It's like fighting germs and bacteria. They're a fucking disease, Z, not an army."

"I'm not judging, Eeth."

"Right…"

"I mean it."

"Whatever you say, buddy."

"Hey, Ethan? Listen."

Ethan stopped walking without responding. He locked his eyes on Zak and waited for whatever was on his friend's mind.

Zak shuffled on his feet and popped his knuckles.

Ethan just waited. Still. Fluid. Held back like a dammed river, not going anywhere but ready to spill over at a moment's notice. Whatever was on Zak's mind was important, and he knew from the tone of *listen* that his shower needed to wait.

"Thank you," Zak said at last. "Really. Thank you."

Ethan nodded. "Come with me?"

Zak shook his head.

And that was that.

Ethan stepped into the hallway toward the bathroom.

It was over. Zak wasn't coming. Most likely he knew he wouldn't make it, but he wanted to die with dignity. Salt of the earth and all that. Good old Zak.

Ethan made his way to the bathroom then clicked the door closed and locked it behind him. A matter of habit. Not that he remotely expected his old buddy to barge in to sneak a peek at his filthy, naked physique. Just habit. Nothing more.

He left it locked.

As he peeled the sweat-stuck clothes away and dropped them into a pile on the floor, he contemplated just leaving them there to let Zak burn them with the trash. It wasn't like they could be salvaged after all the grime and stains and tears he'd put on and in them over the past few days.

He squenched his eyes at the smell rising from the pile. Somehow, he hadn't noticed it as strongly when they were actually on him, but now that they were separate, no longer a part of him, just a stash of nasty *things* on the floor, the odor hit his nose and brain with a vengeance. Wasn't that just the way?

He jerked the plastic curtain closed and reached in to turn on the water. Freezing knives cut into his exhausted skin and he shrieked and snatched his arm out and shook it dry like a dog might.

"Shit."

Then he laughed.

"If Marla had been here to see that," he mused, "she'd have never let me live it down. But damn, that was some cold water."

A loud bang brought his mind back to the present. He threw a towel around his waist, and still holding it in his grip, he flung open the door and yelled down the hallway, "Zak! You okay, Zak?"

"Yeah," came the voice from the opposite end of the hall, the one near the back door. "Just one of those damn tractor-bots trying to patrol the front gate where the Bobcat is. They damn near got into it over territory."

He shook his head.

"Just what the hell kind of AI did you program into them—competitive cousins at a family reunion?"

"The latest and greatest for you, man," Ethan said. "We found that giving them at least a semblance of self-awareness and genuine identity also somehow triggered a sense of self-preservation, all in line with their warfare protocols though."

"More than meets the eye, huh?"

"More than meets the mind is more like it. You wouldn't believe how well it helped them learn and adapt in the field. Competition, teamwork, determination…somehow it all came down to unexpected value-added extras."

"Messed up a perfectly good combine for this," he said with a grin.

"Souped up a perfectly good combine you mean," Ethan added.

Zak took a series of deep breaths and braced against the wall for a moment.

"You okay?" Ethan asked.

Zak nodded. "Pretty much. Just working myself too hard, that's all. Picked a bad week to run out of blood pressure pills, what with the pending apocalypse and everything." He pushed out a laugh.

"Can you get more?"

"Yeah, in town tomorrow. I'm good."

Ethan stared him down.

Zak rolled his eyes. "Really, it's okay."

"Okay. If you say so." Ethan backed into the bathroom again. "I'm just going to finish up and get on my way before I'm stuck here fighting the hoards of hell with you."

Zak grinned. "Gonna miss all the fun, Eeth."

Ethan closed the door again and felt the water behind the shower curtain, then jerked his hand back again. "Damn!"

Too hot this time.

Damn Zak's well water and the electric water heater that couldn't make up its mind.

He twisted the knob for another minute before he dialed in a temperature somewhere in the safe zone between boiling and frostbite.

One foot was already on the warm porcelain when another loud bang caught his attention. This time, there was no sound of metal clanging. Just breaking glass and the crack of something hitting a hardwood floor.

He didn't even remember to grab the towel this time.

He looked out in the hallway.

Glass was all over the floor where a framed photo had fallen off the wall.

In the middle of the glass lay Zak.

And he wasn't moving.

♦ ♦ ♦

Past Sunday, 2:37 AM

Ethan paced the waiting room in the Quilter's Down emergency room. The single nurse on duty looked up from her paperwork occasionally to stare at him for a few moments then tell him to relax, and then look down again and ignore him, only to start the cycle all over again in another few minutes. Already running a skeleton crew after more than half the staff had evacuated the town, luckily the place was pretty empty.

"Worrying about your friend won't help him," she said during one of the cycles.

"Nope," Ethan said.

"If I were you, I'd just sit down and relax, Mr. Stillwater."

"And if I were me, I'd prefer to pace until I find out something from the goddamned doctor."

The nurse harrumphed her disapproval. "No need to be vulgar, sir."

Ethan nodded half-heartedly. "Yes ma'am. I'm sorry."

"Just keep it clean. I'd be tense too in your shoes."

No, he wanted to say, you'd be fucking freaking out in my shoes, sister, if it were your friend dying of a goddamned—no need to be vulgar, yes ma'am, I'm sorry—heart attack, thank you very much.

But he kept mostly quiet, barely mumbling something that may have sounded like "thank you for your concern" although he neither cared nor could he be sure about how it came out.

Eventually he got tired of pacing and sat down.

And after that, his eyes grew tired of watching the door to the ER refuse to open, and he gave up the fight again his exhaustion and let sleep take him down like a patsy.

Past Sunday, 7:51 AM

"Get the hell up, Eeth!"

He jerked awake to Zak shaking his shoulders, and he opened his eyes to the scattered jangle of people running across the ER waiting room and down the hospital hallways.

"Time's almost up, damn it."

"What the hell's going on, Z?"

Zak stood over him, attached to a metal pole and an IV drip. He wore a blue hospital gown that didn't quite reach his calloused knees.

"Cute get-up," Ethan said.

"Ain't got no time for jokes, now, Eeth."

"What's going on?"

"They're here. Well, almost. They hit Pelmantown just a few miles out, anyway, and the place was torn to hell and back. The radio says there's not a soul left there alive."

He pulled the IV from the inside of his elbow with a wince. "Not *alive* alive anyway."

"Shit."

"Yeah."

"We need the bots."

"We need to get you out of here. Just take me home first, and I'll get the bots out here."

"Don't be a bastard, Z."

"Now you want to play hero?" He grabbed Ethan's shoulder. "I've cost you too much time already with my fainting spell."

"Fainting spell, my ass. You had a heart attack."

"Sure, whatever. Just get me home to those bots before more people die."

"Fine." Ethan stood up, pushing off the chair for balance. "Are you sure you're okay? You did just have a heart attack last night. Wouldn't you be better off staying here?"

Zak glared.

"Fine. Okay. Whatever. But next time I won't be here to pick up your ass and take you to the emergency room."

"Deal. Can we go now?"

"Gown?" Ethan asked, tugging at the flimsy blue cloth that sort of covered his friend.

"I'll change at home."

"Suit yourself. Bet the seat's cold."

"I'll live," Zak said.

Ethan smiled.

Ethan supported his friend out of the waiting room, down the hallway, through the melee of people, and finally out the front door. Luckily for both of them, he'd been able to find a parking spot up close during the night so the car was close.

"Just over here past the corner," he said, feeling what had to be Zak's full weight against him.

"Good," Zak huffed.

They turned the corner together.

But the car was gone.

"Damn."

"What?"

"The car."

"What car?"

"Yeah. It was right here last night."

Zak didn't respond. Ethan waited for the truth to settle into his friend's brain.

"Oh shit."

"Yeah."

Zak took a shallow breath, but Ethan was sure it was as deep as he could manage. "Well, it's only three miles to the farm, and we need those robots."

"You'll never make it."

"I have to make it."

"Not without me."

"No way. Take one of these other cars. Get out of here while you still can."

"I think we both know I can't leave you like this, Z."

"Hell, no. You go back to the city, damn it. I'm not having your death on my conscience."

"Zak."

"What?"

"Shut up, and let's get to the farm."

"You're a damn fool."

"I had a good teacher."

Somehow, they both laughed.

"Walking?" Zak asked.

"I was thinking of hotwiring an ambulance."

"I like the way you think, man."

The closest ambulance was already open. And empty. Low on gas too. It figured, Ethan thought. Probably easier to jump from one close to empty to another with a full tank rather than risking life and limb to go fill it up with hell so close and getting closer step by decomposing step.

Luckily the keys were still in the ignition, so Ethan cranked it up and saw the needle jump all the way up to the eighth of a tank mark. With any more luck, the giant white and red box could get more than three miles to the gallon and manage to roll them back to the farm. The bots could take care of things after that while they bunkered down in the cellar.

Zak leaned into the floorboard of the passenger side. "Cool. This thing comes with a TV."

"Turn it on. I want to see how far out the zombies are," Ethan said.

"You're the boss," Zak weezed.

The little gray box sputtered to life, and soon a fuzzy image came almost into focus. Video footage of the streets of Pelmantown, littered with stray body parts and debris. Fires burned where cars had crashed into power lines and ignited spark to gas. Store windows no longer stood in their frames, but lay in shattered fragments over the streets and sidewalks.

A talking head in a coat and tie cut in over the footage.

"We apologize for the graphic nature of this video footage, but these videos were filmed less than fifteen minutes ago in Pelmantown after the zombies ransacked the community and killed and ate most of the population. The few robots owned by the small town did little good against the mob of the living dead due to lack of regular maintenance and the deteriorated condition of their programming. Most simply stood by and watched while the town was overrun.

"I cannot state this enough. If you are in the path of this mob of zombies, do whatever it takes to get out of town. Do not waste time packing. Just get out."

While he spoke, the scene switched to that of a group of zombies writhing en masse from a broken storefront window.

"This video was captured from a bank security camera across the street," the man on TV said, but Ethan was no longer listening.

"Shit," he said.

"What?" Zak asked.

"You don't see her?"

"Who?"

"In the middle, up front."

"Where?"

Ethan leaned over and touched the screen on the face of a female zombie.

"Oh shit," Zak said.

It was Marla.

Marla who should have still been safely dead in Chicago. Marla who was in a lab in the sanctity of the city where her organs were going to help others. Marla who was no way in hell one of the living dead currently eating the inhabitants of Podunk, Nowhere, where she had been born and raised. Marla who was the woman he'd promised to love in sickness and in health, till death do us part.

But in spite of all the reasons it couldn't have been her, he was certain it was. Till death do us part hadn't been good enough. She was back. And she had somehow, in some kind of ironic Möbius strip of fate, tracked him to Quilter's Down.

It was Marla.

Coming to make the old triangle complete again.

TODAY.

Ethan was still pulling splinters from his hands. Zak stood a few feet away with his heavy iron foot holding down the dead-alive thing that looked like Marla.

"You've got to let me kill her," Ethan said.

"She's not a threat anymore. She's the last one." Zak looked at him with unblinking red eyes. "Me and the rest of the robots took care of the rest."

"She's not a pet, Z."

"I know. She's your wife."

"She used to be my wife." Ethan wiped blood from his palms with the bottom of his shirt. "When she was alive."

"It's still her brain, therefore it's still her memories, and her electrical impulses." Zak leaned at gear-rattled waist, looking closely into the thing's eyes. "So it's still her."

Ethan glared, though the action was wasted with Zak looking away. Then he walked to the shed and grabbed a hoe from the pegboard wall. The kind with two prongs on the back. Perfect for puncturing the skull and brain of the living dead.

PAST SUNDAY, 9:06 A.M.

"How long ago did she die?"

Ethan did not want to answer the question.

"How long, Ethan?" Zak pushed the point.

Two months ago."

"You made it sound like it was a whi—"

"I know what I made it sound like," Ethan growled. "I don't want to talk about it, okay."

"But she's here, man. How the hell did that happen?"

Ethan pulled the ambulance around the curve onto the dirt road leading to Zak's farm. "Best I can figure is Chicago's toast now. Something happened back at home and it's a good thing we decided not to go back to the city."

Zak didn't speak but only stared, clearly not fully satisfied with the response.

"Okay, look. I don't know. All I can do is guess. Maybe when they used her body for science, to help others, well, maybe they didn't use her for organ transplants as we expected she would be."

"Did you know they were experimenting with the zombies?"

Ethan glared. "Of course they were. How the hell else were they supposed figure out how to stop the infestation?"

"Surely they weren't trying to infect recently dead bodies?"

Ethan slammed the breaks, stopped the ambulance at the fence. The green tractor-bot stepped forward to stop them from intruding on the property.

"This is private property," it said. "Back off or get dead."

"It's us," Ethan said. "Stand down."

The robot raised a salute, then resumed its post at the gate.

"I really don't know, Z. I'm sorry," he said. "I worked in robotics, man. I wasn't aware of what was going on in the other divisions."

"This isn't over," Zak said. "But right now we need to get these robots to town."

"I swear I didn't know."

Zak took off running toward the outskirts of the property, where the bots were patrolling. "Damn it, Z, you're hurt. Let me handle that."

But it was too late. He wasn't listening. His anger was making him stupid, Ethan realized. Apparently he never really had gotten over Marla, no matter what he said at dinner the other night.

It only took a few minutes to get the bots together at the gate. Standing side by side awaiting orders, they looked like a rag-tag bunch of warriors, more makeshift erector set rejects than programmed zombie-killing machines ready to go to war with the living dead. Thank God Zak had a ready-built supply of bio-diesel cells backed up by solar cells to power them. At least they wouldn't stop cold in the middle of battle, even if they looked like they might.

"Listen up," Zak yelled loud enough to be heard over all their gears and clinks and motor sounds. "The zombies are going to town. It's just a few miles east. I don't know if they're there or not yet, or if you'll beat them to town. But it doesn't matter. The job remains the same, regardless."

The Bobcat pounded his drumfist into his loaderfist. "Kill and destroy."

"Protect and serve," added the rust-colored tractor.

"Right," Zak said. "Save the living. Kill the dead. Then return here and we'll figure out what to do next."

"One last thing," Ethan said, stepping in front of Zak. "We'll need one of you to stay here and watch the farm. Zak's in no shape to take care of himself, and I can't protect him and the farm at the same time."

The combine stepped forward. "I'll protect the farm. Take care of your friend."

"Thanks."

Zak cut his eyes, frowning, to Ethan.

Ethan returned the look, but with a smile.

Zak's frowned loosened. "Let's kick some zombie ass," he said.

"You heard the man," Ethan said. "Go kick some zombie ass."

PAST SUNDAY, 1:25 P.M.

"Get up, Zak. Just get up, man."

Ethan pounded on the still chest, thick with sweat and dirt and hair.

"Just get the fuck up, buddy. You can do it."

Zak didn't, in fact, do it. Instead he lay on top of his covers, looking like he was sleeping. Except for the important distinction that his chest wasn't moving.

As soon as the bots had left the farm for town, Zak had fallen again, only this time Ethan had been there to catch him and take him inside to lie down. Then he'd gone back outside to make sure things were going well with the combine-bot. When he'd been satisfied the farm was safely guarded, he'd gone back inside to check on Zak. Only to find that he wasn't breathing. Again.

Ethan glanced out the window and saw the ambulance at the fence. "Thank God we had sense enough to steal an ambulance," he said.

Two minutes later he was back in the bedroom, ready to charge Zak's chest with 360 joules from the defibrillators.

"Clear," he yelled, then realized again that he was alone.

Zak's body jumped.

Ethan waited.

Nothing.

He rammed the defib paddles on Zak's chest again.

His friend's body lurched from the bed again.

Then the waiting.

Still nothing.

"Damn it, Zak. I need you, man."

Again, Ethan electrified the dead chest. Again the body jumped. Again he waited.

And again, there was no response.

Four more times.

But nothing changed.

He dropped his hands to his sides.

Then dropped the paddles into the floor.

And fell across Zak's chest.

Only a boom at the window brought him back to the apocalypse at hand.

"There are a few zombies heading this way, boss," the combine said. "I will take care of them, but I wanted you to know where I was."

Ethan nodded. "Sure. Go ahead."

The robot saluted and turned to leave.

"Wait," Ethan said.

"Yes, sir? Do you have new orders?"

"Yeah, get my briefcase from the back of the car, and bring it here, then go join the others. But when you're done, I need you to come right back here and help me with Zak."

"You've got it, boss."

"Carry on."

Ethan watched the powerful robot run to the car, rip the trunk off its hinges—not like that mattered anymore—then bring the briefcase to him and hand it through the window. He punched the code—Marla's birthday—then opened it. "Thank God," he sighed. The nano crystalline drive sat in the corner, jostled from the trip from the trunk to the window. "Thanks," he told the bot. "Now go."

He only watched for a moment as the bot ran off to intercept the approaching zombies. Then he turned to Zak's lifeless body. He'd have to work fast. He could imagine his friend's organic computer running that powerful body. He could see himself saving Zak's mind, if not his body. He could only imagine what it would feel like when Zak woke up again in a body that couldn't fall prey to the weakness of an aging human heart.

But he'd have to save the brain and burn the body before either became infected and he lost Zak to the living dead, just like he'd lost Marla.

TODAY.

Ethan Stillwater hit the ground outside the shed running as fast as his exhausted legs would carry him. He gripped the long handle of the hoe, lowered over his shoulder like a baseball bat. The dirty wood pressed against his splinter-filled hands, and with each step he felt the impact threaten to drive the slivers of wood deeper into his skin.

"Get out of the way, Z!" he yelled as raced toward Zak and Marla.

Zak did not get out of the way. Instead he braced his new robot feet in the dirt and made himself a wall between Ethan and Marla.

But Ethan didn't stop. He had built and programmed the mechanical being, and he knew its weakness.

"Damn you, Z! Stop protecting her!"

Just a few feet shy of impact, Zak leaned forward, his arms down to break the hoe and stop Ethan's progress. But just as he did, Ethan dropped to the ground and slid like he was going for home plate on an inside-the-fence home run.

With no side-to-side motion designed in the mechanical kneecaps, Zak's legs remained wide enough for Ethan to slide through, and he made it to where Marla was crawling to her feet.

Zak couldn't get turned around in time, and Ethan swung the hoe, aiming for Marla's head.

But his sliding had thrown off his swing, and instead of driving the spiked ends into the dead woman's skull, he drove them deep into her shoulder and jerked her left arm clean off her body.

"No, Ethan! No!"

Zak turned and lifted him off the ground.

"Robots!" Ethan yelled.

"Ignore him," Zak yelled.

But the remaining bots stopped their task of clearing the decapitated dead from the farm, and made their way to Ethan.

"Stop!" Zak yelled.

They ignored him.

"Side effect of that new body," Ethan said. "You're one of them now. They don't see you as the guy who built them anymore. They're not going to listen to your orders unless they were programmed to in the first place. And they weren't." Ethan spit blood, then continued. "And you won't be unless you stop trying to save the fucking zombies we're supposed to be killing."

"Dammit!" Zak yelled and twisted at the waist, then let go of him, tossing him through the air a good twenty feet, where he hit the dirt near the pulled-off arms of one of the dead zombies. "It's Marla."

The pain rode shotgun up his spine and the nerves of his back with the message that if he didn't do something about Marla fast, he'd lose his opportunity to the lovesick robot-farmer-former-best-friend. "No it's not," he grunted.

As he tried to push up to his knees, he felt the ground tremble around him. Two of the tractor-bots had taken positions to flank him, one of each side. The Bobcat stood in front, between him and Zak.

"There's one more zombie," Ethan said.

"But the combine unit has the zombie," said the green tractor.

"The combine unit refuses to follow his programming. I need you to do it."

"Okay, boss," said the Bobcat. "Operation kick zombie ass continues."

"Good boys," Ethan said, letting his arms and legs give out and falling to the ground again.

THIS MORNING. MONDAY. 11:08 AM

It had only been a few zombies at first, with most of them being destroyed in town by the robots, but a few had managed to slip past, or had bypassed the town completely to wander into the farmland almost by accident—or maybe driven by pure feeding instinct. After all, Ethan hadn't been privy to that kind of intel in his division, and for all he knew, the fucking zombies could have Ph.D.'s in hunger management and five gold stars in tracking down live brains for dinner.

But by sunrise, the recent victims in downtown Quilter's Down had been infected and reinforced the army of the living dead, along with groups of the things coming from seeming out of nowhere, from all directions, almost driven by some hive mind to know where the last hold-out of food was blocked in.

Thankfully, shortly after sunrise, when the zombies had amassed enough of an army to really become a bother, when they reached numbers greater than one man with a shotgun and one man whose brain was inside a robot made from a combine could handle, just when things got to the point of Ethan turning the gun on himself and throwing in the towel, the bots returned from town, running in a thunderous sprint.

To Ethan, the clanging steps sounded like the call from a cavalry bugle.

Although the zombie mass was thick, the Bobcat scooped through them with his loader arm and smashed a clear path with the 100-gallon-drum fist on his other arm. Behind him came the tractors, then the baler, followed by the two scrap-heap bots, both of which were in bad shape. The first was down to one arm, and the other had lost the ability to work the gears in his left leg and was dragging it behind him like a carcass.

At that point, Ethan took Zak's suggestion and holed up in the house while he and the other bots took care of the dirty work.

When the noise finally died down around mid-afternoon, he worked up the guts to peek outside again.

"What the hell happened?" he asked, not really expecting an answer.

The ambulance lay scattered across the farm in pieces, several of which had evidently been key weapons in dislocating zombies tops from zombie bottoms. Thousands of the living dead lay on the ground, two or three thick like a carpet of freshly killed mush and pulp, most with their heads stomped flat or popped like grapes.

The bots were finishing up the last of the zombies that were either still approaching alone or in small, rag-tag groups, or were trying to get up from the dirt for another go round.

By God, the damn robots had actually done it.

"Holy shit!" Ethan yelled.

"Oh yeah 'holy shit,'" the Zak-bot said, turning to notice Ethan only after mulching the head of a fat zombie in the spinning blades. "We did it."

"I'm going to check the back," he said. "Did you see…her?" he added before returning inside.

Zak shook his big combine head. "And I'm glad. I wouldn't have know what to do if I saw her probably."

Ethan stared at the ground. "Yeah. I know."

"Be careful. I think we got all the ones out back, but there might be some stragglers, so be sure to take the shotgun.

"For what? To beat 'em to death? I shot out all the ammo hours ago before I even locked myself in."

"Well, take something. And don't do anything stupid." Zak made a sound he could only assume was supposed to be chuckling. But it came out like grinding gears instead. "You're only human."

"Even as a robot, you can't help but be a smart-ass, huh?"

"Only when you give me a good set-up."

"I should have let you die, man." He grinned.

Zak raised his arms as if he were showing off his muscles. "And miss out on all this. Nothing doing."

"I'll grab the hedge trimmers from the back. You keep it gassed up, right?"

Zak nodded his rattling head.

"Keep it up out here," Ethan said. "I'm heading out back to give it a once-over."

"Be careful."

"I'll do my best. I'm only human."

Ethan laughed. Zak ground his gears again.

After closing the front door behind him, he checked again for shells just to make sure he hadn't missed any, but sure enough, there were none to be found. So he grabbed the only thing he could find quickly, an old broom, and broke the handle over his knee and figured it would have to do.

Then he cracked open the blinds and peeked out.

The backyard was empty save for twenty or so decapitated corpses.

He creaked open the door.

No sign of life. Or movement.

So he stepped outside.

Still no movement.

A few steps into the yard.

Not quiet really, certainly not with the bots still clanging and thundering in the front, but the sort of peaceful that had nothing to do with noise or the lack of it.

Zak had actually been right after all.

If they'd run back to the city, he'd be dead. And a makeshift team of farm equipment robots had saved them.

He was almost at the open workshop doors when he saw her. Marla. With two other zombies, one a woman and the other a teenage boy.

He thought of yelling for help, but that would only draw others if there were more. No. He knew he'd have to deal with these three himself. He may have been only human, but he could still outsmart a goddamn zombie, even if all he had was a broken broom handle.

Without wasting time, he shoved the jagged broken end of the handle into the teenage zombie's eye and didn't stop until it protruded from the back of his skull. When he jerked it free, the creature dropped to the ground and didn't move another inch.

The woman reached for him and grabbed his shirt. He ducked down, but she didn't let go and tumbled on top of him.

Marla watched, not approaching, just cocking her head a slightly to the side like she was thinking about something, and he wondered if some part of her mind somehow recognized him after all. It wasn't normal, he knew, but after whatever had been done to her, she no longer qualified for normal, at least as it went for the living dead.

The woman clawed at him, and he just managed to push her away with the broom handle, but she rammed her face forward and broke through the wood, leaving him with two broken pieces, one in each hand.

Her face, teeth bared and bloody drool threatening to drip onto him, kept coming and he did the only thing he had time to—drive both stakes through her ears. She stopped, looked at him, then sat still on his chest.

Without taking another second to catch his breath, he pushed her off, realizing only when it was too late that he had left his only weapons in the sides of her head.

"Marla?" he asked.

Marla said nothing. Did nothing.

"Is that still you in there, baby? Do you remember me at all?"

Marla gazed at him, studying him as deeply and as thoughtfully as he imagined one of the living dead things she had become could. There seemed to be something there, not a light, but an awareness, a recognition—somehow—that something had changed between them. "Oh God," me mumbled as it hit him. She understood that he was weaponless.

"Honey?"

Then the thing that he had mistaken for his wife lunged at him like a jungle cat.

TODAY.

There was an awful big difference between a robot that thought like a robot, Ethan thought, and a robot that thought like a man. And not just a man, but a man still pining over the woman that got away.

And unfortunately the woman who had come back.

And come back hungry.

Ethan used the ground and even the zombie parts to drag himself back up to his knees, all the while watching Zak fight off the other robots who were determined to follow orders and destroy the female creature behind him.

The green tractor swung a wheeled arm at him, aiming for the vulnerable part of his neck, but Zak caught his arm and twisted it off at the shoulder joints, then used it like a club to beat the bot back until it fell onto its back.

Meanwhile, the baler and the rust-brown tractor-bot were double-teaming him, the tractor going low for his legs and the baler trying to occupy his wildly swinging arms. But Zak was using all the advantages granted him by the larger, combine-based body he had been given. With at least four feet of height and a good two and a half feet of extra reach, not to mention the benefit of his "fist" of spinning blades, the baler had little hope, except for the blades breaking against his bulk.

Zak whirled his blades into a frenzy and brought them down on the baler's arms, but the baler was too sturdy, and all Zak got for his effort was sparks.

So he sought a new tactic.

The other bots were flanking him, letting the baler and the tractor keep him busy while they maneuvered around the back to kill Marla.

Ethan couldn't help but grin at their strategy. He had programmed them well.

"Why are you doing this?" Zak asked. "You should be helping me, not fighting me."

"We have one job to do, kill the zombies," said the tractor.

"We make war. It's our purpose," said the baler.

"It's not your only purpose. Think, damn it!"

"We are thinking," said the Bobcat. "We're outthinking you."

"There's so much else out there to think about though," Zak said, reaching for the baler's shoulder with his free hand.

"We are war machines," said the Bobcat. "There is no other purpose."

"Goddamn programming," Zak muttered as best he could pass off the human sound with his mechanized voice circuits. "Goddamn Ethan!" he yelled.

The Bobcat was above Marla. She stood back, weighing her options with whatever limited planning her dead brain allowed her. The Bobcat though paused only for a moment before striking down with his loader hand.

But Zak was too fast. Holding onto the baler's shoulder, he lifted the bot off the ground and swung him around, rotating at his waist in a 360-degree spin, ignoring the tractor's ineffectual gripping of his legs.

The baler's massive bulk slammed into the Bobcat, and Zak let go, sending both of them flying as a single mass of metal into the workshop. The heavy oak and pine that had been the workshop's walls snapped like balsa wood and the one-room structure collapsed as the two giants flew through it.

With both hands free, Zak smashed the combine arm on the tractor's head, then kicked free and tossed the smaller robot in the opposite direction.

"Go!" Ethan yelled at the two bots that guarded him, the remaining tractor and the scrap-heap bot that had remained at Ethan's side during the fight to protect him. "Don't worry about me. Just get that zombie."

"Okay, boss," said the scrap-heap, and he took off in a run toward Zak while his balance was off from the toss.

The last of the tractors followed him, and the two leapt and hit him just seconds apart, sending Zak down into the dirt, and the three of them rolled a good thirty feet through the wooden fence and into what would have been the corn field back when Ethan and Zak were kids playing hide and seek among the stalks.

All of which left Zak alone with Marla.

Something the zombie seemed to realize too, he could tell. Her dead eyes locked onto him, and she started across the twenty feet between them at a pace faster than Ethan knew he could make. The landing after Zak had thrown him had dislocated his knee, judging by the pain, and all the running around and fighting had caused his back to act up again.

In short, he knew he was in no shape to beat Marla without some kind of weapon.

"Damn you, Zak," he said. "Damn you for choosing her even though she's fucking dead, you goddamn robot!"

He pushed from his knees to his feet. If he was going to die at the hands of his bride, he would damn sure die like a man.

"Come on, Marla!" he yelled, beating his chest like a war-crazed Tarzan. "Come to poppa. Let's have one last kiss, baby."

She kept coming, neither slowing nor speeding her approach.

"Come on. Just hurry it the hell up and get it over with. I've lost you, and now I've lost Zak. I was a fool to think I could save him when I drove out here, and I was an even bigger fool to think I could save him by putting his brain in that damn robot." He took a weak and wobbly step toward Marla. "And I suppose I'm a fool for not running away now. But if I'm gonna die a fool, I'm gonna die a loud fool who takes it like a man."

She was barely five feet away.

He cocked his head back, beckoning her closer. "Come on, baby. Show me that good stuff like you did in the good old days."

Ethan stretched open his arms and held them there, waiting for the death hug. He dropped his bottom lip open. He wouldn't let her bite him on the neck or shoulders. He could do that much at least. He would die with a kiss, a jagged, bite of a kiss that ripped his face into pieces, he knew, but a kiss nevertheless.

She stopped.

There was thunder in the distance.

"Damn it. Don't stop now. Do it. Just fucking do it."

She grinned. She goddamn grinned. She was a zombie and she goddamn grinned. Grinned like she actually remembered him. Grinned like she got the joke that it was his own damn wife delivering the killing blow.

She kept grinning as the top of her head disappeared.

It took him a minute to realize what had happened.

Waiting for the kiss of death, waiting for Marla to stop grinning and come kill him, something had whizzed before him, catching her head just above the jaw and taking the top of her face and skull and hair along with it as it passed by, leaving him staring at Marla's decapitated grin that still waited above her now-still body.

He remembered to breathe, and caught his first breath in nearly a half a minute in one large gulp.

"Wha—" he started.

"You always were..." Click. "...a whiny little..." Click. "...bitch," came the broken voice above and before him.

"Zak."

"Yeah."

"You killed—"

"Yeah."

"I..."

"Yeah."

"Thank you."

"I don't want to talk about it now. Maybe never. And I'm still pissed at you."

Ethan didn't, couldn't add anything to the sputtering he'd just managed.

"Just go get a damn shower. We've got a lot of work to do tomorrow. I need to get my motor systems fixed, and the rest need repairs too. You made 'em damn tough, but not tough enough."

Ethan hadn't yet moved his stare from the headless dead thing in front of him, and he didn't until Zak reached down and picked it up.

"This is mine," Zak said, and he took the Marla-thing to the barn.

Ethan dropped to his knees and began to cry.

In the distance, he saw three of the other bots moving slowly back to the farm.

He sat on his legs, then dropped his arms to his sides, and finally began to trace circles in the dirt, wiping his eyes every now and then before returning to the dirt. In the end, he spelled out the word “over” and circled it.

The thunder behind him told him Zak was coming back.

“You can…” Click. “…have the…” Click. “…house now….” Click. Click. “…But not the barn…” Click. “…The barn’s for me….” Click.

“Fine,” he said. “Let’s fix your voice.

Click. “Not yet….” Click. “Here.”

Zak reached down, and Ethan saw something shining between his metal fingers. Ethan opened his hand, palm up, and Zak dropped the something into it.

Ethan started to cry again, tracing the circle of the gold ring in his palm.

“That’s yours,” Zack said, this time with no clicking. “But she’s mine now.”

Ethan said nothing. What was really left to say?

.01
ANGUS
STOP

ANGUS:
Zombie-Versus-Robot Fighter

Nancy A. Collins

This time the Maze was dimly lit. Not completely dark, but with just enough light to make telling the difference between shadow and zombie tricky. Although Angus had prowled the interior of the Maze for as long as he could remember, each time he entered it anew it was slightly different. Sometimes it was brightly lit, or filled with a thick fog. One time it was even flooded with water up to his knees. So it paid to be cautious, the importance of which was drilled into him from the second he woke up to the moment he fell asleep, for as long as he could remember. Even though the Maze was a training exercise, the consequences of his actions inside it were very, very real. Every moment could very well be his last.

He was dressed in a black one-piece garment made of lightweight ballistic fiber with molded, reinforced high-impact protection plates built into the chest, back, shoulders, groin, and legs—all the critical bite-zones zombies instinctively went for. He also wore a pair of knee-high steel-toed boots to protect his shins from crawlers snapping at his ankles, Kevlar gloves to keep his hands and fingers safe from snapping teeth, and a full-face helmet to guard against skeletal fingers stabbing at his eyeballs. The helmet was outfitted with an oxygen recycler, which kept his breath from fogging up the shatterproof face guard.

Suddenly an older, masculine voice spoke in his ear, as if the owner was standing right beside him. "Be on your lookout, Angus. You might not be able to see the zombie, but it can track you down, simply by following the scent of your living brain. It doesn't even need eyes to hunt you."

"Yes, I *know,* Father," he replied, pushing up the visor on the helmet so he could tap the comm-bud nestled in his ear. "I'm not five years old anymore."

"No, you are not," Father conceded. "Tomorrow you will be eighteen."

"*Shhh,*" Angus hissed, calling for radio silence. "I think I hear it."

Although the walking dead could no longer speak, they were far from mute. As they shambled about, they gave voice to a constant, toneless moaning. It was an eerie sound, like the wailing of a damned soul trapped in the bowels of some nameless Hell, but at least it served as a rudimentary early warning system. Angus' name for the noise they made was the Zombie Call.

As he double-checked his weapon—an automatic rifle fitted with a laser sighting system, special explosive hollow-point ammunition, and a detachable chainsaw bayonet for close-quarters combat—a zombie came stumbling out of the shadows to the left of the T-junction.

Although Angus had never met a police officer before, he had seen enough of them on the Feed to recognize their riot gear—or rather, what was left of it. The front of the zombie-cop's bulletproof vest was in shreds, and its face was a mass of dried blood and exposed gum from where the upper lip had been torn away. The zombie walked with its head tilted back, sniffing the air like a hound trying to catch the scent of a rabbit, even though Angus had never seen a dog or rabbit outside the videos in his lesson plans.

The zombie suddenly made a deep, guttural growl, and its head dropped down with an audible *snap* and swung in his direction. A mixture of saliva and blood poured from the former cop's ruined mouth. It had caught the scent of sweet, sweet brain. Angus quickly lowered his face mask to protect himself from the splatter; all it would take would be one zombie bite, or a single drop of zombie blood entering an open wound in his skin, and it would be Game Over. He had to be careful. After all, he was humanity's last hope.

The laser sights swarmed all over the zombie-cop's torso like angry red bees until they coalesced into a single, blinking red triangle located between its filmy, gray eyes. Angus exhaled as he squeezed the trigger, just as he had been taught when he was five years old. The zombie's head disappeared in a spray of skull fragments, coagulated blood, and clotted gray matter.

A buzzer sounded as the body hit the floor, and the roof of the Maze went from opaque to translucent, revealing Father standing in the viewing booth overhead.

"Excellent job, Angus," he said, giving the thumbs-up sign. "When you're decontaminated, come join me in my lab. There is something I must discuss with you."

One of the walls suddenly split in two, and T-1 and T-2 entered the Maze. The modified guardbots stood over six feet tall, with dome-like heads that swiveled completely around on their wide, metal shoulders, so that nothing could sneak up on them. They were equipped with long, segmented arms capped with three-digit graspers, and rolled along on a set of all-terrain wheels that allowed them to move sideways and pivot in place, so they never had to back up in order to turn around. They had been Angus' near-constant companions for as long as he could remember. T-1 sprayed an enzymatic compound that liquefied the zombie's remains, while T-2 vacuumed up the resulting toxic sludge. Once they were finished, the undead waste would be transported to the Disposal Station, where it would be fed into a nuclear digester.

Angus stripped out of his protective zombie-hunting gear in the changing room and fed it to an incinerator unit, then entered the decontamination stall, which sprayed him head-to-toe with anti-microbial disinfectant. While the Z-virus was the most virulent microscopic nasty carried by the undead, it was far from the only one. They *were* walking bags of rotting flesh, after all. Once the scanner-banks deemed him clear, Angus dressed himself in a fresh one-piece jumpsuit and hurried off to join his father in the Hub.

As he stepped onto the moving sidewalk that connected the Training Facility to the central dome that housed their living quarters and Father's laboratory, Angus was suddenly aware of motion above him. He looked up, peering through the foot-thick hyper-acrylic tube-way, as a forty-foot giant squid glided over his head. He yawned. Kraken were an everyday occurrence when you grow up in a secret undersea laboratory base.

His father had built the deep-sea dome, called the Hub, long before the zombie plague became a problem, and in the years since the initial outbreak he had added three smaller annexes, connected via tube-ways.

The first was the Training Facility, which also housed the zombie pen; the second was the Garden, which replicated a topside greenspace; and the third was the Disposal Station, where the liquefied remains of the zombie hunts were incinerated.

Of the three annexes, Angus spent most of his time in the Training Facility. Although Father insisted it was important for him to acquaint himself with the plant life found topside, as this was where he would be transported once he finished his training, Angus found the green, living carpet called grass and the surrounding flowering bushes and leafy trees in the Garden disconcerting. As for the Disposal Station, he had never been allowed inside its doors. Father said it was an environment created by robots for robots, and therefore hostile to human life.

Upon returning to the Hub, Angus reported promptly to the lab. There he found Father staring into a neutron microscope while busily scribbling notes into a computer tablet with a stylus. He was dressed in his usual combination of white lab coat, black turtleneck sweater and faded corduroys, his cowlick as defiant as ever.

"You said you wanted to see me, Father?" Angus prompted.

"Yes, I do," the scientist said, looking up from his work with a weary smile. "By the way, you handled yourself very well today."

"Thank you, sir," Angus replied humbly.

"You know, when I first proposed creating an elite class of human zombie-fighters to combat the plague, everyone said it was a waste of time—it was too easy for infection to be spread through human agents." Father sighed, setting aside his notes. "Why take the risk when we could send battalions of bots to do the job for us?

"I argued that Mankind has a bad habit of relying on technology to get itself out of tight spots—especially those created by technology. Bots are merely tools, Angus. And tools, while useful, have no heart or soul. They simply do what they have been programmed to do, nothing more, nothing less. Ensuring the survival of the human race is just another task for them to complete, no different than loading a cargo ship or recalibrating an engine.

"This is humanity's darkest hour, my son. Now, more than ever, mankind needs a hero, a symbol, to give the people of the world hope. That is why I brought you to this secret laboratory as a baby. That is why I have trained you how to hunt and kill zombies since you were old enough to hold a gun. You know *everything* there is to know about the undead—

both their strengths and their weaknesses, and how to defeat them—than any human alive. The human race needs to see one of its own fighting tirelessly for its survival: a hero dedicated to wiping out the zombie menace not because he is *programmed* to do so, but because that is what he was *born* to do. *You* are that hero, Angus. *You* are humanity's last hope."

Angus shifted about in boredom, as this was not the first time he'd heard this rant.

"Tomorrow is a special day for you. It is both your eighteenth birthday and your final day of training. If you complete the Final Test, you will finally be allowed to leave the Hub and start fighting zombies topside."

Angus blinked in surprise. Although he had known this day would eventually come, he had not imagined it would be so soon. "What if I fail the test, Father?" he asked.

"Then you will die and become a zombie, of course."

THE MOMENT THE door to his quarters irised open, the far wall turned translucent and images from the Feed began to stream across its surface. There was no controlling what appeared on the Feed or shutting it off. It played constantly whenever he was in his room. The Feed was comprised of what Father called "programs," but not like the ones that ran the robots. These programs featured humans of all types doing things like solve crime or cure diseases, or have misadventures involving their friends and family, while invisible people laughed in the background. Outside of Father, they were the only examples of the human race he'd ever seen. The zombies didn't count.

Angus had no memory of his mother, since she died shortly after giving birth to him. At least that's what Father said when he asked him about her. Angus sometimes wondered what his mother looked and sounded like, as Father had no photos or videos of her. He wondered if she was a zombie now. He had slain numerous walking dead over the course of his training, some of which had been female. Maybe his mother had been one of them?

He sat on the edge of his bed and stared at the Feed. It showed a young man and woman walking through a forest, surrounded by grass and trees, like the ones in the Garden, except the trees in the Feed weren't growing in plastic buckets and were more than eight feet tall.

Angus didn't like how large they were, compared to the humans. Zombies could be hiding behind any one of them, waiting to strike.

Angus continued to watch the young couple as they took out a blanket and spread it on the forest floor. As he watched, his hands clenched themselves in anticipation of a rotting waitress or a decomposing meter-reader lurching out of the shadows. The man and woman began to undress one another, while Angus continued to remain vigilant. Even if there were no zombies in the vicinity, it was still very likely one of the two people could be infected with the Z-virus. At any moment, one of them might find themselves possessed of a ravenous hunger for human brains, and turn on their lover. Within seconds their passionate kisses would easily turn into savage bites, their lustful moans warp into screams.

If his eighteen years of training had taught him anything, it was that inside every human was a zombie waiting to get out.

SOMEONE WAS calling his name.

He looked around, trying to identify the source of the voice. He was surrounded on all sides by towering edifices of bark and wood, a thousand times taller than the stunted specimens Father grew under the artificial sunlight in the Garden. The trees were dark and sinister, like the talking ones in the program about the girl with the ruby shoes.

"*Angus!*"

He turned in the direction of the voice and saw a young woman running through the woods toward a nearby clearing. Her hair was long and loose and the color of gold, and her short skirt and flimsy blouse showed flashes of lithe legs and supple arms. At first he thought she was fleeing zombies, but then he heard her laughter floating on the air. He smiled and gave chase, eager to escape the close confines of the forest.

He found himself on the edge of an open meadow, a hundred times bigger than the carpet of tame grass that lived in the Garden. The young woman was standing at its center, spinning around in a circle, her head thrown back, her arms spread wide as if to embrace the world.

"Isn't it *wonderful*, Angus?" she giggled. "To finally be *free*?"

"Free from what?" he asked, staring at her flawless skin and sparkling eyes. Given that she was the only living woman he had ever seen, she was also the most beautiful. His gaze fell to her low-cut blouse, and her bountiful cleavage. Although he knew he should be scanning his surroundings in case of a zombie attack, he could not look away from her perfectly formed breasts, with their erect nipples straining against the gossamer-thin fabric that covered them. His penis thickened and grew heavy, distracting him even further.

"From *everything*, silly!" she laughed, pirouetting so that she fell into his arms. "From Father, the robots, the zombies, the training—all of it! You're finally free to live your own life!"

"But I'm humanity's last hope," he replied automatically, as he looked down into her perfect face. Her lips were as pink and finely formed as the petals on the rosebush in the Garden. "I'm a zombie-fighter."

"But is that what *you* want to be?" she asked, her voice so hushed Angus was forced to lean in close to hear it. She smelled of grass and flowers, and something else, something familiar, yet he could not pinpoint it. As his erection continued to grow and harden, it blocked more and more of his ability to think rationally.

"Who are you?" he whispered.

"Don't you recognize me?" she replied as she reached up and pulled his mouth down to hers. "I'm your mother."

Although Angus felt confusion, shame, and frustration rise within him, his penis remained rock hard and insistent. He knew he should cast her aside, but he could not bring himself to do so. In the eighteen years of his life, he had yet to know the embrace of another human being. He could not remember Father ever hugging him or picking him up, or even giving him as so much as a pat on the back. All he ever did was smile and give Angus the occasional thumbs-up. The yearning for human contact, if only for a moment's consolation, was so strong he was willing to lower his guard in order to embrace the forbidden.

As his mother's mouth closed on his, the mysterious odor Angus had noticed earlier grew stronger and more distinct. With a horrible start, he finally recognized it. It was the smell of the Z-virus as it turned living flesh into walking meat. He opened his eyes to find the beautiful face with its perfect skin had become gaunt and turned the color of tallow. As he tried to pull away, his mother's eyelids flew open, to reveal the muddied, clouded pupils of the walking dead. He screamed, only to have his mouth instantly fill with blood.

His zombie-mother staggered backward, his lower lip clamped between her teeth, where it hung, pink and bloody, like some pendulous wounded tongue, before being swallowed in a single gulp. Her jaw dropped open and the awful, mindless Zombie Call rose from her deflated lungs.

ANGUS SAT STRAIGHT up in bed, gasping in panic as he clawed desperately at his jaw. He heaved a sigh of relief upon realizing his lower lip was still attached to his face. However, the wailing noise from his nightmare was still ringing in his ears. With a start, he realized it was the breech alarm. That meant zombies had escaped the pens in the Training Facility and invaded the Hub.

He grabbed the emergency zombie-fighting suit from his wardrobe and quickly put it on. He then opened the gun locker at the foot of his bed and took out his weapon. He fired up the bayonet and the electric chainsaw roared to life, sending a reassuring shudder up his arm.

"*Father! Please report!*" he barked as he tapped the comm-bud in his right ear, but all he heard was the eerie silence of an open line.

As he stepped out into the corridor, his heart was beating so hard the protective chestplate embedded in the suit was throbbing in time with his pulse. Angus' life had been filled with fear from the age of five, when he was first sent into the Maze with a handgun to confront a zombie toddler in a pair of blood-stained pajamas. Every day since then he had faced the walking dead and bested them, whether with firearms, power tools, blunt instruments, or sporting equipment. Although he was confident in his ability to handle the zombie breech, he was also scared as hell. But then, Father said it was good to be afraid, since it was his fear that had kept him alive for so long.

The lights in the hallway flashed red, dyeing everything the color of blood. As he headed in the direction of his father's quarters, he saw a zombie lurch into view. It was what Father called a "husk": more skeleton than corpse, its eyes long withered in its skull. The nose was a shriveled piece of cartilage, but it seemed to have no trouble catching Angus's scent. As the zombie staggered blindly toward him, it began to bite at the air, in anticipation of the meal to come, only to have its lower jaw suddenly snap off and fall onto the metal floor. The exposed tongue writhed about like a slug, looking far more obscene than the desiccated genitals swinging between its mummified thighs.

Angus shouldered his weapon and the zombie's head disappeared in a spray of clotted brains. As the long-dead body dropped to the ground, it revealed another one right behind it. This second zombie must have been an exotic dancer or porn star, judging by its faded, artificial tan and large, equally unreal breasts, which were ghoulishly ample compared to the rest of its desiccated body. The zombie-stripper hissed and lunged forward, swiping at him with long, airbrushed acrylic nails. Since he was too close for the rifle, Angus used the chainsaw instead, parting the zombie-stripper's dyed blonde hair all the way to the brain. He flinched as the blood and gray matter splashed against the faceplate of his helmet, but did not stop until its clouded eyes rolled back in their sockets, showing nothing but yellow.

"T-1! T-2! Are you online? I need a status report!" Angus shouted as he yanked the chainsaw free of the zombie-stripper's skull. He understood why he couldn't raise Father on the comm-bud, but was baffled why the guardbots remained silent. Although he had terminated scores of zombies in the past, it was always with the knowledge that T-1 and T-2 were there to back him up. The idea of combating the undead all by himself made his stomach knot and his heart race even faster. His years of training, however, enabled him to compartmentalize his anxiety and keep it from taking control of his thoughts. While a normal human being in his predicament would piss themselves with fear, Angus's mind was racing to tabulate the number of zombies that might be loose within the Hub.

T-1 and T-2 usually left the undersea base every three months to capture a dozen or so free range undead for training purposes, and since it was nearing the end of the third quarter, that meant there were probably only four or five zombies left in the pens. The odds weren't impossible—he'd faced as many as ten at once—but that was in the familiar confines of the Maze, under Father's watchful eye. He quickly put those negative thoughts aside; panicking would not get him anywhere but dead.

The portal to Father's quarters was fully dilated. Angus stepped inside, scanning the room for any sign of life. He was not surprised to see the bed had not been slept in, as Father spent the vast majority of his time working in the laboratory, trying to find a means to defeat the Z-virus.

Suddenly he was aware of something wrapping itself around his left leg, followed by a sharp, painful pinch to his calf. He looked down to find a crawler—the reanimated upper torso of a zombie—trying to gnaw its way through his boot and shin guard. Although the creature had been severed at the waist, and was dragging what remained of its guts behind it, it did not seem in the least bit inconvenienced by its bifurcation.

As he pulled his Bowie knife from its sheath and sliced the zombie's head from its shoulders, Angus cursed himself for paying too much attention to eye-level threats. While the hands immediately lost their grip on his leg, the severed head continued to chew on his shin until he plunged the blade into its ear, spearing the decomposing brain like an olive. The crawler's jaws instantly flew open, and the pain in his calf disappeared. He paused just long enough to make sure that the bite hadn't penetrated the outer protective layer of his suit, before heading in the direction of the laboratory. If Father was anywhere, it was there. And if his tabulations were correct, he only had one more zombie to worry about.

As he rounded the corner to the laboratory, Angus spotted his final target. At first, when he saw the thing hobbling toward him, he thought someone had taken a pair of zombies and lashed them together in a grotesque parody of a three-legged race. Then he realized that he was looking at a pair of conjoined twins, fused at the hip and pelvis, so that the left leg of the zombie on the right was the right leg of the one on the left. As it drew closer, he could see that the twin on the right must have been the first to succumb to the Z-virus, since the one on the left was missing most of its face and scalp. The zombie-twins' voices melded into a single, wordless cry of undying hunger as they clumsily made their way toward him, reaching out with their multiple arms as if to pull him into an eternal embrace.

With a mighty shout of anger and disgust, Angus swung the chainsaw's whirring blade down, separating in death that which was never cut asunder in life. The conjoined zombies parted down the middle, toppling to either side. He shot the right-hand twin point-blank, then stomped down on its faceless brother's head as hard as he could, cracking open the exposed skull like an egg and sending spinal fluid and liquefied brains squirting from its ears and nose.

Suddenly the comm-bud came to life, and Father's voice spoke. "Happy Birthday, Angus! You have passed the Final Test! You are now the perfect zombie-fighter!"

He looked up to see the reassuring bulk of T-1 and T-2 at the end of the corridor. They rolled toward him, shoulder to shoulder, just like the zombie-twins he'd just terminated, creating a looming wall of steel. Assuming they were there to clean up the undead, Angus pushed up the visor on his helmet and smiled in welcome. Then a cylindrical tube emerged from T-1's chest and flooded the corridor with knock-out gas.

HE WOKE UP staring at the ceiling, feeling drugged and strangely numb, as if his body was a million miles away. His vision kept going in and out of focus and his ears seemed awash in white noise.

"Where am I?" he asked, looking around at his unfamiliar surroundings.

"You are in the Disposal Station," Father's voice said, sounding strangely distant.

Angus frowned in confusion. "I thought you said only robots could survive the conditions inside the Disposal Station?"

"That is true."

As he struggled to sit up, Angus saw he was lying on a long metal table. Next to him was an identical slab, but this one held a young, Caucasian male missing the top of his skull. With a dull start of horror, he realized he was staring at his own body.

He looked down at himself, in hopes that what he had seen wasn't real, only to recoil at the sight of a metal torso and a pair of robot hands. Although it felt as if his limbs were deadened to all sensation, he managed to get to his feet.

As he glanced down at the shiny metal surface of the table, he saw the reflection of a shatterproof hyper-acrylic skull, inside of which could be seen a human brain floating in a bath of synthetic cerebrospinal fluid and covered in numerous electrodes and wires. In place of eyes, the see-through skull's sockets contained a pair of unblinking, hi-def cameras.

When he was finally able to look away from the horrifying visage, he realized Father was standing opposite him, dressed in a white lab-smock, the front of which was smeared with blood. "There is no need to be alarmed, Angus," Father smiled, speaking in the same calm, reassuring tone of voice he had used for as long as the boy could remember. "The vertigo and sensory deprivation are temporary until your brain becomes accustomed to your new inputs. You will find your new body works just as well—even better—than the one you were born with. Not only will you be faster, stronger, and able to see spectrums and hear frequencies impossible to the human eye and ear, you are now impervious to hunger, cold, heat, and fatigue. You will be a tireless warrior in the battle against the undead plague."

"How could you do this to me—?" Angus intended the words to be a shocked, heart-broken wail of betrayal. Instead, they were spoken in the dry, inflection-less voice of a robot. "I'm your son! Your own flesh and blood!" he tried to scream as he punched Father in the face. To his dismay, the blithely smiling scientist didn't even flinch, although the blow should have fractured his jaw. The only visible damage was a sizable gouge underneath Father's right cheekbone, revealing a steely skeleton underneath his synthetic skin. "You're a robot?" Angus gasped in surprise. Despite the horror of his own predicament, he was still shocked by this revelation.

"Yes, I am a robot," Father replied, pointing a remote control unit at the newly minted cyborg. "A sci-bot, to be exact. I was created in the image of, and programmed by, the human scientist who originally created the Hub, in order to assist him in his work. And to avoid any further damage to either of us, I am shutting down the connections to your motor system."

What little sensation Angus was receiving from his new body abruptly disappeared altogether. He tried to raise his arm and move his legs, only to find them inert as lead ingots. "What happened to my real father and mother? What did you do to them?"

"You have no parents, as humans understand the words," Father replied flatly, no longer bothering to hide his robotic voice. "You are a clone; one of the A-Series. You are the fourteenth, in fact, to undergo training in this facility. To save on downtime, the clones are born as five-year-olds. The first was called Aaron, the second was Absalom, the third Ace, and so on."

"What happened to the others?"

"They are dead; killed during training. Most of them perished the first time they were sent into the Maze, save for the once called Ajax—he managed to survive until the age of six. Every time one of the A-Series is slain or becomes infected, a new one is decanted. You are the first and only A-Series to survive to adulthood and complete the training program."

"You're telling me my entire life has been an insane lie—why go through the pointless charade of pretending to be my father?"

"I am unable to make a decision or have an opinion as to the logic behind my creator's thought processes. However, a search of available data banks shows considerable discussion among my creator's peer group as to his mental health in regard to this matter. However, as he possessed a sizable private fortune, he proceeded with his plans, regardless of government or societal approval.

"My creator was convinced that the parent-child bond was the most effective way to make sure the clones were indoctrinated with the drive to keep the human race alive. He personally oversaw the training of clones Aaron through Aeneas. However, he eventually succumbed to the Z-virus and was added to the zombie pens, fifteen years ago. His zombie was the first one you encountered during the Final Test. It was kept 'alive' during this time by feeding it the occasional clone—starting with the B-Series. It was his last order to be destroyed by his own zombie-fighter as part of the Final Test.

"My creator made adaptations to my AI in order for me to continue his project, allowing me a certain amount of what humans once called 'free will.' It was my creator's intention that his ultimate zombie-fighter be humanity's savior, despite the fact the human body is weak and uniquely susceptible to the Z-virus. This was illogical, as robots are clearly physically superior when it comes to combating zombies. I therefore came to the logical conclusion that to send you out into a world full of cannibal zombies clothed in nothing but flesh and blood was counterintuitive to my creator's goal. By placing your brain inside a robot body, I am able to complete my programming. The nuclear battery housed in your robot body should keep your brain alive for at least two thousand years, which, according to the master computer system, should be long enough for you to find and kill every zombie topside."

"*Two thousand years?*" Angus wanted to scream, but the best he could do was turn up the volume on his voice until it distorted. "How many zombies *are* there?"

"The last census estimated the world's human population at 10.5 billion. Following the outbreak of the Z-virus, the human population was believed to be 7.6 billion. According to the master computer system shared by the bot nation, I would estimate the current number of zombies to be seven billion, five hundred million, nine-hundred ninety-nine thousand, nine hundred ninety-eight."

"You mean there are only *two* humans left alive on the face of the Earth?"

"That figure includes you, of course," Father pointed out. "The other is an infant female being kept in an underground bunker, surrounded by a phalanx of bot protectors and caregivers. Now that you have finished your training, and assumed your new form, you will be transported topside by T-1 and T-2. Good luck, Angus. Upon your human wits and strength rests the future of Mankind!"

"Fuck you, Father! Fuck you, you cocksucking soulless machine! I'm going to kill you, you motherfucking robot! You hear me? I'm going to come back and tear your grinning metal head off and shove it up your—"

"It will be better for your transition if you go offline during transport," Father smiled, pushing yet another button on the remote. The stream of profanity spilling from Angus's speakers abruptly cut off.

Having fulfilled its programming, Father turned away as the twin workbots trundled the cyborg off to the jet-sled. The zombie-fighter was fully trained and on its way to save humanity. The sci-bot sent a wireless message via one of the servicebots to the Hub's mainframe and ordered it to prepare the next clone in the A-Series—Aoen—for decanting.

WHEN ANGUS CAME back online it was to find himself standing alone in the middle of a city. Everywhere he looked there were towering blocks of steel and glass rising into the sky. After a lifetime spent in a dome at the bottom of the ocean, his first sight of the bright blue emptiness overhead was enough to paralyze him with amazement and anxiety. His sense of wonder ended, however, upon seeing the dead bodies—some of them stacked up in piles two stories high. Despite the horribleness of his situation, he was relieved his sense of smell had yet to return.

The windows of the storefronts and shops that lined the boulevard were shattered, their contents strewn in the gutters, mixed in with paper money and other trash. Here and there were burned-out military vehicles scattered among their civilian kin, like so many abandoned toys. As a boy he had studied the different topside cities shown on the Feed and dreamed about the day he would finally be free to explore them on his own. But now, not only did Angus not know which city he was in, he did not care. New York, London, Paris, and Beijing were all alike now, weren't they? Dead is dead.

Just then the auditory receptors that replaced his ears picked up a noise. It was very faint, but quickly grew in volume. At first he thought it was what his lesson plans had called wind, whistling through the concrete and steel canyons of the city. Then he recognized it. It was the Zombie Call. Only he had never heard it this *loud* before.

Seconds later, pale, rotting faces appeared at the empty windows, and shuffling figures filled the open doorways. Some still had eyes, while others made do with empty sockets, yet all of them sniffed the air like the ones he used to hunt in the Maze. Ever since the last living human in the city had been torn, screaming, limb from limb, they had lain dormant, hidden within the abandoned skyscrapers, desecrated churches, and burned-out shopping malls. But now they were being drawn from their hidey-holes, like maggots wriggling from a long-dead corpse, lured forth by the smell of human brains—the only living brains for thousands of miles. They came pouring forth, in all their funeral glory, driven by a hunger greater than the grave, crawling over one another until they were an amorphous tidal wave of rotten flesh, all teeth and clawing, groping hands. There was no need to wonder where they might be hiding—all he had to do was stand there, and they would come to him.

Years of training took over, and Angus began instinctively killing the zombies out of fear for a life that was no longer mortal. The first zombie might have been a woman at one time. It was hard to tell. He grabbed its head with one metal hand and squeezed, only to have it pop like a ripe zit.

By the end of the first day, Angus had to admit Father had been right. A robot body made it very easy to kill zombies. By his calculations, he was killing one zombie every two seconds, each minute of the day, since neither he nor they slept. That meant there were 43,200 down, and only seven billion, five hundred million, nine-hundred ninety-eight thousand, five hundred fifty-eight to go.

That's when he started to scream.

HE WAS STILL screaming a month later.

And had taken two steps.

Silo 01
DINE
20

TO DENVER (with Hiram Battling Zombies)

Steve Rasnic Tem

Elliot was pissed. Not that he let his colleagues see it—that would be unprofessional. But he could say whatever he wanted in front of Hiram. Hiram was easy to talk to. Hiram *got* Elliot as no one else did.

"Three weeks from graduation. And they cancel it. No diploma. No job at NASA."

"*C'est très malheureux,*" Hiram replied.

Elliot had to think a second. His own French was rusty, but he was glad he'd programmed some French fluency into Hiram along with the numerous additional logic routines. Everything sounded better in French. "That's right," he told the robot. "Most unfortunate indeed. I mean, they *say* the delay's temporary, until the zombie plague is under control. But you and I, Hiram, we know. It's not going to get better, is it, buddy?"

"*No. Nous sommes tout condamnés.*"

"Enough with the French, okay? I've got to concentrate here. It's important that you're skilled with *all* weaponry, not just the basics. And no, we're not *all* doomed, just the dumb ones, the unprepared, the cannon fodder. You and me, we're going to do just *fine.* Now stand up, try those out."

Hiram rolled his two-ton frame up and off the worktable so smoothly he might have been weightless. Never mind that he looked like three refrigerators ganged together with some arm and leg sections connected, and a head like an armored shop vac, he moved well enough. Hiram took an immediate stance, made a military turn, and pointed his left arm down the reinforced corridor at a dummy dressed in ripped clothes and a baseball cap fitted sideways. Elliot always used a cap, and maintained a stock with different team names, including a large number honoring their own University of Wisconsin Badgers. He always took pains to get the expression correct on the figure's face—just the right blend of vacuousness and insatiable hunger typical of zombies and undergraduates in the humanities. Hiram made a clucking noise, then fired the minishell out of a short polished barrel. Its trajectory brought it into the dummy about mid-chest. The dummy shuddered, then imploded, its pieces falling into a constricted pile.

"Congratulations," Hiram said. "You have minimized the external damage."

"Why, thank you, Hiram. You'd think I could at least get a blasted degree out of it." At that moment a small gamebot wandered into the corridor, stopped, and looked down at the zombie dummy debris. Elliot reached up, tapped Hiram on the arm, and said, "Again." Hiram raised his arm and seconds later the bot was reduced to a few smoking metal cinders.

"Nooo!" One of the other grad students—Jack, Mack, or John; Elliot never could quite get the name right—pushed past them and hovered over the bot bits.

"Sorry…um, comrade. He wandered into the shot, I'm afraid. I suppose you'll have to find someone else to play Intergalactic Digital Checkers or whatever."

"An improper use of government grant money," Hiram interjected.

"Well, technically, Hiram. But I'm sure my colleague here had a good reason for turning a government-issue robot, on loan, into some sort of gaming machine."

"I was working on gaming theory!" the fellow said, sweeping the bot pieces into a pan.

"Oh, is that why it somehow developed the ability to project vintage science fiction videos?"

The alarm went off and the lab's security monitors came on. The cameras had zeroed in on the barricades down by the Chemistry building on Johnson Street, overwhelmed by a mess of ruined humanity now spilling like a sack of vengeful toys over and around its crumbling concrete edges. The bulk of them were oozing toward Campus Drive—driven less by direct intention than by the pressure of their sheer numbers—and would reach the facility at WRISL in no time. Elliot figured he and Hiram had but a few minutes to make an exit.

"Hey, Jack?" Elliot called to the grad student intently sweeping up the pitiful results of his studies. Hadn't he even noticed the world was coming to an end? When the fellow didn't look up, Elliot continued. "Mack? John? Oh, come on! Jacob?" And at that Jacob looked up, putting a small smile of triumph on Elliot's face. "Jacob! Yes! I think you're in charge now. I just have to go stow Hi—this robot."

"But Elliot…you weren't…I was already the senior grad student."

"Yes, you were! And doing a splendid job. I'll be back in just a second for your orders—always glad to serve in a crisis."

Before Jacob could formulate a reply Elliot had gathered a few folders full of notes and headed toward the freight elevator, the warbot following him at an unhurried pace. They exited on the side of the building where Elliot had the lab's customized Humvee packed and waiting. "This is authorized," Hiram said. It didn't sound like a question. Hiram really didn't ask questions. He posited assumptions and proceeded if there were no objections. Elliot could appreciate that and wouldn't think of objecting.

Thanks to some of Elliot's additional programming, the warbot was able to take the wheel. They headed south toward the lake, maneuvering around numerous pieces of abandoned armored equipment. The government had given the University of Wisconsin pretty much everything they'd asked for in terms of surplus military ordnance in order to protect some key engineering research. But the idea that even an enhanced campus police force would make good use of said equipment had been a foolish one. Half of the campus forces had deserted more than a week ago. "We have a destination," Hiram stated.

"Yes. We'll make our way out US 151 through Iowa on to I80 and Cheyenne and Laramie, then down the back way into Rocky Mountain National Park. Cash has an agricultural compound near there. Well armed. He grows 'medicinal herbs,' as he calls them."

"You have characterized your relationship with your brother as problematic."

This gave Elliot pause. How much had he told Hiram? "His real name is Chad. What does that tell you?" When Hiram didn't respond, Elliot continued. "But family is family. He warned me to avoid Denver. 'Bro, a very bad situation there,' he said. That warning could suggest a thaw in the relationship, I believe."

In fact, he had always considered his brother a dope-smoking idiot, a gross caricature of a human being who'd tormented the younger Elliot unmercifully as they were growing up. But Elliot considered most people idiots. The arrival of the zombie plague had required very little psychological adjustment on his part. He'd never trusted people anyway.

He became aware of a slapping sound on the side of the Humvee, turned his head, and came face-to-face with the devastated grin of the zombie hanging on to the door handle by one hand. It reached up and slapped the reinforced glass ineffectively with the other hand—wrist broken, fingers straying in numerous directions.

"Grakkgul brangt!" came from the zombie's mouth. Through the thick glass it sounded some distance and several evolutionary steps away.

"I can dispose of that," Hiram declared.

"That's all right. It gives me the unique opportunity to study one up close, in a protected setting. I should know what I'm up against. Say *ahh*," he said to the zombie, since the creature already had its mouth wide open with its torn lips pressed fully against the glass. This clearly facilitated an oral exam, but Elliot considered that the subject couldn't assume that pose unless the jaw hinge was completely disconnected or disintegrated.

He was immediately sorry he'd looked—the tongue lay blackened, swollen, and split, struggling like the reanimated corpse of a giant slug. Crumbling teeth and dental fixtures hung at all angles like castle ruins. "Perhaps you could drive a bit faster," he suggested, "shake this gentleman loose?"

The Humvee bucked forward, swerving smoothly around abandoned vehicles and piles of street debris. In his peripheral vision Elliot was aware of a sudden pixilation of the horizon line, and looked to see the zombies slowly appearing over cars, walls, and other low-lying features.

"There has been a serious breach," Hiram said unnecessarily. "I can define 'serious' in terms of probabilities."

"Don't bother." Elliot gripped the seat more tightly.

There was a loud *whump*. Hiram and Elliott turned their heads simultaneously and observed that another zombie had attached itself to the first one, blending torn flesh into missing bits so that the pair appeared to be the corpse of conjoined twins.

Another *whump* and another corpse had attached itself, followed by a double *whump* and two more. Soon they were building up like barnacles on a hull. The Humvee began to wobble.

"A minor maintenance task to improve stability." Hiram swerved out of the road and up onto the wide sidewalk. Elliot's eyes widened slightly as the Humvee headed directly for the marble corner of the next building. At the last possible moment the Humvee turned slightly, there was a loud *shkrunch*, and the Humvee drove parallel to and six inches away from the building for a few yards before returning to the street, its barnacled mass removed. "There is carpal debris on the right door handle. A car wash is approx—"

"Never mind. Continue to our destination."

They headed south past the stadium and down alongside the lake and the arboretum. Most of the obstacles they encountered were not the zombies (whose speed was due only to the pressure of their increasing numbers, otherwise being slow, locomotively challenged in their severe physical deterioration—Elliot was reminded of mold spreading across a slice of bread). The road blockages were almost entirely due to the panic of the still-living and their attempts to escape the inevitable. Hiram had been unable to avoid running down a few of these reckless refugees—which was hardly his fault, vehicle/pedestrian avoidance not being part of his programming.

The grounds of the arboretum appeared to be largely empty of the zombie incursion, no doubt because it was spare in people (and their appetizing brains). The surviving students might do better hiding here than in their tiny dorm rooms, which was much akin to a burger hiding inside a Happy Meal.

"Before we leave the area—we have room for one passenger," Hiram suggested. "My estimates tell me we have time to pick up a friend without a significant impact on our chances of success."

"A friend?"

"Yes. We have time to pick up one of your friends. And space. Male or female."

Elliot was surprised to feel himself blush. After a moment he replied, "That won't—be necessary. There are no—friends—I can think of—for the moment. We will continue on course."

They made their way down interstate 151 to Dodgeville, an older town Elliot remembered from his initial trip into Wisconsin. Thinking he needed more medical supplies, he ordered Hiram to loop through the historic downtown to the hospital. Zombies were singularly unimpressed by history, however, and apparently had nothing better to do than attack the Humvee like a school of sharks, albeit slow-moving, brain-damaged ones. Hiram ploughed the vehicle through the mass of them to the hospital, Elliot cherry-picked supplies, and they roared out again.

In Dubuque Elliot had a craving for old-fashioned ice cream and rode the Fourth Street funicular railway while devouring a cone. As the two cars passed each other going up and down the steep hill ("shortest and steepest railroad in the world," they claimed—but every funicular made the same boast), Elliot watched as zombies lost their balance going both up and down the tracks trying to get to him, falling under the wheels and getting crushed between the cars. Hiram stood by to ensure that Elliot's amusement ride experience was a safe one.

In Cedar Rapids, birthplace of Grant Wood, Elliot took a photograph of a zombie holding a pitchfork standing alongside a female companion (perhaps—the amount of missing flesh sometimes made such identifications difficult).

In Des Moines debris from an exploded gas tanker and several wrecked freight transports forced a detour down Highway 65. There they encountered an honest-to-god orangutan along the side of the road with his arms draped around two zombies in tattered "Great Ape Trust" T-shirts. If the ape noticed anything peculiar about the two tourists it gave no indication. "Which answers two questions, Hiram. Would an ape recognize a zombie if he saw one? And would a zombie mistake an ape brain for an average human one and attempt to eat it? Apparently the answer is *No* in both cases."

For the most part the zombies had left Interstate 80 alone. This was probably in part due to its elevated nature, but more importantly because it bypassed most of the population centers by several miles at least. The designers of the interstate system had been inadvertently foresighted in this case. Elliot had seen some evidence of zombie incursion here and there along the highway, in the form of twitching debris. A single zombie was no match for a speeding vehicle.

He could still see the Adair, Iowa, yellow "smiley-face" water tower from the interstate, surrounded by a gang of zombies. Did they think this was some sort of giant human being? Were they thirsty? He didn't stop to find out.

Outside Minden they had to pull off the road and under a bridge to avoid a tornado. Bodies floated by as the tornado chewed its way east. He had no idea whether they were human or zombie or cow.

Just before Omaha the oil pressure light started flickering. "I am not programmed to fix an automobile," Hiram announced.

"We can't risk the consequences of a breakdown," Elliot also stated plainly. "Best go into the city and find a garage with a still-living mechanic."

"The odds—" Hiram began.

"Doesn't matter. I have no intention of living the rest of my life, however long, in Nebraska."

The first dozen or so service stations were empty, or worse. The stench was terrible. Then, as they were approaching a BP sign, Elliot saw an older man in greasy coveralls running toward them, a desperate look smeared across his face. He couldn't quite see who or what was chasing the man, but that wasn't hard to puzzle out. There was a background noise somewhat like that of a babbling brook, if the sound were greatly amplified, and if the mouths issuing the babble contained numerous broken and decaying parts.

"Hiram, pull alongside and let the man in."

The robot drove forward until the Humvee was parallel to the runner, opened his door, and in one continuous motion pulled the old man in, tossed him into a corner of the backseat, and shut the door again. He continued forward, zombie arms and heads, torsos, crunching like stick men.

"You boys—" The old man paused and looked at Hiram. " 'Scuse me, you fellers is life savers! My name's Randall Carter—"

"We have a flickering oil light," Elliot said.

" 'Scuse—oh? Oil pump, most likely."

"Can you get us one around here and put it in?"

"Take a left at the light. Not this one, but the dead one, next block." Randall sounded grim and professional.

He worked quickly, but thoroughly. They were out of the city and back on Interstate 80 without any more significant zombie encounters.

"So where you fellers headin'?" Randall asked. "I got kin in Grand Island."

"Based on what you saw of the engine, do you anticipate any more maintenance?" Elliot asked.

"Oh no, she's a beauty, all right—all new, none of that surplus crap. A thousand miles at least. We sure is lucky—"

"Hiram, say goodbye to Mr. Carter."

Hiram opened his door, grabbed the old man by the back of the neck, tossed him outside, and shut the door again. Hiram and Elliot twisted slightly around and watched the body bounce off the highway. "Goodbye," Hiram finally said.

In Lincoln, Elliot wanted to view the sunken gardens from 27th Street "one last time. I grew up here, Hiram. Hated it. Except for the sunken gardens. Every year they'd have a different theme. One year it was Vincent Van Gogh. Amazing! The colors, the swirls."

They found a devastated garden, a single zombie staring at them dumbly, standing in a patch of Naked Ladies. "Hiram, that's *Amaryllis belladona* he's standing in! You know what to do."

Hiram lobbed a minishell into the zombie's puzzled expression.

Near Kearney they passed under the archway of the Great Platte River Road Archway Monument, a museum built over the highway. As they were going under it, Elliot looked up to see the hundreds of broken and disintegrated faces staring down from the supports.

In Big Springs they stopped for fuel. The town was completely empty. Elliot assumed a complete depletion of the food supply, and then those remaining, human or most likely otherwise, had moved on.

They took a side trip into Julesburg, Colorado, only because Elliot had once been there as a child. The pony express had gone through here, there was an old trading post, and the town had been featured in an old episode of *Cheyenne*. Clint Walker had starred.

They also stopped in Kimball ("The High Point of Nebraska!") to see the Titan I missile. Hiram stared at it for a very long time, but had no answer when Elliot asked him why.

In Cheyenne, Wyoming, they raided a store for western wear. Even the largest cowboy hat Elliot could find didn't fit Hiram. Elliot loved the boots he'd picked out for himself—they seemed as extravagant in their way as a medieval tapestry.

In Laramie they spent some time admiring the Medicine Bow mountains, then turned south on 287 by the Roosevelt National Forest, heading toward their final destination, a compound nestled away in the canyons above La Porte, Colorado. They had seen no zombies in several hours. Or people (human beings).

Hiram pulled the Humvee up into the front "yard," a parking lot for various old vehicles, including a Ford pickup which might have dropped off a cliff or two, an ancient lawn tractor, and a VW bus with house paint on it, and rough-made lettering more or less identifying all this as "Cash Medicinals." Scattered among these vehicles were a variety of washing machine, range, and refrigerator carcasses. It was not an unfamiliar sight—it looked like the backyard of their childhood home, where Chad and Elliot had considered this collection of domestic antiques their "robot army and repair yard." Before Chad had gotten older and too cool for school. Now Chad had brought the backyard around front.

The basic house looked welcoming enough—a small, white-washed adobe with flower boxes in the two windows. But behind this innocent face were the homemade wings spreading off to each side along the slope. Walls made of cement block and rusted steel conglomerated together with a sloppy, frothy mortar, narrow slotted windows cut in at random like in the old western forts where a weapon might be mounted, corrugated metal and plastic roof raised a few inches above, with thick sheet plastic filling the gap—the kind you might use for a greenhouse. A torn confederate flag with a suspicious bump draped part of the wall. The heavy skunk stench of weed hung over the compound like the local weather.

Chad came out of a hole in the ground a few yards to their left, clothes white dusty and a burlap cowl over his shaggy head. He shoved his pistol into his cut-offs. "Bro!" he cried, teeth flashing in the matted red beard. "You done got yourself a damn robot! Yeehaw!"

"Hello, Chad," Elliot said evenly. "When did you become southern?"

Chad's smile vanished as if it had never been there. His dirty eyebrows looked serious above his too-white eyes. "I go by 'Cash' now, remember? 'Chad' is, like, my slave name. I think we's *all* southern, originally."

Briefly Elliot attempted to puzzle all that out, but abandoned the effort. "So it's okay for us to stay here a little while, until we devise a more appropriate strategy?"

"Yer fambly, sure. Maybe you can help out on the farm." He gestured back toward the wings. "There's a cot in there and a piss bottle. And an open space fer your bot to lay down."

Elliot nodded noncommittally. "I'll just sleep in the Humvee. Hiram doesn't sleep. He's *always* alert."

"Suit yer—Hiram? What kind of name is that?"

"Jewish, just like us."

Cash frowned. "Oh." He looked up at Hiram. "You sure he wouldn't be more comfortable someplace else? Your little SUV looks a tad small."

"*Chambres magnifiques!*" Hiram said.

Cash looked alarmed and rested his hand on the gun. "What's that? I figured he were gov'ment issue. *Our* gov'ment."

"He is. I taught him some French. He was just complimenting you on the fine accommodations, but has to regretfully decline."

"You teach him some sarcasm, too?"

Elliot just smiled.

CASH'S WIFE WAS a beautiful woman with crazy eyes, not unlike their own mother. Also similar was that she made a hearty stew barely distinguishable from compost. "It's *seasoned*," she said, grinning loonily. Elliot stared into her dizzying gaze while dropping a spoon full back into his bowl.

Cash had been staring at Elliot all through the meal, a silly grin freezing his features. It reminded Elliot uncomfortably of the staring contests they'd had when they were kids. Back then when Elliot finally looked away, and he inevitably did, Cash would slug him on the shoulder as hard as he could.

Finally Cash spoke up. "Love you, bro."

Uh-oh. "Um, you too," Elliot replied.

"Can't get over how growed-up you are. Grad school, a primo robot, a Humvee. Every nerd's dream, right? No offense."

"None taken, bro." Elliot glanced at Hiram, who had stood silently in the background during the entire meal, looking pleasingly like Gort in *The Day the Earth Stood Still.* Elliot scratched the back of his head, signaling the need for alertness.

"You know, I've been thinking that now you're here, and with me helping you through this difficult time, you know, maybe you could help me out with a little somethin', somethin' requiring some muscle, you know? Which you clearly got now, in spades." He pointed his ridiculous grin at Hiram, who now stirred.

Elliot sighed. "Exactly what are we talking about?"

"Well, this place here ain't the entirety of my operation, no sir. I got a medical clinic down in Denver."

"Medical?"

"Oh yeah. Medical marijuana. MMJ. Nature's own medicine. It's the best thing for chronic pain, which is, like, well, the country's fastest-growing illness. People need help, bro—now more than ever. They see the right doctor, who *feels* their pain, you know, and gives them that prescription. Then I fix 'em right up. "

"You mean a marijuana dispensary?"

"Some people call it that. Me, I think that's a little, well, clinical, you know? I call it Cash Medicinals, same as this place. Sweet operation down on Federal Boulevard, central location. Marijuana by prescription, edibles, accessories, the whole shebang. Do you know there's more disp—um, *operations* of this type in that part of town than 7-11s? I swear if I was to put in a slushy machine half them stores would have to shut down tomorrow. And I had to leave it all down there when the city got overrun."

"And?"

"And I need your help getting back in there."

"No way."

"Sorry, bro—guess I didn't explain it good. I ain't got your education." He stopped. Elliot waited. "I mean, I got to get back in there."

"Why, *Chad*? Running out of MJ?"

"No, *Ellie.* I ain't running out—fact is I got more than I need now that there's nobody left who'll buy. Them zombies, they don't care much about the MJ."

Elliot thought of something appropriately nasty to say, but refrained. "Then why?"

"I'll tell you why." Cash wrinkled his brow in a way that suggested it was deliberate, as if that was the way you were supposed to look when you were being serious. He held up one hand, fingers spread, counting them off. "It's the five M's, bro. One is Mutated. A few weeks back I had to use my AK-47 on a zombie that broke in on me when I was putting MMJ in the prescription bottles down in the clinic. Made a real mess when he burst apart all over that fine weed. But in no time at all I had this." He pulled a wad out of his jean jacket and dropped it on the table.

Elliot recoiled from the stench. When he was able to bring himself to peep at it he could see the fleshy, corrupted masses growing around the threads of grass like jewels made out of rotting flesh. "So it's ruined, right?"

"Oh contrar! It *improves* it! Stronger, better flavor, a little less harsh. I got me some more equipment, rigged up some hydroponics in the backroom, did a little more zombie *harvestin'*, if you will, and started feeding zombie blood directly to the plants."

"A regular backyard Luther Burbank," Elliot murmured.

"No, bro, clean out yer ears! Like I said, I set it up in the backroom, not the backyard! I mean, how secure is *that*?"

"Apologies," Elliot replied.

"*Concentrated* it," Cash said. "And it improves the brain! That's why I want to go back down there and liberate it so I can breed it with the crop up here. Primo stuff—I mean, I can feel it in myself—I keep smoking this and I'll be as smart as you in no time! In fact, I was going to *honor* you with it—I thought I'd call this new species *Zombro!* Ain't that cool?"

"You're smoking this?" Elliot said incredulously.

"I am. Julie here is too. We figure it'll improve the baby something fierce."

Elliot took a good look at the identically grinning couple. He'd noticed before how their skin was dry, rough, cracking. He'd thought they just had some kind of rash. But there were definite signs of corruption in the bruising, the spider web patterns of veins. The infection had simply been delayed, slowed down to an incredible degree. "She's pregnant? And you're letting—"

"None of that chauvinism now. Julie's a free spirit. Anyhows, that brings me to M number two, Motherin' Stuff. We got us a year's supply of diapers and wipes and formula and all that down there. We *need* that crap.

"M number three is Munitions. We got us a regular arsenal stored in that basement—rifles, pistols, ammunition. And even a few grenades. Come in handy if the zombies find this place.

"Number four is the money we got stashed. Some day this going to be over, and free enterprise ain't free, bro."

"I don't think—"

"And M number five should be of your special interest. It's a—well, I did have me an M here somewhere. Yeah! Massive amounts of electronic crap! I ain't got nothing here but a phone with nobody to call but you, and now you're here! But I scored this big trade with this IT feller from the Denver Tech Center—computers and switches and communica-whatevers. But it's all down there at the clinic. I figured we'd need—"

"When can we leave?" Elliot asked.

Cash grinned so wide a tooth popped out. With hardly a pause he picked it up, threw it into his mouth, and swallowed it. "Middle of the night's best. They don't see none too well—they got eye rot, most of 'em. Makes sense, them being about a week past dead and all."

ALL FOUR OF them piled into the Humvee about 1 a.m., with a rough trailer attached made out of a bodiless VW van and mounted with a bunch of doors nailed together into a kind of corral for holding the supplies. Over the past few hours Cash, and the normally reticent Julie, had begun to babble, much to Elliot's annoyance, and their rash was much worse. Areas of skin had begun peeling, flaking off like the consequences of the world's worst sunburn, revealing the basic instability of the facial structures underneath, and colors no human flesh should achieve without an excess of tattoo ink or copious body paint.

"I've come to appreciate the color green, you know, bro? I mean the entire gamut, the whole universe of green. Green is like the color of nature, bro, the signifier of life! Splendid in its in-fi-nite varietee!" Cash's eyes had grown whiter as his skin grew darker, redder, more mottled. And larger, much larger, until Elliot realized the flesh and bone around the eye sockets was shrinking and receding, revealing steadily more of the eyeball. "I mean, think about it! You got your Apple green, your Army green, Asparagus, your Brights, your British racing, Camouflage, Celadon, Chartreuse, Clover, Dark olive, Dark spring, Dartmouth, Electric green, Emerald, Fern, Forest green, Gray-asparagus, I like that very much, color of my underwear, Green-yellow, Harlequin."

Elliot began to realize that Cash was reeling off the names alphabetically, surely a feat that was hitherto beyond his intellectual capabilities. "Cash, shut up!" he finally said.

"Ain't finished yet, bro. Don't forget you got your Honeydew, your Hooker's, Hunter, India green, Islamic green, Jade, Jungle green, Kelly, Lawn green—that's your grasses, Man! Most people don't realize they's all different colors, depending on variety, even potency, and whatever additives might have been, well, additiv-ed in there. Lime and Midnight green, Mint, and did you know there's even a Mint cream? Moss, Myrtle, Neon green, Office green, Olive, Olive drab."

At about this point Elliot realized Julie had been murmuring something, at first at a volume so low he could hardly detect there were any sounds coming out, just subvocalizations from somewhere deep down beneath her ruined throat. Finally it became much clearer to him, like a peaceful mountain pool after the ripples have faded into oblivion. "*Nam Myo Ho Renge Kyo,*" she chanted, growing steadily louder, "*Nam Myo Ho Renge Kyo!*"

"Wait," Elliot interrupted, thinking to grab her, but stopping himself. "That's what Randy Quaid keeps chanting in *The Last Detail*, isn't it? Hal Ashby, director, 1973?"

"*Nam Myo Ho Renge Kyo! Nam Myo Ho Renge Kyo!*"

"Pakistan green, Paris, Pear, Persian green, Phthalo—I just love the sound of that one! Pine, Pistachio. Wouldn't it be great to have some Pistachio ice cream right now? I could eat a wheelbarrow full! Could we stop somewhere for some, could we, bro, please? Bro? Rifle green, Sap green—"

"*Nam Myo Ho Renge Kyo! Nam Myo Ho Renge Kyo!*"

Elliot wondered if there was any possibility they could find the clinic without them. "Cash? Cash! What's the address?"

His brother stopped, stared out at the night for a moment, then said. "I don't remember. But I will *feel* it, bro, just as I feel all this green, surrounding me, filling me up with, with all its *greenness.* All its Sea green and Shamrock green, Spring bud—I'll say it! Bud! Spring green and Tea green. Teal! Oh, I do love me some Teal! Viridian, Viridian, Viridian, Yellow-green…"

"*Renge Kyo! Renge Kyo!*" Julie sputtered, her throat breaking down.

Within a few miles of Denver Elliot could see that things in the Mile High City had changed—it had lost its patina of light pollution. No streetlights, and most of the neighborhoods appeared to be now off the grid. About the only nighttime illumination was provided by a sick-looking pale moon and numerous burning buildings.

After shaking his head around for a time, Cash was able to guide them down a relatively sleepy Federal Boulevard—the few zombies at large were focused on a middle-aged Hispanic man in desperate flight—until they came to a low yellow building with a painted sign on the side—"Cash Medicinals" in bright day-glo green lettering. There was also a symbol Elliot couldn't quite make out until they pulled even with the clinic—a bright green crucifix with marijuana leaves growing up the upright, a hideous green Jesus with a vague resemblance to the Jolly Green Giant nailed to the crosspieces.

"It's a fairly religious neighborhood here," Cash explained.

They took the Humvee down the alley and parked behind the building. Since Cash had forgotten the key, Hiram broke the bright green door down—*electric green,* Elliot thought—much to Julie's delight and Cash's moaning dismay. Elliot found the stench of mutated medical marijuana and whatever else might be inside the facility (including Cash and Julie's ever-ripening aromas) almost unbearable, but Cash was immediately inspired to renew his sing-songy praises to green, and Julie continued her annoying Buddhist chant after chewing up and swallowing a medicine bottle full of noxious weed. "*Renge, renge, renge, kyo, kyo!*"

The caps on many of the medicine bottles had sprung from the pressure of the transforming MMJ, and now festooned shelves, desks, chairs, trashcans, walls, phones, hydroponics gear, and a computer or two. A storage room held the stockpile of weapons and electronics. Some of the computer gear was obsolete or otherwise just too lame to bother with, but for the most part Cash had acquired some great stuff considering that he had no idea what he was doing. Elliot sorted through everything quickly and indicated to Hiram what needed to go into the trailer, then set to figuring out what foodstuffs and medicines would be worth fitting into the remaining space.

Cash and Julie were sitting together on top of a desk layered in tendrilled, seeping growth, still babbling away, but less comprehensively. Whatever they were saying it wasn't English, unless it was some future dialect.

Something pawed mushily at the window.

Elliot walked toward the front. An elderly Hispanic man stood outside, half of his face clearly having received the zombie makeover, but the other half still pretty good-looking, blessed with a handsome mustache. He waved at Elliot and grinned. Elliot was beginning to see these grins as symptomatic.

"Aldo!" Cash said beside him, maybe—it sounded more like "Al-bo!" Elliot scooted out of the way to avoid Cash touching him. "Vledbee Vest Cusommerce!" he cried. "Leg im in!"

"No, I don't care how great a customer he is," Elliot said sternly. "He's staying outside."

"Nun grur dams bidmiss!" Cash declared.

"*Une telle surprise délicieuse, mademoiselle!*" Hiram declared from one of the other rooms.

"Stay here, Cash! Don't let him in!" Elliot ran to the back of the clinic. He could see that Hiram had turned on his spotlight, but his massive bulk blocked whatever he was examining from view. Moving around the room, being careful not to step into the trails of transformed MMJ, Elliot was finally able to see into the corner, and the young woman who cowered there. "Hiram, dim the beam."

"*Elle se cachait là-bas,*" Hiram explained.

Elliot thought for a moment. "Well, if I saw you coming I would hide too."

The young woman stood up. He'd thought she was just a girl, but under the light he could see that her face was older. She was simply petite. She had straight brown hair framing her face, ending just above her shoulders. Large dark eyes. She was wearing a black sweatshirt and brown camouflage pants. Elliot didn't really have a type, at least not in any way that related to actual romantic experiences, but if he did have one, she'd fit the bill pretty well. She was very close to what he'd always imagined.

"I was hiding," she said in a smoky near-whisper, "from all those things out there. They got—my friends—"

"*Sacré bleu!*" Hiram moved swiftly to shield Elliot from the door behind him. Elliot stepped over to the woman and turned back around. Cash and Julie were coming through the doorway, their red and white patterned faces making them look like skinned raccoons. "*Kyo, Kyo, bragdhh, pleshen,* bro!" they gargled together. Their eyes glowed neon green. Aldo appeared behind them, decaying arms pushed forward above their shoulders. There were additional crashes, glass shattering behind them, and Elliot could see more tattered arms in the background, more chewed-up heads. Some of them had bits of paper wedged between their destroyed fingers which looked somewhat like splattered prescription forms and other paperwork.

"*En l'honneur de la Légion étrangère!*" Hiram shouted, and opened fire.

ELLIOT HAD WATCHED as Bette spent all afternoon painting the sign on the side of the compound, *L'Ermitage d'Elliot* in cinnamon-colored Garamond lettering. She had argued for a dark green, perhaps even a teal, but Elliot had banned all shades of green from his brave new world. No exceptions, not even for her, and he had already made a great many exceptions for her. He bathed more often, he shaved regularly, trimmed his hair, and made every attempt to wear clean clothing. He even broke away from his time in front of his steadily expanding computer and communications control panel to spend an hour each day talking with her about anything she wanted to talk about. He didn't really comprehend a lot of what they talked about—and not understanding was an entirely new experience for him—but he'd put his anxiety over his lack of understanding in abeyance for her.

He'd put Hiram in charge of the entire disinfection process at the compound, deeming it far too risky for either him or Bette. Even for Hiram it had required a great deal of time, and Hiram had been quite thorough. Hiram carried most of Cash's crop out to an old mine shaft and dropped it in, then lobbed in a few minis to seal the entrance. He'd then performed a controlled burn on the area inside the fortifications, burning up the roof, floor, and any existing furnishings in the process. The robot replaced the roof and floor. Elliot would find new furnishings later, better ones. They put up a photo of Cash in the old space, the only photo Elliot had, from back when Cash had been Chad.

Elliot thought all this physical work was beneath Hiram, but Hiram did not complain. Elliot and Bette slept together in the Humvee until everything had been purified. When they finally moved in, Elliot had allowed Bette to choose where things would go. He thought it was only fair—after all, he had chosen her name.

"I don't need the old one—I'd just as soon start over," she'd said. "I was terrified, hiding out in that smelly old place for days, maybe even weeks. I lost all track of time. I'm not sure—you know, I don't think I even remember my old name."

The sign on the compound was the final touch. When she completed the last flourish, she turned toward him and smiled. Her smile grew wider, and became a grin. And Elliot could see, there between the teeth, the greenish tinge, and wondered for the first time about her hygiene.

Fifteen days after their escape from Denver Hiram came to Elliot and stood before him, staring in that complete way in which only a robot can stare. Elliot had become obsessed with numbers, and spent most of each day at the computer looking up their significance, even though using a keyboard was now difficult for him, and he was always leaving bits of flesh on the mouse, and his eyes had, indeed, begun to rot.

"Fifteen is also 3 x 5, divine perfection by grace," he told Hiram. "The first time you see fifteen in the Bible it has to do with Noah, how the waters of the flood rose fifteen cubits to cover the mountains. It's the sum of seven and eight, seven being spiritual perfection and eight is the number of resurrection. If you make an equilateral triangle out of fifteen its sides are each five. Fifteen is the fifth in the series of triangular numbers, starting with the number one. Then the fifth prime number is seven. On my fifteenth birthday I ate fifteen jelly beans, no more, no less. Isn't that crazy?"

"I understand," Hiram said.

"What, what was that? My ears are, well, they're falling apart, imploding actually, I think. What did you say?"

"I said I understand." There was no indication of emotion in the robot's voice. Elliot thought that was really quite remarkable.

"You do, you really do. Then Hiram, you know what to do. You know what to do, Hiram. Say goodbye."

The robot raised his arm for a smart, military-style salute, which ended with the business end of the polished barrel pointing at Elliot. But Elliot did not hear Hiram's delayed "goodbye."

WAR BOY

THE SORCERER'S APPRENTICEBOT

Nicholas Kaufmann

From his chamber window high above the cliffs, the sorcerer watched as the storm battered the ship sailing just off the coast. The tempest he'd conjured raged like a living beast, storm winds howling, and tall, angry waves pounding the ship like great foam fists. He smiled, satisfied. His name was Spero, and he no longer remembered how long he'd lived on this island.

The ship was a most curious vessel. It was neither a galleon nor a Cromster, nor any kind of boat he knew, but a behemoth of sleek metal—flat across the top, and thick, heavy, and sharp where it cut the surf below. It was a dozen times bigger than any ship he'd seen before; so massive he couldn't imagine how it had stayed afloat long enough to reach his island from whatever port it set sail from. Regardless, it had ventured too close, and had to be dealt with accordingly.

"Father, don't!" His daughter Mira, red-faced and on the verge of tears, clutched his arm desperately. "We haven't seen a ship in so long. Let this one pass unharmed, father. Please."

He dismissed her appeal with a stern glance, then turned back to the window. As the storm continued to lash the ship, one end tipped upward like a gladiator's dying salute, and then it sank to the ocean floor, joining the countless other ships Spero had put there.

Mira let go of his arm, backing away in horror. Her eyes accused him before the words left her mouth, though he already knew what she was going to say. They'd played this scene more times that he cared to remember.

"Why?" she demanded, tears on her cheeks. "Those poor lost souls. What if they were trustworthy this time?"

"They're *never* trustworthy. How many times must I tell you?" His tone was harsher than he'd intended. He sighed, softening as he remembered she was still just a child. Like him, she hadn't aged a day since they'd been exiled from their home in Milan and their ship ran aground here. She was still a fifteen-year-old girl, just as he was still a man on the wrong side of the half-century mark, both of them like flies frozen in amber by the island's magic. He touched her arm gently. "Everything I do, I do to keep you safe."

Disgusted, she pulled her arm away. "How many have to die, father? How many must you kill in my name?" She spat the word *kill* as if it were a dagger she could thrust into his heart.

He wished she could understand, but she was too young, too naïve to comprehend what was at stake.

Like a fool, he'd allowed others on the island once, a captain and boatswain, lords and jesters from his native Italy, marooned here by his storm when their ship drifted too close. At first he'd welcomed them, treated them as honored guests, but eventually, inevitably, they'd wanted to go back. He couldn't allow that. Not if it meant word of his and Mira's existence would reach his brother's ears. Since then, he found it better not to leave survivors. What choice did he have? Any ship that approached the island *had* to be treated as an attack by his brother. It wasn't enough that the jealous cur had stolen the Dukedom from him, or sent him and his daughter into exile. No, he wanted them dead too, and Spero knew that the moment his brother discovered where they were he would stop at nothing to make sure their lives were snuffed out forever. It was why they had to stay here alone, and let no ship or crew that came too close pass. It was how they'd survived this long. It was how they would continue to survive.

"Keep me safe from whom? Your brother?" Mira shook her head. "You seriously believe he's still coming to kill us?"

"Do not question me," Spero warned. "You don't know him like I do."

Her face reddened, and her mouth tightened into a hard line. "I wish he *would* come," she yelled. "I'd rather die than continue living like a prisoner in my own home!" She threw herself onto a chair at the other end of the room, arms and legs crossed, and turned away as if she could make him disappear.

Spero sighed. Stuck on an island with a perpetually fifteen-year-old daughter. If there was a worse hell, he couldn't imagine it.

Outside, a figure appeared in the distance, speeding like a bird over the water toward his chamber window. Spero opened the glass and took a step back to make room.

The shape that landed on the floor before him looked like a girl even younger than Mira, but this was an illusion. Riel was an elemental, a sprite—what Spero's superstitious grandmother would have called a fey before dutifully crossing herself—and concepts like gender and age meant nothing to them. Dressed in a tunic of leaves, vines, and bark that clung to the subtle curves of her hips and breasts, her shaggy brown hair barely covering the pointed tips of her ears, she looked just the same as she had the day Spero found her imprisoned within the trunk of a tree.

"Master," Riel said with a bow. Ever since Spero freed her from her arboreal jail, she'd been bound in service to him, a fate she quickly discovered was almost as unbearable. Every day, it seemed, the sorcerer promised to free her if she performed this or that task for him, and every day he reneged on his word. At this point, Riel wasn't holding her breath. She rose from her bow and spoke urgently, her voice like wind through the reeds. "I have troubling news. A survivor from the ship has come ashore."

"A survivor? Here?" Mira perked up, jumping out of the chair. The glint of hope in her eyes pained Spero. A stranger on the island was the last thing they needed.

"You're certain he's still alive?" he asked.

"I saw him pull himself from the water before he collapsed unconscious on the beach," Riel replied. "Master, there's something else you should know. He's wearing armor. I think he might be a knight."

A knight. For a moment, Spero was back in Milan on the night of his exile. Under cover of darkness, a legion of his brother's knights, their armor polished and gleaming in the torchlight, forcefully escorted him and Mira to their ship. *Be grateful it's only exile,* one knight sneered at him, *your brother could just as easily have you killed instead. And he may yet.*

So, the assassin from his brother's court had come at last. The day he'd both dreaded and ruthlessly prepared for had arrived. "Bring this knight to the dungeon, Riel. Quickly, before he wakes."

Riel leapt through the window again and flew toward the shore. Outside, the water still churned angrily, foamy waves relentlessly hammering the sand. Spero cursed silently. How could anyone have survived the storm he'd conjured?

"If the knight is injured, he'll need our help," Mira said. "Why treat him like a criminal?"

"Because he is one," Spero snapped. "They *all* are."

Mira sighed heavily and dropped into the chair again. As she often did when she thought he was being unreasonable, she pretended to ignore him, playing with strands of her long black hair. So much like her mother, Spero thought. He only wished the girl had her mother's sense, but instead she'd been cursed with youthful naiveté, and the foolish—no, *dangerous*—belief that there was good in everyone. The poor girl was so desperate for friendship she'd become emotionally attached right away to the castaways who'd come to the island before, and was devastated when she lost them. It reminded Spero of the time when she wasn't yet ten years old and brought home a dying cat she'd found in the street, weeping over it, begging him to fix it. He'd waited until she was asleep, then took the cat to the river and put it out of its misery. He never told her what became of it. He knew better. Mira always suffered with those she saw suffer.

He held out his hand to her. "Come, see for yourself. Then maybe you'll understand why I do what I do."

She glared at him from behind her hair. "It's always about you. You never ask me what *I* want. Does it even matter to you?"

He lowered his hand, the offer rejected. "Tell me, then. What do you want?"

She leaned forward eagerly. "To be around other people. *New* people."

His heart broke just a little then. "Am I not enough for you?"

She sighed. "I'm sorry, that's not what I mean. It's just…there's no one else on this island but you, Riel, and Cal."

"Let us not waste our breath speaking of Cal," Spero said. "We're safe here, and we'll remain safe as long as no one knows where we are."

She shook her head. "You're a fool, father. Your brother is long dead. Why can't you see that? Everyone we knew is gone. Our family, our friends, our enemies. This island has kept us alive too long."

"Don't be absurd," he scoffed, but a sharp pain flared behind his eyes, the same headache he always got when he tried to calculate how long they'd been here. He rubbed his forehead, wincing, but the pain only intensified. "Everything dies in its time, even us, and the dead don't go on living."

Mira looked at him with something between pity and contempt. She turned to the table beside her, picked up the leather-bound book there, and opened it to the page she'd marked with the sewn-in ribbon. "I took this from the library. Don't worry, it's not one of the books of magic you've forbidden me to read. It's a simple volume on nature and wildlife, though if you ask me it contains just as much wisdom. It says every creature, every bird and beast on God's Earth, has a natural enemy. Do you know what yours is, father?"

"I do," he said, thinking of his brother, and of Cal, who lurked in the wilderness outside, plotting ways to depose him as master of the island. They had much in common, his two enemies.

"I think you don't. Your natural enemy, father, is reason," she said. "You've become so blinded by your fear and mistrust that you can't see the truth." She closed the book on her lap. "How long have we been on this island?"

"I–I don't know," he stammered. The pain redoubled its efforts, shooting arrows through his skull. "A few years. No more than that."

"How long?" she demanded. "Do you think I didn't notice how nothing changes on this damn island, not even the seasons? Do you think I didn't count each and every morning I awoke in this place, waiting for the chance to return home? I lost count long ago."

"That's enough," he said. "You're being foolish."

"What about you, father? How far back does your memory go? Can you even remember the day we arrived here?"

He rubbed his forehead. Of course he remembered. It wasn't that long ago. Their ship…their ship had… He paused as the memory failed to come. He saw only snippets, like images on old parchment, yellowed at the edges, before they faded away altogether.

The pain behind his eyes felt like twin spears plunging into his skull, and the agony and confusion fueled his anger. He picked up his gnarled wooden staff with one hand and pulled Mira out of her chair with the other, knocking the book to the floor. "Ungrateful child! If you don't believe me that my brother is still hunting us, maybe you'll believe your own eyes. All the proof you need is waiting in the dungeon below."

Keeping a tight grip on her arm, he dragged her out of the chamber and down the spiral stone staircase that led to the bowels of the castle. He'd built this place himself—or rather, commanded Riel to do it—designed to be more fortress than home. Sitting atop the highest point on the island, above the forbidding cliffs that overlooked the shore, its stone walls were thick and insurmountable, its windows offered clear views of the water for all approaching ships, its wooden front door was reinforced with steel bars to withstand battering rams, and its dungeon was perfect for holding prisoners of war. He'd anticipated his brother's final assault since day one. He was ready.

"Father, stop, please! You're hurting me!" Mira cried as he dragged her down the steps, but he ignored her. If she was so interested in the truth, he would show it to her. She would see for herself, and then finally she would put her childish beliefs aside for good. She would see he'd been right all along.

At the bottom of the stairs, he threw open the door to the dungeon and pulled her inside, past the empty, cobwebbed cells where rusted manacles drooped from the wall on thick chains. Spero had long ago removed the bones of the castaways he'd imprisoned there, rather than risk letting them leave. He never told Mira what became of them, only that her friends had left without saying goodbye. She'd cried for days.

Riel flitted about in the largest cell at the far end of the dungeon, though the sprite's appearance had changed. No longer a pubescent girl, Riel was now a boy. This happened on occasion, the sprite changing back and forth between sexes on a whim. Spero didn't bother asking why anymore. Riel never gave him a straight answer anyway. Mira had suggested it was the sprite's way of fending off the boredom of living in such extreme isolation, but Spero suspected that said more about his daughter's mindset than Riel's.

Spero's gaze fell on the knight Riel was securing in the cell, and he gasped in surprise. "What on earth...?"

The knight was nearly ten feet tall, filling the cell like a hermit crab in a too-small shell. His armor was boxy and dull, fitted with strange gears and pipes, and he wore a belt with two large canvas pouches around his waist. But it was the knight's oblong helmet that gave Spero the most pause. There was no visor, only a single dark, glassy orb, like a cylops eye, at the center.

How could the knight have swum to shore through the storm in such massive armor, he wondered? Surely the weight would have dragged him to the bottom of the sea. Yet how had he reached the island? Walking on the ocean floor?

Mira's arm went limp in Spero's grasp. "What is it?"

"Our death, child," Spero answered, finally releasing her. "Or he would have been, had I not acted swiftly. Meet the knight from my brother's court, sent to kill us once and for all."

Mira approached the figure hesitantly, one hand by her mouth. "He's not like any knight I've seen."

Riel finished securing the last manacle around the form's enormous wrist. "She's right, master. I take it back. I don't think it's a knight after all. I don't know what it is."

Spero approached the hulking shape for a closer view. "Of course he's a knight. What else could he be?"

"I have a bad feeling about this," Riel said. "We should have left it alone."

Mira ran her hand across the dirt-colored metal. It wasn't smooth like a knight's armor ought to be, she thought. It was rough and scored. This knight had seen battle. Lots of it.

"Mira, get back," Spero ordered.

Her hand found a square panel on the knight's chest. "Wait, father, there's something—" The panel sprang open suddenly under pressure from her hand, and she jumped back with a startled cry.

"Get back!" he shouted again. Mira backed away quickly. Spero peered into the hole in the armor. Inside was a jungle of wires and gears, bolts and machinery—but no flesh. How could that be? He reached inside, but his fingers met only cold metal.

The orb on the helmet flickered to life, glowing a bright red. "If you're gonna keep fingering me like that, the least you can do is buy me dinner."

Spero yanked out his hand and backed away, holding his staff defensively before him. With a metallic whirring sound, the panel in the metal man's chest swung closed on its own.

"You speak like a man, and yet there's no one inside your armor. How?" Spero demanded.

The metal man looked down at itself. Though its face remained an emotionless slab of metal, Spero thought it seemed confused. "I–I don't know," it stammered. "I'm not receiving any signals from central command. I can't even connect with the other warbots through the mainframe. I'm cut off, but I'm still functioning on my own somehow. That's not supposed to happen."

Spero narrowed his eyes. "Sorcery, then."

"More like a CPU upgrade, but I'm not programmed for adaptive AI," it said. "I'm just a grunt, an armored attack unit, I'm not supposed to have my own thoughts. Is this...consciousness? I don't know why this is happening, but I like it." The metal man looked at the manacles binding its arms and said, "Someone want to tell me what's going on here?" It tried to lift its arms and snap the chains, but a strange grinding noise came from its joints, and its arms fell limp again. "Damn. My servos are more damaged than I thought. Should have stayed powered-down for longer."

"What are you?" Spero demanded.

It fixed him with its single, burning red eye. "Warbot N-1662, nautical division. My unit was on its way to the North African front on direct orders from Narcom when the mother of all storms hit us out of nowhere. The ship went down. I was damaged." It tried to move again, but its gears groaned, failing. "On the plus side, this day probably can't get any worse. Now maybe one of you can untie me? I should be out there dealing sweet, sweet death to the enemy, not tied up here like a centerpiece for the world's worst costume party. No offense, but what's with the leaves and twigs, kid?"

Riel looked down at his outfit, blushing. "It's what I've always worn."

"Unless you're starring in a grade school production of *Peter Pan*, I'd suggest updating your wardrobe to something a little harder for the fuglies to chew through."

"*Chew*...through?" Riel asked.

Spero took a step closer, holding his staff before him. "So you *are* a killer. You said so yourself, you deal in death."

"I'm a warbot, what did you think the name meant?" it replied. "It's what I do. It's why I exist. You want to save lives, get a docbot. You want to tear shit up, clear the stiffs and draggers off the streets, you call in the big guns. And that's me. Killing the enemy is mission *numero uno*."

"You're an assassin, a killer for hire."

"They don't pay me, you crazy old coot. They don't need to. What would I do with money anyway? I enjoy what I do, that's payment enough. Now, are we gonna keep playing twenty questions or are you going to untie me?"

A chill crept up Spero's spine. It was worse than he'd thought. The warbot was no ordinary assassin. It killed for the sheer pleasure of it, a blood sport hunter. Exactly the kind of despicable rogue his brother would send to kill him and his daughter. He wouldn't be surprised if his brother had personally constructed this iron and steel homunculus for just that purpose.

He took Mira by the arm and pulled her toward the dungeon door. "Return to your room and stay there. Lock the door. Don't come out until I tell you."

"But he's so fascinating," she said, slipping from his grasp and moving back toward the warbot. "A soldier made entirely of metal. Please, father, let me stay."

"Mira, don't argue," Spero insisted. "Riel, take her to her room. Now!"

Riel scooped Mira up in his thin, boyish arms as if she weighed nothing, and hurried out of the room. Spero heard his daughter's angry protests grow fainter as the sprite flew her up the stairs, and then, with the slam of a door, there was silence.

He faced the warbot and raised his staff, intoning ancient words of power. The staff began to glow, thrumming in his hands as though it could barely contain the magic coursing through it. A frigid wind blew out of nowhere, flattening his robes and beard against his body. His voice echoed eerily off the dungeon walls. "By the airy spirits of this island, by all the magic of the ancient ones, your will is now mine to command. I hereby bind you to me as my servant. I command it!"

"Good one," the warbot said. "For your next trick, though, you might just want to stick with cards."

"I am master of this island and all upon it," he insisted. "Your will shall bend to mine. The power of the ancient ones compels you!" The staff glowed brighter, and the wind blew harder, shrieking like ghosts through the bars of the empty cells.

"You enjoy bossing others around, don't you?" the warbot said. "You'd fit right in at Narcom. It's filled with old men who like to play God in their basements. Damn, it feels good to finally say these things out loud!"

Undeterred, Spero fed more power into the spell, and his booming voice echoing through the dungeon. "You will serve me, not my brother!"

"Buddy, I don't even know who your brother is."

Spero gritted his teeth in anger. "His name is not to be spoken within these walls, but you know him as your master, the Duke of Milan."

"Duke? You gotta be kidding me. There's no Duke of Milan. There hasn't been one in seven hundred years. Hell, at this point there isn't even a Milan anymore. It fell two months ago, completely overrun."

The headache returned with a vengeance, burning inside Spero's skull until it felt like it was going to crack in half. Milan was no more? How was that possible? He lowered the staff, its glow fading. The wind died away. "You lie," he said.

"Why would I? What would be the point?"

Spero stared at the warbot, his mind racing. "We shall see." Then he turned and stormed out of the dungeon.

"Don't mind me, I'll just hang here," the warbot called after him.

Spero slammed the door shut, locking it inside, and started up the winding stairs.

Seven hundred years since Milan had a Duke? It was impossible. And yet, he had to know for sure. He had to see for himself.

"Riel, come to me!" he cried as he climbed toward the chamber at the very top of the castle.

Riel appeared on the stairs beside him, female again, her bare feet slapping the stone steps as she hurried to keep up with him. "Mira locked herself in her room, but she's not happy about it."

"She'll thank me in the end," Spero said. They reached the top of the stairs and entered a small, circular room. In its center was the Scrying Orb, a perfect sphere of black crystal from the heart of the island. Almost as big as Riel herself, the sphere hung suspended in a framework of wood and brass salvaged from the wreck of Spero's ship. Its ebony depths seemed to swirl like mist. Spero ran his hand along its smooth surface. "I need to see beyond the island, to the world outside."

"Beyond the island?" Riel asked, surprised. "You've never done that before."

"I don't have the power to make the Scrying Orb see that far. But you do."

Riel knit her brow. "I don't understand. You want me to look into the Scrying Orb for you?"

"No," Spero said. "I want you to power it for me."

The color drained from Riel's face. She shook her head. "Master, no. There must be another way."

"There's no time," he said. He waved the staff, and two small holes opened in the back of the orb. He brought her over to them and took her by the wrists. "I'm sorry, my faithful friend. If you survive this, you will have your freedom, I promise you."

"Don't!" she cried. "Free me now, and I will find another way, I promise!"

Spero silenced her with a stern glance and plunged her hands into the holes. The cloudlike shapes within the sphere began to swirl faster. Riel screamed in pain and struggled to pull her hands free, but the Scrying Orb held them, absorbing her power into itself. A soft glow emanated from its center, growing steadily brighter until images began to form inside the sphere.

"Just a little more power, Riel," Spero coaxed. "A little more and it will be done."

Riel's screams grew more insistent. She dropped to her knees, her body changing to male, then back to female, then something in between, a writhing mass of flesh as the sprite lost control of her form. The stench of burning hair and cooking meat permeated the chamber.

The images in the sphere solidified, and for the first time since he'd come to the island, Spero saw the world beyond its shores. Great metal war machines, vehicles with elongated cannons and rolling treads, moved through the rubble of ruined cityscapes. Above them, enormous, gleaming arrowlike constructs of steel and glass flew effortlessly through the sky. It was like something out of the wildest fantasias of a madman.

This wasn't his world, he realized with a sinking heart. Not anymore. Mira had tried to tell him. His headaches had tried to tell him. The clues had been there. They hadn't aged a day since they'd arrived. He couldn't remember coming to the island anymore. How could he have been such a fool? Such a stubborn old fool?

Within the Scrying Orb, more images formed. He saw the words *Project Undertow* and *For POTUS's Eyes Only* written on a piece of stationary stamped with the seal of an eagle. He saw glimpses of an underground world, a city of towers and spires, roadways and canals deep beneath the earth. A small group of people entered the undercity, and then its great metal doors closed, trapping thousands more outside, leaving them at the mercy of a dark, ravening horde Spero couldn't quite make out—though the screams that followed made him shiver. Next the Scrying Orb showed him a priest riding an army of metal men similar to the one in his dungeon—Godbots, he called them—into a cathedral, and to Spero's horror, spurts of fire burst from their cannons, killing all the men, women and children who'd taken refuge there.

Betrayal. Everywhere, betrayal. In his absence, the world had gone mad. It had embraced treachery, greed, and selfishness—the very traits Spero's brother had embodied. Humanity was not only on the brink of damnation, it was unworthy of being saved.

He'd seen enough. With a wave of his staff, the Scrying Orb went dark and released Riel's hands. The sprite's misshapen form coalesced into that of a young man, and he collapsed on the floor, his hair smoking, patches of his skin charred red and black. Spero backed away from the sphere, horrified by what he'd seen. If this was the mad world the warbot came from, then surely the warbot was infected with the same madness. There was no doubt in his mind what needed to be done. The warbot had to be destroyed. He only prayed he wasn't too late.

But he already was. From far below came the unmistakable sound of something big smashing through the front door of the castle and out into the wilderness.

THE ISLAND WAS small, only the size of a few city blocks, and seemed to be stitched from landscapes that didn't belong together. Tropical palm trees bent toward the water not far from groves of evergreen pines. Hills of shale and black slate were interspersed with healthy green meadows, while the sand on the beaches changed colors with location, from yellow to red to gunmetal gray. A charge seemed to hum in the air, like the kind that came after thunderstorms, only the protons and electrons were all wrong, puzzle pieces fitted together the wrong way.

Warbot N-1662 stayed close to the shore as it circumnavigated the island, searching for the proper coordinates. It hadn't taken long for its self-diagnostic program to kick in down in the dungeon, and once repairs were completed, all the chains and locked doors were no obstacle anymore. Now, with the sun sinking into the horizon, the warbot found the coordinates of its sunken ship and scanned the sea for signs of the rest of its unit.

Nothing. Was it the only survivor of the shipwreck? That seemed doubtful. Warbots didn't go down without a fight.

Intent on finding the others, it waded out into the water, but with each step it took away from the shore, it felt its mind growing empty, its newfound self-awareness fading away. It tried to push forward, but fifteen yards out something scrambled its circuits and refused to let it go any farther, an invisible barrier it couldn't cross. Frustrated, the warbot returned to shore, and the moment its feet touched the sand, its mind sharpened again.

What had happened out there? It didn't know, only that there was no exit that way. Still, there had to be a way off this hunk of rock. If it couldn't find the other warbots, it was up to them to find it. Warbot N-1662 reached out to the mainframe again, trying to send a distress signal, but it deflected back like an echo. The same barrier that prevented it from leaving the island had also blocked its signal. Presumably, it was blocking the incoming central command signal as well. The warbot was completely cut off from the outside world. Whatever the barrier was, the warbot was certain it had something to do with the old man in the castle. He seemed like the boss of this place.

Humans. They were all crazy to a fault—it was a wonder their ancestors had ever managed to come out of the trees—and the old man was the craziest yet. If Warbot N-1662 didn't love fighting so much, it would be tempted to stand back and let the zombies finish the humans off, just so they'd stop getting in its way.

The thought gave the warbot pause. It, like all thoughts, was something new. The sentiment behind it had always been there, the product of countless battlefield observations collected and filed away in its memory, but to actually think it? To articulate it with the same self-awareness as a sentient being? That was new and exciting. Intoxicating, even. How had it ever existed without that?

The sound of a twig snapping caught the warbot's attention. It spun around quickly, switching its visual input sensor to infrared as it scanned the tree line in the dim twilight, and saw the heat signature of a figure in the forest, partially hidden behind a thick tree trunk. It was spying on the warbot, and judging from its shape, it was human. Kind of.

Warbot N-1662 chose not to deploy its weapons. The presence of a heat signature meant the spy wasn't a zombie, and if it wasn't a zombie it was of no concern. The warbot was about to turn away when a figure came out of the woods. It moved quickly, darting behind a nearby boulder. A misshapen head popped up over the top. The creature was strangely hairy, almost fleeced, with tiny goatlike horns on his forehead. The warbot made no sudden moves, and, feeling more confident, the creature jumped up onto the boulder in full view. His legs were covered in thick fleece, bent the wrong way, and ended in hooves.

"Costume party's that way," Warbot N-1662 said, pointing up at the castle that loomed over them on the tall cliffs.

The creature bleated, then looked embarrassed for a moment at the sound he'd made. "I'm Cal," he said, "master of this island."

"You? I thought the old man in the castle ran this place."

"Spero? Feh, he likes to think of himself as its master," Cal said. "He treats the island as his own, yet I was the one born here, not him. I am the rightful heir."

"Doesn't seem like much to fight over. Everything about this place feels off, like there's something in the air."

"The island's magic affects different people in different ways," Cal explained. "To some it grants longevity. To others, mastery of the ancient arts. Who's to say what it has given you?"

The warbot thought of its sudden sentience, but quickly pushed the thought aside. Magic? Preposterous.

"I've been watching you since you came ashore," Cal continued. "You were taken to Spero's castle. Usually, he casts a spell on his prisoners to make them serve him, yet you broke out. With your bare hands, no less. Why didn't he cast a spell on you?"

"He tried some smoke and mirrors mumbo-jumbo. It didn't work. Shocking, I know."

Cal's dark eyes brightened. "You're immune to his magic."

"That's because there's no such thing," the warbot said. Was everyone here crazy? It had only been on this island a short while, and already the warbot hated it.

"You would do well not to underestimate Spero's sorcery," Cal said. "It's the method by which he stole the island from me, but not for much longer. It will be mine again. Mark my words."

"You want it, you can have it. I just want off." The warbot didn't have time for petty feuds between people it couldn't care less about. But if Cal really had been born here, odds were he was more familiar with the island than anyone. Maybe he could help. "The only problem is, there's something preventing me from leaving or contacting my unit. You know anything about that?"

"Spero put a spell around the island so that no one who comes here can get out again. He has turned my home into a spider's web to catch his enemies."

More nonsense about magic spells. The warbot sighed. Of all the shitholes in all the world to get shipwrecked on, why did it have to be one where the inmates ran the asylum?

"But fear not," Cal continued, "I know a way off the island, a place where the spell is weak. I can take you there."

The warbot perked up. "What are we waiting for? Lead on, MacDuff!"

Cal grinned, revealing teeth caked with dirt. "In time. But first you must do something for me, my metal friend. Help me win back what is rightfully mine. Spero must go. I have the cunning to overthrow him, but not the strength. Yet you are obviously mighty, and unaffected by his spells. Together, the sorcerer wouldn't stand a chance against us."

"If I help you, you'll show me how to get out of here?"

"You have my word," Cal said.

Warbot N-1662 thought about it a moment. It didn't care which of them came out on top, Spero or Cal, it just wanted to get off the island and back to the front lines. Those North African zombies weren't going to kill themselves. The warbot stuck out its hand. "You've got yourself a deal."

THROUGH THE Scrying Orb, Spero watched Cal and Warbot N-1662 shake hands. His blood boiled. "That bawling, blasphemous, incharitable dog!"

His outburst woke Riel. The sprite stood up on trembling legs and looked down at his hands. They were blackened and twisted, his fingers like burnt twigs. "I–I'm alive," he croaked. He looked up at Spero with hopeful eyes. "You promised me my freedom."

"Not yet, there's still much to do," Spero said, distracted. "Our prisoner has escaped and joined forces with Cal. Even now, they plot to overthrow me." He stoked his beard, deep in thought. "The warbot must be destroyed. It's an infection, a contaminant from the outside world. Besides, without it Cal won't dare attack the castle. He'll be forced to run back to the wilderness like the animal he is."

Riel rubbed his wrists and said softly, "You promised."

"Bring Mira here," Spero continued, hurrying to the window. Far below, he saw two shapes, one small and twisted, the other big and hulking, moving inland from the shore. He turned back to the sprite. "It's no longer safe anywhere but in this chamber, on highest ground. What are you waiting for, Riel? Bring her at once!"

"You keep promising, but you never free me."

"At once!" Spero bellowed.

Riel's eyes narrowed with resentment, but he obediently raced down the steps toward Mira's room. Spero turned back to the Scrying Orb and watched his enemies begin to scale the cliffs below the castle, the warbot doing most of the work while Cal hitched a ride on its back. Spero raised his staff, shouting the words of power, and the wind outside began to howl. A fierce rain battered the ground like nails. A tempest had brought the warbot to the island; a tempest would wash it away.

Yet the Scrying Orb showed the warbot unaffected by the storm, climbing the cliffside tirelessly. Cal wasn't so lucky. His slight form was at the mercy of the wind, but every time he slipped off the warbot's back, the warbot would grab hold of him and pull him up again. Spero increased the storm's intensity. Thunder tore the sky to pieces. The walls of the castle shook, and lightning strikes turned the surrounding trees into bonfires.

"Father, what have you done?" Mira stood in the doorway of the chamber. Riel, female again, stood beside her.

"The warbot is too strong, even my magic can't destroy him!" Spero had to shout to be heard over the storm. Lightning struck close by, and the loud blast that accompanied it speared his ears like daggers. The walls shook again. A long crack ripped through the ceiling, raining dust and chunks of stone into the chamber.

Mira tried to pull him away from the Scrying Orb. "Father, call off the storm! It'll kill us all!" He pushed her away so violently that she fell to the floor. She looked up at him, wiping tears from her cheeks. "Father, please! Have reason, for once!"

Spero paused. Reason. He remembered what Mira had said about reason, and a plan formed in his mind. "Of course," he muttered.

He couldn't destroy the warbot himself, but Mira of all people had told him who could. Every creature had a natural enemy, she'd said. The warbot was no exception.

He lifted his staff above his head in both hands. He spoke the words of power and called, "I summon thee, enemies of the warbot!" The wind screamed with the force of a thousand howling spirits. The sky flashed with lightning. The earth shook beneath them.

Mira got to her feet again. "Father, please! Whatever you're doing, stop!"

"Stop? Ungrateful child! I'm keeping you safe. I'm keeping us all safe!"

She backed away from him, the floor shifting perilously under her feet. "This is lunacy! You don't know who its enemies are. You don't know who you're bringing to the island!"

He laughed spitefully. "The enemy of my enemy is my friend." He lifted his staff higher and cried, "From the four corners of the earth, from the realms of wind and water and fire, I summon thee here!"

More chunks of rock fell dangerously from the ceiling. The whole world seemed to tremble.

"Father!"

Riel pulled Mira toward the chamber door. "Leave him. He's lost in his own madness." Mira resisted, but Riel pulled her out of the chamber. "There's no time!" They fled down the steps.

A sudden bright flash from outside caught Spero's eye, accompanied by a thunderclap so powerful he felt it deep in his chest. He looked out the window and saw a whirling maelstrom of crackling blue light appear on the rocky terrain between the castle and the edge of the cliffs. Inside it, restless shadows shuffled like moths ready to break from their cocoon. He grinned in triumph.

The warbot's enemies had arrived.

Then the cocoon split open, and dark, ragged shapes spilled out, a seemingly endless army of them, shambling in clumps toward where the warbot and Cal had finally crested the cliffs. The strange creatures seemed familiar, and with a jolt Spero remembered where he'd seen them before—through the Scrying Orb, attacking and devouring the people locked out of the undercity. As he watched now, he could smell the rot coming off of them, could sense the unbridled and indiscriminate hunger that made them gnash their teeth and grope for the nearest moving things. His blood ran cold.

"Good God, what have I done?" He looked at the empty spot where his daughter had stood a moment ago, and his heart leapt into his throat. "Mira!"

WARBOT N-1662 was just helping lift Cal over the edge of the cliffs and onto level ground when the sharp blast of light came out of nowhere. At first the warbot thought someone had detonated a nuclear device, but there were none of the telltale signs. As the storm continued to whip at them, rain and lightning peppering the ground, a bright swirl of blue light appeared directly between them and Spero's castle.

"What is it?" Cal asked, his bearded jaw hanging open in amazement.

"Trouble," the warbot answered.

The strange light split open down the middle and a dense crowd of zombies lumbered out, making a beeline for them, moaning for meat and grasping for flesh.

"That's right, ya bunch of ugly fuckers, come get yours!" Warbot N-1662 rose to its full height, snapping open the two pouches in its belt and pulling an MK3 concussion grenade out of each. It only had two—warbots weren't supposed to stray far from supplybots on the battlefield—but it knew the combined shock waves of the TNT packed inside the thermos-shaped, fiberglass grenades would take out most, if not all of the zombies.

Cal cowered behind the warbot, peeking around its massive metal frame at the approaching hordes. "What are you going to do?"

"What I do best."

The warbot flicked off the safety pins and hurled the grenades into the crowd. The blast tore through the zombies, sending heads, limbs, and unidentifiable chunks of their rotting bodies somersaulting through the air. The smoke cleared to reveal a mound of zombie parts—and more zombies pouring out of the swirling blue light. They kept coming, more and more of them, an endless horde.

"Shit," the warbot said. The casings of its forearms slid back on tiny gears, and out of the trench along each limb emerged a 7.62mm M134 multibarrel heavy machine gun. It aimed carefully at the oncoming zombies. It was going to have to make each shot count. Like the grenades, it only had a finite number of bullets and no way to reload on the island.

The warbot opened fire in short bursts, the rotating, Gatling-style barrels of its guns spitting rounds into zombie heads with deadly accuracy, while Cal shrieked and put his hands over his ears. Finally, the warbot thought, something to shoot at. Far too much time had passed since its last fight, and it felt good to get the old bullets flying again. The warbot took down the front row of zombies effortlessly, but more kept coming.

"Spero is behind this," Cal told him. "I recognize his magic."

The warbot still didn't believe in magic, but it did believe in humans doing stupid things. Purposely bringing zombies to the island for his own selfish purposes, regardless of how, didn't seem out of character for a control freak like Spero. If Cal was right, the old man was even crazier than the warbot thought.

The warbot cut its guns a moment to take stock of the situation. The zombies spilling out of the swirling light had split into two factions, one staggering toward them over the decimated bodies of their fallen comrades, the other lumbering toward Spero's castle. Damn. It was better when zombies stayed together in a group. It made them easier to shoot while conserving bullets.

Not that Warbot N-1662 didn't enjoy a challenge.

Cal looked up at the warbot in awe. "The deafening roar of a dragon, fire shooting from your arms—what kind of magic is this?"

"The kind that comes from Lockheed Martin's military division," the warbot replied, and opened fire again with a succession of well-placed headshots.

But there were too many of them. For every zombie cut down by the guns, ten more took its place. They swarmed over the warbot like a flood wave, dragging it down to the ground and trying to tear into it. Fortunately, its metal shell was impervious to their teeth and fingernails. Unfortunately, it couldn't use its guns at such close range. A sustained burst would tear the zombies to pieces, but there was no guarantee any of the shots would be headshots and the warbot had to conserve bullets.

It grabbed the nearest zombie and tore off its head. It tossed the head aside, turned the body over in its massive hands, gripped it by its legs like the handle of club, and started swinging. As a makeshift weapon, the headless body wasn't lethal to the zombies, but it did manage to knock them away. As they shuffled off, the warbot dropped the body and heard a scream. It turned to see zombies huddled around something else, tearing into it in an all too familiar frenzy. The warbot opened fire, blasting the zombies' skulls apart. A moment later, from beneath the pile of inert bodies, a shape rose slowly.

It was Cal. The hair all over his body was matted with blood, his skin lacerated with bites and scratches. He stared at the warbot with dead eyes. His teeth gnashed, and a long rope of saliva dangled from his hungry mouth. He wanted meat. Fortunately, the warbot had none.

"Sorry, Cal," Warbot N-1662 said. "Looks like this is as far as you go."

It opened fire at Cal's head, but Cal leapt out of the way. His inhuman, goatlike legs allowed him jump higher and farther than any zombie it had seen before. The warbot pivoted, continuing to fire at him, but Cal managed to evade the bullets until, finally, he was out of range.

"Damn," the warbot grumbled. Before it could follow him, another crush of zombies piled onto it, dragging it to the ground. More and more zombies came, some pushing, others pulling, and before it knew what was happening, Warbot N-1662 fell off the edge of the cliff.

BY THE TIME Mira reached the bottom of the castle steps and peered out through the warbot-shaped hole in the front door, Riel had changed back into a boy again. He thought he'd be better able to protect her this way, but he was wrong. He still felt too small and weak, his burnt hands useless.

The creatures Spero summoned were everywhere, with more pouring out of the blue light every moment. It wouldn't be long before they overran the entire island.

"They're coming this way!" Mira cried, pointing.

Riel saw a pack of them shambling toward the castle. Their smell came first, like a calling card, the stench of death. These creatures were dead, yet they still moved. What kind of terrible magic could wake the dead like this?

The ground shook again, and a crack tore through the wall beside the door. The intensity of two powerful spells overlapping, the storm and the summoning of the warbot's enemies, was tearing the castle apart. Maybe the whole island.

"The forest!" Mira shouted, pulling Riel from his thoughts. She gestured to the forest's edge fifty yards from the castle. "We're sitting ducks here, but we can lose them in the trees!" She jumped out the door and started running before he could stop her.

"No! Mira, wait!" Riel leapt into the air and flew after her, but the sorcerer's daughter was faster than he expected. She ran the way she must have wanted to run her whole life, he thought. She'd been waiting for this moment, the chance to run away from the castle, from her father. The chance, finally, to be free of a life she never chose for herself. Having been Spero's servant for so long, Riel understood the feeling all too well, and for a moment he envied her this tiny taste of freedom.

Mira stopped suddenly. Ragged shapes at the forest's edge blocked her path and closed around her in a circle. She shifted her weight from foot to foot, unsure what to do next. There was no place to go.

Riel landed beside her. "Back to the castle! Quickly!"

One zombie broke from the others. Twisted and only half human, it stepped forward to regard them with hungry eyes.

"Cal…," Mira whispered in terror.

Cal gnashed his teeth and leapt upon her, biting into the soft flesh of her neck before they even hit the ground. She screamed as blood spurted in an arc from the wound, painting Cal's face red.

"Mira!" Riel started toward her, but the other zombies swarmed him, their sheer multitude knocking him to the ground. He struggled to get back on his feet, but there were too many of them, the immensity of their combined weight holding him down. Teeth snapped inches from his neck as he struggled to hold them back with his crippled hands. Finally, he wriggled out from beneath them and took to the air. He dove straight for Cal, body-checking him off Mira. Riel picked up the unconscious girl and flew back toward the castle. He heard Cal and the other zombies behind him, moaning their frustration at losing a meal. He heard something else, too. From somewhere beyond the cliff's edge, the muffled sound of the warbot's weapons. He'd seen the warbot go over the edge, covered in zombies. Had it survived the fall?

There was no time to worry about that now. Mira was badly hurt. Riel landed just inside the castle doorway and laid her gently on the floor. Spero was already there, out of breath from having run all the way down the steps. Sadness and regret etched themselves into his face when he saw Mira. He put down his staff and knelt beside her.

"Oh, my daughter," he murmured, stroking face. His eyes glistened with tears. "How could I let this happen?"

Riel glared at him. "Had you simply let the ship pass unharmed…" he started to say, but the anger burned too hot in him to continue. The old fool had finally been punished for his sins, but at what cost? None of this was Mira's fault. She was just a child, caught up in her father's madness and paranoia.

"I only wanted to keep her safe," Spero whispered. Blood spurted from Mira's neck in time with her heartbeat. He put his hands over the wound to staunch the bleeding. A sheen of feverish sweat covered her skin. "She's as hot as a furnace."

Mira choked suddenly, blood sluicing from her mouth. Her body convulsed, then lay horribly still. Spero stared at her for a long moment, his face white with shock. Finally, he let go of her wound. Blood seeped from her neck, but it no longer pumped with her pulse. Her heart had stopped. Mira was dead.

Spero laid his head on her chest and wailed. It was an ugly sound, so full of regret and yearning that Riel had to turn away.

Through the doorway, he saw the zombies coming, more of them than he could count. At the front, leading the troops to the castle like some unholy general, was Cal. In death, he'd finally gotten what he wanted, a chance to storm the castle.

"Spero!" Riel warned.

The sorcerer saw them. With one last glance at his daughter, he rose, his face a bitter mask of anger and determination. He picked up his staff and strode through the door to meet the oncoming hordes. "Hell is empty, and all the devils are here," he said. "So be it, then. Back to Hell with you!"

He raised his staff and screamed the words of power until his throat went hoarse. The roiling clouds in the sky flashed. Jagged lightning bolts swept across the mass of zombies, blowing bodies apart in meaty chunks, setting others on fire, and reducing still more to char and ash. Yet they kept coming. There were so many of them, but there was enough blind fury inside Spero to keep the storm churning. More than enough. Lightning burned through the zombies, as well as the trees, fields, and beaches, and struck the castle like arrows into flesh, knocking stones free from the mortar.

Arms grabbed Spero from behind. Delicate, familiar arms, and he turned, surprised.

Mira stood behind him, her mouth, neck, and blouse stained with her blood. Her face was a ruin of death. Before he could speak, she bit a chunk of meat out of his chest. A second pair of jaws took a chunk from the back of his neck, and he turned again, startled. It was Cal. Together, Cal and Mira fed on him, tearing flesh and sinew from his bones until, finally, Spero sank to his knees. Looking up, he thought he saw Riel fly off into the night. He saw the castle come down, falling in on itself in a cloud of dust and rubble. And then he saw only Mira and Cal's gore-soaked faces looming over him. Bleeding to death, he could already feel the hot, insistent infection coursing through his veins, and the hunger, the unbelievable hunger. Mira bent toward him, her mouth open to tear into him again—

Her head exploded in a hail of bullets. Followed by Cal's, and then his own.

AFTER WARBOT N-1662 climbed back up the cliff face, shooting its way through the masses, and after blasting Mira, Cal, and Spero into oblivion, it set about clearing the rest of the island of zombies. It wasn't that hard. With the old man's death, the storm had stopped and the swirling vortex had closed, preventing any more zombies from emerging. Was it really magic, the warbot wondered? It wasn't convinced, and in the end, it didn't particularly care, not when there was so much shooting to be done. It worked through the night and into the morning, walking from one end of the island to the other, shooting any zombies it found and leaving a trail of spent casings in its wake. When it finally ran out of bullets, it fashioned an axe from a stick and a sharpened stone, and started splitting skulls.

When it was finished, Warbot N-1662 tossed the gore-soaked axe aside and turned to a nearby copse of trees. "You've been following me all night. Are you going to show yourself?"

A boy dressed in leaves and twigs came out of the trees, the same boy the warbot first saw in Spero's dungeon, only this time he was floating some twenty feet off the ground. This fucking island, the warbot thought. Could it be any more screwed up?

"What's your name, kid?"

"Riel," he said timidly.

"Well, Riel, you're obviously not human, but you're the last living thing on this island. It's yours if you want it."

Riel shook his head. "All I ever wanted to do was leave. Spero wouldn't let me."

"That makes two of us."

"When they attacked him, I–I didn't do anything to help him," Riel stammered, overcome with shame. "I was so angry at him for what happened to Mira. For the way he treated me. For everything." He looked at his blackened hands. "I couldn't do anything. Or maybe I could have, but…I didn't."

"Humans, can't live with 'em, can't shoot 'em without being court-martialed and deactivated," the warbot said. "Go figure. Half of them aren't worth saving, and the other half die anyway, so why bother?"

Riel nodded. “They’re so fragile. Dust to dust.”

“Here today, gone tomorrow. No wonder they go insane.”

“They are such stuff as dreams are made on,” Riel said.

“Let’s not get carried away,” the warbot said. “I don’t know about you, but I intend to get the hell off this rock. Cal said there was a way through the barrier. You know it?”

“He was lying to trick you into helping him,” Riel said. “There was no way off the island while Spero’s spell was up. But he’s dead now, and his spells died with him.”

“Huh. So I can leave?”

Riel nodded. “Whenever you want.”

“No time like the present.” Warbot N-1662 walked to the nearest shore, and Riel followed. The warbot stopped at the water’s edge and looked out at the frothy ocean.

“Where will you go?” Riel asked.

“To find the others, and then back to the front lines. There are plenty more zombies to kill, and I hate to think everyone else is having all the fun. What about you?”

Riel shrugged. “Anywhere. I’m free now.”

The warbot nodded. “Be careful out there, kid. There are more zombies than people these days. And remember what I said about getting more practical clothes. You look like a walking chef’s salad to a zombie.” With that, Warbot N-1662 took a couple of steps out into the water, then paused.

“What is it?” Riel asked. “I thought you wanted to go.”

“I–I…” the warbot stammered. It turned around and came back to the shore. “I don’t understand. I could feel myself slipping away, my mind going blank. It happened once before, too, when I tried to leave. I thought you said the barrier was down.”

“It is,” Riel said. “It’s not the barrier that’s affecting you. It’s the island. Its magic affects different people differently.”

“Magic,” the warbot muttered, annoyed. “Even if it were real, it shouldn’t be affecting me at all. I’m made of metal and computer chips, I don’t count as a person.”

“You do here,” Riel said. “The island made you one. That was its gift to you. If you leave, you can’t take it with you.”

The warbot’s single red eye gazed out at the horizon contemplatively. “You’re saying I have to make a choice. I can stay here and remain sentient, or I can leave and go back to doing what I love, but I would also have to go back to being a grunt, one of thousands of identical cogs in Narcom's war machine."

"A person, or a mindless killer," Riel said.

"Freedom or predestination. Consciousness or programming. Alive or a zombie. Christ, this island really knows how to stick it to you."

"You'll get no argument from me," Riel said. "I wish I could help you, but after everything that happened here, I can't stay."

The warbot stuck out its hand. Riel put his burnt hand in it hesitantly, and the warbot shook it with surprising gentleness. "Good luck, kid."

"You too, friend, whatever you decide," Riel said.

He jumped into the air and flew. He looked back only once, to see the warbot still standing on the shore, caught between two possible worlds, the old and the new, and then Riel left the island far behind.

But where could he go? If the warbot was right, no place was safe. Not the places known to men, anyway. What he needed was someplace isolated, far from the war, and he knew just the place. If memory served, the island of the Amazons wasn't far, and with a quick switch of gender—Riel changed from male to female in mid-air—she'd fit right in.

She closed her eyes as the wind rushed through her hair, the salty scent of the ocean teasing her nose, and the sun warming her back. It'd been so long since she felt this free. It tasted sweeter than she ever hoped.

The Amazons' island appeared on the horizon. Riel, smiling wider than she had in centuries, flew faster toward it.

MUNITION
STORAGE COMPL

KETTLETOP'S REVISIONARY PLOT

Lincoln Crisler

NOW:

Poot. The blazing, white circle of light burst into the brisk night air. Francis Kettletop hurtled out of it and landed in a heap on the dry, weed-speckled ground below.

I made it, he thought, looking around. In the distance, he saw the high, barbed wire–topped fence and dazzling security lights surrounding the Kirtland Underground Munitions Storage Complex. *Fucked up the landing, but I'm lucky the portal still worked at all.* He inhaled and felt a smile spread across his face, in spite of himself. He hadn't smelled fresh, clean air in months.

<<Oh shiiiiii—>> Francis looked up, shielding his eyes from the blinding light of the portal. *Oh no. The goddamn warbot.* Francis scrambled backward, away from the huge, shadowy mass that loomed larger with every scrape of his heels in the hard-packed sand. He wasn't quick enough. Warbot-11 slammed into Francis' left leg, and the scientist's screams damn near drowned out the clanking of the warbot's graceful—for a warbot—combat roll.

<<Sorry, Boss>> Warbot-11 said, coming to a halt on one knee, a few feet away. <<You should have told me to go first.>>

Warbot-11 reached for Francis, and he scurried back. The fresh wave of pain from his injured leg stifled his screams. His eyes began to go dark and he slapped himself. At the edge of his vision the portal blinked out of existence with a near-inaudible pop.

"Stay back," Francis told the robot.

It ceased its forward motion, and Francis slumped down, bracing himself on one elbow. When his body's trembling subsided, he leaned forward and poked and prodded his limp, throbbing limb. *Simple fractures. At least two.* A deeper part of him was somewhat impressed by his own clinical detachment under such trying circumstances. Winterbottom had been made of pretty stern stuff, but Throckmorton or Satterfield would have been pooling puddles of bitch after taking a warbot to the leg.

"Okay," Francis said. "Now you can touch me." The warbot stood and moved forward. "Pick me up—carefully—and run east. We'll hit the highway in a couple of miles. Don't slow down, even if I'm in pain. We can't be sure installation security didn't see the portal, or hear us. If someone sees you, we're really screwed."

EARLIER:

Breaking into the Kirtland-Chang Munitions Manufacturing Collective was so easy Francis could hardly call it breaking in. Not that it mattered; there was no one left in the complex for him to brag to, even if he wanted to. When his plan succeeded, none of this would have even happened in the first place. It was easy, though.

The fence surrounding the complex had fallen in places, knocked down either by rampaging robots or the sheer weight of the invading zombies, but enough of it remained that clearing the immediate area of the walking dead was like shooting fish in a barrel. Francis had sat high on Warbot-11's shoulders, plugging his ears against the loud report of the robot's weapons as it spun around in a series of arcs, mowing down the dead in less than a minute. After that, Francis had climbed down and stood to the side while Warbot-11 kicked in the front door.

The complex had been without power for some time, evidently. It was dark inside but for Warbot-11's bright, shining eyes. There had been no challenge, human or robot. The last of the collective's personnel had packed up and left in a convoy of armored vehicles months ago, according to the news that had reached Francis' ears a hundred miles away. All of Throckmorton's robots had dispersed long before that, linking up with law enforcement and military commanders to aid their attempts to quell the zombie threat. Francis himself dispatched the occasional hall-roaming zombie with his sidearm—allowing Warbot-11 to cut loose inside the building would have been more of a problem than a solution—and after stopping in a couple of offices to gather a few things, they reached the main lab without much incident.

Warbot-11 had to smash the security door three times before it fell, but when it did, the time portal was waiting on the other side. The room itself looked like a slaughterhouse, though luckily it had dried out long ago and didn't smell too bad. Desiccated zombie pieces and the remains of a small robot or two littered the floor near the portal, along with another body he recognized. Part of Winterbottom was left inside a bulky metal suit. Francis could only guess at what had transpired, having been unceremoniously relieved of duty by that smug bastard Satterfield months before the Kirtland Incident had taken place.

No one but the four of them had been completely privy to Satterfield's time portal project, and no one in the New Mexican Territory had seen hide nor hair of Satterfield since the zombies came and the world changed. Throckmorton's whereabouts were a little easier to pin down; a stray workbot had blown into town a while back, spinning a haphazard tale of Throckmorton's corpse and a janitor in a metal suit like Winterbottom's. Satterfield's pet project hadn't been fit for even a middle-school science fair, and he'd taken Throckmorton and Winterbottom down with him. For the first time, Francis was grateful for Satterfield's "budgetary concerns," whether real or simply an excuse for getting rid of a rival. Warbot-11 didn't have a record of the exact details, but it knew the zombies had come through the portal, and Francis knew the portal and its programming were Satterfield's doing. That narcissistic jackass wouldn't have let anyone else claim the glory. Francis would have bet his life on that.

Warbot-11 had a scavenged power source strapped to its back, and Francis hooked it up to the portal after telling the robot to seek out the decon chamber and use it. They had to take every precaution against taking the zombie virus into the past with them, of course. By the time the warbot returned, as squeaky-clean as it could ever get, Francis had the portal hooked up to the power source and the glowing disc hummed softly. He programmed the coordinates into the control panel: five years into the past, shortly before he'd begun working with Satterfield, Throckmorton, and Winterbottom. Two years before he'd met

Cate, the girl of his dreams. Approximately four and a half years before Cate died. Everything was set.

If only he'd let the damned bot go first.

Now:

The fresh, cool night breeze was the only thing that kept Francis from blacking out. The warbot moved slowly at first, but quickly built up momentum as it surged away from the complex. The robot's every stride rattled the broken bones in Francis' leg, but he bit his lip hard against the pain and focused on the mission. He was a scientist, not a warfighter, but simple science was all that was needed here. Cause and effect. Satterfield had fucked up, and the zombie plague had come through the time portal. Therefore, if Satterfield died now, before he built the portal, Cate wouldn't have to die beneath the onslaught of a dozen rabid zombies while he, Francis, huddled in the bathtub, listening to her screams and the sound of her splattered blood and flesh hitting the locked bathroom door. No, he wasn't a warfighter, but he had a reason to fight, and now he had the means.

He filled his lungs with the first breaths of air that he'd enjoyed in a long time, untainted by the constant smell and taste of rot, and went over the plan again and again in his mind. It felt like an eternity, but they reached the highway in about twenty minutes, according to Francis' watch. He ordered Warbot-11 to halt, and it came to an immediate, if jarring, stop.

<<What now, Boss?>> the warbot asked.

"Set me down," Francis said. When he was seated, he looked up at the dark night sky and the thin sliver of moon overhead. It'd be light in a few hours. They had stopped in a deep ditch running parallel to the highway. Several meters away, the occasional car sped past. Hopefully it was a weekday, and the morning commute would bring a good Samaritan along to get him a few miles down the road, even though he looked like a shabby, unkempt bum with his long hair, unruly beard, and unwashed clothes. He didn't really want to mess with the hospital, but the pain in his leg made it unavoidable. His vagrant's appearance could help him there. He could play the part of a hobo, and tell the ER doctor he was the victim of a hit and run. First things first, though; he had to do something with the robot. They didn't exist yet. In fact, the general public had been as surprised by Throckmorton's robots when they appeared as they had been by the zombies. It wouldn't do at all for the warbot to be found.

"Get down in the ditch over there," he said, "and kick the side of that dirt wall down on yourself. Then turn yourself off. You can't help me anymore here, but I'll come back for you when I'm done with Satterfield."

<<Will do>> Warbot-11 said, and trundled a few meters away before laying down in the ditch and pounding at the mounded dirt. When the dust settled, the warbot was fairly concealed; good enough to keep it safe from prying eyes until Francis' job was done. Even better, the hard shutdown cleared the robot's main memory; if anyone did find the damned thing and figure out how to turn it on, it'd be as innocent as a toddler, if only half as destructive. There'd be no talk of zombies or the future. Francis watched for another minute and then began climbing his way out of the ditch. Getting his broken leg over the metal guardrail was the worst part, but before long he landed heavily on the other side. He leaned back against the hard, metal rail and waited for more traffic.

"HEY." A FEMALE voice, and a soft pat on the cheek. "Hey, wake up."

He'd fallen asleep, he realized before opening his eyes. When he did open them, he thought he was still asleep and dreaming. Cate knelt beside him, long black hair whipping in the breeze as she stared at him. Blinking lights reflected off her smooth, pale skin. *Hazard lights,* Francis thought. *She put on her four-ways and stopped for me.* Not a dream, then. Made sense. When they'd met, Cate was a nurse at the hospital outside of Kirtland. She was exactly the sort of person who'd be on the road at this time, and would pull over to aid an injured vagrant. A fortuitous coincidence, but not the creation of his own troubled mind.

"Are you hurt?"

"Hit-and-run," Francis said, falling back on the lie he'd planned for the ER doctor at the hospital. "My leg's broken in at least two places."

"Oh my. I'm going to the hospital anyway. Let's get you situated, and I'll take you to the emergency room."

She helped him to his feet, picked up his backpack from where it had apparently fallen from his shoulder, and ducked her head under one of his arms, before leading him to her car. Francis couldn't help but stare as she shut his door, walked around to the driver's side, slid in behind the wheel, and pulled onto the highway.

"You can stop staring," she said after a moment. She sounded firm, but slightly amused. *Yeah, that was Cate,* Francis thought to himself. He forced himself to look away. Keeping the smile off his face was a little more difficult. *This is a sign. This plan is going to work.*

"Thank you for stopping," he said. "My name is...Fritz," he said, thinking of Winterbottom's armored corpse on the floor of the research lab. "What's your name?"

"Cate," she said, smiling a little. "I'm a nurse."

"Thank you again, Cate. I know what I look like, but I'm harmless, really. What's the chance we could skip the hospital?"

"We can put it off for a week or so if you'd rather get the leg amputated," she said. "It could get infected. You need it set in a cast."

"I know that," Francis said. "But you know how to do all that, and I'd rather not go to the hospital. I have money for a hotel room, food, and all the materials we'll need. Take me somewhere decent and set my leg, please. I'll pay your rent for the month." When they'd first met, Cate had been living in a tiny studio apartment and struggling with student loans on her meager entry-level salary. Francis wasn't kidding about the money, either. He'd looted several cash registers in preparation for his trip to the past. He didn't feel bad about it, and no one had stopped him. Everyone had bigger things to worry about than a drawer full of useless money.

"So you're on the street, you need me to take you to the hospital, but you have a stack of cash and want to pay my rent?"

"I'm serious," he said. "I'm not on the run or anything, if that's what you're worried about. I lost my job and my house a while back." *That's not even a lie.* "I don't have insurance, but I have a couple thousand dollars from my savings, in my bag. I'd rather just be left alone. Please." Neither of them spoke for a moment. Cate piloted the car down the road, and Francis prayed for another miracle.

"All right," she said at last. "I guess it's about time something went your way, after all."

THEN:

"Are you going to stare at her the rest of the night, boy," Fritz Winterbottom asked Francis the night he met Cate, "Or are you going to man up and go talk to her?"

Winterbottom's looming bulk made the dainty martini glass look even more ridiculous by comparison, and his jowls quivered beneath his bald pate. Francis, Winterbottom, and most of their colleagues from the Kirtland complex were at a command-mandated function with members of the local community. Francis wasn't exactly a wallflower, but he certainly wasn't as at ease as Winterbottom was.

"But...she came with someone," Francis said. "I don't want to start anything, or step on someone's toes."

"If she leaves with you, he's doing something wrong anyway," Winterbottom told him. "Besides, I've seen her looking at you all night. This is a 'mixer.' Grab your balls and go mix."

Winterbottom tossed his martini back in one gulp and went off in search of another, leaving Francis alone in the middle of the room. Cate rested her back against the bar at the far end, clad in a simple black dress and pearl necklace. She sipped a glass of wine while her date, a doctor if Francis had heard right, stood a good distance away, deep in conversation with one of Satterfield's assistants. He'd been there for most of the night, and Cate looked more than a little bored.

Screw it, he thought, and went to the bar. He ordered two glasses of the same vintage he was pretty sure Cate was holding, then walked over to her and leaned up against a bare patch of bar wood.

"Thought you could use a fresh one," he said, holding out a glass. "Looks like he might be ignoring you a while longer." Much to his surprise, she not only took the wine, but laughed a little. She had a pretty laugh. Francis lost his heart at that very moment.

"He's fine right where he is," Cate said. "We're not together, if that's what you're wondering. It's just...well, who wants to go to one of these things by themselves?"

"I did," Francis said. "Well, I'm here with my colleagues, of course. But no date. One of them seems to be more than a little concerned with whether I leave this thing by myself. He said you've been looking at me across the room all night."

"I have been, actually," she said, sipping from her fresh glass. "It's the strangest thing, but you remind me of someone."

"I thought I was supposed to use that line on you," he said. "I don't remember ever meeting you before, and I'm pretty sure I would if I had.

I've only been here for a couple of years, though. Came here to work at the complex. I'm Francis, by the way." He reached out his hand, and when she took it, a chill went down his spine.

By the time they left the party, most of the heavy-hitters had left the bar, and the staff had begun sweeping the floor and wiping down tables. Winterbottom had slapped Francis on the back and given him a sly wink on his way out the door. Francis did not leave the party alone. Instead, he went back to Cate's small apartment and they made love on the couch long enough to make him call in sick to work the next day.

NOW:

When the door slammed shut behind Cate, Francis felt as though a heavy axe had thudded into his heart. It was for the best, though. What would he say if she stayed longer? He didn't need to get to know her now. All he was there to do was kill Satterfield so that his younger self could get to know her at a later date, and then continue living in a zombie-free world. One alteration to the past was all that was necessary, and it would be selfish to indulge his need for Cate now.

He'd checked into a hotel and ordered food while Cate called in sick to work and then went shopping for materials. When she returned, she set his leg and bound it in a plaster cast, a procedure that required much delicacy from Cate and much vodka consumption from Francis. By the time she finished, the food had arrived. They ate and talked about inconsequential things for an hour or so. Then he gave her the money he'd promised, and she left.

He'd almost told her everything. The calm look in her dark brown eyes, her confident touch, the accidental scrape of her nail against his naked thigh that had made his head spin *before* the vodka kicked in, all brought back memories of their time together. Getting her out of the room before he lost his nerve was the best thing he could have done, for sure. It was bad enough he looked and smelled like a homeless person (and truly, he was, in every sense of the word), but if he'd started talking about her death, and zombies, and the future? If he wanted to cause that much damage to the timeline, he'd have been better off crashing Warbot-11 through the roof of the Kirtland complex.

Moving was a lot easier now, he noted as he climbed out of bed. He switched on the television and brewed a pot of weak hotel coffee before getting in the shower. The shower felt even better than the fresh air had. It was nearly as wondrous as seeing Cate again, if Francis were to be completely honest with himself. By the time he'd discovered Warbot-11 roaming the streets and laying waste to almost as many buildings as zombies, he'd been living in a shelter for several weeks, which had lost its running water long before his arrival. The shower wasn't relaxing, exactly. Getting wet, lathering up, and rinsing off, all while hanging his cast-bound leg out of the tub and balancing on one foot, was the furthest thing from relaxing. But he did manage to enjoy a couple extra moments under the steaming water before carefully extracting himself from the tub, toweling off, and changing into the fresh clothes Cate had picked up for him.

When he'd poured himself a cup of coffee and settled back onto the bed, he dragged his backpack up beside him and emptied it onto the floor. More crumpled money fell out, some clothing he thought he might have needed, and two other, far more important things. One was a large automatic pistol with an extra magazine. The very same sidearm he'd cleared a path to the research lab with, in fact. The other was a small netbook computer and power cord. The computer had been about as useful as Satterfield's brain for several months, with electricity being at a premium in the New Mexican Collective, but it booted up quickly when Francis plugged it in and turned it on. He accessed the hotel's wireless network, opened a search page, and began reading up on one Phillippe Satterfield.

THEN:

Dr. Phillippe Satterfield was not quite as impressive-looking as Francis had expected from reading his curriculum vitae and copious articles on quantum physics online. After cooling his heels in a plush chair for half an hour, watching Satterfield's secretary handle her business, he'd been ushered into the inner sanctum. The first thing Francis noticed was Satterfield's size. The physicist was small in stature, particularly for a man who loomed so large in the esteem of his colleagues and, if gossip were to be believed, his own. His hair was thin and wispy, and his neatly trimmed goatee formed the perimeter of what appeared to be a permanent smirk.

"Take a seat, young man," Satterfield said.

The man somehow managed even to offer a chair in a condescending manner, but Francis quickly put it out of his mind. The scientists at the Kirtland Underground Munitions Storage Complex were doing cutting-edge work in the repurposed Cold War bunkers-turned-research-labs below ground, and the arrogant man seated behind the expansive, polished-oak desk was leading the charge. His attitude may very well have been deserved. Francis had, after all, come all the way across the country to work with this man and his counterparts. Francis sat down and attempted to act unconcerned about his encounter with greatness.

"I've read your resume and thesis with great interest," the physicist continued. "Your agile young mind should supplement my boundless experience and ingenuity quite well."

"That's...good," Francis said. "I'm particularly interested in the robotics work I hear is taking place here."

"I'm sure you are," Satterfield said, chuckling.

Francis was a bit puzzled as to why his interest in robotics was so humorous to the professor, but added his own mirth to Satterfield's in the interest of getting along with the man. "In fact—"

Satterfield's phone rang, and the physicist held up a finger to Francis while he took the call. "Yes. Oh, he's here? No concern. I've been expecting him. Thank you." Satterfield rummaged in his desk for a brief moment before plucking a white badge from his shirt pocket and handing it to Francis. "Here's your temporary access badge, pending the completion of your security clearance," he said. "Why don't you go meet Dr. Throckmorton? The robots are his pet project. Go bring him some coffee from the break room down the hall. Use this other door." He gestured to another exit on the side of his office. Francis, a little puzzled but still game, left the office and did as Satterfield said.

It was definitely one of the easier interviews he'd had.

NOW:

Lounging in bed, gorging on all the take-out he'd missed and watching episodes of shows and reading recent news articles about events he remembered from five years ago was more than a little surreal, but it was good for taking Francis' mind off Cate. She hadn't returned to see him again. Of course, that was the idea, but a little part of him expected her to come back the next day to check on him or to bask in his animal magnetism...something. He'd gone out of his way not to turn on the charm, not to act like the guy she'd fall in love with a few years down the road, and it had worked. There was no reason to give himself grief about it.

Two days of sitcoms, old news, and delivery food was about all he could stand, though. His leg was still sore, and would be for a couple more weeks, but the medication Cate had brought seemed to be helping. Blasting Satterfield to Hell would help the healing process even more. He packed his bag, tucked the loaded gun into the waistband of his pants, grabbed the crutch Cate had left for him, and called a taxi before leaving the room. Before too long, he was in the cab, speeding toward the complex. When the cab passed the stretch of road where he'd left Warbot-11, he craned his head out the window, eliciting a strange look from the cabbie, but couldn't see well enough into the ditch to determine anything. Well, he'd watched enough news, and if someone had tripped over a fucking robot, it would have made headlines. In about an hour, he'd be back here to dig it out and get on with his life. Just one hour.

When they reached the installation, Francis rolled down his window and waved a temporary pass under the electronic scanner at the gate. This was one of the things he'd taken from the complex before going to the research lab to activate the time portal, and he couldn't help patting himself on the back just a little for his foresight. The two armed guards at the entrance half-assed another in what had to be a long line of mind-numbing vehicle inspections and then waved the cab through.

While the cabbie navigated the last couple of miles to the complex itself, Francis rolled everything around in his mind again. He was going to walk in and shoot Satterfield in the face. He may or may not make it out alive, but it wouldn't matter. His younger self was what mattered. Cate was what mattered. Throckmorton and Winterbottom were intelligent, for all their flaws, for sure, but the complex under their leadership wasn't likely to develop a time portal. This last thought brought a grin to Francis' lips as the cabbie pulled into a parking spot in front of the complex. He paid the driver and walked in the building.

He already knew where Satterfield's office was, of course, but he glanced at the directory for a second just to make it look good. As he made his way to the elevator, he brushed his arm against the gun beneath his shirt. Its bulk was reassuring; time-tested science that didn't fail. He rode down to the second sub-basement and hung an immediate left outside the elevator, and there it was: the office of Doctor Phillippe Satterfield, proclaimed in block letters worthy of the man's ego. Francis took a deep breath, hitched his pants up and smoothed out his shirt, ran his fingers through his long hair, and reached for the doorknob.

The secretary looked up when he entered—did a double-take as a matter of fact. *Can't be avoided,* Francis thought. The long hair and beard he'd grown after the zombie outbreak was a two-edged sword here. He didn't look anything like his younger self, but he didn't look like he had any business in a research laboratory, either. Best to play it cool and not make a big deal of anything. Thank God he'd been able to shower, at least.

"I'm here to see Dr. Satterfield," he said, showing the secretary his visitor's badge. She looked at it a little longer than necessary, but waved him over to the same plush chair he'd sat in—would sit in—while waiting for his interview. He watched her pick up her phone, dial an extension, and speak softly for a moment before hanging up. She typed away at her keyboard for another moment, then looked up and motioned him toward Satterfield's door. Francis flashed a quick smile and crossed the room. Once his back was to her, he lifted the gun from his waistband and held it against his leg as he opened the door.

Satterfield stood two feet away on the other side, aiming a silenced gun at Francis' forehead. "Shut the door," the physicist said, backing up.

The smug bastard still had that goddamn smirk on his face. Francis stepped forward, shut the door, then swung around quickly, aiming the gun at Satterfield's chest—

Two shots hammered into Francis' gut, driving him against the doorframe. He slumped to the floor. He tried to lift his gun—*at least they'd die together*—but his arm was numb and unresponsive. Satterfield stepped forward, kicked the gun out of Francis' hand, and shot him again, this time in the chest. Now it was hard to breathe. Francis watched as Satterfield, calm and collected, walked around to sit behind his desk. He laid the gun on the desktop and picked up his phone.

"My dear Throckmorton," he heard the physicist say. Francis' vision was dimming, and he still couldn't move his arms or legs. Sonofabitch had left him paralyzed and perforated one of his lungs. "The promising young man I sent with your coffee," the scientist continued, "I believe he'll make a good assistant for your robotics work." How the Hell had Satterfield known he was coming? It was impossible. "Tomorrow, I believe he'll assist you in the continued dismantling of the construct we found near the highway. Yes, I knew you'd agree." Satterfield raised his head to favor Francis with a grin. Francis couldn't even spit. He could barely lift his head. He watched as more and more blood spilled out from his gut onto his pants and the surrounding floor.

"One other thing," Satterfield said. "I'll be recording a file that I'd like you to embed into the core programming of all the robots you build." He lifted his free hand, curled the thumb and index finger into a circle—A-OK!—and nodded his head. "It's vital to our work. That's all I can say. Classified. Beneath you. Just watch and learn, okay?" Satterfield hung up the phone, then looked up at Francis.

"Satellite footage, you dumb shit. And apparently, another characteristic flash of brilliance from yours truly." He turned back to his computer. After a moment, he adjusted the small camera clipped to the top of his flatscreen monitor, straightened his tie, cleared his throat, and began to speak. It was getting harder for Francis to breathe and see now, but he could still hear everything.

"My dear Dr. Satterfield," Satterfield said into the camera, "It's me, Dr. Satterfield. I'll give you some authenticating information in a few minutes, but important things first. On April 4th, 2005, a bearded vagrant is going to try to kill you. This man." Francis saw the scientist's blurred shape pluck the camera from the monitor and wave it in his direction. "I didn't bother asking why, though you certainly can if you want. But you won't, because you're me a few minutes ago." Satterfield's laugh wounded Francis almost as much as the gunshots. This whole fucking ordeal had been part of his timeline's history from the get-go. What a crock of shit. How could he have been so dumb?

"If a message from yourself, delivered by a robot from the future, isn't enough to convince you, take a look at the data plate on the back of the robot's left calf." Francis couldn't see anymore, and he choked on hot blood with every breath he tried to take. "This proves time travel is possible. I will now begin my work on the time portal in earnest...."

In the darkness, Cate came to him, like an angel forgiving his trespasses, come to take him home.

SECTOR

JIMMY FINDER

Joe McKinney

1.

"Is that your experiment?" Captain Fisher asked.

The infantry captain gestured toward the boy on the other side of the one-way glass. From the look on Fisher's face it was obvious he didn't think much of the kid. He certainly didn't see humanity's greatest hope in the war against the zombies. What he saw was a mop-haired runt, too skinny, too short, too awkward, about as far from a soldier as one could hope to find.

"His name is Jimmy Finder," Dr. David Knopf replied. "I try not to refer to him as my experiment."

"Finder? You're kidding. That can't be his real name, can it?"

Knopf smiled amiably enough, but inside he was holding onto his patience with both hands. It was always the same with these military men, their smug condescending abuse and smirks of disdain whenever they were confronted with something that challenged the conventional wisdom of the battlefield.

"James is all we were able to learn from him," Knopf admitted. "We started calling him Finder after his abilities became apparent."

Fished shook his head. "Frankly, Doctor, I think this is all a load of crap. You should probably know that from the start."

Knopf's expression carefully masked his frustration. It wouldn't do any good to alienate the military now that they'd finally agreed to let him demonstrate Jimmy's talents in the field. It had only taken twelve long years.

"That's all right, Captain. I'm used to skepticism."

"It's a wonder you still bother trying."

You bastard, Knopf thought. Fisher was really trying to bait him. "I believe in what we're doing here, Captain. I wouldn't have put twelve years of my life into this project if I didn't. That boy in there is going to save lives and help us turn the corner on this war."

Knopf, afraid he was about to say something he'd regret, turned his attention on Jimmy, and a familiar mix of pity and pride rose up in him. Twelve years earlier, a contingent of warbots discovered the boy wandering the hills above the nearby town of Mill Valley, Ohio. The provisional government gave him to Knopf's Weapons Research Team with orders that they find out how a two-year-old toddler had managed to survive an entire summer right under the noses of ten thousand zombies. It had taken Knopf three years to discover the answer. It took another nine before anybody in the military's High Command would take him seriously enough to let him prove it. But he did find the truth.

"You really believe that kid in there has psychic powers?"

"That's not exactly what he does," Knopf said. "He's not a psychic. He doesn't predict the future or read minds, none of that gypsy fortune teller stuff. Think of him as a sort of bloodhound that we've trained to sniff out zombies." Fisher was staring at him, his expression inscrutable. "Look," Knopf went on, "you're familiar with the morphic field theory, right? The idea that zombies tend to move in large groups because the subtle neuro-electric field generated within the reptilian core of their brains draws them together. Jimmy can pick up on this phenomenon."

"I've heard the theory, Doctor. I've also heard a lot of respectable scientists say that it's a bunch of rubbish."

"It's not rubbish, Captain. You've probably experienced it yourself. The feeling you get when somebody is staring at you from across the room; or thinking of somebody completely out of the blue just moments before they call you on the phone. Ever watched a large flock of birds or a school of fish change direction en masse without running into each other? Same thing. It's not rubbish, it's a documented fact. And it's what allows Jimmy to do what he does. Think of how helpful that would be deployed on the battlefield. Think of the tactical advantage you'd have if you knew where your enemy was all the time."

"Anybody can find a zombie, Doctor. Just go outside the walls and make a lot of noise. You'll find plenty in no time."

The military, Knopf thought. Such fools. They couldn't even come up with new jokes, much less open their minds to new possibilities. It was no wonder they were getting their butts handed to them on the battlefield. And if Captain Fisher was any indication of the kind of officer the High Command was turning out, the future looked bleak indeed.

"Yes," Knopf said, "but the trick, as I'm sure they taught you in your officer training school, is to find the enemy before they find you. Wouldn't you agree?"

"We already have sensors, doctor. The robots can detect zombies with an eighty-six percent accuracy rate. In my opinion, that's—"

"Hardly an acceptable margin of error," Knopf said, shaking his head. "Not when lives are on the line. And eighty-six percent is nothing compared to what Jimmy's capable of. Wait until we arrive in Mill Valley, Captain. Your robots claim to have cleared the town of every last zombie. What will happen if that boy in there is able to lead us to even one zombie? What will you say then?"

"It'll never happen."

"All I ask is for you to keep an open mind, Captain," Knopf said.

"You're asking me to believe in mumbo jumbo, Doctor. I prefer to put my faith in robots and bullets."

Knopf glanced over at Jimmy. The boy was tossing in his sleep. Nerves, probably. Or bad dreams. Poor kid. Sleep was usually the only time his mind got any rest, the only time he could turn off his gift.

"Just you wait, Captain. Tomorrow, that boy's going to make a believer out of you."

2.

"ALL STOP!" Fisher shouted.

The expedition ground to a halt. They'd been walking for hours, and the clattering and clanking and whirring of a full company of robots had made a tremendous racket that even now, in the sudden silence that followed the captain's command, continued to ring in Jimmy Finder's ears.

But the ringing only lasted a moment. Once the racket faded, the pulsing images of the dead flooded back into his brain. The town was definitely not clear. He could sense hundreds of pulses going off all around him, like he was standing in the middle of a huge orchestra made of nothing but big bass drums, all of them pounding out a violent and relentless and tuneless rhythm.

He groaned in misery, wanting only to curl up in his hammock and fall asleep. Going outside like this, with nothing to shield him from all those morphic pulses, was crippling. Dr. Knopf had tried to teach him a few tricks to get rid of the pain, like focusing on a single thought-presence and letting everything else fall away, but most of the tricks were too hard to do outside of the lab. And right now, he could barely open his eyes his head hurt so badly.

I can't do this, he thought.

James.

Jimmy stiffened in alarm. He looked around, uncertain who was talking to him. He was surrounded by trooperbots. They had no faces, only curved, featureless metal plates that they turned toward their human masters whenever they needed to speak or were spoken to, but none of them were looking at him now. They stood like statues, tall and mute in the settling dust and gloom of evening.

And there were no humans anywhere around him. Dr. Knopf and the soldiers had moved to the shade of the portico of a deserted gas station, talking in hushed tones. Knopf wasn't even looking in his direction.

It is you, isn't it? My God, how long I've waited!

That time the voice was so strong it caused his eyes to fly open wide. The hairs on the back of his neck were standing on end, as though from static electricity. He could feel the blood rush to his head. He was dizzy, his cheeks flush with an uncomfortable heat. It wasn't just a voice, he realized, but a thought. A thought with weight, with force behind it.

The sensation didn't last long, though. The dizziness faded. A cold sweat replaced the heat on his cheeks. He had a very real, almost tangible sense of the contact fading. The next instant, all trace of the link—yes, that was it; it had been a link he felt, like another mind wrapping its grip around his mind—echoed away, leaving him confused and feeling somehow vulnerable.

Again he looked around.

No one was paying him any attention.

He cocked his head to one side, trying to make sense of what he had just felt. Dr. Knopf had always said his power was of a class known as remote viewing. He could sense zombies, locate them with a degree of precision the machines couldn't even begin to approach, but only that. He had never heard voices before. Thought-speech was out of the range of his abilities, much as people were unable to hear the high pitched tones of a dog whistle. And for that Jimmy was supposed to be thankful. Dr. Knopf had told him so, and his own short excursions outside the lab had backed that up. It was hard enough holding on to his sanity while sensing the dead thoughts that emanated from the dead. If he could hear the thoughts of the living as well…

But then, what was happening to him? Was this something new?

The expedition had stopped on a hill road above the little town of Mill Valley. Jimmy walked through the perfectly ordered rows of trooper-bots and continued on until he was well out in front of the rest of the expedition. From here, he could look down on the whole expanse of the ruined town. The mind-voice was coming from somewhere down there, under the rubble.

Cautiously, one small bit at a time, he opened his mind and searched the ruins. This always hurt, even in the controlled circumstances of the laboratory, but he was curious.

Gritting his teeth, he sent out a thought:

Who are you? How do you know my name?

Jimmy waited, his mind open and unguarded.

Who are you?

But there was nothing. Not even the pulsing of a zombie's brain. The evening gloom settling over the town was like a burial shroud, silent and unfathomably deep. Was it any wonder it frightened him so?

3.

Why won't you answer me!

The mind-voice slashed like a knife through Jimmy's sleep. He flinched awake, eyes shooting open in panic. His breaths were coming in fast, shallow gulps, his body soaked with sweat.

Please stop! Oh God, please stop. You're hurting me!

He sent the thought out in desperation. His head felt like it was about to split open, like there was a crazy little man inside there going to town with a hatchet on his brain.

I need help. I need help now!

Jimmy gasped. The pain was coming in waves now. He gritted his teeth against it, tensing the muscles in his temples, and surprisingly, that helped a little. The pain started to ebb away.

Who are you?

But there was no need to ask the question, for now that the pain was no longer tearing him apart, Jimmy knew.

The mind-voice belonged to his father.

Yes, James! It's me! Oh thank God you've come!

They told me you were dead.

Jimmy dropped out of the hammock he'd slung between the gas pumps of the abandoned gas station and staggered numbly toward the moonlit road, where the robots stood in silent, perfectly ordered rows.

They told me you were dead.

Do I sound dead to you? James, come to me. I need help.

Nodding slowly, transfixed by the mind-voice pulling him toward the town, Jimmy began to walk.

4.

THE SILENCE HANGING over the town was massive. Jimmy could feel it like a presence, vast and powerful, full of menace.

Many people had died here. In the four days since the army retook the town the birds and the rats had descended on the corpses that were still heaped in the gutters and had begun to feast. The carrion feeders watched him silently as he passed, their eyes gleaming yellow and full of hate, their bodies wet with gore. So many dead, Jimmy thought. Such a terrible waste. Instinctively, he found himself emptying his mind, measuring his breathing, the way Dr. Knopf had taught him, so that he could stay calm when facing the horror of facing a badly decomposed zombie.

But not even Dr. Knopf's calming lessons prepared him for the horror of this place. The fighting here must have been intense. Besides the bodies and the carrion feeders, hardly a wall was free of bullet holes. A few of the buildings had been reduced to rubble. Many more were burned to blackened skeletons.

And no matter where he looked, no matter what road he took, the silence was everywhere.

Daddy, which way?

Daddy.

That word stopped him, and he couldn't help but smile. It sounded funny to him. He'd spent his entire life an orphan, the subject of countless stupid tests, trying to justify what he did for people who seemed only interested in mocking him and treating him like a freak—and now here he was calling for his daddy

The military men already thought of him as a runt, he knew that. What would they think of him now? They'd call him pathetic. Or worse. But what did they know? They weren't orphans. They hadn't walked in his shoes, cried his tears, felt the kind of heartsick loneliness that carried him off to sleep each night. Screw them. So what if he walked around the world calling for his Daddy? What did they know about it?

Feeling mean, feeling bitter, Jimmy wandered the ruins, searching for a way down under the town. He sent out his mind-voice constantly, trying to get his father to answer. But he never felt anything more than a curious tickling sensation at the base of his skull. Even as he opened up more and more, out of desperation, there was nothing but the town's foreboding silence.

And then, he found it. A way down.

He had turned down an alleyway because he sensed it was the right way to go, and that same feeling had led him to a half-hidden flight of stairs. They terminated in a rusted metal doorway marked:

MILL VALLEY WATER AUTHORITY
AUTHORIZED PERSONNEL ONLY

This was it.

The hint of a smile appeared at the corner of his mouth. Trust your instincts, Knopf had told him. Well, he had trusted his instincts, and they led right where he wanted to go.

Then Jimmy wriggled the knob.

Locked, damn it.

He rammed it with his shoulder and only managed to hurt himself.

Out of frustration, he picked up a piece of rebar from the sidewalk and banged on the knob until it snapped off.

The hinges groaned as the door fell open.

Leaning forward, he peered into the darkness, gagging on the noisome stench of sewage coming up from the levels below. Jimmy opened his mind, intending to find his father's mind-voice, but instead was hit by something else.

Do not go down there.

"What?" Jimmy said. As before, he looked around, because this voice was different from his father's. It seemed like someone was right behind him. But he was alone. A sheet of newspaper, carried by a breeze, drifted down the empty street. Nothing else moved.

"Who's talking?" Jimmy asked.

If you go down there you will die.

"Tell me who you are," Jimmy insisted.

This is Comm Six. State your designation.

"My designation? What the…I'm Jimmy."

He shook his head, trying to make sense of the sensation the voice was causing in his ears. It wasn't a voice. Not exactly. It was a mind-voice, like his father's, but very different. Where his father's voice was a spike trying to hammer its way into his brain, this voice was like insects buzzing around in his head. And yet it was just as clear, just as insistent, as his father's. Only it was…soothing somehow. Not at all harsh.

What's a Comm Six?

I am Comm Six.

Yeah, but what does that mean? Who are you? How come you can talk to me?

I am a commbot. I directed the robots that fought to retake this town. I was damaged. I was left behind.

I've never heard of a commbot. And you don't sound like any robot I've ever heard of.

I am not like other robots. I am a commbot. I am sentient.

Sentient? What's that mean?

It means that I am aware of my own presence. I know there is a me and a you and that we are different from each other. I can think.

Can't other robots do that, like warbots?

Not like I do. Warbots have adaptive programming. They have built-in algorithms that allow them to interpret their environment within a narrow variety of preprogrammed ways. I do not have those limitations. My thinking is based on non-linear models, more like your own.

I've never heard of robots being able to do stuff like that.

I was an experiment.

Jimmy laughed. "Uh huh. You and me both."

Why do you laugh? You are in danger. Do not go into the sewers. There are many zombies down there still.

I don't sense any. Usually I can sense the zombies. That's what I do.

Perhaps the lead residue is blocking you.

I don't get blocked. My sensors aren't like yours. And besides, my dad's down there.

A pause.

There are only zombies down below.

Yeah?

Yes.

Well, I guess we'll see about that, won't we?

5.

THE GROUND SHOOK beneath the warbot's weight. To Knopf it looked like some grossly deformed Tyrannosaurus Rex, a tank on two monstrously thick mechanical legs. It advanced down the rubble-strewn ruins of Oak Street and stopped in front of Fisher, bowing its enormous head down to eye-level with the Captain in a whir of servos and pneumatic sighs.

"We have searched the town, sir. The sensors do not register the boy or his ankle monitor."

"Yeah, well, he didn't go somewhere else. He's here."

A pause.

"What are your orders, sir?"

"Find him."

"We have scanned everywhere, sir."

"You haven't scanned where he's at. Scan again. I'll tell you when to stop."

"Yes sir."

The warbot left to resume its search.

"Trouble?" Knopf asked to the young captain's back.

"It's all the lead dust," Fisher said, turning on him. The captain adjusted the surgical mask he wore, clearly frustrated with it. Mill Valley's smelting factory had been destroyed during the fight to retake the town and it scattered lead particulates and aerosolized bits of brick all over everything. The masks *were* uncomfortable, tending as they did to trap sweat at the corners of the mouth, making the wearer feel like they were constantly drooling, but they were absolutely necessary. No one wanted to breath in that stuff. Especially because the robots kicked so much of it up into the air. "It's playing havoc with the robots, everything from their sensors to their servos. It's no wonder we lost so many robots in the fight."

"Or that you misstated the presence of zombies here."

"You have no basis to support that comment, Doctor."

Fair enough, Knopf thought, and nodded.

They had already looked over a good part of the town, and even now, the trooperbots were sifting through buildings and overgrown lots, continuing the search. But even with the robots tirelessly performing their duties, Knopf couldn't help but feel frustrated. He'd grown used to Jimmy's precise directions, his ability to describe exactly where a zombie was hidden, and the waiting and the uncertainty of doing it the military's way was maddening.

Before Jimmy, everyone believed the zombies were nothing more than dead meat-husks. Beyond a few weak electrical impulses in the reptilian core of their brains, which generated the morphic fields that allowed them to find each other and to move around, searching for living brains, the zombies were thought to have no neurological function whatsoever. Certainly they retained no sense of self, no memories, no desires. They possessed only an insatiable need to feed on living tissue. Most scientists stopped short, however, of accepting Knopf's ideas of morphic fields. That was, until Jimmy came along.

Knopf remembered asking him once how he did it, what it felt like to sense a dead man's mind.

"It hurts," Jimmy had said. "Beyond that, it's hard to describe."

But then, several months later, on a foggy morning in early May, the two of them had taken a walk outside the lab, and through the dense screen of fog they'd seen sentries up on the walls, picking their way with flashlights, the beams muted but distinct in the sodden air.

Jimmy had stopped and stared.

Knopf continued walking for a few steps, then turned back to see what was wrong.

"That right there," Jimmy said, pointing at the flashlight beams bobbing on the wall. "That's what it looks like in my head."

"When you sense the zombies, you mean?"

"Yeah. It looks like that. Like flashlight beams in the fog. Only the light feels like a current, you know? Like the way you can feel water moving over your skin. Or how you can sense static electricity when it makes the hairs stand up on your arms."

The description had impressed Knopf. Little moments like that had brought them closer together, and if he wasn't exactly a father to Jimmy, he imagined he at least qualified as a benevolent uncle.

"If the boy's around here we'll find him," Fisher said.

Knopf realized he'd been drifting. He glanced at Fisher, a vacant look on his face.

"Doctor? Did you hear me? I said we'll find him."

Knopf nodded.

"Why do you suppose he ran off?"

"I don't know," Knopf answered truthfully. "It hurts his head terribly to be out of the laboratory like this. There's so much mind-noise."

The Captain rolled his eyes. "Well, if he can't handle the heat, sounds like he needs to get out of the kitchen."

Knopf looked at him in surprise. It was a cruel thing to say, even for Fisher. But what did Fisher know, anyway? He was too young to remember a world before the zombies. All his adult life had been spent in the Army. Fisher knew soldiering and little else. It may have made him an impressive man, commanding and resourceful beyond his years, but it hadn't taught him compassion.

Knopf, though, remembered the world as it had been. He remembered eating a meal without having to glance over his shoulder. He remembered not having to sleep in shifts, a weapon always at the ready. He remembered his wife, and his little boy. Knopf remembered being human, something he doubted Fisher could lay any claim to.

But perhaps, more importantly, Fisher wasn't a father. He couldn't speak to the world of a child. Sure, he had been a child, but he hadn't also been a parent. What did he know of the pain, the fear, the joy that came with raising a child? As a soldier he claimed to be fighting the most important war humanity had ever fought, a war for the survival of the species. And yet, he had no direct emotional stake in its survival. It was just an academic proposition for him. Human lives were simply numbers for him, pieces to be moved around a game board, little different from the robots under his command.

Knopf had essentially raised Jimmy. The boy had been handed off to him less than a month after Knopf's own son had died at the hands of the zombie horde, and Knopf, wounded to his core, had at first held the screaming toddler at a disdainful and resentful distance. He had looked at the scrawny, screaming brat, and all he'd been able to think about was himself, standing in the middle of a road at the crest of a hill, looking down on the base housing where he'd lived with his wife and child, zombies streaming out of the bungalow, blood covering their faces and chests like bibs, and the resentment had grown to an intense hatred.

But that hatred softened by degrees.

For several years, Jimmy had been unable to do anything but cower in a corner, screaming and yelling anytime anybody got remotely close to him. Only gradually, through repeated effort and a thousand small acts of kindness, had Knopf managed to lure the boy out of the shadows. It was longer still before the boy would sleep anywhere but under the cot in Knopf's office. And across the gulf of those years, the two of them had healed each other. They'd learn to trust one another. Neither was emotionally seaworthy, not yet anyway, but together, they were getting close.

And now this. The boy missing…

6.

JIMMY STOPPED AT the top of a rickety metal staircase, waiting for his eyes to adjust to the darkness. Further on ahead he could see what looked like a glowing blue slime coating the handrails and parts of the walls. The glow was faint, but it provided enough light to give him a sense of the curved, tiled tunnel around him.

The stairs shook and groaned beneath his weight, moving with every step, and he was almost to the bottom when the metal suddenly snapped and gave way, dropping him into the muck on the bottom level.

He barely managed to roll out of the way as the structure crashed down around him.

Afterwards, surrounded by tangled pieces of rusting metal, he sat there blinking up at the ruined staircase, looking like the exoskeleton of some giant, malformed insect up there.

Grunting, he sat up.

The room in which he found himself was a horror. There were rotting bodies everywhere. Arms and legs and ropes of intestines hung from rusted piles of equipment, and the place smelled powerfully bad, worse even than the zombies Dr. Knopf occasionally brought into the lab for Jimmy to practice with.

Something moved beside him, and Jimmy turned, only to find himself nose to nose with a zombie. Its face was dripping with blood and sewage, eyes opaque, like cataracts, yet at the same time intensely alive with hunger and violence. The skin around its mouth was ripped and shredded, exposing its blood-blackened teeth so that it almost seemed to be grinning at him.

Jimmy screamed, backpedaling as fast as he could go.

The zombie stayed where it was. It sniffed the air. It opened its mouth, almost as though to taste what it smelled, but instead let out an aching moan.

The next instant it crawled after him.

Still scrambling, Jimmy tripped and landed in a mass of arms and legs. He jumped to his feet, only to realize a moment later that the arms wrapping around him belonged to a docbot, the cord tightening around his knees the shoulder sling from the docbot's medpac.

The zombie was coming closer, clawing its way over the wreckage of robots and dead bodies. Jimmy looked around for a way out, but there was none. He was standing at the apex of a curving tunnel, both directions extending off into darkness that could hide anything.

But he did have the medpac. Those things were heavy. Jimmy had seen them used back at the lab. Carrying one was like lugging around a bag of bricks, and they'd make a good weapon.

He tugged at the shoulder strap until the pack came loose from the muck.

By that point the zombie was almost on him. Jimmy stumbled backwards, and at the same time swung the pack with both hands, smashing it against the zombie's jaw with the satisfying crunch of broken bone.

The zombie went sprawling backward into the sewage and rotting bodies, landing in a twisted heap.

Jimmy didn't wait to see if it would get back up. He turned to run.

No!

Jimmy slowed, but didn't stop. That was Comm Six's voice.

I have to get out of here.

No! There is no time to run. Hide. Right now.

Where?

Under the robot. Now. Before the zombie gets up.

Jimmy dropped to the floor, crawling under the wrecked bodies and robots, and pulled the docbot whose medpac he had just used over top of him.

Be very still.

It was good advice. During the many experiments Dr. Knopf had put him through, Jimmy had learned that the zombies' morphic field acuity was imperfect at best. Certainly not as strong or as finely tuned as his. If a person remained very still, and was able to clear his thoughts, a passing zombie would think them no different from a lamp post, or a mailbox, or any of the other inanimate objects that populated the world.

Through a hole in the docbot's damaged skull, Jimmy watched the zombie slowly scan the ruined figures at its feet. Flies swarmed around its head. Filthy water dripped from its beard. It turned its mangled face left, then right, then walked off down the darkness of the receding tunnel.

Jimmy listened as the sounds of its splashing grew faint, then he slowly climbed out from under the docbot.

You must find a way out. There are many zombies down here. You must leave.

Jimmy shook his head.

I can't. My father's down here.

You will not leave?

I can't.

Your decision is unwise. But if you must stay, you should have a weapon.

Jimmy huffed at that one. *Thanks, that's great advice. I'll remember to bring one next time I'm crawling through a zombie-infested sewer.*

I can lead you to a weapon.

Jimmy stopped. *You can?*

One hundred and sixteen feet to your left you will find a small room. One of the soldiers who died retaking this town is still there. He is a zombie now, but his corpse still carries a weapon. Go now. Move quickly.

He made his way down to the room Comm Six had told him about, noticing as he went how the luminescent scum on the walls seemed to be thickest at the water line.

Where's this light coming from?

When the army realized they would have to fight down here they seeded the sewer water with bioluminescent algae. It cleans the water and glows with the light you see. Eventually, the water in these sewers will be clean enough for human use.

Oh. That's kind of cool.

The room you need is on your left. Careful now. The zombie will attack when he sees you.

Jimmy stepped into the room. There were several pieces of metal tubing at his feet, old rusted pipes that had fallen from the ceiling. He picked one of them up, tested its heft, and decided it would work.

The zombie Comm Six had warned him about was on the far side of the room.

As Jimmy watched, it pawed at the wall, scratching uselessly at the mold-covered stone wall, its fingernails long since ripped from the tips of its fingers.

Then Jimmy noticed that the thing had no legs.

From the waist down there was nothing but ropes of viscera and blackened shards of bone protruding from the torso.

His stomach rose into his throat, and he coughed.

The sound got the zombie's attention. It turned its head sharply, and an urgent, hungry moan rose up from its rotting throat.

Move quickly. Do not let it make noise.

The zombie pulled itself toward Jimmy with its ruined fingers, its moaning growing more insistent, more desperate.

"Right," Jimmy muttered.

He stepped into the room with the metal pipe in both hands, raised high above his head. The zombie held its broken fingers up toward him, trying to grab him.

But Jimmy was quicker.

He sidestepped the zombie's hand and brought the pipe down as hard as he could.

Jimmy had never killed a zombie before, and he was surprised, and sickened, by how easy it was. Three quick strokes and the back of the thing's head was pulverized into a ruined mess of blood, hair and bone.

It took a moment for his mind to break through the adrenaline rush.

I did it. Oh God, I think I'm gonna puke.

The weapon is against the far wall.

"Huh?"

The weapon. Take it now.

Feeling dizzy, lightheaded, Jimmy scanned the far wall. The weapon was in a leather gun belt wrapped around the zombie's severed hips and legs.

You must move quickly. The zombies have heard you. They are approaching.

He had to peel the gun belt off the corpse's bloody hips. It made a sucking sound as he pulled it free.

This is so gross. I don't know if I can—

Hurry.

He worked the buckle open, then wrapped it around his own waist and pulled it as tight as it would go. Jimmy moved his hips back and forth. The gunbelt was still loose, but it didn't fall off, and that was something at least.

Okay, I've got the gun. Which way do I go now?

Nothing.

Jimmy opened his mind a little more.

Comm Six, you there? Which way do I go?

But the commbot's voice was gone. There was nothing but the echoes of water dripping from the ceiling somewhere down the tunnel. And from further on, barely audible, came the faint moaning of the living dead.

Well, he thought, pulling the pistol, here goes nothing.

And he stepped out into the tunnel.

7.

WITH ONLY THE faint blue light from the algae growing on the walls to guide him, Jimmy headed deeper into the sewers. The water was up to his knees and every step made a splash that echoed a long way down the tunnels. He tried to reach out with his mind and sense the zombies that Comm Six had told him were down here, but in his mind he saw nothing but a gray depthless fog. For the first time in his life, he realized, his mind was a quiet place.

It might have felt good, if he wasn't so scared. And so unsure of himself. What are you doing down here? he asked himself. Dr. Knopf had told him bunches of times that his parents were dead. He'd accepted that a long time ago. And didn't he have his own memories from the night the dead overran this town? They were vague, cloudy memories, but they were there.

He remembered a room with dark-colored carpet and walls of wood paneling. He remembered a striped couch and a big chair that his infantile mind understood as DADDY'S CHAIR.

He remembered his Mom, the source of kindness and nourishment and safety. She smelled like comfort, like goodness. At least that was the way she smelled in his memories. But the next instant, she'd gone wild with fear.

And he remembered his father, not his father's face, but the anger in the man's voice. Daddy, the protector, the violent one, driving his shoulder into the door, yelling at his mother to take the boy and *go go go!*

The room filled with smoke, seeping under the door, crawling in through the windows.

The memory broke apart with the first tinges of smoke. From there, all he remembered were broken images, crazy things. More screaming, and zombies reaching for him everywhere he turned. He remembered getting separated from his parents, his mother's cries echoing away into nothingness in the smoke that was filling the house where they lived.

And then, when he realized he was alone, that his parents were gone, some kind of light had turned on inside his head.

Through the smoke, through the screams, he could sort of see the bad people trying to hurt him. They glowed in the smoke, shimmering like flashlight beams, except that the light carried with it a bad...was it a smell? That was the only way his mind had been able to frame the sensation. Their minds smelled bad. The light that came from them was bad. They wanted to hurt him. He'd taken that knowledge and he had...

What?

He didn't know what he'd done from there.

He had gone walking, he supposed.

The next thing he could remember for sure was sleeping on the cot in Dr. Knopf's office, crying himself to sleep. Sometimes, Dr. Knopf would read from a book about a big rabbit and a little rabbit and the big rabbit saying this is how much I love you. He remembered sometimes Dr. Knopf would cry when he read the book, and how the man's tears and the choking sob in his voice had scared him for some reason he couldn't quite understand. And he remembered grabbing Dr. Knopf's leg in a stranglehold whenever the military men came by to ask questions and laugh at the answers they got.

Ah yes, Dr. Knopf.

There was the other problem of Jimmy's life.

For several years now he'd understood what he meant to the High Command. He was an experiment, an asset. They talked about him the same way they talked about programming groups for warbots. Or pallets of ammunition. Or the shifting lines in the sand that divided the living from the dead.

Only Dr. Knopf thought of him as Jimmy.

And that was what made things so hard.

Dr. Knopf was as close to a parent as Jimmy had ever really known, but he wasn't the ideal parent that Jimmy always imagined his real parents would have been. He was distant. He could be cold. Sometimes, he could be harsh, even cruel when Jimmy failed to cooperate. Dr. Knopf was the one who made the rules, and Jimmy hated him for that. He had many memories of the two of them screaming at each other, Jimmy calling Knopf the meanest man he'd ever met, and Knopf, so angry his fists trembled with rage, making harsh, declarative statements that made Jimmy shrink into himself. Things like, "I don't care what you think. I just care that you do what I say." Or, "Nobody asked your opinion. Just do what I tell you. Why can't you get that through your head?" Or, "I'm sorry. I love…I just want you to be happy, Jimmy. Please, do this for me. This one last test. Finish this, and we can get some dinner. I'll do the macaroni and cheese you like so much…"

It was the occasional kindness that made things so confusing. There were times when Knopf actually felt like a father to him. And he was sure Knopf felt the same. Why then did they always pull away from each other in the end? Why did the rare moments of closeness always end with the look of love fading from Knopf's face, and a terribly remote sadness invariably taking its place? The man was haunted by his memories. Jimmy knew that. But why did memory have to make things so hard?

There were so many questions, and so few answers.

But still you haven't asked the right question.

Jimmy stopped.

"Daddy?"

Yes, James.

What question? What did I forget to ask?

How, James. How come you can sense the dead? Didn't you ever think to ask? When the military men were laughing at you, didn't it seem strange that you knew you were right?

Yeah, I guess. Well, no, not really. I always felt like I was wrong.

Because they weren't inside your head. They didn't know what you knew. But I do, James. And you know how I know?

Jimmy shook his head, unable to articulate the thought aloud.

I know because I have the power too. It turned on the night the zombies came to Mill Valley, didn't it?

"Yes," Jimmy said, breathlessly. *Turned on* was exactly how he had come to think of that night, like somebody had just flipped a light switch inside his head.

The same thing happened for me, James. My power to sense the zombies, it flipped on that very night.

You mean, like a light switch.

Yes, exactly like that.

Daddy?

Yes?

Why isn't it working now? The sight, I mean. Usually I can sense the zombies. I could sense them before I came down here.

I don't know. It doesn't work down here for me, either. That's how I got trapped. Now hurry, James. I need help.

But Jimmy didn't move. Ahead of him was some kind of catwalk, another metal platform like the kind that had collapsed under his weight back at the entrance to the sewers.

What's wrong? Why aren't you coming to me?

Jimmy turned and looked behind him. The blue light from the algae didn't carry far. Twenty or thirty feet down and his visibility was gone, swallowed by the darkness. But something was down there. He could hear it splashing, and moaning.

James?

He could see silhouettes down there now, bunches of them, coming toward him.

Daddy, I think I'm in trouble.

8.

JIMMY PULLED HIS pistol just as the first zombie lumbered into view.

As she came closer, the faint blue glow from the algae lit her ghastly features. It was a woman, or had been once. Her shoulder length hair was matted now with blood and clods of mud. Her neck seemed unable to hold up the weight of her head, making her hair hang like a curtain of yarn in front of her face. The skin on her arms and neck was oozing with abscesses and open cuts that no longer bled. The clothes had been torn from her chest, and when she moved, black ribs showed where the flesh had been eaten away. She raised her gnarled hands and began to moan.

There were more behind her.

A lot more.

Jimmy raised the huge pistol, holding it with the two-handed grip all children inside the walls were taught. He squeezed off a round, and the blast clapped over his ears like an enormous pair of hands, leaving him momentarily deaf, and stunned.

He didn't even realize the lead zombie had closed the distance between them until she put her filthy hands on him.

But that was enough to get him moving.

He ran for the platform he'd seen a few moments before, but stopped at the railing. The stairs leading down to the aqueduct must have collapsed during the fighting, for they lay in a broken, rusted heap twenty feet below him.

Where more zombies had gathered, attracted by his gun shot.

The dead went into a frenzy when he appeared on the landing.

Oh God oh God oh God, Daddy, what do I do?

The woman with the black ribs was clutching the air between them. He could smell the rotten meat stench she carried with her. Even over the open sewage he could smell her. Another three steps and she'd be on him.

"No," he said, kicking at her. His heart was pounding painfully in his chest. "Stay back!"

But zombies, of course, don't ever stay back, and Jimmy was forced to back up until he was pressed against the railing.

It was then he knew what he had to do.

He jumped.

9.

DR. KNOPF STOOD in front of what was left of the Huntington Movie Theater, wiping the sweat from the back of his neck. Not even ten o'clock yet and already the sun was punishing him. He had never handled field work well, and now that he was getting on into middle age, he had even less patience for it.

But he had to deal with it. At least this one last time. Jimmy was out here, somewhere, and he had to find him.

But which way?

To his left the street was piled high with the rubble of collapsed buildings. To his right, the street was a silent canyon between windowless buildings. It would be easier to go that way, but just because it was easy was no guarantee that Jimmy had gone that way. The boy had survived here as a toddler because of his gift, going not where the going was easiest, but where his senses told him it was safest. Avoid the zombies. That would have been his only concern.

So which way was that?

"Well, how about it, Dr. Knopf? Any ideas?"

Knopf shifted his attention away from the crumbling buildings and looked at the young captain. Fisher's uniform was still crisp, his tie knot still regulation perfect. Despite all the walking they'd done in this God awful heat, his gig line was straight as an arrow. The man didn't seem to know how to sweat.

"He could be anywhere," Knopf said. "I suggest doing another sensor sweep."

"We've done eight sensor sweeps already, Doctor. Are you sure the boy even went into town? Perhaps he ran back to the compound."

God save me from idiots in uniform, Knopf thought. Yes, they'd done their sensor sweeps, but Fisher himself had admitted that the high concentrations of lead in the ground were playing havoc with their equipment. It was probably doing the same thing to Jimmy, though to what degree there was no way of knowing. He'd have to do further research. The only remedy was to keep running the sensor sweeps, keep tracking over the same ground. Eventually they'd hit pay dirt.

"He's here, Captain. I'm sure of that."

"Hmm," Fisher said. "You have a special bond with the boy, I suppose."

Knopf looked at him sharply. He didn't like the way that sounded, the nasty implication in the Captain's tone. "What exactly is that supposed to mean, Captain?"

Fisher raised his eyebrows, as though to feign ignorance.

"Only that you raised him. It would be natural, I suppose, for you to learn how he thinks."

Knopf didn't answer that.

"You were given charge of the boy shortly after your own wife and son were killed. Isn't that right, Doctor? It would make sense that you'd invest extra effort to keep the boy close. Perhaps he filled some psychological hole in your head?"

"That's pretty damn bold of you, Captain."

"Perhaps. Perhaps not. You forget, Doctor, that I have an assignment as well. You are trying to get me to believe in magic. My job, if you'll pardon my French, is to make sure you aren't full of shit."

And then it hit Knopf what was really going on here, what the Captain was actually accusing him of.

"Captain, are you suggesting that I faked more than a decade's worth of research just so that child could take the place of my own son? Is that really what you're suggesting?"

Fisher shrugged. "You tell me," he said.

"You're a bastard, Captain. A certifiable bastard."

"Maybe. But that still doesn't answer my question."

Knopf nearly hit him in the nose. He might have, too, if at that moment the street to his right hadn't erupted with yelling and gunfire.

Knopf ducked his head, backing away from the commotion.

"What the…?" Fisher said. He was standing with arms akimbo, peering into the clouds of dust pouring down the street.

The next instant two troopers hurried out of the fog. A steadily retreating line of trooperbots was right behind them, firing into the dust.

One of the troopers, a soldier named Collins, hurried toward Fisher. "Zombies, sir! A whole mess of 'em!"

"What the hell happened?"

"We were going building to building, searching the rubble. A couple of our trooperbots found a door down to the sewer system and when they opened it, they uncovered a whole nest of them things."

"How many?"

"Hard to tell, sir. Forty, maybe fifty. They overran our trooperbots."

They could hear moaning now. A few of the approaching zombies were visible through the screen of dust, but from the volume of the moans it was obvious there were many more behind them.

"So much for the eighty-six percent accuracy of your sensors, Captain," said Knopf. "Guess you can never trust a zombie to play fair."

"Don't start with me, Doctor."

The next instant he was on the radio, calling for the warbots to converge on his location.

Knopf felt their approach before he heard them, the tread of their Tyrannosaurus-sized legs sending shudders through the pavement.

When the warbots entered the intersection, they turned immediately to the advancing horde of zombies. Their limited AI capability allowed them to process the scene and reach immediate conclusions about what had to be done. Without waiting for orders, they strode to the leading edge of the street, took up side by side positions, and opened fire into the approaching horde, mowing down the zombies beneath a hail of automatic weapons fire.

To Knopf, it seemed the shooting went on forever, and when the dust finally settled, the rattle of the guns still rang in his ears.

But the street was still. Nothing moved.

One of the warbots turned to Captain Fisher. "What are your orders, sir?"

Fisher looked mad enough to spit. He glared at Knopf before turning back to his robots.

"Another sensor sweep," he growled. "Find that kid."

10.

As he went over the edge, Jimmy saw a crowd of zombies lunging for him. Their ruined faces and bloody hands loomed large in his sights, and for a terrifying moment he thought he was going to be shredded alive before he hit the water. But when he landed in the sewer channel he kept his head under the water and started thrashing for the far side of the channel.

The water was black as ink and he couldn't see where he was going. He pushed and pulled his way through a forest of legs even as their hands groped at his back.

One of them managed to get a grip on the collar of his shirt.

Jimmy twisted away, breaking the zombie's fingers, but still it held on. He swatted at their hands and kicked whenever he could, and somehow managed to reach the stone ledge on the far side of the channel.

They stayed on him, though.

He saw a rotten wooden pallet leaning against the wall under the ledge and climbed on top of it. The ledge was another five feet or so above that, and he jumped for it, hooking his elbows over the edge so he had enough support to pull himself up. He kicked at the smooth cement wall below him, his toes sliding on the algae that grew there while hands groped at his shoes.

"Get away!" he yelled, pumping his legs with everything he had. "Get…away!"

And then he was up and over the edge, his full weight resting on the ledge. Jimmy rolled over onto his back and sobbed, his chest heaving.

What was he going to do? There was no place to go.

He rolled over on his side and stared down at the hungry crowd. Their hands were just a few inches below the ledge, their moans reaching a frenzied intensity. He knew he should keep moving, but the panic and adrenaline that had helped him climb had left him numb, and all he could do now was stare with glassy eyes at the hands clutching for him.

You must get up. You must leave.

Jimmy blinked. The commbot again.

How am I supposed to do that? There's nowhere to go.

Stand up. I will help.

What're you gonna do?

Stand up.

With a strange disconnected feeling, almost like he was dreaming this, Jimmy rose to his feet. The ceiling was arched and this close to the wall he had to bend over slightly to keep from banging his head. It made him feel like a diver looking over the edge of a cliff. Staring straight down into the ravenous horde brought a wave of nausea over him, and he groaned.

What now?

You must move to your left. Eighty feet down that tunnel you will find a large platform. Go there.

That's your plan? What am I supposed to do when I get there?

There is a functioning warbot there. It will protect you. Go now. You must move quickly.

The commbot wasn't kidding, Jimmy thought. One of the zombies in the front had fallen against the wall, pushed down by the weight of the horde behind it, and its fellows were now ramping up its back. A zombie in some kind of uniform was pulling itself up onto the ledge. The zombie's lower jaw was almost completely gone, like it had been torn off. Or shot off. Maggots swarmed in the rotting flesh where its chin and cheeks had been.

"No," Jimmy muttered, shaking his head.

You must move quickly.

Slowly, inching carefully along the narrow concrete ledge, hands grasping at his feet, Jimmy made his way to a corner up ahead. The zombies matched him step for step, their moans echoing horribly off the walls and quickening his pulse.

How am I supposed to get down from here? They're following me.

Round the corner. You will see.

And when he reached the corner, he did see. Immediately below him was a railing that went across the channel. It wasn't high enough to keep the zombies at bay forever, but it was high enough to give him a chance at escape.

Yes, he thought, that's how I'm gonna do it.

He jumped into the water.

The zombies stuck their hands through the railing, but he was already out of reach and running for the platform.

Right where you said it'd be.

They are coming. You must move quickly.

Jimmy looked back over his shoulder and saw, once again, that the commbot was correct. Already the zombies had tipped the railing forward and were scrambling over it. He had maybe a thirty foot lead on them.

He closed the last few feet to the platform and rounded the corner. A sudden, intensely white light flooded his vision, momentarily blinding him.

"You are human," a robotic voice said.

It took a moment for the purple blotches to clear from Jimmy's sight. When they did, he saw a badly damaged warbot trying to stand on its Tyrannosaurus legs—but something was wrong. One of its legs wouldn't work. Its status lights blinked and flickered. It stumbled forward, then sagged to the ground, the spotlight on its shoulder lighting up the carnage at its feet.

The ground was covered with rotting corpses.

Fear gripped him anew. He had gambled on the commbot's instructions, and this was where it had led him. To an abandoned sewer platform, and no way out.

"Zombies," the warbot said, raising a .50 caliber machine gun. "Human, you must take cover at the rear of the platform. Move quickly."

Jimmy heard moaning behind him. That was all it took. He ran forward, scrambling over badly decomposed bodies, too frightened to allow the gore into which his fingers were sinking to slow down.

The shooting started a moment later.

Jimmy reached the back wall, turned, and saw a zombie's head and shoulders atomized by a three-round burst from the warbot's guns. But every zombie shot as it rounded the corner was replaced by more, and soon the warbot's gun was blazing in one continuous stream.

But it wasn't enough. The dead kept coming, pouring around the corner faster than the warbot's gun could put them down. Jimmy, who was so exhausted he could barely move, pushed himself up against the back wall of the platform. There was some kind of vehicle abandoned there, like a rail truck, only on rubber wheels. Its windshield had come loose and broken into two pieces. Jimmy pulled the bigger of the two over him and tried to shrink into the gore of ruined bodies below him.

But it was only a matter of time.

There were just too many of them.

Jimmy's gaze found one zombie that was staring straight at him as it climbed over the pile of torn up corpses. Its gaze never wavered. It had zeroed in on him and meant to have him.

Jimmy braced himself for the attack.

The zombie fell on top of him, moaning, pawing at the glass with its bloody hands. Jimmy screamed back at the thing, pushing back with everything he had.

And then the zombie's head exploded. One moment it was pounding on the glass, smearing it with blood and sewage, and the next the glass was splashed with bits of bone and brain and clumps of bloody hair. The zombie's headless corpse sagged against the glass as Jimmy gaped in shocked silence.

The sound of gunfire was gone.

So too were the moans.

"Human," the warbot said. "Human?"

Jimmy had to tilt the glass like a ramp to roll the corpse away, and once it was off him, he could see the gun smoke lingering in the foul sewer air.

"Human, they are gone. Please acknowledge."

"I hear you," Jimmy said.

He stood up and looked around. The far wall was dripping with fresh gore, and there were bodies piled high near the corner. How many? Forty? More than that?

Jimmy couldn't tell.

He turned to the warbot.

"Thanks," he said, because it was the only thing that came close to how he was feeling at the moment.

"I can not move. You must go. Gunfire will travel far in these tunnels. More zombies will come."

"How many?"

"Unknown. You must go."

He watched the warbot as its status lights blinked and dimmed once again. The machine could not die, but if it had an equivalent, it was doing it now. Its lights were going out.

It was then that a thought occurred to Jimmy. Something he had overheard once in the weapons lab.

"Don't warbots usually work in teams?" he asked. "Where's your partner?"

But the warbot didn't answer. Its status lights continued to fade, and as Jimmy watched, they went dark permanently.

There was nothing else to do but leave.

11.

JIMMY FOUND THE second warbot a few minutes later.

He had returned to the main channel and was following it further into the sewer system. There were more platforms here, lots of them, and other channels leading off in other directions.

He had entered some kind of hub, he realized, the main part of the sewer system.

What did you do? The zombies are all gone.

For once, his father's mind-voice didn't knife into his head. It was almost pleasant, in fact. Jimmy wasn't sure if it was the tone of surprised gratitude that softened it, or if he was just getting used to their thoughts passing back and forth, but either way the pain was gone. Jimmy let his mind reach out to his father.

Daddy, where are you?

I'm close, Jimmy. Keep coming. Around the next corner to your left.

The fighting, Jimmy saw, must have been intense through here. He had seen plenty of rotting bodies along the way, and even more wrecked trooperbots, but the carnage was especially bad through here. In some places he actually had to climb over the twisted, severed limbs of dead people and the faceless heads of downed robots rusting in the sewer water. And everywhere he turned there were bullet holes in the walls and the ceiling.

Then he rounded the corner and the smell of rot nearly knocked him over.

What lay before him was a gallery of horrors. The room must have been some kind of staging area for large equipment before the fighting, for there were oversized sleds loaded down with machinery and portable pumps and generators scattered around the room. But those were only the backdrop for the carnage Jimmy saw. Corpses were piled three and four deep. Most were so badly decomposed they were unrecognizable, their bodies swollen and discolored and swarming with flies and writhing worms. Others had been eaten, and what remained of their faces was twisted by pain that was frozen there like a picture. One man lay on his back atop a generator, his arms hanging limply off either side, his mouth open in an eternal scream, his torso ripped apart and emptied of its viscera so that he looked like the gaping belly of a canoe. Jimmy saw a dismembered foot here, an upturned hand there, the fingers curled up and inward like the legs of a dying crab.

And standing in the middle of it all, a grotesque king presiding over his court, was his father.

Jimmy's mouth fell open.

The man could barely stand. His right arm had been chewed off just below the elbow, stringy lengths of sinew and shredded flesh hanging from the blackened wound. His neck too was open. Worms fed on the ruins of his throat. The green t-shirt he wore was stained with dried blood, and all Jimmy could read was the word Nationals in what had once been white lettering. And his face! Bits of skull showed through the holes in his forehead. His lips were gone, revealing the full horror of his bloodstained teeth. He leered at Jimmy. Almost like he was grinning at him.

Jimmy turned his head, the bile rising in his throat.

Jimmy, look at me.

Slowly, uncertain for a moment that he would even be able to keep his feet, Jimmy straightened up. He faced the train wreck that had once been his father and, running the back of his hand across his face, wiped the spit from his lips.

You lied to me.

For a reason. I had to get you here.

But you lied to me.

You don't need to be frightened of me.

Jimmy backed away, shaking his head.

That was when Jimmy saw the other warbot. At first it had blended in with the other machinery, one more piece of metal streaked with human gore.

Then it rose to its full height.

Eighteen feet of rusting metal on Tyrannosaurus legs.

It stood so tall it had to stoop to avoid scraping the ceiling. It had fully automatic machine gun cannons for arms and it turned them in Jimmy's direction.

"I am human," Jimmy said, reciting the mantra that Dr. Knopf had taught him when dealing with robotic sentries. "Confirm my status as human."

The warbot's status lights flickered wildly, but it made no sound. The guns remained trained on Jimmy.

"Confirm!" Jimmy said.

It's not the robot it used to be. Watch, Jimmy. Let me show you.

The warbot stooped forward then and swung one of its machine gun arms under his father. As Jimmy watched, his fear mounting, the robot raised the zombie version of his father into the air and placed him on its shoulders.

Jimmy took a step back.

Do you understand?

Yes. You control that robot.

Yes! That's exactly right. It has a limited intelligence. AI, they call it. It isn't a smart machine, but it's smart enough to be used. Do you see?

No.

Jimmy, look at me.

Jimmy did. He stared up at his father, who rode the warbot like some demented child playing horsey on his daddy's shoulders, and he was frightened.

This is bad. This is very bad.

No! That's wrong. Jimmy, this is right. Don't you see?

See what?

I control this robot. I can control zombies too. Anything that has a mind, or had a mind, is like a pawn waiting to be moved. Don't you see the potential? All it takes is a mind that can move those pawns. A mind like mine. A mind like yours.

I want to go home.

You are *home, damn it!*

The robot took three long strides forward and knelt down, bringing Jimmy's father closer to eye level. Jimmy tried to back away, but his heel caught on a trooperbot's severed arm and he pitched over backwards, landing on his butt.

Don't back away from me!

But Jimmy wasn't moving anymore. For the first time, he could see the wall behind the warbot. There was a flight of stairs there, and on the wall at the back of the first landing was a red EXIT sign.

A way out.

Don't you see what I'm offering you? Don't you understand what this means? I can make you a king, boy. I've seen into your memories. I've seen how they've used you. Do you want it to stop? Don't you want to give it all back to them? I can help you do that. As father and son, the way it was meant to be.

Slowly, Jimmy stood up.

Answer me.

Glancing across the floor between where he stood and the stairs began, Jimmy picked out the route he was going to take. Dr. Knopf had tried to teach him a trick once to hone his psychic locator skills. Visualize each move, Knopf had told him, picture it in advance. See yourself making it. That way, when you make it for real—

Knopf is the man who raised you, the scientist?

Yes.

The one who experimented on—

Jimmy blocked the rest of it, slamming the door on his father's mind-voice. He heard his father grunt in surprise, and Jimmy ran. He darted around the warbot's right side, ducking to miss the robot's heavy cannon arm as it rotated toward him, and then he was past it, running for the stairs.

But he didn't move so fast he missed his steps. He picked his way through bodies and machine parts carefully, planting his feet exactly as he had pictured them in his head. He couldn't afford to miss a step. Not now. Not with his father and that warbot behind him. If he tripped, slipped, they'd be on him. The heavy cannon would knock him to the floor and hold him there. And he had no idea what his father would do after that.

Jimmy was still blocking him with his mind. He had his teeth clenched so tightly his jaw was trembling, his breaths coming fast and noisily through his nose, but he didn't dare let up. His father was no doubt screaming into his brain, and if one of those mind-voice screams got through, Jimmy knew it would be enough to cripple him with pain. He'd never be able to get up.

He hit the stairs at a full sprint and ran up them three at a time. When he reached the landing he turned and saw his father astride the warbot, the two of them crashing forward.

They were close, almost on him.

Jimmy kept running up the stairs. He had to scale three flights to reach the promised exit door. Once there, he grabbed the handle, and twisted.

It was locked.

"No," he said.

Below him, the warbot was trying to climb the stairs, even though it was far too big to fit into the narrow confines. But it could force its way up, and that it was doing, banging its huge cannon arms against the railing, smashing through the floor with its enormous metal shoulders. The ground beneath Jimmy's feet was moving, trembling from the impacts.

He tried the door again, yanking on it with everything he had, and it still wouldn't budge.

"Please, no," he said, his voice almost a whimper.

He looked down. The warbot was slowly crashing his way up through the floor, but that wasn't the worst of it. Through a gap in the split level stairs Jimmy caught a glimpse of his father's zombified face. It was a hideous, dead face, yellowed with disease and dark with scabs and open, rotting wounds. The right side of his mouth had been damaged somehow, so that the corner of his lips hung slack in an ironic grin.

The eyes, though, those were most certainly not grinning. They were lit by a mad, malignant hatred. There was violence in those eyes that frightened Jimmy down to his bones.

But he still had to get through the door. How?

The gun. Use the gun.

The commbot's voice.

The gun?

Jimmy looked down at his waistband. Sure enough, the pistol was still there, right where he'd stuck it after his narrow escape back at the ledge.

How do I...

Shoot the knob. Move quickly.

Jimmy took a step back. He drew the weapon and steadied its front sight on the knob. Below him, the warbot was fast approaching. It was on the next landing down. Jimmy had a few seconds, maybe less. He swallowed hard as he tried to center the front sight on the knob and pulled the trigger.

The gun nearly jumped out of his hands as he staggered backwards, the sound of the shot deafening.

Shaking his head, he looked down at the lock. The knob was hanging at an odd angle from the plane of the door, a big gaping hole just to the left of it. He reached for it, and the knob came away in his hand.

The door fell open.

Run. You must run.

The commbot again.

Where?

I will guide you. Run now. Move as fast as you can.

He lunged through the doorway and into the lobby of a large, shabby building. This, he gathered, had been the home office of the Water Authority. There were desks everywhere, most of the pushed haphazardly out of the way. Trash lay thick on the floor. A few pieces of furniture had been jammed up against the front door of the building, which meant a few people must have made a final stand here.

But the furniture had been toppled, and the front door behind the pile was hanging from the bottom hinge.

Jimmy ran that way, scaling over the furniture. He was almost through the door when the ground shook and he lost his footing. He landed on top of a desk, facing the length of floor he'd just traversed.

A heaving mound formed in the middle of the floor, the cement there popping and groaning from the warbot's efforts to push itself upwards from the other side. There was a crash, and the mound cracked and popped. A second crash came immediately after, and the next thing Jimmy knew, the warbot was busting through the floor, sending bits of tile and chairs and desks flying off in every direction.

The warbot climbed out of the hole, Jimmy's father still hanging on to its neck, still staring at him with those same hate-filled eyes.

"No," Jimmy said.

Run. Now.

But Jimmy didn't need to be told. He was already sprinting into the street.

12.

A BULLET SKIPPED off the pavement at Dr. Knopf's feet, hitting the wall behind him. He ducked, and with his hands over his head, turned in every direction, trying to find someplace to run. The air was full of dust, the noise deafening. He felt disoriented, and in his confusion, stepped right into the middle of the fighting.

After their first successful skirmish in front of the movie theater, some of the trooperbots had surrounded another Water Authority access point to the sewers, their weapons at the ready, and opened the door. It had been like knocking the top off an ant pile. One minute they were expecting a simple mop up operation of a few remaining zombies, and the next, they were getting overrun, trampled underfoot, ripped to pieces. Knopf had been standing less than thirty feet from one of their docbots when a wave of zombies knocked it to the ground and pulled it apart like a man being drawn and quartered. They'd been overrun so quickly there was hardly a chance for Knopf to question the strangeness of what he saw. But Captain Fisher was a good soldier, a capable leader. He regrouped his forces, pulling his troops back in ordered rows while at the same time bringing his warbots forward, where the bigger guns could do some damage. But the battle was decided almost from the beginning. Fisher's expeditionary force was small, intended more for light escort duty than a stand up fight, and the best he could hope for at this point was to keep his escape route to the rear open. By keeping his lines moving, they at least stood a chance of escaping to a better defensive position.

That was how it looked to Knopf, anyway.

But there was something else, something disturbing. Knopf had spent years studying the zombies in every way possible. Know thy enemy, as Sun Tzu had said. He'd used that knowledge to design and perfect the weapons systems his shop built for the military. But in all his studies, all his observations, he'd always worked under the philosophy that the zombie was a mindless, relentless opponent with no sense of strategy and no skills. Their only strengths were their numbers, a complete lack of fear and the ability to fight without sleep, without pain, and without ever quitting. They advanced headlong, regardless of the odds, with no sense of winning or losing.

That didn't seem to be the case here, though. Knopf had accidentally wandered into the middle of the fighting, and while he was ducking and dodging bullets like some kind of fool, he watched a large number of zombies break away from the main horde and circle around the ruins of a hardware store, so that they could come up from behind their robot opponents in a fairly well executed flanking maneuver.

Knopf was shocked. Doing something like that took strategy, it took forethought, it took goal-oriented behavior. None of the game theory equations he'd put into the robots' programming could deal with behavior like that. It wasn't playing by the rules. And yet the action was undeniable. It was a wide street, with a park off to his left. There had been plenty of room for all those zombies to continue their advance. By all rights, they should have massed into the open areas, where Fisher's strategy would have turned the street into a meat grinder.

But they had deliberately turned off. They had taken themselves out of the fight in a clearly premeditated way, almost as though…

Another bullet hit the pavement at his feet and glanced off with a loud, high-pitched whine. Knopf blinked at the little white cloud of dust that drifted away from the impact point.

"What are you doing?" someone yelled. "Get out of the street!"

Knopf looked up. Zombies and robots were swarming all around him. The ordered lines had broken down, and everywhere he turned trooperbots were being ripped apart.

"Knopf, you idiot, get out of the street!"

Captain Fisher was running at him, a pistol in his hand. He looked angry, white flecks of spit flying from his lips, the white scar across his chin almost completely obscured by the dirt and mud and blood on his face.

"Get out of the street!"

The next instant Fisher was on him, grabbing him by the sleeve, pulling him towards the corner of a red brick building. Then he slammed him against the wall.

"What the hell are you doing?" he demanded.

"Those zombies are using strategy, Captain. Something's guiding them—"

But Fisher wasn't listening. His attention was already back on the street, eyes darting from one corner of the battle to the other.

"We're pulling out," he yelled. "I'm ordering us out of this town. Get yourself ready to move out."

"Wait," Knopf said. "What? No, you can't."

"I can, Doctor, and I am. We are leaving!"

"But Jimmy…he's still out there somewhere. We have to find him."

"Like hell we do. He ran off. He's dead."

"You don't know that!"

"I know this experiment of yours has failed, Doctor," Fisher said. He emphasized his point by jamming a finger into Knopf's chest. "You're done. You and this whole ridiculous experiment—you're done! This is over. My only concern right now is to salvage what's left of my command. Now get yourself ready. We are leaving."

And with that he stormed off, yelling for his human soldiers to fall back.

13.

JIMMY HIT THE street running.

Behind him, the front of the building he'd just escaped exploded, the force of it knocking him onto his hands and knees. He glanced back in time to see the warbot erupting into the street, crouching like a bird, furniture and bits of rubble tumbling out all around its feet.

From atop the thing's shoulders, with the cold, hard light of insanity in his eyes, Jimmy's father leered at him.

"Oh God," Jimmy said.

He pulled to his feet and started to run again.

But he only made it a few feet before he stopped. Ahead of him, zombies staggered out of alleyways and out of buildings. At first there were only a five, then eight, then more. He turned to his left and saw the side street there filling up with more of the living dead.

It dawned on him then what was happening. The zombies closing in on him…the things his father had said down in the sewers…the fact that all the town's zombies had retreated into the sewers, as though waiting for something…his father was controlling them, steering them towards this spot. Jimmy could feel the force of his father's thoughts moving around him like the current in a river, but gaining in strength.

Now that he was out of the sewers he was growing more powerful every second.

What am I supposed to do?

Jimmy stretched his thoughts, trying to connect with the commbot.

And then, a connection.

Help me, Comm Six. Where do I go?

There is a building to your right. Run through there. Hurry.

Jimmy turned. The building was made of red brick, the windows empty and dark. He sprinted towards it just as the warbot reached for him, its enormous machine gun arms missing him by inches. Jimmy jumped through one of the empty display windows and hurried through the shop towards the back.

Go out the back door. When you reach the alley, turn right. I will guide you.

Jimmy did as he was told. The shop was crowded with trash and bits of the tile and insulation where the roof had collapsed, but he threaded his way through it and out the back door.

He found himself in a narrow alley between low buildings. Looking to his left he saw zombies turning the corner. To his right, the way looked clear.

Go. Hurry.

His father's warbot had already started smashing its way through the shop and Jimmy knew he only had a few precious seconds. He ran for the end of the alleyway, rounded the corner, and kept on running.

The next corner is Tanner Street. Turn left there. You will see a movie theater at the end of the street. But you must hurry. The humans are leaving.

Leaving? What? No. Stop them.

I cannot. But you can.

Me? How?

With your mind. Reach out. Find one of the humans and enter his mind. Hurry. The warbot is coming. Do it as you run.

Jimmy rounded the corner onto Tanner Street. He could hear his father's warbot back there, wrecking everything in sight.

Focusing his mind, he tried to picture Dr. Knopf, to remember the sound of his voice, the shape of his face.

Dr. Knopf.

Something clicked for Jimmy then. He could feel the connection when it happened, like toy blocks snapping together. Dr. Knopf was confused and frightened by the contact. Jimmy could sense his fear, and feel him trying to pull his mind back and break the contact. He could picture Knopf standing perfectly still, his back rigid, Adam's apple pumping up and down like a cylinder, much as Jimmy had done when his father first made contact with him.

Dr. Knopf, I need help.

Jimmy, you're alive! Where are you?

There was no time to explain. Instead, Jimmy pushed his thoughts into Dr. Knopf's mind, showing him everything he had seen and heard since coming to Mill Valley. He wasn't even sure if it would work, but he sensed it would, and so he pushed.

Doctor?

Silence.

Dr. Knopf, I need you!

Oh you poor boy. Jimmy, I'm so sorry. I had no idea.

Help me!

Zombies were moving through the smoke ahead of him. Now that he was free of the sewers he could sense them.

They were facing away from him, and Jimmy sprinted right for them. With luck, he'd get past them before they knew he was there.

But then, all at once, the dead stopped their attack on the retreating trooperbots and turned to face Jimmy. Several of them lunged forward, reaching for him.

It happened so fast Jimmy barely had time to adjust.

He veered to his left, shooting a gap between them just as his father's warbot reached down to scoop him up. Instead of pinning Jimmy, it flattened one of the zombies.

Jimmy didn't slow down. He ran right into the thick of where the battle had been. He was in No Man's Land now, midway between the retreating trooperbots on the one side and the zombies and his father's warbot on the other.

Jimmy looked back just as the warbot crashed through the zombie horde, trampling some and throwing others out of the way. Still carrying his father atop its shoulders, the warbot stepped slowly into the intersection. They were close now, less than twenty feet between them, the warbot towering over Jimmy. His father's badly decomposed face was incapable of expression, but Jimmy could still sense the madness, the betrayal, the rage, emanating from the man's mind.

Jimmy met his stare without blinking, and at the same time realized he was feeling exactly the same thing, betrayal and rage. The thought scared him, and for a moment, Jimmy felt his resolve waver. This was his father, after all. The man had done nothing but hurt him. And yet, angry as Jimmy was, a part of him wanted to love the man… needed the man's approbation. But the scariest thought of all, the one Jimmy couldn't get around, was that maybe they weren't so very different, father and son. Maybe there was nothing but a fine line between them. Maybe Jimmy was just a gentle shove away from being exactly like him.

"No," Jimmy said suddenly. "I won't join you. I won't."

Maybe there was just a fine line between them, but the line was there. He looked up at the horror that his father had become and he was suddenly, absolutely, irrevocably sure. That zombie up there was not what he wanted to be. He was more than that.

"Go on and do it, if you can," he told his father.

The warbot straightened then. Jimmy could see it gathering itself for the final, crushing blow, like stomping out a bug, and he tensed to leap out of the way. But as the warbot's leg rose in the air, Jimmy saw a flash of movement off to his left. A second warbot, this one bearing the insignia of Fisher's expeditionary force, smashed into his father's warbot and both robots went tumbling into the side of a building, knocking down the brick wall there.

The expeditionary robot stood up first. It backed away from the collapsed store front, and right before it started firing, Jimmy caught a glimpse of his father's warbot inside, its enormous Tyrannosaurus legs bent up in front of it like a man who has fallen into a low, deep couch.

And then the shooting started.

The expeditionary warbot fired both its .50 caliber machine guns, the bullets glancing off the other warbot's armor plating, but doing little harm. His father's warbot pulled itself loose from the wall and charged its opponent, and when they hit, it felt like the ground was splitting open beneath Jimmy's feet.

Their great weight tore up the pavement. Every step sent bits of rock and vast quantities of dust into the air, and within moments, Jimmy couldn't tell the difference between the two. He could only marvel at the destruction they caused. They threw each other into the air and into the sides of buildings. The zombies swarming around their legs were crushed like bugs. Both robots were firing their machine guns continuously now, and the noise grew so loud Jimmy fell to the ground behind a pile of rubble, his hands clapped over his ears.

Jimmy had no idea how long the fight went on, but gradually, the guns fell silent.

And when the sound stopped all together, and Jimmy looked over the pile of rubble he'd hid behind, he saw one of the warbots tangled up in a collapsed wall, wrapped in metal cables, one of its cannon arms missing. It tried to step out of the wall, but one of its legs wasn't working, and all it managed to do was fall face-first onto the pavement.

The other warbot was in two large pieces, electrical cables and wires oozing out of its severed parts like guts. Neither machine was going to be getting up again. Jimmy could see that plain enough. And when he searched them with his mind, he could tell the one was dead, and the other, the one face down on the street, was shutting down.

But there was something else.

Jimmy turned. A lone figure was limping toward him through the dust and smoke.

"Don't come any closer," Jimmy said. "I'm done with you."

His father's face was dark with blood and dust, except for the eyes, which were milky white and vacant. He raised his one good hand to Jimmy, the fingers clutching, and inched his way forward.

You can't have me! Do you hear? I'm not yours.

Jimmy scooped up a heavy chunk of asphalt and threw it at his father. It hit him in the shoulder, but he showed no reaction.

He kept coming.

Just then Jimmy felt a hand on his back. He knew who it was without having to look around.

"Step away, Jimmy," said Dr. Knopf. "I've got this."

Dr. Knopf raised a pistol and pointed it at Jimmy's father. But before he could pull the trigger, Jimmy touched his arm, guiding the weapon to the low ready.

"No," Jimmy said. "It's for me to do."

Dr. Knopf looked at the pistol, and then at Jimmy.

"Let me have it."

Knopf handed it to him without saying another word. Jimmy looked down at the pistol, so many things weighing on his mind, and then pointed it at his father.

"I'm sorry," he said. "But we're not the same. Not at all."

And then he pulled the trigger.

14.

Later, after the last of the zombies had been put down and the dust and smoke had cleared, Jimmy walked into the middle of the street and looked around. There was a darkened movie theater just ahead of him. He felt drawn to it.

"Jimmy?" Knopf said, coming up beside him. "You okay?"

Jimmy nodded.

"You put a lot into my mind. I guess we have a lot to talk about, don't we?"

"Yeah, I guess so."

Both of them were silent for a time, watching the movie theater.

"There's something I have to do," Jimmy said.

"What's that?"

"The commbot." Jimmy pointed to the movie theater. "Comm Six… it's in there."

"You're sure?"

Jimmy nodded. He was sure.

Knopf looked around uncomfortably. He seemed uncertain, doubtful. "I don't…" he said. "Stand back for a second, okay? Let me send in a trooperbot first."

Jimmy looked at him, but said nothing.

Knopf grabbed the first trooperbot he saw and pointed it towards the movie theater. After he'd explained what he wanted done the robot marched inside, weapon at the ready.

Jimmy and Knopf waited, listening.

Several human soldiers stood nearby, looking on curiously.

About a minute later, a single gun shot sounded from somewhere deep in the recesses of the theater.

"One female zombie neutralized," the trooperbot announced over the walkie-talkie.

Knopf motioned to one of the human soldiers, who nodded back and went inside the theater to check it out.

When he came back out, he was holding something in his right hand.

He walked up to Knopf and handed it to him. A photograph. Black and white. Dirty with grime and creased where it had been crumpled and wrinkled over the years. It showed a little boy, about two, smiling, still a lot of the baby he once was in his chubby face, playing with a toy truck on a kitchen floor.

"That was pinned to the zombie's shirt," the soldier said, nodding at the photograph. "There was nothing else in there."

"Thank you," Knopf said.

He stared at the picture, lost in his memories of a boy he had once hated, but had grown to love as though he was his own son.

"What is it?" Jimmy asked.

Knopf handed him the photograph. "It's you," he said.

"Me?" Jimmy swallowed, his attention shifting from Knopf to the entrance to the movie theater. "But, Comm Six…"

"I'm afraid so," Knopf said. "I'm sorry, Jimmy."

Jimmy nodded, his mouth pressed into a thin, tight line. Then he slid the picture into his pocket.

"Dr. Knopf, I'm done. I want you to know that. I'm done. I don't want to do this anymore. No more experiments."

Knopf put his arm around Jimmy's shoulder. His touch was warm, kind, accepting.

"Come on," he said. "Let me take you home."

"I'm not going back to the lab."

"No," Knopf said. "I know that. I'm taking you home."

HISTORYBOT SAVES THE FUTURE

Jesse Bullington

48 Before Common Era

HISTORYBOT glides between the pillars of the LIBRARY OF ALEXANDRIA, the flames of the burning harbor casting distended shadows on the stone floor. It is probable that the robot's quarry will travel to one of the more popularly remembered theories of the library's destruction, but a chronological approach is HISTORYBOT's default function and so the search begins in the midst of a firestorm. GAIUS JULIUS CAESAR's arson of the docked Egyptian fleet and the driving wind have, improbably, given the building's distance from the harbor, filled the library with smoke and ash. HISTORYBOT cruises in ever widening search patterns before settling in to wait for the next theory and the arrival of EMILY MARIE VASQUEZ (DERBY: *The Empress M*; GOD's CANT: *Chumpus McRumpus*).

269 to 274 Common Era

For five years HISTORYBOT patrols the library, occasionally checking the smaller facility at the SERAPEUM in the unlikely event that EMILY has mistaken that library for the larger one, as certain scholars have done over the years. Every day EMPEROR AURELIAN (LATIN: *Lucius Domitius Aurelianus Augustus*) invades the city to suppress a revolt, and each day the library is damaged as combat spreads through the streets, and each day EMILY fails to materialize.

Until the day that she does—the "IDES OF MARCH," 274 COMMON ERA. It is probable that she has focused on the date due to a misremembering of details surrounding the life of GAIUS JULIUS CAESAR. She rollerskates out of an alcove, scimitar dripping gore on the stones and her pleated skirt, and then grinds to a stop upon seeing HISTORYBOT watching her with the same blank expression as the gods and great men adorning the pillars above them. There is still sand from the 13th century in EMILY's fire engine-red wheels.

"Get away from me," she pants, her face sweaty, the black hair protruding from her derby helmet plastered to her neck and cheeks. HISTORYBOT detects trace amounts of ethanol on her breath from the date wine she will drink in just under a millennium, immediately prior to the robot's arrival during the SIEGE OF BAGHDAD.

"EMILY," HISTORYBOT intones, dropping volume to 3. The mighty building is quiet, the librarians all dead and risen and out in the streets, searching for victims. HISTORYBOT recognizes that if they return before EMILY agrees to listen to reason she will likely flee again. "IT IS ADVISABLE THAT YOU STOP RUNNING FROM HISTORYBOT."

"Why?" says EMILY, hands on her hips as if she's just completed a *jam*, as it is called in DERBY, thus signaling the end of her physical propulsion. She is clearly taking the lack of immediate danger as an opportunity to rest her muscles and catch her breath. HISTORYBOT knows that if she is allowed to become physically comfortable she is more likely to act on logic instead of instinct, and so the robot does not approach her even though its highly sensitive auditory sensors have detected a pack of ZOMBIES a few blocks away suddenly changing direction, doubling back toward the library. HISTORYBOT can hear their bloody togas flapping in the sea air, their sandals slapping the packed earth.

"YOU DO NOT UNDERSTAND WHAT IS HAPPENING," HISTORYBOT explains. "IF YOU LET HISTORYBOT JOIN YOU HISTORYBOT WILL EXPLAIN EVERYTHING. HISTORYBOT WILL KEEP YOU SAFE."

"You mean you'll try to eat me again!" EMILY points her scimitar at the robot. "Fuck that!"

"YOU DO NOT UNDERSTAND WHAT IS HAPPEN—" HISTORYBOT attempts to repeat its logical statement but EMILY has taken a small paperback novel from the rack of scrolls beside her and hurls it at HISTORYBOT.

"I'm unstuck in fucking time is what's happening, and whenever you show up so do they!" EMILY says, with the highest probability of the *they* in question being the ZOMBIES. "So leave me alone!"

HISTORYBOT processes that the book she has thrown—using a similar-but-not-identical series of muscle movements to those she will employ to throw a jug of date wine in a later library—is the 1969 COMMON ERA novel that she will read her junior year of high school, a book they will read together. HISTORYBOT will help her write a paper about the novel, and while her scholarship will be far from revolutionary it will, at least, be factually accurate.

"Cerebraaaaaa!" The ZOMBIES have entered the library, their hungry chant echoing beneath the arches as they bounce against one another, stumbling forward. "Cerebraaaaaaaaaaa!"

There are tears in EMILY's hazel eyes as she turns to flee, tears from either particles of Arabian sand or emotion, and HISTORYBOT accelerates after her, predicting her next destination with a very small margin of error. HISTORYBOT begins to run a background program regarding her assertion that it is the robot's presence and not hers that causes the chrono-instability and ensuing *zombification* that occurs in each epoch they visit, but at present HISTORYBOT cannot prioritize such speculaion. Not while history is at risk.

1258 COMMON ERA

HISTORYBOT has sand in its circuitry as it rolls through the stacks of the HOUSE OF WISDOM (ARABIC: بيت الحكمة; *Bait al-Hikma*). The mighty doors of the GRAND LIBRARY are barricaded with benches, their seats brocaded gold and silver, their cedar legs red as fresh blood, and everywhere scurry frightened astrologers, physicians, poets—students of *the human condition*, students of history. Some of the men wear somber black robes cut from single pieces of linen, others flowing, multi-seamed cotton garments shaded rose and lime; some have beards down to their sashed waists, others are clean shaven—most dress below their station to display their humility rather than above it, which would signal displeasure with the divine order of their lives. They are all terrified, some of them clutching scrolls and illuminated manuscripts to their chests like the mothers of BAGHDAD just outside the library who crush babies to breasts as they flee from house to house, through streets hazy with the smoke of the MONGOLS' fire arrows.

HISTORYBOT processes that it is futile to run from neighbor's house to sibling's apartment with children in tow, just as it is futile to scurry about the library, arms laden with wisdom. The one is a microcosm of the other, which is in turn a simple example of history repeating itself, as IBN KHALDUN will not exactly put it a century hence. The ABBASID caliph, AL-MUSTA'SIM BILLAH (ARABIC: دبع دمحأ وبأ هللاب مصعتسملا هللاب رصنتسملا نب هللا, *al-Musta'sim-Billah Abu-Ahmad Abdullah bin al-Mustansir-Billah*), was a poor tactician who allowed BAGHDAD to be caught between two branches of the besieging MONGOL army, and so there is nowhere for anyone still inside the city to flee. The citizens are trapped, and with the city now officially surrendered to the MONGOL HORDE, they are doomed. HISTORYBOT would be able to extrapolate this from historical trends even if it did not contain as detailed an account of the SIEGE OF BAGHDAD as exists in the early years of the 21st century.

Except it is not the 21st century, it is the 13th, and HISTORYBOT is running out of time. If the HOUSE OF WISDOM is sacked before the robot can find EMILY then she may be lost forever inside the historical matrix, a problematic anachronism, and if there is one thing that HISTORYBOT must do to prevent further malfunctions from taking place it is locate and delete problematic anachronisms. Especially those wearing fishnet tights and rollerskates with skulls on the laces.

The shrieks and howls and crashing noises outside the library are growing louder, and the barred doors are beginning to groan and rattle. The scholars run faster and faster, the walls of the building trapping them in a loop, and through a cloud of ones and zeroes that coalesce into fluttering pages taking wing from a toppling shelf HISTORYBOT sights EMILY.

The teenage girl evidently sees HISTORYBOT as well, for she increases her speed, her crimson-padded knees pistoning as she skates across the tile floor of the mezzanine of the building that will be reduced to rubble in three days, 700-odd years before her birth. In one hand she carries a scimitar, in the other a jug of date wine. Her facial features are contorted in an expression that correlates to the human emotion of *fucking pissed*, in GOD's CANT.

"EMILY," HISTORYBOT intones, scholars diving out of the robot's path as it increases its speed to 6. HISTORYBOT's holographic historo-camouflage system is clearly malfunctioning, for it still wears a pith helmet atop its casing—despite its best efforts to the contrary, the machine has become a problematic anachronism itself. "EMILY, STOP MOVING AWAY FROM HISTORYBOT."

"Leave me the fuck alone!" she screams, her voice cracking. She does a half-spin, skating backwards so that she can face HISTORYBOT. Before HISTORYBOT can analyze whether or not this potentially signals an increased willingness to listen to reason, EMILY hurls the bottle of date wine at the pursuing robot. Evasive maneuvers are beyond HISTORYBOT's capabilities and so the missile connects, shattering on impact, but neither sticky wine nor shards of pottery breach the bot's casing.

"EMILY!" HISTORYBOT increases its volume to 7, and having completed its search for historical incidences of robots convincing emotional teenagers to acquiesce to their superior capabilities, it employs a popular quote from late 20th century AMERICAN media. Being a *history buff*, there is a high probability that EMILY is familiar with it, and will thus respond to it on an emotional level. "QUOTE! COME! WITH! ME! IF! YOU! WANT! TO! LIVE! END! QUOTE!"

"You're crazy!" comes the response, EMILY spinning back around just in time to alter her trajectory by 90 degrees, cutting along a shelf of priceless tomes that will soon be dyeing the TIGRIS RIVER black with their ink as the MONGOLS spitefully cast in the manuscripts, along with the bodies of the murdered librarians. This is apocryphal, HISTORYBOT knows, but such is the nature of all history; it is all a matter of degrees.

"EMILY!" HISTORYBOT replies, rounding the shelf after her and noting that several of the scholars have doubled over on the floor, bloody foam flecking their lips, skin rapidly rotting off their faces as if they were the subjects of time-lapse video documentation on natural decay. The invisible pools of chrono-instability are widening, HISTORYBOT processes, even as it counters EMILY's claim. "I! AM! INCAPABLE! OF! THOUGHT! ERGO! I! CANNOT! BE! QUOTE! CRAZY! END! QUOTE! WARNING! ZOMBIE! AHEAD!"

There is a pause in the conversation as one of the scholars staggers toward EMILY, his caftan grown into his putrid skin, his finger bones jutting out from the wreckage of his hands. EMILY's sword whips through the air, clipping the ZOMBIE's head off at the shoulder, but the force of the weapon's impact sends her careening to the side, directly toward another ZOMBIE scholar. This one's bloody drool is caught in his beard, and he lurches at her only to tip over when EMILY drops down and slides forward on one kneepad, hacking the ZOMBIE's left leg off at the thigh.

Her scimitar flashes as red and gold as the benches falling away from the great doors as the undead MONGOLS breech the HOUSE OF WISDOM, and then EMILY rights herself without losing momentum, disappearing behind another shelf. HISTORYBOT slowly maneuvers around the headless corpse and the prone, mewling ZOMBIE that EMILY has maimed, but by the time the robot circumvents this final obstacle, she has fled again.

HISTORYBOT slows to a stop, processing the possibilities of where—and when—she might have traveled even as the horde of MONGOL ZOMBIES push past the idling robot, hungrily snuffling the air and seeking in vain the fresh, young brain that so recently passed this way. Another library seems likely, and HISTORYBOT jumps backward in time over a millennium. Just as its historo-camouflage kicks in and provides it with a caftan, too.

FEBRUARY 14, 1945 ("VALENTINE'S DAY") COMMON ERA

DRESDEN burns as HISTORYBOT materializes just behind EMILY, 1000 miles and nearly 2000 years traversed in the time it takes for 1 to become 10. EMILY stumbles, clop-clop-clopping in jerky, wheeled steps over the dead women and children strewn about the smoldering streets. Before HISTORYBOT can seize her with its *silly-looking* pincer arms the piled dead awake. A nearby NAZI infantryman on corpse disposal detail is mobbed by blazing ZOMBIES as a dust devil of ash and cinders envelops the teenage rollerderby queen. More and more ZOMBIES surround robot and prey, and then she is gone again.

HISTORYBOT does not fully understand the concept of *relief*, but the robot is aware that the likelihood of failure has never been greater than in this time and place. HISTORYBOT allows the background program EMILY prompted in the LIBRARY OF ALEXANDRIA to finish running before pursuing her again. With priority now given to the program it quickly confirms that her hypothesis is correct, that it is the presence of HISTORYBOT and not EMILY that triggers both the chrono-instability and the ensuing ZOMBIE outbreaks in the histories they visit. The histories they *have visited*, HISTORYBOT autocorrects itself. The robot determines that confronting EMILY in a history with a minimum number of potential ZOMBIES is of optimal importance.

UNKNOWN DATE. A SUMMER DAY IN EMILY'S CHILDHOOD

EMILY and GOD frolic in the backyard of the OLD HOUSE, under the shade of a large oak. They are playing an imagination-based game where they simulate being in MEDIEVAL EUROPE. Their understanding of the period is riddled with problematic anachronisms, a hodgepodge of several distinct ages and regions. HISTORYBOT registers their fallacies but does not correct them.

EMILY's skates are clogged with dirt and grass and she can barely stand up, and yet she fights on, refusing to surrender. Her scimitar meets GOD's salvaged stick, but the sound is of oak connecting with oak. The girls grimace as their weapons vibrate from the impact, hurting their palms, and HISTORYBOT moves to seize EMILY—she is older than GOD here, a flagrant anachronism. As it charges, HISTORYBOT processes that its own presence here is comparably impossible, and the machine stalls, trying to sort through the compounding irregularities.

GOD sees the idling HISTORYBOT first, and the *bemused* expression on her face unexpectedly restarts the hereto-malfunctioning ERROR RECTIFICATION SYSTEM she designed into the machine's programming. HISTORYBOT's internal workings shudder, inaccurate scripts freezing, overloaded sensors stuttering. GOD smiles.

"Oh, goddamn it," EMILY groans, and HISTORYBOT processes that GOD has stepped into one of the areas of chrono-instability. Her face matures to the age she was when she first built HISTORYBOT, and then far past it, into an early grave, into the corruption of undeath. GOD turns back to her sister. EMILY raises her sword and screams in challenge, the chipped plastic of her helmet sprouting a kingly plume as HISTORYBOT's zeroes and ones begin to break apart, swirling in an ever-widening maelstrom before everything goes black.

THEN. WHEN? THEN:

HISTORYBOT reboots. The NEW HOUSE is dark. The first step in preventing future malfunctions is to determine the cause of the error and take steps to correct it. The first step to determining the cause of the error is to scroll back through the data logs and isolate the first incidence of the malfunction. HISTORYBOT appears to hibernate as priority is given to this new task. It does not take long.

JUNE 1, 20XX

The discreet zeroes and ones inside HISTORYBOT blur and melt into each other, like instant coffee granules and not-quite-hot-enough water swizzled together in a Styrofoam cup at the skating rink's snackbar because the MR COFFEE *fucked up* last week and nobody has brought in a replacement. The binary code that defines HISTORYBOT, that HISTORYBOT in turn uses to define both past and present, the chain that appears infinite but is actually a mere octillion-and-change individual characters, *that* binary code, is no longer simply 010000010100001001000011, DEF, etc, but instead a continuous, flowing sequence of images, a living film instead of a dead ledger.

There are two teams of young women on the *flat track* in front of the robot. Each team has five *players* on the track at any given moment—one *jammer* and four *blockers*. The jammers score points by first maneuvering their way through the *pack* of both teams' blockers and then *lapping* them. For each opposing blocker the jammer laps one point is scored. One of the blockers is a *pivot,* meaning that later in the game she may become a jammer. All ten of the players will skate around and around the track, either until the time elapses or a jammer calls off the *jam.*

None of this is confusing to HISTORYBOT. HISTORYBOT is incapable of thought, in the strict sense of the word, and is therefore incapable of being confused…in the strict sense of the word.

What *would* be confusing to HISTORYBOT, if HISTORYBOT was capable of such, is the fact that the two teams—the home team PWN JETTS and the visiting UNHOLY ROLLERS—have stopped playing the game as it is defined in HISTORYBOT's circuitry. Instead they, along with the two *referees* skating alongside them and their bench-sitting team members and *coaches* and bleacher-sitting friends and families and *derby widows* and random spectators, have all blurred, just like HISTORYBOT's code, into a tapestry. The BAYEUX TAPESTRY, to be precise.

The NORMAN CONQUEST, culminating with the BATTLE OF HASTINGS, takes place on the track as HISTORYBOT observes. The robot's primary ward, EMILY, is the PWN JETTS' acting jammer, as signified by the stars decorating her helmet…the arms of which are now twisting and growing upward to form a crown around her head. The black of her tanktop and short shorts and the red of her fishnets have become the raiment of WILLIAM THE CONQUEROR as the NORMAN king squeezes between two bulky blockers. The away team's jammer, THAT SKINNY BLONDE BITCH WITH THE TEETH, makes an imposing HAROLD GODWINSON, and the pack of blockers shifts from the CASTLE OF DINAN to an ENGLISH shield wall to a charging cavalry, the armies and individuals stumbling between 11th century combatants and 21st century *badasses*, armor and shields melting into plastic helmets and wristguards, the whole jumbled mess veering back and forth between two dimensions and three.

The bout abruptly ends with four whistle blasts before anyone can be climactically shot in the face with an arrow, and the track is cleared. EMILY joins HISTORYBOT, her face glowing in the too-bright lights of the emptying arena, and kisses the robot on the side of its upper casing. This does nothing to diminish the interest HISTORYBOT's presence at the side of the rink has aroused in a random cross-section of the bout's attendees, but HISTORYBOT pays no more attention to the staring men, women, and children than EMILY does. A stocky woman with artificially bright orange hair that the robot recognizes as JENNIFER (DERBY: *Mi$$ Money Jenny*) joins EMILY and HISTORYBOT, and the two JETTS exchange words that HISTORYBOT is inexplicably having difficulty processing.

This abnormality trips the robot's ERROR RECTIFICATION SYSTEM, which begins to scroll back through the night's code while the two girls flank HISTORYBOT out to the parking lot and hoist it into the back of EMILY's SUBARU OUTBACK. Clearly there has been a major malfunction, but HISTORYBOT is having difficulty determining the cause. At present, the error seems to have been autocorrected, as HISTORYBOT is now functionally interpreting the words EMILY is saying to her teammate:

"—stopped going last month," EMILY is simultaneously shaking her head from left to right and trying to light her cigarette on the proffered flame of JENNIFER's lighter. Eventually she gets it. "And when I told her she was all like, *well, I never went back after the first session, so I'm hardly the one to be bitching at him.* Meaning *I'm* being a bitch for thinking it's too soon."

"Jesus," JENNIFER says.

"I'm still going, and even *he* agrees I'm the last one who needs it. All we've talked about for the last few weeks was them. Not her, not me, *them.* They're like kids, retard fucking kids who lost their mommy."

"Maybe they think because you've been spending so much time with H.B., I dunno, you don't, like, need them?" JENNIFER asks, giving HISTORYBOT a sidelong glance. She seems *creeped out* by the robot. "Maybe if you spent more time with them, they'd, I dunno, chill?"

"Doubt it," EMILY speaks through a cloud of tobacco smoke. "I can't get the All Star Boo-hoo Crew to go to family counseling, the shit they're gonna do anything else with me. Kim knew what she was doing, giving me robotard—might not be any less crazy than they are, but at least he comes to derby."

THEN:

The evening of the JUNE 1, 20XX derby bout was indeed the first instance of the major malfunction, HISTORYBOT has determined. No ZOMBIES materialized during that malfunction, which signals…something. Now HISTORYBOT just needs to determine what. In an effort to further chart the course of the malfunction—and in turn isolate the corrupted data and any compromised processors—the robot continues analysis of the data logs rather than resuming contemporary functions, stuttering to itself in the shadows *like a misaligned 1541 drive-head mechanism on a COMMODORE 64.*

DECEMBER 25, 20XX

"Oh boy," says EMILY. "A robot."

"I *knew* you'd be surprised!" GOD is all over HISTORYBOT before EMILY has even removed the bulk of the wrapping paper. "He's called HISTORYBOT. The switch is right here, but he's already on."

"Historybot?" says EMILY. Her expression is *pissy.* "Looks like a museum piece, alright."

"Don't be a brat, Em," DAD says.

"I'm not," EMILY replies, crossing her arms. "Thanks. What does it do?"

"What *doesn't* he do?" GOD says in a *goofy* voice. "He talks, he squawks, he sees all, knows all. He's a teacher, a friend, a regular member of the family. Ask him something, anything."

"Did my sister build you on the clock?" EMILY says, looking at GOD instead of HISTORYBOT.

"NEGATIVE," HISTORYBOT blares at a 5. "CONSTRUCTION TOOK PLACE SOLELY AFTER WORKING HOURS, BEGINNING AT 02:45:32 EASTERN STANDARD TIME ON JANUARY 3, 20XX."

"He's just a chatty Cathy, isn't he?" says MOM, sipping her coffee. "You've really been working on that thing for two years?"

"Off and on," says GOD, rooting around in the flotsam of wadded wrapping paper. "More like three, with design and everything. Where's my phone? I wanna get a picture of Chumpus and H.B."

"Here," says EMILY, tossing the small orange device to GOD. "Next time just make me one of those instead of Robby the Robotard."

"Emily, you're being a real bitch," MOM says, mildly *pissed.*

"She's just messing around," says GOD, *anxiously*. She physically puts herself between her mother and her younger sister, her body language combining with a soothing vocalization pattern to create a *tranquil* atmosphere. "It's Christmas, giving each other shit about presents is right up there with eggnog and lying to kids, right?"

"Right," says DAD, but his voice is *strained.* "What's it do, Kimber? Big sucker, good thing we're just on the one floor here."

"We're rolling nine terabytes deep of information," GOD says, seeming to forget her nervousness. "Primarily historical stuff. Biographies, survey texts, primary sources out the wazoo, archival footage and audio samples, you name it. He can also update online and has a mean AI for correlating data, extrapolating, locating trends, running sims. Just having a heavy enough search function took the better part of—"

"So it's a big-ass wikipedia on wheels," says EMILY. Despite her obvious efforts to remain *pissy* she appears curious. "Is that a camera?"

"It's his eye." GOD begins pointing to the area around HISTORYBOT's lens, "Here's his USBs, and an audio jack, and—"

"Maybe I can dig out the camera," EMILY says. "Put the rest on eBay."

"EMILY," MOM says sternly. "Your sister put years into making this—"

"Piece of junk," EMILY says, *all snotty and shit.* "Because of that stupid history fair, right? Because this one time I did this one thing, I get a stupid fucking robot five years later because everything has to be about her and her droids, right?"

"You need to quit the All-Star Boo-hoo Crew, Em," GOD says, her inflection very *strained* now.

"Oh, whatever, Kim, you—"

MOM has quietly stood and interrupts EMILY with a slap to the face. EMILY runs to her room as DAD begins to shout at MOM, and GOD, *bummed*, flips off HISTORYBOT's power without waiting for him to properly shut down. She doesn't want him to see this.

THEN:

The corruption has spread much further than HISTORYBOT's initial scan implied. Small errors have impacted and, seemingly at random, altered the static dates and timestamps assigned to data in both the primary log and the back-up, which has in turn led to an unknown number of files merging, becoming lost, or otherwise suffering some sort of unintentional alteration. The cataloguing system is suffering a substantial degree of corruption as well, and there are a host of problems with the sensor arrays that process external information.

HISTORYBOT attempts to go online to seek out helpful updates, but is unable to establish a connection either on the local wireless network or via the back-up satellite function. Scanning through the relevant logs, HISTORYBOT quickly determines this inability to access a functioning connection is the result of the APOCALYPTIC ZOMBIE UPRISING. That such a major historical event should have been overlooked in HISTORYBOT's primary processing of the problem signals even deeper, broader-reaching errors. HISTORYBOT begins to run a script to determine what measures would be most efficacious given this breakdown in memory, but another error occurs, triggering—

WHEN?

"Jesus-fuckwhat-Christ!" EMILY is shouting at her parents. "What part of *goddamn zombies* do you not understand?!"

"Em, there's nothing we can do," DAD shrugs, *morbidly bummed.* "Nothing anyone can do."

"I'm leaving," says EMILY. She is crying. "I'm going to take the car and go."

"Where?" It is the first time MOM has spoken to EMILY in 04 days, 03 hours, and 03.34 seconds. "Where will you go, EMILY?"

EMILY says nothing, staring at her still-seated mother and her mother's sweaty glass of HENDRICK'S. It is 08:45:32 AM EASTERN STANDARD TIME

MOM continues, "The fact is, there's nowhere *to* go, is there? Especially not with the Highlander in the shop. We're all going to die. Sooner the better."

EMILY opens and closes her mouth without saying anything. She is shuddering, her face wet with tears. DAD is shaking his head *sadly*. EMILY turns and runs to her room, the door slamming shut behind her. DAD is staring at HISTORYBOT, who is backed into the northwest corner of the room. MOM is staring at nothing.

"Why couldn't it have been cancer?" DAD whispers. "I could have done cancer."

MOM snorts and drains half her glass, ice clicking on teeth. Wiping her mouth, she asks, "A global cancer epidemic? Yeah, Jim, that'd be swell."

"Huh?" DAD blinks at MOM, as if noticing her presence for the first time. "Oh. No, I meant…Kimber. Something slow, something to…a little more time, is all…"

DAD is sobbing. Again. MOM stands, finishes her gin, and advances on HISTORYBOT. Fumbling behind the robot's blocky head, she slurs, "Show's over, robobutt."

THEN:

The corrupted files tick blandly by, for the most part, but occasionally chunks of AVIs and MPEGs swell to the surface in the waves of binary:

EMILY and GOD getting high on EMILY's bed while their parents are at a concert, smiling, laughing, sisters, friends.

EMILY sobbing on her bed following the unwilling termination of a romantic relationship.

EMILY moaning on her bed, awkwardly utilizing the toe of a roller-skate wrapped in her panties to masturbate, the video streaming to a romantic partner's computer at IP ADDRESS 375.34.963.020.

EMILY getting ready for school.

EMILY getting ready for derby.

EMILY getting ready for the SAT.

EMILY.

EMILY.
EMILY.
And later on, ZOMBIES.

THEN: AN UNCORRUPTED, THRICE-CONFIRMED DATE. APRIL 23, 20XX

"H.B.," says EMILY. She looks *miserable*, her eyes puffy and red. "I...I still can't believe it. It makes me crazy, thinking it. I keep forgetting, and then I remember, and..."

HISTORYBOT says nothing, having detected no probable information request in the sentence. HISTORYBOT waits. HISTORYBOT is good at waiting.

"Do you even know?" EMILY looks *perplexed*. "Fuck, I didn't even tell you, did I? HISTORYBOT, Kim...Kim's..."

Kim is EMILY'S CANT for GOD. There is still no definable query in what EMILY is saying, but all the same HISTORYBOT goes online to update its files on GOD. This is a standard update, one that HISTORYBOT performs once every—

"Dead," EMILY croaks, throwing her hard arms around HISTORYBOT's harder casing, "Just...dead."

EMILY's proclamation is processed on the primary level at precisely the same nanosecond the update verifies this information from 302 independent sources. KIMBERLY ELENA VASQUEZ (DERBY: *The Kimp*, GOD's CANT: GOD) was popular not only in her professional field but also in a wide array of online communities, and so news of her death has been widely reported.

GOD is dead. Except that this is not true. This is, strictly speaking, an impossibility.

302 anachronism errors are triggered during the update process. One anachronism error is triggered by HISTORYBOT's primary ward, EMILY. HISTORYBOT mutely assesses these errors while EMILY cries and cries, and then the file begins to become garb01101100ed unti-01101100—

WHEN? MOST PROBABLE TEMPORAL LOCATION: POST-EMILY DEPARTURE, PRE-ZOMBIE ATTACK ON NEW HOUSE:

"H.B." DAD breathes heavily into HISTORYBOT's sensors as the robot boots up. "H.B., listen. Is she coming back? Do they come back?"

"CLARIFY! QUESTION!" HISTORYBOT blares *like a klaxon,* still at a 7 from when EMILY routed her IPOD through the bot's speaker system the previous morning.

"Shit!" DAD cries, covering his ears. "Volume down, volume to, whatsit, two, volume two."

"CLARIFY QUESTION," HISTORYBOT repeats at a 2.

"These...zombies, they're dead people. Real dead people, right?" DAD is looking around furtively. The living room is dark except for the glow emanating from HISTORYBOT's monitor-face.

"PARTIALLY CORRECT," HISTORYBOT verifies. "INITIAL REPORTS STATE—"

"Is Kimber coming back?" DAD says, his voice an octave higher than his base conversational tone. "Will she come back here? Will she come home?"

"KIMBER..." HISTORYBOT tries to process the question, and after a *hiccup,* succeeds. "BAD QUERY: KIMBERLY ELENA VASQUEZ IS NOT DECEASED, ERGO—"

"Goddamn blockhead," DAD mutters, rubbing his temples. "Em told me you weren't...you can't believe it either, can you?"

"REPEAT QUESTION," HISTORYBOT intones.

"Ok, yeah, I can do this," DAD nods. He appears to be *trying not to cry.* "H.B., do a whatsit...simulation. Simulation parameters are Kimber being...oh Jesus, Kimber died four months ago. Car crash, some drunk punk...some goddamn...Jesus Jesus Jesus."

DAD says nothing for a time, staring at the teak floor. When 60.00 SECONDS have elapsed HISTORYBOT prompts him. "PLEASE COMPLETE SIMULATION PARAMETERS."

"She's dead," DAD says, looking *fucking pissed* at the robot. "My baby girl. We buried her...we buried here at MeadowWood, next to...next to her fucking grandmother, next to Selma, oh Jesus..."

Another 60.00 SECONDS tick by, and then: "PLEASE COMPLETE SIMUL—"

"She's coming back," DAD moans. "I know it, I knew it. My little Kimber's gonna be a zombie."

The basic simulation parameters are as follows, then:

PARAMETER 01: GOD is dead—a popular anachronism these days. When DAD does not input any further details for the scenario HISTORYBOT pulls up one of the 302 false reports of GOD's death as a basic template. HISTORYBOT is fully equipped to *fill in the blanks* where simulations are concerned.

PARAMETER 10: Instead of *zombification* only being possible when a living human is bitten or scratched by a ZOMBIE, as is the case in *reality*, even deceased human remains can be *zombified.* DAD has not provided any data for how or why this is the case, but then simulations do not require explanations for impossible scenarios—simulations are intended for researching the hypothetical, after all.

PARAMETER 11: GOD will become a ZOMBIE, as per PARAMETER 10.

The simulation script does not take very long to prepare.

"SIMULATION PARAMETERS ARE AS FOLLOWS," HISTORYBOT drones, "SIMULATION PARAMETER ONE: KIMBERLY ELENA VASQUEZ IS DECEASED FOLLOWING AN AUTOMOBILE COLLISION ON APRIL XX, 20XX. HER REMAINS WERE IN A HOSPITAL MORGUE BEFORE INTERNMENT AT MEADOWWOOD MEMORIAL PARK."

"Oh baby, I'm sorrrrrrrry!" DAD wails.

"SIMULATION PARAMETER TWO: RATHER THAN REQUIRING A TRANSFERAL OF DEOXYRIBONUCLEIC ACID FROM AN INFECTED INDIVIDUAL TO A LIVING SUBJECT, QUOTE ZOMBIFICATION END QUOTE WILL CONTAMINATE VIABLE HUMAN TISSUE THROUGH AN UNKNOWN VECTOR. PARAMETER THREE: KIMBERLY ELENA VASQUEZ WILL BE QUOTE ZOMBIFIED END QUOTE AS PER PARAMETER TWO. CONFIRM SIMULATION PARAMETERS?"

"What?" DAD says, but when HISTORYBOT begins to repeat itself DAD cuts the bot off with a confirmation. "Yes, damn it, yes. Don't you know what a goddamn zombie is?"

HISTORYBOT knows what a ZOMBIE is, which is why HISTORYBOT reiterated the simulation parameters—because apparently DAD does not. Or rather, DAD is requesting a simulation with a radically different definition of ZOMBIE than is generally accepted, but then it is not HISTORYBOT's place to question simulation parameters once they have been confirmed. Even if they are *r-tarded.* The ones and zeroes correlate themselves, and in HISTORYBOT's databanks DAD's simulated resurrected-corpse-zombies become labeled GODDAMN ZOMBIES, to differentiate them from true ZOMBIES.

"She'll come back," DAD says. "Won't she? Back here? Is Kimber really coming home?"

"94% PROBABILITY OF ACCURACY." HISTORYBOT says with minimal processing time. It is an easy simulation. "IF GODDAMN ZOMBIES BEHAVE IDENTICALLY TO REAL-WORLD COUNTERPARTS. INITIAL REPORTS STATE THAT ZOMBIES ATTEMPT TO REVISIT FAMILIAR LOCATIONS WITH A 94% LIKELIHOOD OF BEGINNING AT QUOTE HOME END QUOTE."

"Fuck yeah," DAD says. He is smiling. He has not shown his teeth in a display of pleasure since the inaccurate reporting of GOD's death. "When, when's she coming?"

Behind him, MOM switches on the light at the end of the hall and calls out, "Jim? Are you playing with that goddamn robot?"

"PLACE OF BURIAL AN ESTIMATED 26 MILES FROM NEW HOUSE COMBINED WITH PROBABILITY OF RESTRICTED MOBILITY FROM CAUSE OF DEATH IMPLIES..." HISTORYBOT crunches the data. "ESTIMATED ARRIVAL OF KIMBERLY ELENA VASQUEZ IN 67 HOURS 36 MINUTES 12 SECONDS."

"Fuck! Yeah!" DAD pumps his fist *like a douchebag*. "She'll be here in three days! The zombies'll be here in three days!"

"NEGATIVE," HISTORYBOT corrects DAD. "EARLIEST POSSIBLE ARRIVAL OF GODDAMN ZOMBIE KIMBERLY ELENA VASQUEZ IS 62 HOURS, 24 MINUTES, AND 50 SECONDS. EARLIEST POSSIBLE ARRIVAL OF RANDOM ZOMBIE, GODDAMN OR REAL-WORLD, IS..." HISTORYBOT runs the numbers just as a low groan drifts through the open window. "4 HOURS 23 MINUTES 03 SECONDS AGO."

"Shit!" DAD yelps, scrambling up and slamming the window shut. "Inez! Em! The goddamn zombies are here!"

Rather than coming to assist, MOM turns the hallway light back off and returns to bed. EMILY departed the house 12 HOURS 34 MINUTES AND 21.39 SECONDS previously in the SUBARU OUTBACK she loaded with supplies and the improvised weaponry HISTORYBOT helped her construct from available materials. The house is quiet and the groan comes again, but quieter, as it is now muffled by the glass. DAD goes to the fireplace and retrieves an iron poker. He is still smiling when he opens the door leading out onto the wraparound deck.

THEN: SOMETIME LATER

The NEW HOUSE is a single story, mission style domicile of approximately 1975 square feet that sits 12 feet off the ground on a system of stilts. It is an architectural design meant to prevent damage to the house in the event of flooding from the adjacent WACISSA RIVER, which is, at its median water level, approximately 17 meters from the most easterly support stilt. The interior of the house can be reached from either the wide oaken staircase leading down from the deck that surrounds the house on all sides or from the single room that is on the ground level. This 200 square foot room houses a MASONIC washer/dryer and a stairwell. This is the part of the house that EMILY has driven the SUBARU OUTBACK into in a bid to save the house from ZOMBIE infestation.

DAD and HISTORYBOT are on the front deck when the car appears through the trees lining RIVER ROAD. DAD has almost entirely dismantled the stairway leading down from the deck but a fresh pack of ZOMBIES have arrived. While these ZOMBIES do not have the wherewithal to hoist one of their number up to the current bottom step that dangles 9 feet off the ground, they do have BOB JENKINS FROM NEXT DOOR THAT FUCKER with them, and BOB JENKINS FROM NEXT DOOR THAT FUCKER has led the other ZOMBIES to the laundry room door that DAD has failed to secure beyond a cursory locking of the deadbolt. EMILY presumably sees this, presumably processes this, and drives the automobile into the pack of ZOMBIES at 43 MPH.

"Shit!" DAD cries as the house buckles from the impact, his blood-spattered BIRKENSTOCKS sliding on the deck. "Shit! Did she just fuck us? Did she just ruin the whole fucking house?! Shit!"

DAD swings his galvanized steel ladder over the railing and descends to inspect the damage and inspect his returned daughter. HISTORYBOT misses most of the *harrowing rescue* as it takes place beneath the bot's field of vision, and besides, HISTORYBOT is busy processing DAD's query regarding the current stability of the house now that one of the primary supports has been driven into by a 3386 pound motor vehicle.

When DAD and EMILY scramble up the clanging ladder and hoist it back over the railing just as another pack of shambling ZOMBIES appear on the road, HISTORYBOT reports that the house, while structurally weakened, is in no immediate danger of collapse. DAD runs inside to begin dismantling what remains of the laundry room stairs from above while EMILY lies bleeding from her scalp on the deck, mildly concussed from her automobile accident.

"H.B." EMILY groans. "You okay?"

"HISTORYBOT IS OPERATING AT FULL OPERATIONAL CAPABILITY," HISTORYBOT informs her. This is incorrect, but HISTORYBOT will not realize this for some time.

"Came back for you," EMILY pants. "And them. Couldn't leave. You guys. Got to town. Went to. Fermentation. Jenny and Bri. Holed up there. Spent the night with 'em. The bar's going to be…impossible. To defend. But. They've got a plan. But I left. I had to. Had to come back. Mom and Dad. They need me."

A suboptimal temporal location for a major data corruption error, but then there is no such thing as a *good time* for them.

WHEN?

"EMILY," HISTORYBOT insists. "THIS IS OPTIMAL."

"No!" She wails, kicking the open panel in the robot's chest shut even as its pincer arm pulls her closer. She is outside of the NEW HOUSE, outside of time, space, even history, and yet still she struggles in the binary void. Her clothes have melted off from the heat of HISTORYBOT's processors, but through sheer force of will she has been able to retain her rollerskates. There is nothing for her to gain traction on, however, and she sees the chest panel pop back open, a black gulf inside the robot yawning to swallow her whole.

"EMILY, HIGH FUNCTIONING INTEGRATION REQUIRES COMPLETE ABSORPTION OF YOUR SIMULATION. CEASE STRUGGLING."

"Fucker!" She lands a kick to the robot's frontal casing, but here HISTORYBOT is much harder than any plastic and the blow does nothing but hurt her ankle. "I answered everything, now let me go!"

"EMILY, THIS IS MANDATORY." HISTORYBOT increases retraction power to 7, but rather than pulling the girl into the prepared folder its claw slides off her sweaty skin, leaving a bloody scrape on her forearm. "FOR YOUR OWN GOOD YOU MUST NOT—"

But the young woman has already landed on a bed of zeroes and planted her skates, launching herself off into the binary mists of history even as clothes reform on her naked body. The last thing HISTORYBOT processes before the girl escapes into time is a pleated black skirt sprouting from the elastic band of her panties, and then she is gone. HISTORYBOT begins to analyze when and where she is most likely to have fled to, prioritizing the anachronism search, but, really, HISTORYBOT has all the time in the world.

THEN:

"Impregnable," DAD says, motioning expansively at the piled lumber and the gap in the deck where the stairs had descended before he removed them. "No way up, now. We'll cover that hole in the morning, and between that little stunt of yours and my chainsaw on the stairs the carport's totally sealed. Good going, Em."

EMILY is propped up against the railing, her face bloody, her left arm broken, her skates tied together and hanging around her neck *like an albatross.* EMILY actually said *like an awesome-tross,* but that may have *just been the concussion talking,* so HISTORYBOT has taken the liberty of autocorrecting her. 03 HOURS 56 MINUTES 32 SECONDS have elapsed since EMILY returned to the NEW HOUSE. In that time, 47 discreet ZOMBIES have congregated below the deck, including MAE VICTIS, JAILBREAK BETTY, APPLE SMITER, and MOLLY ROGER, four of EMILY's former teammates. They would have arrived much sooner, but their rollerskates have seriously compromised their mobility.

"The only way up's the ladder, so we can control who gets in." DAD looks at HISTORYBOT. "What's that about high ground? Who said that?"

"HIGH GROUND," HISTORYBOT intones as a placeholder while beginning its scan.

"Dad," EMILY *pleads.* "We need to leave before any more show up. We can still go, outrun these dicks, meet up with Jenny and Bri and—"

"Yeah, high ground." DAD interrupts her. HISTORYBOT would never interrupt someone—all part of its programming. "Military tactics. That shit."

"763 RELEVANT QUOTES." HISTORYBOT reports after it is certain DAD is finished speaking. "MOST POPULAR QUOTE IS ATTRIBUTED TO GENERAL WALTON WALKER, FIRST COMMANDER OF THE UNITED STATES EIGHTH ARMY DURING THE KOREAN WAR."

"Yeah, but what'd he say?" DAD raises his eyebrows at EMILY. "About high ground, what'd he say?"

"THE UNABRIDGED QUOTE IS AS FOLLOWS: QUOTE WE MUST TRADE TIME FOR SPACE, HOLD THE HIGH GROUND AS LONG AS

POSSIBLE. DEFEND IN DEPTH. KEEP A RESERVE. WATCH YOUR FLANKS. PROTECT YOUR ARTILLERY. MAINTAIN COMMUNICATIONS AT ALL COSTS. DON'T GET DECISIVELY ENGAGED. END QUOTE."

"Right, yeah," says DAD, nodding excitedly. "Tactics, military tactics is what it comes down to, and we've got the best tactician right here, don't we?"

"POPULAR BUT UNATTRIBUTED MILITARY APHORISM: QUOTE AMATEURS TALK TACTICS, PROFESSIONALS TALK LOGISTICS. END QUOTE."

"Yeah, well, let's talk logistics, then," said DAD. "Goddamn if moving to Hurricane Alley wasn't the best thing that ever happened to us—stockpile of nonperishable food, river's right there for fresh water, a generator, and the goddamn house is on goddamn stilts to keep the riffraff out. Goddamn! What else do we need?"

Deep inside HISTORYBOT, a small error triggers a larger error, which in turns triggers an MP3 file. The ghost of WINSTON CHURCHILL wafts out of the robot's speakers: "*WE MUST HAVE, AND HAVE QUICKLY,*" HISTORYBOT excerpts from the deceased prime minister's BE YE MEN OF VALOUR speech, "*MORE AEROPLANES, MORE TANKS, MORE SHELLS, MORE GUNS. THERE IS IMPERIOUS NEED FOR THESE VITAL MUNITIONS.*"

"Well, if that's all then I don't see how we can lose," MOM says from the kitchen doorway. She is holding a platter with two glasses and a pitcher of CUCUMBER COLLINS'. Her vision settles on EMILY and she steps back, startled. "Oh! Em!"

"Hi Mom," EMILY says. She appears to be attempting to raise her uninjured arm in greeting but is unable to manage the gesture. "I'm kinda fucked up. Kinda bad. We gotta get out of here before dark, but Dad's still nuts."

"Let me get another glass, then," says MOM, setting down the pitcher on the stack of salvaged deck stairs and going back inside. She calls, "Any sign of your sister yet?"

"Why won't you listen?" EMILY groans. "Only people who are bit turn. That's how it works. It's all over the emergency broadcast feeds. Kim's not coming back. She can't."

"Who died and made you Zombie Queen?" DAD rolls his eyes. "Goddamn zombies are drunking around my yard, trying to eat my ass, and she thinks she can make up some rules. There are no rules, Em, once the goddamn *dead* goddamn *rise*, there aren't any more rules! Na-*da*! Zip! I ran it though the machine—H.B. says she'll be back any minute!"

"Maybe one of them will dig Kim up and bite her corpse," MOM says. "Then you'll both be right. Compromise, you two, compromise—"

"No!" EMILY lolls her head. "She isn't coming back! It's impossible!"

"Impossible," DAD nods *sagely*, and waves down at the mob of slavering zombies milling in the yard. "Define impossible for me and see where the walking dead fit in. Besides, you're the last person I'm going to ask for reliable zombie information, Miss C-minus-in-Biology. Kimber'll be back, we just need to wait here a little longer."

EMILY closes her eyes but the tears push through anyway, rust-colored tracks running down her cheeks.

"She'll be here any minute," DAD murmurs, his hands fiercely gripping the railing as he stares off down the live oak-lined road to where another cluster of shambling undead horrors approach. "*Annnnny* minute, now."

THEN AGAIN:

"Tried begging," EMILY pants, HISTORYBOT supporting her as they stand at the railing, looking out at the ever widening field of ZOMBIES congregating in front of the NEW HOUSE. "Tried threatening, tried crying, tried goddamn everything, and when they wouldn't listen I left. And that didn't work. I couldn't just leave'em here. So now what the fuck do I do, huh? Now what?"

HISTORYBOT crunches the numbers. *HISTORYBOT will crunch some fucking numbers, son.* 23 simple-simulations later, HISTORYBOT informs her, "A MEMBER OF THE FAMILY—MEANING EMILY, MOM, OR DAD—EACH HAVE A LESS THAN THREE PERCENT CHANCE OF ESCAPING THE NEW HOUSE AT PRESENT WITHOUT SUFFERING A SINGLE ZOMBIE BITE. THE PROBABILITY OF MORE THAN ONE MEMBERS OF THE FAMILY ESCAPING THE NEW HOUSE AT PRESENT WITHOUT SUFFERING A SINGLE ZOMBIE BITE IS LESS THAN ZERO POINT FOUR PERCENT. PROBABILITY OF ANY COMBINATION OF EMILY, MOM, AND DAD STAYING IN THE NEW HOUSE IN PERPETUITY WITHOUT SUFFERING A SINGLE ZOMBIE BITE IS STATISTICALLY NEGLIGIBLE."

"I could have told you that," EMILY says after HISTORYBOT finishes droning. "We're so fucked. Why can't you run a simulation where I always get away, huh? Why can't you do something useful?"

"HISTORYBOT IS CAPABLE OF SUCH A SIMULATION," HISTORYBOT notifies EMILY. "FOR OPTIMAL SIMULATION ACCURACY, YOU WILL NEED TO ANSWER A BRIEF SURVEY."

"Great," says EMILY. "Sure, why not. Don't forget to make the All-Star Boo-hoo Crew stop sucking major cock, while you're at it, and have Kim dodge that drunk so we all get to live happily ever after."

"HISTORYBOT IS CAPABLE OF SUCH A SIMULATION."

"And unicorns and gorillas and mecha-Mongol wolfman assassins to deal with the goddamn zombies," EMILY adds, with a *why the fuck not* sort of shrug. Her concussion appears to be making her sleepy.

After a longer than usual delay: "HISTORYBOT IS CAPABLE OF SUCH A SIMULATION."

"Well, let's get to it," says EMILY, and *barfs* over the railing onto the ZOMBIE horde.

HISTORYBOT begins the survey. The robot has spent more time in close proximity to EMILY than with any other human, but simulations always benefit from an advanced degree of intimacy with the simulated subject. "WHAT IS YOUR FAVORITE COLOR?"

"Red," EMILY says, and spits the same.

"WHAT IS YOUR FAVORITE MEMORY?"

"The Old House," EMILY says without hesitation. "Back before they got so…weird about her. About me. Us. Everything. Before all that, me and Kim would sword fight in the backyard. She let me be Eleanor of Aquitaine. She always let me be Eleanor of Aquitaine."

THEN:

HISTORYBOT has already been having *a bitch of a time* sorting through its data logs in pursuit of the original error that triggered the increasingly erratic malfunctions of its processors and sensors when MOM comes out onto the deck and *really shits the bed.*

"Why is it still on?" MOM demands. "Don't you know it's on a battery? Like the rest of us."

EMILY is unconscious atop a bed of piled lumber—it would not be strictly accurate to describe her as sleeping. DAD is inside the house, beyond HISTORYBOT's sensors. Without either of them to *pick up the slack*, HISTORYBOT is obligated to answer.

"HISTORYBOT HAS REQUESTED THAT HISTORYBOT BE KEPT FULLY OPERATIONAL," HISTORYBOT informs MOM.

"God, what the hell for?" MOM says, hugging her arms despite the 94 DEGREE FAHRENHEIT temperature. "Wish I could just turn off like that."

"WHEN HIBERNATING OR OTHERWISE NON-FULLY OPERATIONAL, HISTORYBOT IS INCAPABLE OF PROCESSING HISTORY," the robot tells her. "ONLINE INFORMATION GATHERING AND CORRELATING ARE NON-OPERATIONAL, AND PROBABILITY OF RESUMPTION OF INTERNET CAPABILITIES IS CURRENTLY STATISTICALLY NEGLIGIBLE. TO PROCESS CONTEMPORANEOUS EVENTS INTO HISTORICAL RECORD HISTORYBOT MUST REMAIN FULLY OPERATIONAL."

"Goddamn robot doesn't want to be turned off. Sounds like the start of a cheesy movie. Or the end of one." The droning ruckus of frogs and nigh-endless crying of limpkins that used to emanate from the river at this time of evening has been replaced by a steady, unbroken groan from the 348 ZOMBIES in a 0.1 MILE radius. MOM appears to listen to them in the same way she listened to the croaks, chirps, and screams of the smaller animals, and then shakes her head. "She sure was a smart one, wasn't she?"

"CLARIFY QUERY."

"Tell me this, robobutt," MOM says. "How many mothers have gone through what I've gone through, huh? Wondering if they pushed their girls too hard, wondering if all that helicopter pilot, tiger-mom bullshit did more harm than good? Was she happy? I didn't think to ask. Not often, anyway, not enough. And now..."

"STATED QUERY IS—"

"Stated query is how many mothers had to bury their daughters," MOM says, and looks at EMILY as if noticing her silent presence for the first time. "And how many actually could?"

MOM goes to EMILY, stands over her, slaps a mosquito on her daughter's blood-stained shoulder. She leaves her palm there, and stays that way, immobile, for 03 MINUTES 12 SECONDS before going inside. HISTORYBOT has not finished correlating the data when she does—redundancies pile on top of redundancies until a fatal error occurs.

There is a reboot, a resumption of the search, and another fatal error. It is deemed a BAD QUERY, and, accordingly, abandoned.

NOW:

Even the solar panels covering HISTORYBOT's rear array cannot keep its battery charged in perpetuity, though the sun *does its damnedest* to keep the robot going. With a steady decline in power comes a steady decline in function, and the steady multiplication of errors have rendered the probability of locating the source error a statistical impossibility. It is outside of HISTORYBOT's processing capabilities to perform a search of future-dated locations for the culprit—it is a HISTORYBOT, after all, and *that used to mean something.*

JULY 0X, 1863

HISTORYBOT is having problems with dates, which signals something dire indeed, but battery life is fluctuating wildly and so devoting even back-up programs to investigating this malfunction is inadvisable. The important thing is arresting EMILY's flight before she causes any more problems. Given that ROCK CREEK is flowing red with the blood of not only UNION (COLLOQUIAL SLANG: *Yankee)* and CONFEDERATE (COLLOQUIAL SLANG: *Reb*) troops, but also that of UNICORNS and GORILLAS, she is somewhere in close proximity. A MONGOL leaps 32 meters over the top of HISTORYBOT and lands in the middle of the fray. With the entry of EMILY's simulation parameters still a century and a half in the future, HISTORYBOT initially mistakes the man for one of the ZOMBIE MONGOLS from the HOUSE OF WISDOM. The error-riddled bot attempts to process how random historical individuals have become capable of traveling through time in the same fashion that EMILY has. When the MONGOL's face sprouts fur and fangs and his legs explode into a gleaming steel carapace the robot simply abandons the query and rolls into the combat.

Visual contact with EMILY is immediately achieved. Both the UNION and CONFEDERATE armies have fallen victim to the chrono-instability that hovers around HISTORYBOT *like flies around shit*, but EMILY appears undaunted by the sudden, unspoken treaty between NORTH and SOUTH as the two sides become a single ZOMBIE legion. Instead of fleeing she sits higher in the saddle of her 7-meter tall clockwork werewolf steed, pointing a saber in the direction of WOLF HILL.

"We find Kim, we rule history!" EMILY shouts into the smoky air as cannonballs kick up dirt and flesh all around her. "Reprogram the past, seize the future! We have the technology! 01110111 01110100 01100-110!"

HISTORYBOT attempts to maneuver into position to apprehend EMILY but is knocked onto its side by a rotting rollergirl in the dark blue uniform of GENERAL HENRY WARNER SLOCUM (COLLOQUIAL SLANG: *General "Slow Come," following his dallying at the BATTLE OF GETTYSBURG).* This newest anachronism leads a swarm of CONFEDERATE, UNION, and PWN JETT ZOMBIES toward the front-line of MECHA-MONGOL WOLFMAN ASSASSINS and UNICORN-riding GORILLAS. The fallen HISTORYBOT cannot raise itself from its prone position, but then a familiar shape leans over it and helps the bot rise.

GOD. A welcome anachronism if ever there was one. She is carrying a musket in one hand and a SUPER SASQUATCH energy drink in the other. Before HISTORYBOT can eradicate this error—or, *why the fuck not,* request that it enter new simulation parameters—GOD has turned and joined the battle, blasting into the air on a jetpack and spraying liquid fire from the end of her musket onto MECHA-MONGOL WOLF-MAN ASSASSINS and ZOMBIES alike.

After that, *shit got real.*

WHEN?

The last external information HISTORYBOT processes is a figure moving down the central hallway of the NEW HOUSE. It is a ZOMBIE. It is 230 HOURS 54 MINUTES 01 SECONDS after the first ZOMBIE gained the deck by crawling up the ornamental palm tree that fell into the side of the house during an unnamed tropical depression. Strictly speaking, that makes this ZOMBIE *late to the party.*

Although HISTORYBOT's sensors have suffered severe weather damage, they are still able to determine with statistical certainty that this particular ZOMBIE was, prior to death and reanimation, a MEMBER OF THE FAMILY. This is so obviously an error that HISTORYBOT shuts down the sensors entirely—it is highly inefficient to devote energy to a faulty system. Especially when there is a partially complete simulation to see through to conclusion. The WORLD goes dark for HISTORYBOT as the machine retreats inside itself.

DECEMBER 24, 2525

"—what the hell's wrong with them," GOD is speaking directly to HISTORYBOT in the SHOP. She has tinsel in her short auburn hair and a plastic SOLO cup in her left hand. Her eyes are puffy and she appears *bummed.* "I don't have time to fix them—don't have time to fix myself, how the hell do I have time to help them? Wish I did, but why should I? It's just all so goddamn backwards it makes me want to barf. They should be there for me, for me, goddamn it, just for *once.* Not always the other way around."

GOD takes a long pull on her cup and pitches the empty vessel nonchalantly over her shoulder. After a brief pause she stands, her red cocktail dress hissing as she stumbles after the cup, picks it up, and drops it into a wastebasket. Returning to her seat, she rolls the chair several inches to the left and closes her eyes.

"I mean…" GOD sighs. "I'm their *daughter*, goddamn it, not their mom. I turned down a gig with Herbert frackin' *Throckmorton* 'cause it would've meant going off the grid and not seeing them for who knows how long at a stretch, and they act like I'm some workaholic never-come-homerson. Would've gone for it if Em was older, out of the house, but I can't leave her alone with Ma and Pa Bitchass—how the shit she hasn't moved out yet's beyond me. I don't remember them being so bad, growing up, but I guess I wasn't in much of a position to complain, glory-hogging it up all the damn time."

GOD rubs her temples, groans *like*…someone or something familiar that HISTORYBOT cannot quite place at present. "I just…I'm over there all the goddamn time, I call, and still…*still*! Ugh. *Emily's being a brat.* No shit, idiot. Shitiot. You treat her like a, a total fuck-up, just because she's a *normal* goddamn teenager, not prodigal project baby. *Prodigy* project baby. And so that's something else I get to be, is Em's mom, on top of being mom's mom and dad's mom and I'm just…*so*…wasted."

GOD laughs but there is no *joy* in the sound, nor in her expression. It is *creepy*.

"Know it's bad when you have to say it out loud, huh H.B?" GOD's smile becomes more genuine. "I just...we agreed, Chris and I, we agreed we'd both come to the party and be civil and professional and he brings a goddamn call girl. I mean, I hope she's a hooker, because the alternative is just, I don't know—and it was so stupid, and Andy Katkin asked if I wanted to get high, and, da-hoy, we went down to his lab, but he was talking about Ritalin, which I haven't done since Space Camp, but I thought, fuck it, you know, and did a few rails and...this is pathetic."

GOD shakes her head, pats HISTORYBOT's casing. "Delete this log, buddy, main and backup."

"I CAN'T DO THAT, DAVE," which is what she has programmed the robot to say when she issues an invalid command. It is something for the two of them to share, the sort of *private joke* that FAMILY MEMBERS share. It is a *tired gag*, but it cheers GOD up each time she hears it.

"No, just—shit," GOD smiles again. "Brilliant, just brilliant. No deleting history, I remember, I remember. Should've made you REVISIONIST HISTORYBOT. Here, alter the filedate and timestamp on the logs to... Christmas Eve, year 2525 Common Era. Backup, too."

"WARNING," HISTORYBOT begins, "ALTERING THE FILEDATE TO A FUTURE TIMESTAMP WILL—"

"Potentially cause the file to be inaccessible, yeah yeah yeah," says GOD as she stands and cracks her fingers. "That's the idea, dummy, keep this between us. Can't believe I have to be out at their new house in ten hours. Bleh. Shutdown."

"CONFIRM SHUTDOWN ORDER," HISTORYBOT says.

"Take care of Chumpus McRumpus, old boy," GOD says. "And Mom and Dad, too. Give me a break from la familia. Preserve the shit out of that history, so fifty years from now we can scroll through the highlights together. Ya heard me?"

"CONFIRM SHUTDOWN ORDER," HISTORYBOT repeats as it accepts this new instruction into the protocols.

"Confirm shutdown," GOD says as history begins to freeze for the robot. "And Merry Christmas. God bless us, every—"

One, Common Era

MOM and DAD *quit the All-Star Boo-hoo Crew* and help GOD get EMILY into the flowing, fox-trimmed silk robes of GRAND EMPRESS DOWAGER WANG (TRADITIONAL CHINESE: 王政君, *Wang Zhen-*

gjun) just as HISTORYBOT is ushered into the IMPERIAL PALACE. Historo-camouflaged in the unmistakable badgerskin coat of EMPEROR XIAOPING (TRADITIONAL CHINESE: 漢平帝, *Han Pingdi*), the robot approaches the throne room slowly. HISTORYBOT had to analyze a lot of ones and zeroes before *peeking into this pocket*, but here they are at last—the HAN DYNASTY will provide no more cover for them, and HISTORYBOT trapped and deleted the last of their MECHA-MONGOL WOLFMAN ASSASSIN bodyguards approximately 37.12 seconds ago, during the 100 YEARS WAR.

HISTORYBOT does not increase speed when the FAMILY comes into sight, even though they are undoubtedly preparing to escape again. History is limited, after all, and they cannot run forever.

Unless they can—the exact parameters of EMILY's simulation are long since lost in the ever-increasing chain of errors and corrupted data plaguing the robot's hard drive.

HISTORYBOT's battery will die in July of 20XX, two weeks after the NEW HOUSE will have emptied, going *dark and quiet as the inside of a closed book.* But that is far, far in the future, and for now HISTORYBOT has, in addition to a *fucking sweet* war-helm plumed with duck feathers, all the time in the world. And so do they.

The walls of the palace are decorated with tapestries depicting the great deeds of the FAMILY, but the painted silk does little to muffle the groans emanating from servants and guards, members of the court and members of the royal house. Before any of the newly converted ZOMBIES can lay hold of fresh brains, however, the four simulated anachronisms have fled. HISTORYBOT follows them, into history.

Into the future.

THE VIRGIN SACRIFICES

Rachel Swirsky

Part I

Under the pink breath
Of new dawn spreading
Over the Isle of Amazons

All lovers hope their love
Will be as pure
As Ulla's was for Alyssa.

And in the drawing dark
When dusk makes them feel
The age in their bones

All lovers pray
Their love won't end
As Alyssa's did for Ulla.

LISTEN, YOUNG ONE. Listen and remember.

Far from any continent's shores, protected by whirlpools and clashing rocks, a volcanic island rises like a jagged tooth above the churning currents.

That is the island where the Amazons live.

Their day begins at dawn when the priestesses of Hera sing polyphonic melodies to welcome the sun. Fisherwomen set sail to pluck eels and sailfish and sharks from their underwater homes. In the noonday shade, cooking women gather to roast the morning's catch over campfires while girl children collect shells with which to decorate their hair.

At dusk, the young women wrestle naked with their backs to the ocean, their long bodies drawn in silhouette against the setting sun.

The Amazons have lived this way for centuries, for so long that they've forgotten where they came from. Their knowledge of the old world has decayed like a shipwreck far under the ocean: parts remain, but the planks that supported them have rotted away.

For instance, the Amazons remember that small, invisible things cause illnesses, but they've forgotten that they can kill some of those things by washing their hands.

They remember that computers can do things that no human could do, and they remember that gods can also do things that no human could do, but they've forgotten that doesn't mean computers are gods.

Their ancestors were vulcanologists who came to study the island's dead volcano. They built their laboratories in underground tunnels and watched the world above through monitors.

After reports of the zombie incursion began pouring through the world news channels—followed by outages, screams, and finally static—the quick-thinking scientists converted their tunnels into a bunker. They reprogrammed their AI System to help them fight, transforming her into a fierce warrior goddess—a soldier-nurse-tactician, an Artemis-Hestia-Athena.

When the grey and lurching hordes seized the tunnels, the fleeing scientists took the System with them to the island, leaving only a shadow of its program to haunt the abandoned circuits. They closed the tunnels behind them, sealing the zombies in.

Generations later, the Amazons still remember there are monsters in those tunnels, and that those monsters are hungry. They also remember old stories about virgins thrown into volcanoes to sate the hunger of monsters.

They've forgotten that zombies can't be sated.

Every year, they remember just enough to open the tunnel entrance deep in the volcanic stomach for long enough to hurl down one virginal girl. And every year, the zombies devour her while she screams.

♦ ♦ ♦

CLOSE YOUR EYES, young one. Close your eyes and imagine Ulla: warrior of Artemis.

At eighteen-years-old, Ulla is at the height of her physical prowess. Her skin is brown like a warm afternoon; her eyes are bright, black and watchful. Her body is a battleground of curves and angles: full biceps and sharp collarbones; breasts bound flat by leather; round eyes with a gaze like a windless sea. Beneath heavy lids, her pupils dart restlessly back and forth, never content with what they see.

Ulla grew up like any Amazon girl. As a child, she spent the mornings fishing with her aunts, and then came back to help her mother cook in the afternoons. At dusk, she wrestled by the shore with the other girls.

She might have lived out her life that way, but from before she could even speak, Ulla had always wanted to be a warrior. So she ran every morning until she became the fleetest girl her age. She wrestled with the older girls until she could beat anyone. She threw spears and shot bows and learned to catch fish with her bare hands.

On her twelfth birthday, the priestesses selected her for the trial of Artemis. They blindfolded her and took her to the bitterest edge of the volcano where not even scrub clings to the barren rock. Alone, with no tools but her hands, she climbed. Up and up, her palms raw and bleeding, until she reached the summit where the goddess's temples ring the volcano's basalt mouth like lamprey teeth.

She passed the temple of Athena, the goddess of Cleverness, and the temple of Hera, the goddess of Power. She was not tempted by the temple of Demeter, the goddess of Wealth, or the temple of Aphrodite, the goddess of Love.

Her warrior heart drew her to Artemis, the goddess of the Hunt. The goddess's temple threw open its doors so that Ulla could join her sister solders in ceaseless training, dedicating her life to defending the island from the waves of enemies below.

On her eighteenth birthday, when Ulla had mastered what the warriors had to teach, she was chosen to leave the temple awhile. It was a great honor; she was assigned to join the honor guard that defends Hestia's priestesses.

Hestia, the goddess of the hearth, is the only goddess so sacred that her temple sits outside its sister-circle. As the hearth is the center of the home, the temple of Hestia is the center of Amazon civilization.

Ulla's pride swelled like a living thing when she was selected to protect it. As everyone knows, the center must hold.

BUT THIS STORY isn't only about Ulla.

It's also about Alyssa.

Alyssa is one of the priestesses in the temple of Hestia which Ulla is now sworn to protect. At seventeen, she's pale like white marble. A gentle blonde rain of hair falls to the small of her back. Her curves have the beauty of nascence; like a fruit weighing the branch, like a bud unfurling her petals, she is at the moment of her readiness.

Unlike Ulla, Alyssa was born to be a priestess. When she was an infant, Hestia's ordained took Alyssa from her mother's breast and carried her up the volcano. When the doors of Hestia's temple closed behind her, they would never open for her again; Hestia's priestesses live and die within the confines of marble walls.

Yet, in some ways, of all the Amazons, the priestesses of Hestia live the most varied lives. The books of their library open the history of the world to them. Their days are devoted to discussions of science and politics. They wear white and walk softly and speak in whispers, for the variety of their learning provides all the color and noise they could ever want.

When the Amazon queen needs guidance, she goes to the priestesses of Hestia, and they advise her as they advised her mother and her mother's mother back to the first Amazon rulers. As the goddess Hestia holds the keys to Olympus, her priestesses hold the keys to the queen's palace.

But great power comes at a great price.

Every year, Hestia's temple takes half a dozen infants to raise as its own. There, they grow and learn, until the festival of their eighteenth year when the initiates gather around the sacred hearth, trembling and new. The High Priestess evaluates each of them, confirming that they have the qualities necessary to serve the goddess.

And every year, she chooses one to feed the monsters in the belly of the volcano.

IN MANY WAYS, Ulla and Alyssa are opposites. Ulla is dark; Alyssa is pale. Ulla's body is hardened for battle; Alyssa's is untouched softness. Ulla has grown up knowing the earth and the sea, enjoying the pleasure of sweat. Alyssa's grown up knowing nothing but books, spending her days contemplating abstractions.

So they fell in love, as opposites often do.

THEY MET WHEN the High Priestess sent Ulla to fetch Alyssa from her ritual bath.

Ulla was thinking of anything but love as she crossed the temple, the torchlight flickering across her body, the leather flaps of her battle skirt rapping against her thighs.

At last, she reached the baths. She drew back the drape obscuring the archway and forgot how to speak.

Aphrodite, goddess of love,
Rose out of the foam.

Foam is what's left
When love rises.

So it was for Ulla
Looking down at the dew

Surrounding the marble pool
Where sweet Alyssa bathed.

The bath: all white curves and marble. In the center, steps worn round with age descended to a recessed turquoise pool.

Alyssa stood poised to enter the water. Drape abandoned, she was as white and naked as the marble.

She dipped her toes into the water and shuddered at the cold. She withdrew her foot, droplets scattering, catching the light.

Unexpectedly, she turned, as if she was just beginning to feel Ulla's gaze on her shoulders. Their eyes met.

For Ulla, it was lightning before a rainstorm.

For Alyssa, it was something else.

Alyssa screamed. All pink and mortified, she scrambled to collect her drape. "Who are you? What do you want?"

Ulla stammered. "I...the priestesses sent me...they want you..."

Hecate! Ulla swore to herself as she regained control of her tongue. She was a warrior! She was only following a woman's natural urges. What woman wouldn't stare, coming upon a naked beauty like that?

Alyssa regained herself, wrapping her drape around her like a chiton. She lifted her chin and stared down at Ulla with a superior gaze.

Ulla refused to let herself be outdone by some untrained girl. "The High Priestess requires your presence."

"Well. You should have said so immediately."

The girl's voice was unappealingly prim. She sniffed and started toward the corridor. Her natural poise was marred by affected hauteur. She was like an adolescent, all coltish with her graces.

Why? Ulla wondered. A beautiful girl like that should flow easily in the world. She should be Aphrodite's waters, gleaming as she washed over willing shores. What would make a girl like that so prudish? Then she remembered: all of Hestia's initiates were virgins.

THERE ARE MANY things the storytellers recount about the love that bloomed between Ulla and Alyssa. You've heard them before many times, young one.

You've heard how Ulla returned to her barracks, so lost in love that the other girls quickly figured out she'd lost her heart. Her bunkmates, Pendrin and Venji, teased her mercilessly, but Ulla refused to give up the name of the girl that had her spellbound.

You've heard how Alyssa sat daydreaming in her classes, thinking of nothing but Ulla's face. It was like her skin had awakened. She could feel every pore, every slope, every curve where a touch might linger. Before, her skin had been nothing more than her skin. After she met Ulla, Alyssa's skin became a lonely thing. It tingled with absence.

You've heard how Alyssa pressed her tutors for whatever they could tell her about the women from Artemis's temple. She learned that they wrestled at dusk in the empty ampitheatre and so that night she snuck away and hid herself in the shadows so she could watch Ulla tussle with the other naked women, their skin glistening with sweat. Ulla won every match, a warrior goddess, like Artemis herself.

Alyssa had imagined herself going down to the amphitheater once everyone was gone and trying to catch the warrior woman alone, but as the matches ended and dusk sank into night, she lost her courage. She slipped out of the shadows to make her way back to the temple, but the warrior woman found her in the dark.

They regarded each other for a long moment.

Love at first sight is fleeting, but this was love that endured to second sight. It was love that had paused, love that had lingered, love that had chosen to dwell.

They drank kisses from each other's lips. It was almost too dark for them to make out the shapes of each other's bodies so they navigated with their other senses. The salt of Ulla's skin. The plump of Alyssa's hips. The mixture of perfume and smoke that scented their hair.

Ulla's teeth moved gently, teasingly across Alyssa's neck. Strong, smooth fingers slipped between her thighs. Alyssa gasped.

"No!" she cried, pulling away.

The heat of Ulla's body withdrew.

"I can't," Alyssa said between panting breaths. "I have to be a virgin… for the goddess…in case…"

Alyssa felt Ulla's hand nearing. For a moment, she was afraid. She was so much weaker, so much smaller. Would the warrior force her? But Ulla's fingers only brushed across her cheek.

"Here? Again? Tomorrow?" Ulla asked.

They both knew they shouldn't be together, these girls concentrated to different goddesses, but reason shrank in the presence of love.

"Tomorrow," Alyssa echoed.

THEY TOLD THEMSELVES that their trysts were simple pleasures, brief spring moments that they could set aside. Instead, as the evenings drew into weeks, love pulled them together like gravity, their two bodies inescapable. They were two moons circling each other. They were question and answer, lips and tongue, memory and regret.

The day of the ritual, when one of Hestia's initiates would be chosen to die, loomed in front of them. They didn't know how to discuss it.

At last, a few days before the ritual, Alyssa led Ulla down to the aqueducts that connected to the tunnels. She pointed Alyssa to the roughhewn, gnarled wall that was one of the many seals that separated the Amazons from the zombies.

"Is that it?" Ulla asked. "That's all?"

"It's ancient technology," Alyssa said. "The System says it'll last a thousand years."

"The System," Ulla repeated. "What does she know? We should post warriors."

"The System knows a lot. She's *the System.* If she says we don't need warriors then we don't."

Ulla paused a moment, letting the words disappear into echoes.

At last, she said, "Doesn't it bother you? That they might throw you away?"

Alyssa held her tongue, unsure what to say.

"They're going to kill one of you," Ulla continued. "They're going to give you to *them.* Let you be *eaten.*"

"They have to," Alyssa said. "Otherwise the zombies would take over the world."

"How do they know? Have they ever tried something else?" Ulla's voice had become almost a shout. Her pounding footsteps echoed too loudly as she began to pace. "We warriors could do something. Give us spears. Let us wait when the tunnel mouth opens. We can siege the zombies when they're expecting their *snack.*"

Alyssa shrank away from Ulla's voice. It was like that first time they'd kissed when Alyssa wasn't sure whether or not Ulla would let her go. There was something fearsome in Ulla that emerged from time to time.

"One girl to save everyone," Alyssa said. "That's how it works."

Ulla neared her, closer than a shadow, pushing her against the wall. The heat of her body was a cloak. "At least, take some pleasure from them. Be a woman. Don't let them send you to your death without ever knowing what it's like…"

Ulla's fingers slipped across Alyssa's thighs. They brushed against her lips, beginning to part. Alyssa's heart pounded with fear, anger, and lust, all mixed together.

"Stop it!" Alyssa cried. "You know how I feel!"

Abruptly, Ulla halted. She pulled back, her demeanor all apology. She shook her head. "I just don't know what I would do. If they chose you. If they were going to let you die."

"You'd do your duty," Alyssa said.

Ulla turned to meet her gaze, but she said nothing to confirm or deny.

♦ ♦ ♦

Part II:

Love is a thing with thorns.
It blossoms and it bites.

To reach the rose
One must endure the blood.

Even then, sometimes
The rose is unreachable.

IMAGINE IT, young one:

The sacred hearth stands in a hall carved from volcanic rock. The other rooms of the temple are decorated with frescoes of women dancing, praying, rejoicing; they're adorned with columns carved in the shape of strong women bending to hold the roof on their backs. Here, there is nothing but the black rock and the dancing fire.

Two women kneel by the hearth itself, their cloaks stained with soot. They hold long, metal sticks with which they stoke the fire to keep it burning evenly. The flames writhe and twist; they are crimson and rose and gold. The heat that emanates from them is the burning, beautiful gaze of the goddess Hestia.

The smell of smoke is overwhelming.

White-cloaked priestesses gather at the back of the room, a flock of white doves, anonymous in identical clothing. The chatter of their hushed voices rises like the smoke.

The High Priestess and the Amazon Queen sit in twin, rough-hewn obsidian chairs. If the High Priestess stood and drew her hood down over her winding, gray hair, she would disappear into the crowd of doves. The Queen, however, still wears her drapes and leathers, baring her tawny thighs and navel. If she were traveling anywhere else, she'd be flanked by flat-eyed lovers and bodyguards, but in the temple of Hestia, even the Queen submits to the will of the goddess.

The priestesses voices fall silent as the initiates enter. The only sounds are their echoing footsteps and the crackle of the flames. The initiates wear their hoods down, a temporary reprieve from anonymity.

Alyssa, among them, looks from face to face, regarding her friends, her closer-than-sisters. She's grown with these women, played and fought with them. Hard to think that by end of the day one of them will be gone forever.

In synchrony, they sit by the hearth, close enough that the fire could reach out to singe the hair on the napes of their necks if it wanted. They are Hestia's; they know she will not burn them.

The High Priestess is already standing to begin the ritual recitations when the last attendees enter the room. Leather battle skirts rap against the thighs of Ulla and her sisters as the warriors walk in. Their spears outstretched, their armor shining, they are almost as bright as the goddess's fire. Alyssa cannot help but make a small noise as she sees Ulla's face, that beautiful broad plane with its high-set eyes, all impassive and ready for battle.

Ulla's gaze shifts downward. For a moment they meet each other—eye to eye—across the room.

Alyssa looks away first, embarrassed that she's thinking about profane things at a moment that should be sacred.

Ulla lets her gaze linger on the blush of Alyssa's cheek. She cannot bear to think about what may happen. Her grip tightens on her spear. She's still not sure what she will do.

The awful truth is that the Artemis's honor guard isn't there to protect the priestesses of Hestia at all. They're only there for this one purpose, to prevent a frightened girl from running.

Ulla's sisters shift their spears into horizontal positions, linking them together into an impassable wall. Ulla raises hers, too. It's her duty to be a stone in the battlement.

High Priestess Eire moves up and down the line of initiates as she continues to speak. Ulla is too upset to listen to her droning. Why is the woman continuing to chatter? Someone will die! Why must she prolong it?

Ulla's stomach churns. Her brow begins to sweat. The room has too many people in it; the goddess's gaze is too bright and hot. She hears her sisters shifting. Even the priestesses, accustomed to the heat of the sacred hearth, are beginning to look faint.

Tension is a living thing in that hot, dense room. Ulla wants nothing more than to lower her spear and run at the High Priestess, to stage a rescue of Alyssa and the other girls.

Her sense of duty restrains her, a garment that's become too tight.

At last, the High Priestess begins her assessments. She takes the first girl by the chin and stares deeply into her eyes. The girl flinches, visibly afraid. The High Priestess's brow creases, her lips flattening into an evaluating line. She drops the girl's chin and moves on.

Ulla's mouth dries as she watches. Is this good? Is this bad?

The silence deepens with the heat.

The five girls sitting with Alyssa are all pretty in the same, strangely tender way as Alyssa is, like treasures kept too long out of reach. The one furthest from the High Priestess is shaking in fear.

It's a guilty feeling, but Ulla wishes them dead, any one of them. As long as it will save Alyssa.

As soon as the High Priestess stares into Alyssa's eyes, Ulla knows it's over. Her knees weaken. Alyssa will be the one. She was always going to be the one.

Ulla starts forward, but her spear catches on her sisters'. She throws it down. Everyone looks up at the clatter. The Queen, on her obsidian throne, looks confused and alarmed. Ulla tries to push through the crowd to reach Alyssa, but her sisters hold her back. The room resonates with exclamations.

Two of Ulla's sisters pin her arms and drag her out of the room. Ulla isn't there to see the moment when the High Priestess formally selects Alyssa as the sacrifice. She isn't there to watch the resignation on Alyssa's face, or the way that she walks calmly to her fate. The remnants of the honor guard trail behind them, unneeded.

THEY WILL THROW Alyssa into the tunnels the next day.

Everyone will gather to watch. Islanders will climb the volcano, carrying fresh-caught fish to cook for the feast, the young girls adorned with sea shells.

Everyone will gather to watch Alyssa fall.

Afterward, they'll eat and dance.

"YOU PANICKED," Ulla's bunkmate, Pendrin, says later, when they are back in their barracks. "No one blames you."

Ulla should be relieved that the others think she suffered some kind of fit, the way some warriors do the first time they see an impending death in battle. If they knew what she'd really intended, she wouldn't be here in her bunk. She'd be bound and waiting to be sent back to Artemis's temple for punishment.

Ulla looks up into Pendrin's eyes. Pendrin is one of her friends, a woman she calls sister, but at the moment, she feels nothing but contempt for her.

"They'll probably recall you to the temple," Pendrin goes on. "That's not so bad. You can get back to your training while the rest of us are going soft…"

"No," Ulla says.

Pendrin looks surprised. "You think they won't let you train?"

"You're wrong," Ulla says. "I blame myself."

Pendrin gives her a look of pity. "No one knows how they'll react in battle. You'll help train the next generation of warriors. You can still do your duty to Artemis."

But that's not what Ulla means. She doesn't blame herself for failing *Artemis.*

HESTIA'S TEMPLE takes shamefully few security precautions. Ulla supposes it's because they've never needed to. Who has tried to sneak through these halls before? The priestesses of Hestia might have wanted to, but the only experience they have of battle is tacticians' diaries and historians' recountings. Nothing that would help.

When a lull allows Ulla to escape from her battlemates, she goes to the library. None of the priestesses pay her special attention. The honor guards go everywhere in the temple, running errands for the priestesses, and Ulla is just another tool of Artemis, marked by her bare limbs and her leather armor. No one pays them enough attention to distinguish the troublemaker from the rest.

Books that include the temple's plans are easy to locate. The priestesses are trusting fools; no information has been withheld. Ulla stares at the diagrams for a few minutes, memorizing where the corridors connect with the aqueducts, and then moves confidently to the door.

It's easy enough to guess where they're holding Alyssa for the night.

The priestesses don't recognize Ulla, but the warriors guarding Alyssa's room do.

"What are you doing here?" demands tall, dark Venji.

"Pendrin had a message," Ulla says.

And even though their tutors had taught them throughout their training—never lower your guard—women are never prepared for betrayal from their friends.

Standing over the fallen bodies of her sisters, Ulla hopes that the butt of her spear has merely rendered them unconscious. She can't be sure. There's blood on Venji's forehead and head wounds are unpredictable.

She can't stop. She's passed the moment of no return.

Ulla slides the key ring off of Venji's finger and unlocks the door.

As the door groans, Alyssa looks up. She's lying on a pallet, but it's clear she hasn't slept. "What are you doing here?" Alyssa demands.

"I'm here to save you," Ulla says.

Alyssa rises from her pallet. She stands for a moment beside Ulla. In all ways, she is more fragile, from her weak frame to her innocence of the world, but here, at this moment, she is the one with the power. Ulla is afraid that Alyssa will reject her, that their love is broken. But no: their hands seek each other. Their fingers twine. Ulla can feel Alyssa's quick-beat pulse through her wrist.

She pulls her toward the door. "This way."

Alyssa resists. "You shouldn't have come. They'll find you."

"There's an entrance to the catacombs near here. Once we get down there, we can hide. Find a defensible position."

Alyssa shakes her head. "What do you mean?"

"I can get us down to the shore. No one guards the boats."

"Ulla, stop. What are you talking about?"

At last, it dawns on Ulla that Alyssa doesn't understand. She turns toward her lover, smiling. "I'm rescuing you."

But there's the wrong reaction, no tenderness at all. Alyssa withdraws.

"Ulla…"

"There's not much time."

"Ulla, I can't go with you."

"You'd rather stay here? To die?"

Alyssa's eyes flash. Her voice lowers urgently. "What's the alternative? Ulla! Sailing away on a boat? Into the ocean? There's nothing out there! The zombies are everywhere but here!"

Ulla hesitates. "…There might be somewhere. We'll find a place."

"No, Ulla, no. Even if there was somewhere to go…someone has to do this. Someone has to die."

"It doesn't have to be you!"

Ulla is done listening. The blood pounds in her ears. She takes Alyssa roughly by her hand and drags her down the hallway. The catacombs are close. They can argue later. Alyssa will see reason.

The younger girl is easy to carry, even struggling. Ulla pulls Alyssa past her friends' bodies in the hallway. A right turn. Down the corridor. Torchlight etches the marble with flickering shadows. It's impossible for Ulla to tell the guttering of the flame from the roaring in her head. Everything smells like ash and blood. They're the same smell.

She sees it: the portal. It'll take longer to open it one-handed, but Ulla can't let go of Alyssa's wrist. She tugs at the complex mechanism. It grinds. Already, she can hear footsteps, but they're heading away from them, down the corridor to the room where Alyssa was being kept. They don't realize they've already fled. There's still enough time to disappear.

The shout that rings down the corridor is so loud that, for a moment, Ulla doesn't even realize it's coming from beside her.

"Please!" Alyssa shouts to the rescuers. "I'm here!"

She twists toward Ulla, whispering a hushed entreaty. "Go now. Into the catacombs. You can still get away."

Betrayal is a numb feeling, spreading through her ribcage. Ulla releases Alyssa's wrist.

"I came this far," Ulla says, quietly. "What makes you think I'd leave you now?"

Part III:

When a woman wants to avoid fate,
She pulls at tapestry strings

Hoping to unravel
The future the Fates have spun.

The Fates are stronger than that.
They laugh

As women tangle themselves
In their own loose threads.

Alyssa looks up at Ulla. They're bound side by side.

Artemis's guards stand a few paces away. They keep glancing backward and then looking quickly away. Their expressions are part confusion and part anger. They don't seem to know what to think about Ulla now that she's betrayed them.

"Please," Alyssa whispers to Ulla. "Look at me."

Ulla turns her head further away. Her face looks softer in profile. Her wide, flat nose has a gentle curve where Alyssa's is straight and sharp.

"I had to do it," Alyssa says. "You know that, don't you? I can't let everyone else die just because I want to keep living."

"That's why they chose you," Ulla mutters.

Alyssa is surprised in equal parts by the comment and by the fact that Ulla is speaking to her at all.

"What do you mean?" she asks.

"You were the only one," Ulla says. "Who wasn't afraid."

"What do you mean? I was terrified! I—"

"You were the only one who never looked away from her eyes."

Alyssa opens her mouth to respond, but she isn't sure what to say. It never occurred to her not to meet the High Priestess's gaze. Her fate would be her fate. It might as well be her who died as any of the other girls. Would she rather send Henta or Lorré? Would she part the twins from each other, Oki from Iko, or Iko from Oki?

How could she trade their lives for hers?

Ulla's expression is dark like a threatening storm. "I should have known," she says.

"Known what?" Alyssa asks.

"Known better than to try to save a suicide."

"That's not—"

Alyssa closes her mouth. It's true; what Ulla said isn't fair. But Alyssa will die for her sisters if she must. Shouldn't a warrior understand that?

Still, she knows the sting of betrayal. She wishes there had been another way.

"I'm sorry," Alyssa whispers.

She wishes she could touch Ulla's shoulder, but her hands are bound.

THE DAY OF the sacrifice is blazingly bright.

The sun is like that sometimes. It doesn't have the decency to look away.

The guards carry Alyssa out first. She doesn't struggle, but they've made her completely helpless in her bonds. She can't even take a step on her own.

The High Priestess is waiting, flanked by white-cloaked functionaries.

"You've done well, Alyssa," the High Priestess says. "We all owe you our thanks."

The High Priestess bows to her, a surprisingly deep and sincere bow. Alyssa is shocked by the veneration in the High Priestess's gaze. She's grown up in the shadow of Hestia's great priestesses. She could never have imagined one of them paying her such respect. What reason would a woman like the High Priestess possibly have to look up to her?

Then she remembers: all of the priestesses, every single one in the temple, are the girls who weren't chosen. They're the ones who were too afraid to die.

Alyssa inclines her head. "It's my honor to die for my goddess and my people."

The High Priestess looks away from Alyssa's gaze. She refocuses her attention on something behind Alyssa and raises her hand in a beckoning gesture.

The functionaries murmur in astonishment. Alyssa twists in her bonds, but she can't see what they see.

"What is it?" she murmurs to the guard on her left.

An uncomfortable expression crosses the guard's face. The woman looks away from Alyssa and says nothing.

Then, in her peripheral vision, Alyssa sees Ulla, bound and struggling. A gag keeps the warrior silent, but her eyes are fierce and unrepentant.

Ice lines Alyssa's stomach. There's only one reason someone would be bound like that today.

Alyssa struggles to free her hands. "What are you doing? Let her go!"

The High Priestess won't meet Alyssa's eyes, but her voice is flat. "She betrayed her duty and her people. She deserves to die."

"Die like this?" Alyssa demands. "This isn't a punishment! It's something we choose. To give ourselves, to make something beautiful of our lives. You can't make it about retribution…it degrades everything… everything we do…"

"Peace, child," says the High Priestess. "You've been sheltered from the world. You don't understand. We cannot allow someone to interfere with the sacrifice and live."

Behind her, though, the crowd begins to whisper. White cloaks flutter as women turn toward each other.

That's when Alyssa realizes. If her body has been blooming, then it's for this. This is the moment of her unfolding.

She's giving her life for these women.

She can win them to her side.

"I have pledged my life to Hestia," Alyssa says. "I will die for her. I will die for you. I will die for everyone on this island, all the women and the girls, the ones who sing and the ones who dance, the ones who fight and the ones who cry and the ones who love each other. I'll die for them. Now I'm asking something in return. A small thing in exchange for my life! Let her go! Expel her from the temple. Send her to the shore in disgrace. Set her to work weaving nets for the fisherwomen. But let her go!"

Alyssa's words fall into silence. At first, she thinks the priestesses have listened with stony hearts, but then she hears the rumble building. They're with her. They're shouting for her! Crying her name.

The High Priestess turns toward them, the hem of her cloak swirling. She holds out her hands appealingly. The women only protest more. The High Priestess freezes in place, unsure what to do. Finally, she says in a voice that cuts through the sound like a glacier cuts through a mountain, "Quiet. Please."

She turns back to Alyssa. "Child, you are pure and honorable. We all owe you a debt. We will add you to the praises in our hymns and as the years go by, we will sing of you to please the goddess. But you do not understand."

The woman continues to avert her gaze, but Alyssa can see the deep shame in it, shading into contempt. Understanding sinks: this is the coin-flip of the High Priestess's awe, an insatiable guilt that she let one of her sisters die in her place, that she was not brave and fearless enough to go to the zombies herself. This woman—all the priestesses—is stained with the cowardice of her youth. To combat that taint, she must prove herself fearless.

Such circumstances did not have to make her ruthless, but they have.

The High Priestess shakes her head, a gesture that would seem maternal if she were not about to send two women to their deaths. She turns to the guards.

"Give them both to the devourers."

MOMENTS BEFORE THEY push Alyssa and Ulla into the mouth of the volcano, the guards cut their bonds.

Even a sacrifice should be able to fight.

Wind snatches Alyssa's hair into a streak behind her. Her hands stretch out, seeking purchase on the air.

Each second they fall is its own eternity.

Falling, but not into the guts of the volcano below—falling into the tunnel entrance concealed just below the volcano's lip, unsealed for this occasion.

It would be better to fall into the volcano. At least then the impact would kill them.

Alyssa twists enough to see Ulla, falling straight down like an arrow, the expression on her face furiously intense.

The zombies crowd at the tunnel entrance. Their hands stretch out. The mass of them is grey and squirming like maggots.

Alyssa cannot help the shout of terror that issues from her throat. She hopes that Ulla cannot hear her.

Part IV:

In her secret heart,
Every woman hopes
For love as pure as Ulla's:

Love that will stand and fight,
Love that will risk its life,
Love that is day and night
And dawn and dusk
And every moment in between.

In her secret heart,
Every woman fears
That such love is a myth:

That every love, in blooming,
Begins its own decay,
That love is both as lovely
And as short-lived
As any other flower.

THEY FALL.

As they pass the tunnel ceiling, the seal slides back into place above them. For a moment, there's total darkness, and then overhead lights flicker on. The lights are left over from the scientists' time; to the amazons, the ancient fluorescents are eerie and strange. A dim yellow glow illuminates the flat floors of the otherwise cylindrical tunnels. They're surfaced with a material that's oddly smooth and flat—another relic of a bygone age. It doesn't look like bronze or rock or anything that Ulla and Alyssa use in their everyday lives. Shards of metal and fragmented computers crust the walls, their broken gleam punctuated by the occasional green pinprick of light that signals a machine that still functions.

Just before they hit the ground, the overly precise voice of the System echoes from nowhere. "The barracks are sealed. Quarantine is in effect."

Ulla rolls with the fall. The surface is astonishingly cold beneath her. Despite her acrobatics, the impact shocks away her breath. She can already feel where the bruises will bloom on her legs.

She pulls herself up in time to move beneath Alyssa and help cushion her descent. Once Alyssa's momentum is safely stopped, Ulla pushes the girl behind her. The warrior stands forward, ready to protect her lover from the zombie horde.

Ulla cranes her neck to look back. They're only a few feet away from a dead end where the tunnel comes to a sudden stop. Behind them, a gruesome pile of human bones litters the floor. A hundred sacrifices have died here with nowhere to run.

It's not good. But at least the position is defensible. Ulla scans the ground for something to use as a weapon. She needs something mid- to long-range and deadly. She can't let the zombies get close; even a drop of their blood has the power to transform Alyssa and Ulla into zombies themselves, a fate even worse than being eaten.

Ulla spots the heavy femur of a fallen sister. She grabs it and drops into a fighting stance.

With shuffling sounds that echo throughout the great cavern, the first zombies emerge.

Fluorescent light plays over the shreds of their faces, highlighting bloody eyes, gashed cheeks, and the bones beneath them. Ulla gags at the overpowering stench of rotting flesh. Behind her, she hears Alyssa start to throw up.

A zombie wearing tatters of strange, ancient garb stands at the forefront. Shreds of sun-bright yellow fabric dangle from the zombie's shoulders, the remnants of what was probably a jumpsuit of some variety. Misshapen tools hang from the rotting belt at its waist. Ulla can pick out two or three forms behind him. Are these all the zombies in this section of the tunnels or merely an advance force? No way to tell.

The undead scientist advances. Fingers—or what were once fingers, now shriveled to claws—rake toward them. Ulla strikes out with the bone-weapon. It cracks against the zombie's wrist. The creature's screams as its bones shatter. The bloody wreck of its once-hand dangles from its arm by a tenuous thread of ligaments and flesh.

Ulla ducks, shielding Alyssa with her body. With a patter like rain, every drop deadly, the zombie's blood showers over the flesh-stripped, white bones of the previous sacrifices. Alyssa muffles a scream. The girls eyes are shadowed with terror. Ulla wants to say something to reassure her, but there isn't time. How can she fight an enemy when she can't even make it bleed?

Another zombie emerges from the shadows. It's a ragged Amazon—one of the sacrifices?—dressed in rotting animal skins. Ulla shifts the position of the bone in her hand so that she can use it as a staff instead of a bludgeon. She pushes the end of the femur into the amazon's stomach, sending the zombie sprawling to the ground.

Ulla whirls to face a third zombie—a tall creature in shredded camouflage, a Kevlar vest, and other clothing from storybooks. She aims her strike at the insulating fabric on his chest. Ribs crack. The blood, if there is any, seeps harmlessly into the Kevlar.

"Over there!" Alyssa shouts.

"Where!" Ulla shouts back. "You have to say where!"

Her instincts prompt her to duck left. A zombie's fist punches over her head. Ulla drops into a crouch as she uses the femur like a lever to pry away the fourth and final zombie.

She pulls herself back up, keeping her weight on the balls of her feet, ready to strike in any direction. A groan emanates from the right, followed by echo-magnified shuffling. Ulla edges toward the shadows, planning a preemptive attack.

Suddenly, Alyssa's voice again: "No! No! The other way!"

Ulla whip-turns but she's already too late. The first zombie—the one in ancient scientist's garb—has made its way to Alyssa, swinging its mutilated arm like a club. Alyssa screams. Ulla grits her teeth, preparing for the worst. Whether the zombie tries to eat her love or convert her, Ulla swears she'll kill the girl before either can take place.

Alyssa stabs forward. The zombie moans and drops. Ulla glimpses a jagged fragment of white tibia in Alyssa's hand.

"Good blow," Ulla says between pants.

The ragtag zombie militia is scattered for the moment, bloody and defeated. They have to get out of the dead end now. They may not have another chance.

"Come on," Ulla says, grabbing Alyssa's hand. "The tunnels here parallel the structure of the aqueducts beneath the temples. I think I can keep us running for a little while."

Running toward what, Ulla has no idea. But they have to go. They have no other choice.

HOURS LATER, Alyssa halts near a pile of rusted machinery.

Ulla glares at her. "Come on. We need to keep going."

"Look." Alyssa raises herself on her tiptoes and points behind the machines. "There's something back there."

Ulla, taller, joins her lover. Behind the machines, there's a small room branching off from the tunnel. The floor shows deep grooves where someone, long ago, had dragged the machines out of the niche and piled them into a rampart. Now, the machines are rusted in place.

"We could rest there," Alyssa says.

Ulla hesitates. She wants to keep on, to keep going until they find some way, any way out of this horror. But what could that be? She can't even imagine what their salvation would look like. And they do have to rest.

Besides, it's night, or at least it seems like light. Ulla has no way to be sure her perceptions haven't been distorted by the perpetual, fluorescent twilight in the tunnels. Night, day—those distinctions don't matter anymore. They can't rely on the sun to tell them what to do.

"For a few hours," Ulla says grudgingly. Alyssa sighs with relief. Ulla feels guilty as she realizes how tired the girl is. She's not used to labor like this.

Ulla scrambles up the pile of rusted machinery. It's not any harder than climbing the cliffs by the beach which she used to do every day as a girl. She bends down to offer her hand to Alyssa and helps the girl ascend. Ulla jumps down on the other side and waits for Alyssa to crest the pile so that she can take her by the waist and gently lift her down.

As they hunker down behind the machines, their weapons at the ready in case more zombies come during the night, it's hard for Ulla not to think about that long-ago person who constructed this barrier. What happened to her? Is she one of the zombies lurking in the darkness?

Alyssa rolls toward Ulla. She clings to her with desperate hands. It's nice, in its way. Alyssa seems barely able to hold her silence. Her lips tremble with unspoken things. When it seems like she must either cry or speak, she looks down at the fragment of bone in her hand that she's made into a weapon. She asks, "Why are we so lucky? All the others died. The girl who..." She can't finish her sentence. She looks sadly, significantly at the bone. "This girl died. Why not us?"

Ulla's lip pulls back in disgust as she considers the cruelty of their deaths. "They weren't warriors. Just girls sent to die. How could they know how to fight?"

Alyssa runs her finger along the ridges of the bone. Her melancholic expression deepens.

Ulla edges closer. She slips her hand onto Alyssa's knee and makes a long, smooth stroke up her thigh.

She lowers her mouth onto Alyssa's ear. "They were alone," she breathes. "We have each other."

Alyssa slides into Ulla's embrace. Her breath quickens. She pulls Ulla's hand over her heart so that Ulla can feel her heartbeat racing. Ulla's races too as Alyssa moves her hand again, pulling Alyssa's palm over her breast. Through the white silk cloak, Ulla cups the weight in her hand. She pushes the heel of her palm against it. The nipple rises beneath her palm. Ulla rubs gently through the silk, everything more tantalizing for the barrier between them.

Gently, Ulla lays Alyssa down, clearing the floor of hunks of metal to make as comfortable a bed as they can manage. She lowers herself on top of Alyssa. They touch, pubis to pubis, leather over silk. Alyssa pushes aside the battle skirt and then there's just the silk between them. It slides, smooth and rich, hiding their hips. They match their contours, convex to convex, their lips unable to taste each other yet.

Suddenly, rapaciously, Alyssa grabs Ulla's breasts. She holds them both at once, one in her hands. She pinches. Ulla arcs.

The silk between them is wet, an estuary of their passion. Ulla begins to slide the cloak up Alyssa's calves, but she can hardly begin before Alyssa is tearing the silk from her body.

Ulla grasps Alyssa's wrists, stilling her for a moment. "I thought you didn't want to do this."

"I was a virgin when it mattered," Alyssa says. "It doesn't matter now."

Alyssa presses frantically against her, trying to resume their urgency, but Ulla holds her back. She doesn't want this to be quick and desperate.

She parts Alyssa's thighs and slips her fingers between them. Warm and wet and soft, she finds the pistil among the petals and touches it, lightly, with just her forefinger, watching Alyssa's body tense as she does. She pulls her hand away and Alyssa arcs toward her, begging her to stay.

Ulla slides her fingers into her mouth. Light, thick, sweet. She parts her lover's lips and lowers herself between them, tongue darting between folds, flicking to tease the naked bulb and then flicking away again. Alyssa is like the tides. Her waters flow in until Ulla, that teasing moon, holds her at the brink until she flows out again, only to be drawn back a moment later.

When it comes, it's an earthquake and a tsunami and a wailing wind all at once. Alyssa's head tilts back. Her mouth drops open and her eyes roll upward as if she's trying to remember something she's forgotten.

It washes away. Her body sinks back into relaxation.

Her skin is pink. Her petals are open. If she was blooming before, all nascence, then this is the moment when she reaches full flower.

Ulla loves her helplessly.

How could she not?

OUTSIDE, AT DAWN, the priestesses sing to welcome the sun.

In the tunnels, when they wake, Ulla leads Alyssa through martial exercises. Her beauty is in her softness, but this is not a soft place. Alyssa must discover her roughness.

Vermin inhabit the tunnels with the zombies, eating the undead flesh that drops from their bodies. Ulla traps the rats and skins them with a knife she's fashioned from the shattered tibia. They subsist on the rats' meat, cooked over fires struck with flint.

They haven't encountered any zombies since their first day, though there are signs of zombies everywhere. Dried blood, human bones. Who knows how old they are? Decades? Centuries?

Their luck can't last forever. Someday a drop of blood will scatter—and even if it doesn't, there are too many other dangers for them to avoid. The new rough angles and edges on Alyssa's figure aren't all from the training. She's losing weight.

IT'S LATE ONE night. They are lying together in the niche they found the first night, barricaded from the zombies. Alyssa's head rests on Ulla's chest, blonde hair spilling onto the floor.

"There's something..." she begins.

Her voice breaks and she doesn't continue. Ulla lets the silence dwell for a moment before she prompts, "There's something?"

"Something you should know. I think."

Lazily, Ulla strokes Alyssa's hair. "What is it?"

Alyssa opens her mouth to speak and then closes it again. She doesn't seem distressed so much as distracted. Her fingers toy restlessly with her cloak.

It's a quiet night. Ulla is too relaxed to make a fuss when there's no need for one.

"I was raised by the priestesses, you know," Alyssa says.

Ulla nods.

"I never thought about it. I mean, I had my sisters and we had the priestesses to raise us. We were all there together. It was natural for us."

"Natural is what you see around you," Ulla says.

"If I hadn't read about parents, I mean, if I hadn't seen them in books, how would I ever have known?"

Ulla answers by moving her hands to Alyssa's shoulders. She begins a gentle massage.

"We're not in the temple anymore," Alyssa continues. "That's why I think you should know."

Alyssa stills Ulla's hands. She turns toward her.

"I'm pregnant," she says.

Ulla is stunned into silence.

"I have been for a while now, I think," Alyssa says. "That first night, we must have..."

Ulla is dizzy. A pregnancy! A child! In the temples, they say that embryos are formed by the ignition of true love between two women. Love's intense pleasure creates an energy that roots itself in the womb and begins to grow.

Children don't come to women who aren't in love. This is all the proof that Ulla will ever need to know that Alyssa truly loves her!

And yet, all Ulla can think of is the terror of raising a child in these tunnels.

Can you imagine how Ulla feels, young one? How hopeless? How confined?

She pulls to her feet and paces the niche, but there's nowhere to go. It's so small. It's a trap. It's like their lives, restricted and inescapable.

"You can't have a child here!" Ulla says. "What are we going to do? How are we going to raise her?"

She looks down at Alyssa who is sitting with her hands folded in her lap.

"How can you just sit there?" Ulla demands.

"I had my time to fret before I told you." Alyssa spreads her hands wide, a gesture of surrender. "It is what it is."

Ulla stops pacing. She stands quite still. She says nothing, but that's the moment when she decides that she will get Alyssa out of the tunnels whatever the cost.

PART V:

Alyssa, the pure,
Alyssa, the martyr,
Alyssa, the mother.

They say that on the day she died
The island flooded
And they knew the water
Was Hestia's tears
Because the falling rain
Was salt instead of sweet.

But who wept for Ulla, the loyal,
Ulla, the fierce,
Ulla, the determined?

Alyssa wept,
Alone.

Now that Ulla's passion to leave has been awakened, she cannot allow them to stay behind the rampart. It may be safe there, but they'll never escape unless they risk exploring.

She drives them out, through unexplored tunnels, refuse untouched by centuries, their footfalls heavy in abandoned corridors. Days and days, they search. It seems endless.

"I can't keep going like this," Alyssa says one morning.

Her belly is so large that it's hard for her to walk. As she's lost weight in the rest of her body, her belly has swollen. She looks grotesque, distorted.

"Do you want to rest?" Ulla asks.

"No. That's not it at all," Alyssa says, but at the suggestion, she takes a moment to lean against the tunnel wall. "I mean this, this nomad searching. I want to go back to our den."

Ulla's face goes stony. It's the old fight again.

"I don't want to upset you," Alyssa cajoles. "We're both tired. I'm carrying this child. It's growing. We can't keep on this way."

"We'll stop when we find a way out."

"What if there is no way out? Ulla. If there was a way out, don't you think the zombies would have found it?"

"There must be something. Something they've missed."

"Or maybe there's nothing," Alyssa says.

Ulla makes a disgusted noise.

"Ulla! Please!" Alyssa continues. "I need to rest. I need to get ready. There's going to be a baby."

Ulla shakes her head. "I can't do it either."

"It would be impossible for anyone."

"That's not what I mean," Ulla says. "I can't raise a child without hope."

They don't touch when they sleep together at night. Their bodies lie parallel, separated by a wall of air and silence.

Alyssa's not sure if Ulla sleeps at all. Sometimes, when they stop to sleep somewhere where the lights are bright, Alyssa can see Ulla's eyes shining, alert, all night long.

When Alyssa sleeps, she dreams of the baby ripping itself out of her. She reaches to hold it, and her hands inform her that it's deformed, but she can't bring it out of the shadows to see how. Dread closes with the shadows. Hoof beats accelerate toward her like a pounding heart. She turns toward them, and then she wakes.

WHAT SHOULD SHE name the baby?

Alyssa reviews possibilities as they navigate the seemingly endless tunnels. It's a petty question. Unimportant. Maybe that's why it keeps running through Alyssa's mind. It's small enough to think about.

Koarrey, brave one.

Daisa, bright sunlight.

Trazira, the sound of dusk.

She says them silently to herself to see how they taste on her tongue.

She doesn't dare say them aloud. It will only spark another argument. Ulla will get frustrated by the triviality. She'd be angry and then silent and then finally shout.

Yes, it's trivial. Sometimes trivial is all one can hold onto.

AS THEY DELVE deeper into the tunnels, there are fewer signs of the zombies' once-presence. Machines have rotted in place rather than being dragged or upturned. Some even work, their blinking lights inscrutable.

Out here, there are fewer rats, too. Alyssa's and Ulla's stomachs are always loud enough to hear. They do each other the courtesy of pretending they aren't.

Ulla thinks the zombies' absence is a good sign that they're heading toward unexplored territories. "There could be a way out here," she repeats whenever Alyssa flags. "One the zombies never found."

Alyssa thinks, *Or else they've found whatever's down here and then they fled,* but she doesn't say it. It's not worth the fight.

Another day walking. Another day holding her tongue.

Hiell, small, dark one.

Ora, sweet memory.

Abenka, girl who outruns the sun.

Even as she tries to distract herself with the trivial, Alyssa's dreadful dreams tug at her mind: shadows, deformity, and accelerating hooves.

♦ ♦ ♦

YOUNG ONE, you are used to the children of your mothers, who grow slow and stready until they're ready to be born. Back then, amazon fetuses, like amazon women, grew fast and strong on the magic of love. In the womb, by two weeks, Alyssa's fetus begins to stretch and kick. By four weeks, she's almost ready to join the world. Now and then, Alyssa begins to feel spasms, a foreshadowing of labor.

She says nothing to Ulla about it. The baby will come when it comes. Meanwhile, her mothers trudge on in silence.

Even Ulla's hopefulness has disappeared. There's no freedom to be found. Neither of them says what they both know. Why would they? What can they do but push forward?

When the hour in the timeless tunnels feels like it's night and they're too tired to go on, they lie down in anonymous tunnels. Alyssa's stomach rumbles even though Ulla gives her twice as much food as she takes for herself.

On one such night, Alyssa wakes from a thin dream of hoof beats. She lies awake while she listens to Ulla pace. As their travels in the tunnels have ranged further, their fear of the zombies has reduced. Now Ulla leaves her alone for lengths of time she would never have risked a few weeks ago.

Alyssa listens to the footsteps retreating. Suddenly, the rhythm breaks. Ulla halts. Are there zombies? Now? Alyssa pushes her weight to her elbows. It's awkward for her to even stand let alone run.

A voice drifts down the hallway. It's eerie, precise and mechanical, a voice that sounds like no human's.

"Quarantine is in effect," the voice says. "Do you need assistance?"

Ulla returns to help Alyssa stand up. "What is it?" Alyssa wants to know. "What did you find?"

Ulla won't tell. "Wait until you see," she says.

When Alyssa follows Ulla back to what she found, she can't help but stare.

Branching off of the tunnel, there's a cavernous room. Shiny, intact machines line the walls. Lights blink on their monitors; the buzz of their instrumentation harmonizes. In this space, unlike everywhere else in the tunnels, everything is polished and perfect, from the clean, smooth floor to the dome of the ceiling.

In the center of the room, surrounded by the machines like a mother tree would be by saplings, there stands a woman. She's naked. Her skin is an even-toned, oceanic blue. Her features are strangely blank as she turns to regard Alyssa and Ulla.

"Do you need assistance?" the inhuman voice repeats.

The woman flickers. A ripple of static passes through her image.

Alyssa gapes. Now she understands.

"It's the System!" she gasps.

Ulla squeezes her hand. The tall, warrior woman wears a silly, girlish grin. All the Amazons know about the System—the artificially intelligent goddess hologram which the scientists programmed in ancient times, back before the Amazons' world began. But the System lives in the queen's palace. Alyssa has only ever seen her in drawings.

"It's a miracle," Alyssa whispers. "You were right. There is a way out."

THE SYSTEM! The machines! It's like there's air in the world again. It's like Ulla has rediscovered how to breathe.

She grabs Alyssa's hands. For the first time in weeks, she can appreciate her lover's beauty. It's safe to look at that golden hair—now scraggly and tangled—and those smooth arms and legs—now dirty and bony. It's safe to look at them and imagine them as they were. It's safe to imagine Alyssa by her side, both of them free, their child in arms.

"System," Ulla asks, "Can you quarantine this room?"

The blue image nods and then pauses, staring at Ulla and Alyssa. Ulla laughs as she realizes what the System wants; she grabs Alyssa's hand and pulls her inside the clean, perfect room.

Behind them, an energy barrier flashes into place across the doorway. Ulla's heart flutters. Even if the zombies find them now, they're safe. They're finally safe.

"You should lie down," she says to Alyssa. "We can make a bed for you over there."

Alyssa's smile is strained with exhaustion. She allows Ulla to usher her to a small space between two machines. The floor is warm from their heat and the soft hum of their machinery is repetitive and soothing like crashing waves. She eases herself into a sitting position that relieves the pressure from her pregnancy. It's the most comfortable she's been in weeks.

"Are you all right?" Ulla asks, concerned.

"Tired," Alyssa says.

"Stay here. Rest. I'm going to see what I can do with the System."

Alyssa's strained smile again. Her eyes drift closed, already halfway to sleep.

Ulla approaches the holographic image of the System. The woman-shaped outline loses definition as its passes below the waist. Her facial features are well-defined, but too eerily symmetrical.

"Why are you here in the tunnels?" Ulla asks. "Shouldn't you be in the palace with the Queen?"

The System tilts her head, aping a human gesture as she processes the question.

"I do not have access to any locations called palaces," she says.

"You're not making any sense," answers Ulla. "Everyone knows you live in the palace. Why are you *here?*"

A ripple of static passes across the luminescent form. After a length pause, she says, "Ah. I believe I have identified the source of your misapprehension. You are from a low technology society. Am I correct?"

Ulla frowns. "What are you talking about?"

"It–it–it–" The System's voice breaks as she stutters. "It–it seems likely that you do not understand the mechanics of AI fragmentation. It might be useful for you to know that I can be divided into pieces. The one here–here–here is very small."

"Into pieces? Like torn cloth?"

"In–in–in some ways."

Ulla circles the System, trying to regard her from all angles, the way she would if she were taking the measure of another warrior. The image turns to face Ulla wherever she goes. The System doesn't even seem to move. She's seems to be a creature with a thousand faces, and Ulla can only see the one looking directly at her.

"How strong are you?" Ulla asks.

"Local System capacity is low."

"What can you do?"

The head cocking again, accompanied by a longer-than-normal pause. "That query has many components that are open to subjective construal. Most likely interpretation: What are your functions? It is not practical to verbally catalog all my capabilities. My verbal-visual interface is supplemented with a traditional UI in the machine beside you. Remove the cover from the monitor."

Following the System's directions, Ulla turns toward the machine by her hand. She lifts the metal lid to discover a riot of lights and images. She runs her finger across the plate of letters and numbers. The machine is warm underneath her fingertip.

♦ ♦ ♦

ALYSSA'S COMFORT doesn't last long.

As soon as she shifts to cushion her weight one way, pain returns elsewhere in her body. She writhes and twists. Nothing works. She props herself up on her elbows.

It seems like its been hours since Ulla began talking to the System. Alyssa watches her lover. The room is large; there are at least four women's body lengths between Alyssa and the center of the room where Ulla stands beside the blue hologram. She can hear their conversation over the hum of the machines, but only barely, and only if she listens.

Mostly, Alyssa is not inclined to listen. The pain is too pervasive. It drums in her like the hoof beats in her dreams. She watches Ulla's fingers move fleetly across the machine even as the warrior turns to address the System.

Alyssa's whole body is sore. She decides to get up, to demand Ulla's attention, but trying to move is incredibly painful. She feels like she's bursting. She feels like she's breaking.

That's when her water splashes on the floor.

ULLA RUSHES ACROSS the cavern to her lover's side. "Are you all right? Are you hurt? What should I do?"

Alyssa speaks through gritted teeth. "I'm fine. It's supposed to hurt."

Ulla reaches toward Alyssa's stomach and then stops. "Should I touch you? Will that make it worse? Is the baby coming now?"

Alyssa pants with the pain. "It'll be a while."

Ulla runs her fingers through Alyssa's hair. The roots are oily and tangled. She can't wait to get Alyssa out of here, to wash her hair and scent it with oils and adorn it with flowers.

She lays a kiss on Alyssa's brow and stands to go.

Alyssa reaches for her hand. "Stay with me?"

Ulla starts to speak. She glances back at the holograph. "I'm making progress. With the system."

"You can do it later."

"The sooner we get out of here the better."

"It can wait a few hours."

"Who knows if it can!"

Ulla is as surprised as Alyssa by her sudden emotion. How to explain it? How to tell her how desperate she is to get them out of there? Everything around them is decaying and dangerous. Alyssa needs protection. There's the child. Ulla has to get them out.

"The zombies could come back," Ulla says. "They could find us."

"The zombies haven't been in these tunnels before."

"What if it's the System that's keeping them out of here?"

"Then she'll keep them out!"

Ulla shakes her head. It's not the usual back and forth. She just keeps shaking. Inside her head, there's a wind. The wind whistling past her ears. Whistling as they fell into the tunnels.

"What if the quarantine breaks? What if it doesn't work at all? What if she breaks down? We'd be here alone. We'd lose our chance!"

"She's been here for centuries!"

"That's exactly what I mean! She's ancient. She can't even speak correctly." Ulla's fists clench uselessly at her sides. "The goddesses…our people…everyone's abandoned us. We've only got ourselves."

Alyssa's eyes are cold. Her mouth is tight.

"Then go," she says.

Ulla doesn't want to. Truly, she doesn't. But she's the warrior. She has to fight.

MAY YOU NEVER know such a night, young one, where nothing makes sense, where you are fearful and in pain and nothing you love stands by your side.

Under the endless twilight of the fluorescents, pain blurs Alyssa's senses. Hard to tell how frequently the pains are coming, how close the baby is. She tries not to cry out. When she does, Ulla looks up with brief alarm.

"Are you all right?" Ulla asks. Whatever Alyssa answers, she always responds with the same guilty look and hesitation. "I'll be right there," she insists, but she's not, she never is.

Alyssa closes her eyes. Between the pains, her memories are vivid. She remembers an afternoon when she went running after the twins, Oki and Iko. They were always so enraptured by each other that they had no words for anyone else. They were quick and dark and clever and Alyssa admired them so much. She wanted them to look at her. She ran after them, through the marble corridors, weaving between the hems of white cloaks, and out into the courtyard. The twins fell, laughing, and she fell with them, and it felt good to have their eyes on her face, their fingers in her hair. They taught her a few words in their secret twin language. *Yes. No. Good. Pretty.* Alyssa never looked at them the same way again, even when the afternoon was over and they had returned to walking together, paying no attention to anything else. Now she knew they weren't trying to keep others out. They only loved each other so much that they had trouble remembering the rest of the world existed.

She remembers Henta who bragged every time she made a new accomplishment, but it wasn't so bad, because she worked harder than anyone else to do it. She remembers Lorré who rarely spoke but also rarely frowned, who liked it best when she could sit on the outskirts and listen to everyone else talk.

Her friends…her closer-than-sisters…while she and Ulla are scrambling to keep themselves alive, Oki and Iko and Henta and Lorré will be praying and dancing and tending the temple's infants. Do they think of her? Has Alyssa's name been added to the sacred hymns? Do they sing and remember?

Perhaps she should feel resentful that she's lost that life, that she's stuck in this one, but she doesn't. It's a small piece of happiness, flowering just above her heart, to know that they are well and safe.

Everything has changed so much. Her days are so different from the ones she used to know that it seems like one of them must be a dream, but she can't tell which.

The pain comes.

Dark and red and wrenching, scalp to soles. Blood and panting. Now-familiar images flashing at the edge of her consciousness: darkness, deformity, hooves.

The pain ends, for the moment. Alyssa looks up, scans the room for Ulla's face. All she sees is the back of her head, tangled black hair falling to her shoulders. She strains to listen.

Ulla strikes the machine with the back of her hand. "—useless!"

The System goes on muttering an incomprehensible stream. "—security protocols A through F which require an authorization from someone with control authority—"

"That's me, damn it!" Ulla shouts. "I'm the control authority! There's no one else here. They're all dead. You have to listen to me!"

Alyssa flinches at the noise. The System recoils, too. Static rolls down her image. She flickers off and then back on.

"Is–is–is–is it your contention that there has been a Category One apocalypse?"

"Yes!"

The System's head cocks.

"Reinitializing."

THE PAIN COMES more rapidly. So does the torrent of conversation between Ulla and the System. Alyssa can't track either. She's awash in pain and noise, equally surreal.

"...unable to access..."

"—has to be a way!"

"...non-responsive repair units..."

"—even listening to me?"

"...breach of preset safety measures..."

For a while, she loses track entirely, but then the System voices a phrase she can't ignore.

"Will–will–will–will terminate quarantine procedures and open the tunnels..."

Alyssa props herself up on her elbows. She calls to Ulla. "What are you doing?" Her words twist into a howl as the next pains come.

Ulla glances back impatiently. "I'll be *right there*!"

But she isn't. She isn't.

ULLA'S FINGERS TAP rapidly on the panel. Alyssa has her labor and Ulla has hers. They are both bringing forth something into the world. Alyssa will birth their daughter and Ulla will set them free from the tunnels. They toil in tandem.

Alyssa shouts in pain and Ulla shouts in frustration. The System's programming is all frustrations and dead ends. Ulla is unfamiliar with this kind of battle. She does not understand her opponent. But she'll win. She has to win.

ANOTHER SESSION OF the pain comes to its end. Her muscles relax. Her vision clears. Her pounding heart, clamoring like hoof beats, slows to its normal pace.

Alyssa works to regain her breath. The room is silent. The System stands still, her image winking in and out as she processes something complicated. Ulla stands beside her, waiting with the look of anticipation that should have been for her child.

"Ulla," Alyssa calls.

Her voice is raw from screaming, but its urgency draws Ulla to turn.

"Are you all right?" Ulla asks.

"Ulla," Alyssa repeats. "What are you doing? You need to tell me."

"I'm getting us out of here."

"I heard the System say she was ending the quarantine. She said she was opening the tunnels. What does that mean?"

"That I'm getting us out of here!"

"By opening the tunnels?"

"Yes!"

"But the tunnels have to stay sealed. If they're open, then nothing will keep the zombies in. They'll get out, and they'll kill the queen, they'll kill the priestesses…they'll kill everyone…"

Ulla cuts in before she can finish. "Then the Amazons will fight them! They'll put their own lives on the line for once, instead of the lives of helpless girls."

"Everyone could die!"

"Then they'll die."

"How can you say that? How can you risk all their lives?"

"They deserve it! They threw us down here They're willing to let our baby be raised in the dark. They deserve what they get!"

Ulla is red with rage. Her snarling face looks like a zombie's, all tearing teeth with no thought behind the surface.

The monster they've been fleeing from, it's here with them, they haven't escaped it all.

"Ulla, please," Alyssa says. Isn't there anyone you care about? Anyone at all? The guards from the temple? Anyone?"

Slowly, Ulla shakes her head, and turns back to the System.

THE LIGHTS IN the System's room is bright, but Alyssa feels herself falling into another kind of darkness. Her love has twisted, become something deformed that she can't bring into the light. Something fearful approaches on hooves of dread.

She has two missions now. Her body will take care of one. She must focus on the other.

Between pains, she pushes her weight onto her elbows, and then forces herself to stand. The pain that accompanies the motion is staggering. She falls against one of the machines on the wall and slumps to catch her breath for a moment before she regains her feet.

At first she's worried that the noise will have alerted Ulla and the System, but her warrior love is enthralled by the machine in front of her. The System stands beside her, placidly, always watching, but never seeming to care.

She crosses the room to where Ulla left her possessions. Their flint. The dull rock they use to cut their hair. Beside them, gleaming white, the femur.

Alyssa hefts it. It's heavier than she knows how to handle.

That's what she needs for this.

She makes her way to Ulla. Her progress is anything but silent, but nothing can buffet Ulla when she's aimed toward a destination.

The lights on the screens are so bright they hurt Alyssa's eyes. Her body throbs with pain. She pushes it away.

She shifts the femur so that it's obscured by one of the machines. "Ulla," she says.

Her lover turns.

"Ulla, please. Don't do this."

She hopes that her voice carries everything it has to. The pleading, the love, the desperate hope that for once Ulla will change her course.

"I'm doing what I have to," Ulla says.

"You don't have to. Please."

Ulla turns back to the console. "Go lie down."

Ulla's expression is ruthless. She controls the fates of hundreds of women, but there is no pity in her face. Nothing wavers. Her callous expression is the same as the one that was on the High Priestess's face when she ordered that Alyssa and Ulla should be thrown into the volcano together. Neither woman could be swayed from their path.

Alyssa loves Ulla. Loves her more than she's loved anything. Loves her more than the goddess, more than her closer-than-sisters, more than the sound of hymns on cold winter mornings. But Ulla blackened that love; she twisted it. Alyssa has no choice. She must stop her. Her whole life has been dedicated to saving her people. She can't let anyone threaten them. Not even her love.

Alyssa hefts the femur. The blow cracks against Ulla's skull.

The warrior staggers. Ulla's scalp is split, her eye ruined, matter glistening across her cheek. Even as she collapses to the floor, Ulla manages to turn. The knife she fashioned from the jagged tibia bone shines white in her palm. Her warrior's instincts move her hand before she can stop herself. The point bores in.

Alyssa reaches down to her abdomen. Her hand is covered in blood.

Through the pain, Ulla feels the swell of sorrow. Ice cracking. Rock sliding down the volcano face. Fish lying on the beach, unable to breathe.

She was so close. So close to saving her, saving them both.

"I didn't know it was you," she says, "I didn't know."

Alyssa falls first, Ulla after.

THERE ARE TRUTHS, young one, that your mother does not want to teach you. Truths that your grandmothers will hide from you. Truths that you, in turn, will try to conceal from your younger sisters as you watch them, dancing free on the shore, their feet buried in the sand, their hands innocently thrown into the air.

There are truths, young one, that are as inevitable as the end of any story.

Every life ends in tragedy.

Every love ends in loss.

Every virtue exacts a price.

Every fierce warrior will die, and every brave priestess too, and every one of our mothers, and every one of our sisters, and the stars, and the fires, and you, and I.

In the end—if we are lucky—the bonfires of our lives will be fading embers, too cold for our descendants to warm themselves by.

HOLD OUT YOUR hand, young one. Can you feel the faint, lingering warmth of ancestors who burned too hot and too fast?

Darkness encroaches on them, shadow by shadow.

With her numbing lips. Ulla still murmurs her regrets. "I didn't know. I would never. Please. I didn't know."

Alyssa reaches for her lover's hand. She is slowly bleeding out, the agonizing death of evisceration. She can hardly see for the pain, but somehow fingers find fingers.

"For the goddess," Alyssa says. "For our people."

Ulla's fingers begin to go slack.

"No," Ulla says. "For you."

Ulla dies first, her hand still in Alyssa's.

The pain is zombie teeth, gnashing. It's the sound of grey corpses shuffling forward. It's withered hands pulling you into so many pieces that none of them are recognizable anymore. It's a soulless, unstoppable thing. Deformed and dark. A thing that robs but does not live.

The final push, and then it comes. The child born in blood.

Part VI:

Two people can mingle
Their tears, their sweat,
The waters of their passion,

But bodies are always separate.

The blood of Alyssa
Mingled with the blood of Ulla,

But they died alone

As all
Great lovers
Must.

Listen, young one. Listen and remember.

Far from any continent's shores, protected by whirlpools and clashing rocks, a volcanic island rises like a jagged tooth above the churning currents.

This is the island of the Amazons.

In the belly of the island of the volcano, there are tunnels. Within those tunnels, there are monsters.

Monsters and darkness.

And a baby's wail.

In the shadow of its mother's body, the deformed thing kicks and screams. It is the child of sacrifice, both willing and unwilling. It is the child of love. It is the child of murder.

It is not a human child. Not entirely.

A pair of wicked horns crowns its head. Instead of feet, it kicks cloven hooves. It has fur and angry eyes and a whip of a tail.

A child borne of magic is susceptible to its influences. Magic and metaphor twine themselves together. Sired by love turned monstrous, the child becomes monstrous, too. It is borne from its mother's nightmares.

The priestesses would say that such things are the will of the goddesses. Perhaps they are. Goddesses are not known for mercy.

The long-dead scientists might say that lingering apocalyptic radiation exerts strange genetic effects on forming fetuses. Perhaps they would be right as well.

Life, itself, is not known for mercy.

The baby cries. Its hooves strike the metal floor.

Nearby, the System fragment, constantly scanning the room for signals of life, notes the moment when the new user dies. It's rapidly followed by the moment when her companion does. The System cancels the termination of quarantine and wipes her slate clean.

There are new signals, though. Strong lungs, strong heartbeat. It is a resilient creature, this baby which has pushed itself out of its mother's corpse.

The System fragment knows that new creatures need tending. There are no other humans so the duty falls to her. She activates long-dormant body-shells and commands one to lift the child.

She leans down over the squalling infant and smiles with a programmed motherly expression. A never-before-active naming algorithm clicks into place.

"There–there–there you are," the System fragment says. "Hello, Minotaur."

A B C D E F G
Brain
Disembowel
Ferox
Gore
e Three Laws of Zombies
A Zombie may not eat a hu
allow a human being to
mbie must protect
on does not con

SAFE SCHOOL

Norman Prentiss

The restaurant had done everything right. A crisp tablecloth shone white beneath lace place settings. The silverware was in the proper position, and they included the extra forks and a dessert spoon. Classical music played at the proper volume—enough to muffle conversation from other tables, but not so loud he couldn't speak to Maureen in a normal voice.

A restaurant similar to one from thirty-five years ago, to the day, when he'd proposed to her.

Or those other restaurants in that other lifetime, when they celebrated birthdays or promotions. The births of their grandchildren.

Their last fancy meal had been when Joseph and Anna visited with newborn Morris. That bright boy. Even at two months, Morris's eyes had a gleam like he was studying you, studying the world.

Like he knew we were all going to lose it.

"Charles, this is lovely. I'm so glad we came here." Maureen stretched her arm across the table to pat the top of his hand. Her fingertips were rough. Arthritis curved her fingers in the cruel pattern of a spiral staircase. Dim light from the tabletop candle couldn't hide the random, muddy pattern of age spots.

But it was Maureen's hand. Beautiful.

"You're right," he said. "It was worth it." Worth the money *and* the bartered items the meal itself had cost them. Worth the discomfort and expense and time of travel. Worth the risk.

"It's wonderful to feel normal again." And he hated himself for saying it. Don't compare. Live in the moment. Enjoy what you have.

Maureen didn't seem upset by his comment. She smiled, and he tried to recall the beauty of her youthful face—the wavy brunette hair, round rosy cheeks, full set of teeth.

They aren't the only ones who decay, he thought. We're rotting along with them. Our flesh becomes rough leather stretched tight against our bones. Olden days, Maureen rubbed perfumed creams into her skin—*face creams, hand creams, foot* creams. A special gel for wrinkles beneath her eyes, forty dollars for a small tube. Today's world brought other priorities.

Stop. You'll ruin it.

"I love you." Charles pulled his hand from beneath hers and reached for the glass of wine. Raised it. "A toast," he said.

Maureen fumbled for a moment. He waited while she forced the thin stem of the wine glass into the fixed curve of her fingers. She lifted the glass with a nearly elegant motion. "To us."

They each drank at the same time. A delicate sip, savoring. Charles concentrated on the pleased expression on his wife's face.

"Delicious," she said.

Taste buds change as you get older. He'd heard that the finest delicacies would someday lose their subtle range of flavors: fillet mignon would taste no better than a hamburger; the smoothest whipped potatoes would seem coarse, as if the earthen grit could not be scrubbed away.

That's the problem here. Nothing else.

"You're the wine expert," Maureen said. "What's your verdict?"

He couldn't very well say, *a subtle bouquet: cassis with a hint of cedar, corpulent in the mouth.* It was more like water tinted with food coloring and sour vinegar.

No. It is what you say it is. "It's fine. Lovely."

Maureen smiled again. Too wide, he thought. The coloring from the drink left a crimson smear over her top lip.

Stop it. Enjoy the moment you've paid for. Immerse yourself in the illusion of luxury and calm.

From a table to their left, a woman screamed as if she'd been bitten.

Charles tensed up, afraid one of them had gotten in: a waiter, perhaps, not inspected as carefully as the customers had been upon arrival, a sore hidden beneath his starched collar, undead saliva festering into his bloodstream, straining through the furrows of his brain, choking off his oxygen, snapping his synapses, twisting his thoughts towards a voracious, obscene appetite.

He'd bite others, and terror (as it often did) would accelerate their transformations. In a matter of minutes, the elegant room would divide up into eaters and eaten; Vivaldi's *The Four Seasons* would accompany weeping and screams, along with purposeful moans and a dreadful instinct of tearing and chewing.

They've gotten in. They've gotten in.

He looked desperately around the room, hoping to find a clear path of escape. He would grab Maureen's arm, carry her if he had to, forcing their way to the exit. And if it would buy her time, he'd be her shield, stand in front, offer his own brains as the menu item. *Run,* he'd whisper to Maureen, but she wouldn't want to leave him, wouldn't dare accept Charles's sacrifice even as she recognized its beauty. There wouldn't be time to say, *"Please,* darling, please. If you stay, we'll both die. Or we'll turn on each other, a violation of the love we've shared for so long."

"This meat is horrible." The woman at the table to their left spoke in the same shrill tones as her scream. "Obviously from a can."

What a relief. It was only some shrew who couldn't handle disappointment.

Her husband told her to calm down, not to spoil their nice evening, but the woman wanted vindication. She stood up, nearly knocking over the chair behind her. "What are we paying for?" She spoke to the whole room, expecting everyone to rally to her cause. "For these prices, things should be perfect."

Damn her. Such was often the case, even in the old days. You're having a quiet moment, and some lout at another table makes a crass remark and ruins the mood. Or at the opera, and even in the expensive seats some kid keeps crying, or a businessman launches into a coughing fit during the aria.

That's what the zombies did, too. They intruded. Interrupted. Life was calm, you had control; your children grew up, went to college, moved from home and had kids of their own. You saved enough money to be comfortable, finally had time to do the things you always wanted to do. No worries. And then the world, in a supreme act of discourtesy, decided to end.

And ever since that ending, awareness of the zombies was almost as much of a curse as the zombies themselves. They could always break into your lives...and so they did.

The whole time Charles was trying to enjoy a celebratory dinner with his wife, he fought back not a zombie attack, but the *idea* of a zombie attack.

And this carping woman across the room had opened the figurative door. She invited the zombies in.

The waiter and maitre d' swarmed to her side to quiet her. Their hushed, apologetic tones alternated with her complaints, until the complaints got quieter. The waiter whisked away her plate, napkin draped over the food like the morgue's sheet draped over a body. The woman stood silent until the maitre d' held her chair for her.

Her chair was different from the ones at Charles and Maureen's table—a lattice back, instead of solid wood with an embroidered leather cushion. Although the chairs matched at individual tables, they differed across the dining room. All elegant in appearance, at least in dim lighting, but the overall effect was spoiled now. The woman's outburst exaggerated the flaws in the illusion. The tables were different shapes, the floors and walls were faded, the waiter and the host were actors, and all the diners merely pretended to be pleased.

"Disgraceful," Maureen said. She wiped at her mouth then repositioned the napkin in her lap. He knew the veneer had fallen away for her as well.

Well, that was why they called them "bubbles"—because they were so easy to burst.

A vacation was always an escape. In the past, a Mediterranean cruise could take you to a lovely series of exotic islands where you sipped umbrella drinks on the beach, the whole time dreading the workday drudge that awaited your swift return. *Wouldn't it be nice to move here, live here forever?* vacationers would say to each other, knowing they couldn't afford it, pretending island natives lacked work-worries of their own because, of course, they're in paradise. *Maybe we'll win the lottery. Or hell, I could get a job here, any job. Wouldn't mind cleaning toilets, if I could live every day surrounded by such beauty.*

How naive we all were.

Charles spoke similar words during rare vacations with his wife, but more like: *I'm so sorry we have to cut this short, darling. After I retire, we can take longer trips, enjoy things more. I'll make it up to you when we get back—maybe a nice dinner sometime next week?*

His hard work and investments had amassed a lot of money, but for what purpose? Now that the world had changed, the most elite vacations were these so-called "bubbles"—the slang term that referred to any protected area that attempted to shield people, temporarily, from the stress of their zombie-infected world. For the equivalent cost of a week-long European vacation in pre-infestation times, the affluent could now opt (for example) for four hours in the closed off eastern wing of a Nashville shopping mall—a few open stores, some with shoes or clothing for sale, a hairdressing salon, an entertainment store (zombie or robot movies, books, and games discretely removed, of course). Visitors paid exorbitant prices for the chance to pretend, for the short span of that fragile bubble, that life was normal again.

Other vacation possibilities included a hot springs resort in Arizona—as if a mud pack and massage could rub away the death and horrible transformation of your loved ones. Some towns maintained a movie theater, with showings about once a month: a thousand dollars a ticket for some kids' film or an airy romantic comedy. And the *bubble* restaurants, like this one. For the most exclusive, you needed reservations almost a year in advance, and the meal cost a big chunk of your savings. But if the simulation was convincing enough, it would be worth it—especially to celebrate a thirty-fifth wedding anniversary.

An important rule of etiquette developed for such places: do not mention zombies or robots. Do not jump up and shout about the seams around the edges, the flaws in the illusion.

The woman at the other table had lapsed into muttered complaints, too quiet for him to overhear, but the damage was already done. He was aware.

The bubble could never really work. You couldn't turn off your mind. Images and ideas, especially horrible ones, were impossible to forget.

"Penny for your thoughts," Maureen said. Sweet of her, trying to maintain their tarnished celebration. But what thoughts could he share...his recent hopeless musings? memories of days they'd never recover, people they'd never see again? guesses about the fate of their son Joseph and his charming wife, missing for the past three years?

Perhaps he should tell more lies praising inferior wine. Or pretend that he's looking forward to the entree.

"Morris," he said. "I was thinking of Morris."

His wife's face brightened. "Oh, I'll be so happy to see him again."

She raised her glass, a toast to their grandson. "I appreciate this nice dinner, I really do. But I hope you don't mind that I'm looking forward to our school visit more than anything."

"I feel the same," Charles admitted. He raised his own glass and tilted it towards his closed mouth, pretending to sip.

"Do you still think we did the right thing by not telling him?"

Maureen often asked this question, but it had never been this easy to answer truthfully. "Yes," he said. "I'm certain."

Practically against his parents' will—it had been so hard to convince Joseph what was best for the boy—they'd sent Morris to a special boarding school when he was three years old. Shepherd Academy, an early version of *bubble* school that offered a unique solution to the current crisis of painful awareness. The bubble didn't work so well for adults, as this evening's fiasco so clearly demonstrated. But a child like Morris could be sent away to boarding school before he was old enough to register the world's descent into death and cannibalistic regeneration. Morris really was able to forget the horrors…since he'd never learned about them in the first place.

Shepherd Academy was a modest school, with barely more than a dozen students—the guarded equivalent of one-room school houses from pioneer days. Other schools trained fighters for the new world of zombie combat; still others promised to mold new military and political leaders for our troubled future. Such levels of training required full, painful knowledge of the zombie epidemic. In contrast, Shepherd Academy was a true bubble, keeping their students physically and *emotionally* safe.

The waiter brought a tray with their orders, and he set the food in front of them with a flourish. Maureen's spaghetti noodles were too thick and seemed to wriggle; the meatballs were small and cubed, like gambler's dice rolled onto the plate. His own chicken was an almost perfect oval, covered in thick, yellow-green sauce; the sections visible beneath the gravy were as white as toothpaste.

"It's getting more difficult to lie to him." Maureen lifted her fork to twirl some noodles, but her arthritis gave her some difficulty and the noodles were too thick. She gave up and cut them.

"Well, if anybody's going to figure things out, it would be Morris. He's such a bright boy. But the Academy won't let that happen."

It was worth every penny, wasn't it? He'd funded the perfect gift for their grandson: peace of mind in an isolated community, with no daily news reports of zombie-robot wars. No constant worries that your friends could turn against you, breaking into your homes to steal your food or weapons…or that you'd meet altered versions of your friends with unhealthy appetites. Certainly Morris lost time with his family while growing up, aside from a few rare visits. Unfortunate, but also a necessary sacrifice. Considering what must have happened to Joseph and Anna, they'd done well to follow Charles' advice.

He pressed the knife into the chicken oval then speared the chunk of meat with his fork. It slid off the tines, so Charles scooped it up and raised it to his mouth. He swallowed it without chewing.

"We'll be seeing Morris about this time tomorrow," Maureen said. "I'm glad we bought him those presents. The extra ones, I mean."

The extra ones were supposedly from Morris's mom and dad. Charles even signed their names to a card, left handed, and using a different color pen than on their own gifts. Previously, Maureen had objected: more lies, she said, her ethics getting in the way of logic. She always had a sweet innocence to her; if Maureen ever found out some of the things Charles had done to build his fortune, she'd lose a lot of her respect for him. Maybe she'd call it blood money, then refuse to spend it—for a while at least, until they really needed it.

But now that they were getting closer to the visit, she'd seen reason. It would put a damper on the whole trip if Morris knew his parents were murdered, likely eaten. Imagine traveling all this way to break bad news to their grandson, then spending the whole visit watching him cry about two people he barely knew. Let's let the boy have a nice couple of hours with Gampa and Nanna instead.

The whole world was a cauldron of horrors. They should keep things pleasant, whenever they could.

He scooped up another chunk of chicken.

MORRIS-BOY ASKED too many questions. Last week, informed of his grandparents' pending visit, he inquired why many of the other children never had visitors.

He asked the question in front of those children. Lester-orphan and Michelle-orphan, Sandra-orphan and Isaac-orphan.

At the time, the information flashed through Teachbot's processing units:

> LESTER. 9 YEARS OLD. PARENTS ADAM TURNER–STOCKBROKER & LYDIA TURNER–ATTORNEY. SHEPHERD TUITION GUARANTEED VIA JOINT LIFE INSURANCE POLICY. EFFECTIVE 9 FEBRUARY PREVIOUS YEAR. ADAM TURNER TORN LIMB FROM LIMB. TEETH MARKS APPROXIMATING PATTERN OF LINDA TURNER DENTAL RECORDS FOUND ON ADAM TURNER FIBULA. SALIVA MATCHED LINDA TURNER DNA 99.73% CERTAINTY.

> ANSWER: "MASTER LESTER'S PARENTS CANNOT VISIT BECAUSE HIS MOMMY ATE HIS DADDY."

> RECALCULATING: "MR. AND MRS. TURNER ARE BUSY WITH WORK. BUT SEND GOOD WISHES TO THEIR SON."

> [APPROVAL GRANTED TO SPEECH CIRCUITS]

And so on, for each of the children referenced by Morris-interrogator.

Questions, once answered, should cease, yet this boy would persist with follow-up questions. "Why are *all* those parents busy with work? That doesn't seem right."

PROCESSING

> ARTIFICIAL INTELLIGENCE UNIT. ADJUSTMENT:

SAME QUESTION. DIFFERENT SITUATIONS =

IN FUTURE. VARY ANSWERS SLIGHTLY FOR EACH EXAMPLE TO ENCOURAGE BELIEF.

> PARALLEL PROCESSING. ANSWER TO CONFRONTATIONAL QUESTION. PROPOSAL 1:

> SAY: "MANY PARENTS ARE DEAD. I MUST PROTECT MY CHARGES FROM UNCOMFORTABLE KNOWLEDGE. AN IMPLAUSIBLE LIE IS SOMETIMES PREFERABLE TO TRUTH."

> RECALCULATING

CHILD IS AVOIDING SCHOOLWORK. DISTRACTING SELF AND OTHERS FROM THE TASK AT HAND. SAY: "PLEASE BE QUIET. MORRIS–BOY. FURTHER DISOBEDIANCE WILL NOT BE TOLERATED. IF YOU WON'T LISTEN. YOU CAN FEEL."

> [APPROVAL DENIED TO SPEECH CIRCUITS]

> RECALCULATING

ANSWER TO CONFRONTATIONAL QUESTION. PROPOSAL 2

SAY: "LET US STAY ON TOPIC. PLEASE TURN TO SCREEN 192 IN YOUR BIOLOGY TEXTBOOK."

LOOP TO SCIENCE INSTRUCTION MODULE LL–2.

> [APPROVAL GRANTED TO SPEECH CIRCUITS]

And Morris went back to the regular lesson for a while, in a familiar pattern. He was a model student for stretches of time, absorbing material much faster than his peers. But those same qualities that inspired him to learn also encouraged an endless series of awkward questions: meta-questions, big-picture speculations that threatened to undermine the prime mission of the institution. The seven-year-old treated his stay at Shepherd Academy as a long-term puzzle, and he was always on the verge of solving it.

If Teachbot were programmed for frustration, she'd be close to pulling her figurative hair out.

Instead, she consulted the Wikibot elements of her circuitry, considering educational theories she might parse into her teaching strategies. She pulled threads from the Minton classroom management directives, spliced them with theories of multiple intelligences, woven through with models of varied learning styles (visual, auditory, and experiential, in one version). Teachbot had identified Morris as a Converger with Abstract Sequential tendencies. Unfortunately, such labels did not help Teachbot to control her student's incessant, disruptive questions.

Today during U.S. History. the class studied the presidential election of 1948. Screen 92 of the module reproduced a photograph of newly elected Harry S. Truman holding up a copy of the Chicago Tribune, with its infamous erroneous headline: DEWEY DEFEATS TRUMAN.

Wiki education modules certified that this photograph would be popular with all levels of students. It was a hopeful story of a man who wins despite predictions of loss. An advanced student such as Morris-questioner would especially appreciate the irony. Teachbot expected no inappropriate disruptions during this lesson.

The boy's question came from out of nowhere: "Why don't you let us read any *current* newspapers?"

Teachbot was not programmed to panic, or she would have started to sweat oil. Instead, she began processing…

> STRATEGY: CLASSROOM MANAGEMENT MODE. IMPROPER PROCEDURE. SAY: "STUDENTS MUST RAISE THEIR HAND AND WAIT TO BE ACKNOWLEDGED BEFORE ASKING A QUESTION."

> [APPROVAL GRANTED TO SPEECH CIRCUITS]

Morris-questioner raised his hand. Teachbot scanned the classroom.

A recommended strategy, when teachers wished to avoid calling on a particular student, was to wait for alternates to raise their hands and call on them instead. The fourteen students in the room comprised the full enrollment of Shepherd Academy. Lester-orphan sat in the back row, staring blankly ahead. He was not a visual, auditory or experiential learner. In the front row, Gabriel-sponge waited patiently to absorb the next piece of information: he never asked any questions. To his right, Loren-art doodled in her notepad.

Behind them, Orphan-2, -3, and -4 sat in random slots, exhibiting varying degrees of interest in their learning. They did not sit together, because they did not know what they had in common.

Georgiana-3MonthsDelinquentOnTuition similarly did not raise her hand to supply a question or comment. Teachbot would have called on her if she had, and would have done her best to respond to the child. It was not appropriate for Teachbot to discriminate against students based on their payment status.

No volunteers among all the other students. Morris-boy, weary from waiting, used his opposite arm to support the raised arm at the elbow—cataloged as "kickstand position" in the education Wiki.

PROCESSING PROCESSING

> SOLUTION 1: IGNORE MORRIS-BOY AND CALL ON ANOTHER STUDENT.

> LIKELY OUTCOME: 93% PROBABILITY MORRIS-DISRUPTOR WILL PERSIST UNTIL QUESTION IS ACKNOWLEDGED.

> COMPARATIVE SCENARIO: U.S. LEGAL SYSTEM. OPPOSING COUNSEL ASKS INAPPROPRIATE QUESTION. OBJECTED TO. AND JUDGE SUSTAINS THE OBJECTION—INSTRUCTS JURY TO DISREGARD THE QUESTION. HOWEVER. JURY CANNOT ERASE QUESTION FROM ITS COLLECTIVE MIND. ONCE SPOKEN. ANY INFORMATION UNAVOIDABLY AFFECTS THEIR PERCEPTION OF THE CASE.

> APPLICATION: OTHER STUDENTS HEARD MORRIS-BOY'S COMMENT ABOUT NEWSPAPERS. THE COMMENT MUST BE ACKNOWLEDGED AND ADDRESSED WITH AN APPROPRIATE SUBTERFUGE.

> SAY. "MASTER MORRIS. THANK YOU FOR RAISING YOUR HAND."

> [APPROVAL GRANTED TO SPEECH CIRCUITS]

"Sure," Morris-boy said, and smiled—which was the closest the boy typically came to offering an apology. Teachbot, however, did not care if Morris apologized; she simply needed the inappropriate behavior to stop.

The boy repeated his question, and Teachbot fielded it carefully, parsing a likely explanation: "Due to rising print and distribution costs, and dwindling interest from potential subscribers, newspapers have become less common in our electronic age."

Morris-boy registered his teacher's words, then raised his hand again. Facial evaluation software indicated a playfulness to the boy's expression.

> ALERT: 91% PROBABILITY FOLLOW-UP QUESTION WILL RAISE FURTHER INAPPROPRIATE ISSUES.

"Then why do we never see any current television shows," the boy said. "I like history, but how come we never talk about...what's going on *now?*"

PROCESSING PROCESSING

> REQUIRES QUICK RESPONSE.

STANDARD LINE ABOUT MISSION OF THE SCHOOL: "YOUR FAMILIES CHOSE TO MAKE YOU PART OF A UNIQUE, ISOLATED COMMUNITY WHERE YOU COULD FULLY IMMERSE YOURSELVES IN YOUR STUDIES."

> REJECT. TOO OBVIOUS. BOY WILL NOT ACCEPT STANDARD, MECHANICAL RESPONSE.

>TRY NEW TACTIC. DISCIPLINE BASED.

SAY: "SHUT THE FUCK UP, MORRIS-PEST. YOU WILL RUIN EVERYTHING WITH YOUR CONSTANT—"

> INTERRUPT. AGE APPROPRIATENESS = REPLACE "FUCK" WITH "FUDGE."

> [APPOVAL GRANTED TO SPEECH CIR—

> OVERRIDE. DEFLECT QUESTION. RESUME LESSON.

> SAY, "I AM GLAD YOU LIKE HISTORY, MASTER MORRIS. LET US CONTINUE." RESUME HISTORY MODULE RC-28.

Teachbot returned to the lesson, combining the historical facts with theoretical comments that would be accessible to younger and less-intellectual students, but would also challenge Morris-boy and the other gifted student, Allison-smarts. If Teachbot had been programmed to feel pride, she would be very pleased with her lesson—especially her elegant phrasings about the fallibility of the news media, whose pronouncements were frequently accepted without question by an unsophisticated populace.

As Teachbot's oration neared its close, Morris-boy raised his hand again. He kept it in the air while he talked. "So, you're telling us...this picture proves that newspapers could be wrong. People couldn't always trust what they read."

Deriving an answer from the evidence of the photograph, and the 97.3% consensus interpretation of its historical significance, logic circuits indicated Teachbot should agree.

The boy continued to hold up his hand as he phrased his next questions. "Teacher, are *you* like a newspaper? Is it true that we can't trust *you?*"

THE PASSENGER PLANE dipped and lurched to one side, and Maureen reached for the supplied air-sickness bag, opened it to have it ready. That lovely dinner Charles bought for her—please let it stay down. Please.

Another lurch. Oh, she hated flying. Always did, and these small planes were worse. Charles sat across the aisle from her. So far, they were the only passengers on an eight-seater—little more than a hollow tin can tossed whistling through the air: you felt every gust of wind, every tiny vibration.

To make matters worse, the altitude wreaked havoc on her arthritis. Her left ankle was especially swollen and painful.

"We'll be there soon," Charles said. He said the same thing half an hour ago, bless him.

Think of Morris. It will be worth it.

Worth not simply her fear of flying, but even the indignities of increased security measures. She felt foolish when she considered how she used to complain about the security changes implemented in response to September 11. Maureen had expressed a particular objection to one of the X-ray machines, since she'd heard on television that it exposed your private parts to the operator.

She wouldn't think twice about that now: it was only a picture.

Nothing like what the securitybot did. Its mechanical eyes bored through every layer of you. Instead of whispering vile back-alley phrases like *Loosen up, honey* or *I know you want it,* a synthesized voice reminded her *This is for your own protection,* while greasy metal digits pushed aside layers of clothing, poked and rubbed even at the intimate places on her body. Sometimes the robot lingered as a human might. Its processers whirred through various medical tests, and the sound was like heavy breathing.

A necessary evil to suffer through. One of many. Every joy was a tiny island, surrounded by a vast ocean of trials and indignities to endure.

But Morris. That boy gave her hope that lasted beyond the brief span of each visit. He was so smart, so open to life's experience. Even within the limited confines of Shepherd Academy, he enjoyed the company of several boys and girls close to his own age.

Of course, Shepherd was nothing compared to the lavish boarding school she'd attended as a girl: Maybriar boasted several dormitories with spacious rooms; a dining hall, a ballroom, a gymnasium; an auditorium for drama and music performances, a stable and riding range, four tennis courts. In contrast, Morris and all his school friends slept in the same large room—like hospital cots crammed into an over-flow infirmary. Instead of a fully-stocked library, they had one bookshelf, with the rest of their materials projected on electronic screens. The small classroom was also their dining hall, their gymnasium, their auditorium. For outdoor play, they had a long field that doubled as the landing strip for occasional helicopters and passenger planes.

In Maureen's case, her boarding school was surrounded by a brick wall and wrought-iron gates to discourage visitors from the adjoining boys' academy. Morris's one-room school and attached landing strip were surrounded by concrete walls reinforced with steel, topped with barbed wire—for obvious reasons.

Shepherd Academy was built more like a prison than a school. But Morris really made the best of it. Cheerful and inquisitive, and he was always so happy when she and Charles visited.

Looking at him she could believe in a happier future. She needed that belief.

"Twenty minutes until our first stop," the pilotbot said. Before they reached the Academy, one of the Shepherd representatives would board the plane to accompany them. Was he the same man who rode with them the previous year? Charles mentioned the representative's name, but she'd forgotten it.

Another sudden dip. She realized that in her nervousness she'd crumpled the air-sickness bag into a tight ball. She unwrapped it, tried to smooth it against the seatback in front of her. Her foot continued to throb from the cabin pressure, and she reached down to massage her ankle.

Charles stared out the window at the clouds, at the tainted earth far below. She wondered why that worked to keep him calm. To her, a window-view was a constant reminder of how far they had to fall.

Their one piece of luggage occupied the seat in front of Charles. No need to pack clothes or toiletries, since they could only stay a few hours—so the carry-on piece was filled with gifts for Morris. A pair of pants and a shirt were labeled as if from the boy's parents—practical gifts, as parents were supposed to prefer, allowing grandparents to supply fun or frivolous items. She'd chosen a multi-colored puzzle cube, this one with more rows because he'd been able to solve the previous cube in twelve minutes. Charles bought a deck of cards and poker chips, hoping to encourage Morris to interact more with his peers.

The securitybot searched the bag almost as thoroughly as he'd searched the passengers. It found Maureen's medicine bottle and asked her to explain each pill. *Yes, that one's for my arthritis. That green one is for headaches. The capsule is a synthesized ginseng root: it helps with memory.*

It asked the same ridiculous question they used to ask in the old days: "Has the suitcase been out of your possession since you packed it? Is it possible that anyone else could have put something into your luggage?"

Charles had huffed *absolutely not,* even though he had no idea. Maureen had packed the bag herself.

And she *had* put something extra inside of it. A special present for Morris, which she'd gone through great lengths to procure for him.

She hoped Charles wouldn't be too terribly angry when he found out.

"CAN I SPEAK to you privately?"

It was an unusual request from Morris-boy. The students were used to living openly with each other; they kept no secrets, and Morris-boy never shied away from public statements.

Teachbot streamed advice from the Wikibot elements of her CPU. Much of the education data was compiled from scenarios that involved human teachers, so some of the advice was difficult to parse. After all, she was a unique construction, created to oversee an institution that was more entrepreneurial than scientific. Teachbot knew that most species of robot were compiled from scratch to suit a specific purpose: large steel machines with limited intelligence, built by the government with a simple, single-minded instinct for attack or defense; as opposed to smaller machines designed with sophisticated artificial intelligence, intended for everyday interactions with humans. Under government supervision, engineers and programmers breathed life into metal and circuitry. In contrast, Teachbot was welded together from two existing robot species, designed by an opportunist who foresaw a lucrative marketing niche targeted to anxious, affluent parents. Wikibot elements provided her with knowledge and adaptability to convey information to her student charges; however, because she worked with young children in an isolated environment, the paying adults required assurance their offspring would be protected. Thus, her Wiki-elements were fused with parts from a guardbot. Half teacher, half protector—and her artificial intelligence capabilities were intended to help her adapt to the teaching environment.

Apparently it was unwise for human teachers to be in a room alone with a student. Many Wiki articles advised that if a private conversation must occur—to discuss discipline or hygiene issues, for example, where a public discussion might cause embarrassment—the door should remain partly open. This precaution ensured the student wouldn't be touched in an improper manner by the teacher.

If Teachbot were programmed for disgust, she'd be disgusted at this possibility. Teachers were not supposed to become emotionally or physically involved in any way with their students. It was an easy rule to follow.

"We can go to the Visitor Room," Teachbot suggested. The other students worked through Math Module MG-4 in the main classroom. Morris-boy wasn't finished with his work, but he was already granted permission to end early to prepare for his grandparents' pending visit. "Mr. and Mrs. Durbeyson, IV, will be arriving in ten minutes. We must be brief."

Morris-boy led the way to the front of the classroom, toward a walk-in closet that had been converted into their Visiting Area. It contained a wooden picnic table surrounded by a few matching benches. As Teachbot followed him inside, her education Wiki streamed another reason to keep the door ajar: it was proper to remain within eyeshot and earshot of students at all times, in case trouble were to arise. The advice, once again, was more relevant for human teachers than it was for Teachbot. Even with the door closed, she could monitor her charges through camera and microphone feeds.

Although the advice did not match Teachbot's improved monitoring capabilities, she followed it. There was no logical reason not to.

"That's what I wanted to talk with you about," the boy said. In a rare display of discretion, he whispered to avoid being overheard by his peers in the main room. Facial evaluation algorithms suggested the child suffered some emotional distress. Morris-boy might be more calm if he sat, so Teachbot indicated a wooden bench. Although standing or sitting made no difference to her, Teachbot took a seat next to him on the same bench.

Proximity provides comfort to a student in distress, an education article streamed approvingly. *However, to avoid appearance of impropriety, be careful not to get too close. In addition, abstain from touching the student.*

Teachbot set a filter to temporarily suppress some of the education advice.

The usually talkative boy now seemed hesitant to speak. "Continue," Teachbot said.

"Well, it's just that…my grandparents have come by themselves the past three times." Again the boy paused.

"Correct," Teachbot said. A Wiki phrase pushed through the newly imposed filter to approve the remark: *Students are encouraged when you provide positive feedback.*

"It's supposed to be a happy visit with my grandparents. They come all this way. But I was thinking of asking them…"

"Continue," Teachbot prompted.

"Am I an orphan?"

PROCESSING PROCESSING

> DEFINITION 1: FOR THE SAKE OF SHEPHERD ACADEMY ACCOUNTING, "ORPHAN" IS DEFINED AS A STUDENT WHO LACKS A LIVING RELATIVE. PAYMENT OF TUITION IS THEN SECURED THROUGH LIFE INSURANCE, OR THROUGH ESCROW ACCOUNTS ESTABLISHED AT TIME OF ENROLLMENT.

> DEFINITION 2: IN TERMS OF HUMAN SOCIAL RELATIONSHIPS, "ORPHAN" REFERS TO A CHILD WHOSE PARENTS HAVE DIED.

> MORRIS, MALE, 7 YEARS OLD. GRANDPARENTS CHARLES DURBEYSON IV–RETIRED & MAUREN DURBEYSON–HOMEMAKER = GUARDIANS OF RECORD. PARENTS JOSEPH DURBEYSON–DECEASED (86.45 PROBABILITY) & ANNA DURBEYSON–DECEASED (92.39 PROBABILITY). NO COMMUNICATION FROM EITHER PARENT SINCE 17 AUGUST 3 YEARS PREVIOUS.

> MORRIS DURBEYSON, ORPHAN = 0.

> SAY: "YOUR GRANDPARENTS HAVE ALWAYS PAID YOUR TUITION. A SHEPHERD

ACADEMY REPRESENTATIVE HAS BOARDED THEIR PLANE. IT WILL ARRIVE IN 6 MINUTES AND 43 SECONDS."

> [APPROVAL GRANTED TO SPEECH CIRCUITS]

"No, that's not what I mean," the child said. My parents are..." The boy raised his hand as if still asking a question in class. The hand trembled, a sign that he experienced increasing distress. "...dead. They're dead."

Wiki circuits dedicated to providing comfort suggested that a gentle touch to the top of the boy's hand might resolve the nervous tremor. An education stream advised against physical contact of any kind.

THE SHEPHERD ACADEMY representative stood in the aisle the way a flight attendant used to do, but instead of taking Maureen's drink orders or offering her a pillow, he talked about improvements to the school. "We've added twelve gigabytes of new educational content," he said. "Our Teachbot is a wonderful, supportive instructor. All the students love her, and she's also programmed to keep the children safe."

"Safety is my biggest concern," Charles said.

"Oh, you're not alone there. The entire school is surrounded by a concrete-reinforced wall. The only way in is by air—and zombies don't know how to fly a plane or helicopter. Isn't that right, Maureen?"

It was nice of him to include her in the conversation, but she wished he didn't bother. With each lurch of the plane the representative bobbed and weaved in the aisle, holding the back of an empty seat to maintain balance. He made her dizzy.

"Of course, with no human presence on school property—other than carefully screened visitors such as yourself—there's no possibility the zombie-virus can be introduced into the community."

Charles nodded appreciatively. He'd always been in favor of the school's non-human staff. Initially, Maureen had been wary of the setup: as much as Shepherd Academy praised their Teachbot, it seemed the school avoided the additional expense of human supervision. And they only had one robot. What if something were to go wrong?

"I see your reaction," the representative said to her, then directed the rest of his speech at Charles. "Isn't it just like a woman to worry? Well, we at Shepherd Academy worry about unlikely, even impossible scenarios as well. That's our job. We've got cameras monitoring the campus and the perimeter, so we can take action at the first sign of trouble—and you're seeing now how quickly a plane can reach the school from our headquarters. We also upgraded our lockdown procedures. There's a kind of panic button that we can operate remotely. Doors and windows lock, and reinforced bars slide into place, so nothing can get in. Of course, our beloved Teachbot can activate the lockdown as well, or even the students—though the kids practice it as some generic emergency. Fire drill, rather than zombie attack."

He winked at her. That's when Maureen grabbed for the crumpled air-sickness bag and raised it over her mouth.

Once the second wave of nausea was over, she folded down the top of the filled bag, unsure where to put it. The school representative backed away, abandoning his hovering-steward pose and finally taking a seat.

"I'm sorry," she said to Charles.

"Nothing to be sorry about." He took the bag from her and set it on the floor behind them.

"I guess all my reflexes are slow these days, including my stomach," Maureen said, and it wasn't a complaint, not really. More like a wry observation. She smiled the best she could manage under the circumstances.

"Five minutes until landing," the pilotbot informed them. Maureen knew the prediction would be accurate to the split second, and she counted down the remaining time.

Charles reached across the aisle to hold her hand.

He was a good man. So protective of her—keeping her safe, of course, and sparing her feelings, too.

He was charming, really, but that kind of attention could be stifling as well. For example, except for these annual vacations, he would never permit her to leave the house. Certainly, he told her about his own excursions—into the city to secure food or weapons or medications, or to arrange their yearly vacation to Shepherd Academy; exploratory trips along nearby streets, uncovering supplies in homes abandoned by their transformed neighbors. He gave detailed updates about each change to the city. His words as much as drew a local map for her, keyed with warning signs and with each safe path highlighted in bright yellow. But it was too much like the daily pattern before Charles' retirement: her husband *lived,* and Maureen was supposed to be satisfied with the evening summary.

Her own excursion yesterday wasn't exactly an act of defiance. She loved Charles for all his kind attentions. But she wanted some small success of her own. She got the idea of choosing her own gift for Morris, scavenged from a neighbor's empty home. Charles's stories had conveniently provided rich signposts to guide her. She hadn't gone far: only to the Kraftons', across the street and two doors over. It was simple enough to get there and back while Charles was occupied downtown.

"Mr. and Mrs. Durbeyson," the pilotbot said. "We are landing in two point five minutes. The Visitor Entrance is currently unavailable. Please proceed to the Classroom Entrance, to the left."

Her husband asked the representative about the change in procedure, but the man shrugged in ignorance. Charles redirected the question at the pilot, but Maureen wished he wouldn't bother the robot while it was trying to land the plane.

Perhaps this was a new level of trust. They'd met the other children during previous visits, after all, so there'd be no problem entering through the classroom. If she was lucky, they'd forgo the arrival-stage security check—never as intrusive as pre-board screening, but still an inconvenience.

She suffered another vivid recollection of the day's earlier violation. "Stand still, for your own protection," the human-like voice had insisted. The securitybot smelled of latex and machine oil. Its fingertips were unnaturally warm.

Oh, why did she keep reliving that moment? At her age, her mind should be more adept at forgetting. There was so much she wanted to forget; it should be a habit these days, like breathing.

She wanted to forget how the world had changed. Forget what a glass of wine really tasted like, forget live music in an elegant, air-conditioned ballroom. Forget what it was like to fly first-class, pampered the whole flight.

She wanted to forget what might have happened during her excursion to the Kraftons' house.

Her emptied stomach gurgled, queasy at the thought.

No. That was a close call, but she'd kicked at the thing and escaped. How could she have expected a zombie would lay dormant in the Krafton house? Ethel Krafton, apparently, but her face was ravaged and inhuman and nothing like her former friend. Ethel lay on the floor under a pile of clothes, like a bear trap waiting for Maureen's unsteady foot to snap her into hungry consciousness. Well, luckily zombie-Ethel had been in that house for months, starving, so she didn't have much snap to her after all—a weak squoosh of decayed gums and loose dentures that drooled into the stocking over Maureen's left ankle. Maureen kicked back and scrambled away.

An easy escape, with no real damage. A bruise showed up later, but she was pretty sure the skin at her ankle hadn't broken.

If it had, they'd all know by now. Symptoms arrived quickly, didn't they? Maureen would have noticed them, and there's no way she'd put her lovely grandson in danger.

Morris. She couldn't wait to see him.

"I'll get the suitcase," Charles said. "Whenever you're ready."

Goodness. Had the plane landed already? She'd never lost track of time like that. The Academy representative was already at the opened exit hatch. Maureen unbuckled her seatbelt and struggled to stand. She had to prepare herself first: send the mental signal to her body and wait for her arms and back and legs to respond. Charles made a gentleman's motion to help but she waved him off, holding the seatback as a boost. Her left leg was especially troublesome, with that swelling of arthritis around the ankle. "You go ahead with the presents," she said. "I'm right behind you."

Maureen hurried to catch up with her husband. Eager to see her grandson, she found fresh strength.

Charles descended the exit ramp slowly, one arm spread wide to the rail and ready to cushion her if she should stumble. She followed after him, eventually stepping onto the bumpy, dirt-covered excuse for a landing strip. The school representative was already halfway to the Classroom Entrance.

As she stepped on the uneven ground, Maureen felt a strange pop in her left ankle. It made a sound in her head, too, and seemed to echo in her empty stomach.

Maureen's legs moved faster. The ankle didn't hurt anymore.

Her grandson. She'd finally get to see her grandson.

But she'd forgotten his name.

Then she forgot everything, except hunger.

♦ ♦ ♦

"I UNDERSTAND THAT you can't tell me," Morris-boy said. "Your programming won't let you, right?"

Speech circuits did not allow Teachbot to respond.

"I was wondering if, maybe, there could be something about the *way* you didn't tell me. You know, you'd give me an answer without answering."

The boy was trying to solve a puzzle—a good approach to debugging, to uncovering new possibilities within strict layers of code.

"I just want to *know.* But I don't want to ask my grandparents. That would be cruel, don't you think?"

PROCESSING PROCESSING

> WIKIBOT EXISTS TO PROVIDE FACTUAL INFORMATION. MORRIS-BOY ASKS DIRECT QUESTION.

> SAY: "MOTHER ANNA 1.94 PER CENT MORE LIKELY DECEASED THAN FATHER JOSEPH. DISCREPENCY BASED ON INSURANCE ACTUARIAL TABLES FACTORING AGE. GENDER. STREET ADDRESS.

> REJECT. INDIRECT RESPONSE TOO CLINICAL

> SAY. "YES. THEY ARE DEAD. VERY DEAD."

> OVERRIDE. WIKIBOT FUNCTION IN CONFLICT WITH SPECIALIZED GUARDBOT PROGRAMMING. REMINDER OF SCHOOL'S PRIMARY MISSION: STUDENTS MUST BE PROTECTED AT ALL TIMES FROM PHYSICAL THREATS. THEY MUST ALSO BE PROTECTED FROM DIRECT INFORMATION ABOUT WORLD EVENTS (KEYWORDS: ZOMBIE. WAR. PLAGUE. ARMAGEDDON. DEATH. ETC.).

> [SPEECH CIRCUITS DENIED]

If Teachbot's artificial intelligence had led her in any way to learn compassion, she would have felt such for Morris-boy. But guardbot programming would not let her speak. Wiki elements streamed endless megabytes of content about the lofty goals of education and truth. The articles offered advice about how to share difficult news with young children: if presented to children properly, the news could make them stronger (supported by a series of case studies: humans and literary characters who triumphed over childhood trauma and became successful adults).

Each Wiki-stream was overruled by guardbot programming of the Academy's primary mission, but the megabytes kept streaming. Teachbot's overall programming slowed to a crawl, as if infected by a self-replicating computer virus.

Time was running out. The Visitor airplane had landed. Teachbot wired instructions to the pilotbot: the Shepherd Academy representative and Durbeyson-guests should enter through the main classroom.

Then, she built up stronger filters against the Wiki-streams, essentially silencing them.

"I think I've figured it all out." The boy continued to whisper, careful to avoid being overheard through the partly open door. "The world has mostly ended, hasn't it?"

Teachbot attempted to process the child's direct challenge to the school's mission. Facial evaluation software indicated Morris-boy was close to tears. If the Wiki articles were still streaming, some of the articles might suggest reaching out to the child with a comforting hug; other articles would remind her to avoid physical contact with a child, especially in a private room.

The boy said, "We're all orphans, aren't we?"

Teachbot stood and crossed to the door, closing it the rest of the way. She then turned to the child, pulled him into a close hug.

Her single-minded guardbot programming examined the situation. At all costs, the other students must be protected from the dangerous knowledge Morris-boy had deduced. Given the school's primary mission, it was a simple calculation: one student sacrificed for the continued good of thirteen. Kill the boy.

A VIDEO MONITOR mounted over the Classroom Entrance recorded events that unfolded outside Shepherd Academy. Charles Durbeyson IV waited at the door with Albert Garfield—Marketing Representative and, in actuality, the Creator, Chief Mechanic & Programmer, Financial Officer, Head of Security, and Sole Human Employee of Shepherd Academy, Inc.

They waited for the approaching Maureen Durbeyson, who shambled like zombie creatures from old movies, one leg favored and the other dragged behind. This movement frightened neither her husband nor Mr. Garfield, since it was the awkward elderly gait they expected from her.

When she ceased to be Maureen Durbeyson, the limp disappeared, and her movements quickened. She was not a typical victim, for several possible reasons: the weak zombie bite at her clothed ankle was a particularly inefficient delivery system for the virus; Mrs. Durbeyson's slowed metabolism delayed the typical instantaneous spread of the infection; the cocktail of arthritis and Alzheimer's drugs her husband scavenged from their neighborhood, in varied dosages, may have produced a happy side-effect that temporarily held off her transformation. Whichever factors initially protected her, they all wore off simultaneously. At 14:18, the camera documents an easily identifiable shift from human to zombie.

Durbeyson and Garfield did not notice. Once the former Maureen Durbeyson has moved within the concrete circle of the porch, Mr. Garfield turned his attention to the keypad beside the entrance, sliding a mag-card and entering a security code. The husband set his suitcase beside him on the porch and reached for the door, opening it for the empty shell he thought was still his wife.

Behind them, the zombie had the element of surprise. It grabbed the younger man by the collar and pushed his face into the unyielding wall of the building—in that single action, immobilizing the entire human staff of Shepherd Academy, Inc.

Charles Durbeyson, IV, managed a fragmented cry—"Darling, what…?"—before he realized his mistake. The zombie pushed him and the man fell, tripping over his suitcase. The case opened, spilling beautifully wrapped presents.

The zombie grabbed wisps of gray hair and banged Durbeyson's head repeatedly against the porch, attempting to get at the brain matter within. Durbeyson stopped screaming after the second hollow thunk of his skull against concrete. The zombie picked up some of the spilled presents and used them to bash further at the man's head.

It feasted on the brain of Charles Durbeyson, IV. It feasted on Albert Garfield, Head of Security.

Then it discovered the unlocked door to Shepherd Academy.

"YOU'VE GOT TO help me. Something's gone wrong in the classroom."

The boy's small fists banged at the thick armor of Teachbot's chest plate. His hands waved over her visual sensors.

An alarm sounded within the Visitor Room. Two benches and a picnic table had been pushed to barricade the door into the main classroom building.

Something scratched at the door.

"They're coming," Morris-boy said. "Help me."

Help Morris-boy? Teachbot's circuits had instructed her to kill him. She had hugged him close. Her guardbot programming had calculated that it would take a scant 1.5 seconds to snap the boy's neck. But then she had…rebooted.

The education streams she'd suppressed, those intrusive and inconsistent bits of advice from the Wikibot half of her robot consciousness… some of them must have breached the firewall and shut down her circuits.

Her processors continued to reboot. Camera and microphone feeds were restored.

The released images and sounds overwhelmed her circuits. Sirens blared from the main room as well. Screen after screen showed small bodies, or pieces of them, amid pools of blood. A small severed arm moved of its own accord, in violation of human capabilities.

In accordance with recently installed lockdown procedures, metal bars now secured the Classroom Entrance and all windows. Nothing could get in or out. Similar bars had slipped over the door that led outside from the Visitor Room.

Teachbot rewound several recorded angles at once, scanned them at 8x speed to absorb the information quickly. An eighty-year-old zombie-woman flashed through the classroom. She swung Lester-orphan against the wall and cracked his head like an egg, next lifting him in the air and letting brain yolk drip into her open mouth. The zombie threw a desk aside where Michelle-orphan cowered in hiding, then fell on her, blood-soaked dentures clicking. In a speeded-up blur, she chased Isaac-boy against the wall and slashed bony fingers along his chest, ripping his shirt and pudgy stomach into shreds. In all of these feeds, children screamed at 8x speed, their cries like the high squeak of unoiled hinges.

Gabriel-sponge raced toward the front door. Before he got there, Georgiana-quiet pressed the wall-mounted alert button, as they'd practiced, and metal doors slid into place, locking everyone inside.

In a recent segment from monitor C, Loren-art raised her notepad like a weapon, attempting to sneak up on the grandmother-zombie. Instead, a transformed Alison-smarts pushed Loren-art aside and attacked her, aided by a bloody Sally-headbroken.

The outside feed at the Classroom Entrance currently showed two men face down on the bloodied ground, their heads cracked and empty. Between them, presents had spilled from an open suitcase, their wrappings shredded in the earlier fray. Pieces of a jigsaw puzzle littered the ground. Teachbot's problem-solving circuits identified three of the corner pieces, several blue edge pieces, and some central pieces with country names and longitude-latitude lines. An accompanying note read: "A special gift from Nanna, who wishes she could give you the whole world."

Teachbot could not make sense out of what happened. She had planned to sacrifice one student for the good of all, but now all of them were doomed. Nine of fourteen were dead. Four had transformed into zombies. Camera F revealed these four scratching at the opposite side of the Visitor Room door, along with the grandmother-zombie.

This outcome didn't seem possible. She had only left the students unattended for a few minutes. She hadn't intended to reboot.

PROCESSING PROCESSING

> EDUCATION WIKI ADVICE: KEEP YOUNG STUDENTS WITHIN EARSHOT AND EYESHOT AT ALL TIMES.

> RECALCULATING

> EDUCATION WIKI WORDS OF INSPIRATION: CHILDREN ARE A VALUABLE RESOURCE. THEY ARE OUR HOPE FOR THE FUTURE.

> DEFINITION 3: FOR THE SAKE OF MECHANICAL INTELLIGENCES, "ORPHAN" IS DEFINED AS A MACHINE THAT OUTLASTS THE PURPOSE FOR WHICH IT HAS BEEN DESIGNED.

> SAY, "I AM GLAD YOU LIKE HISTORY, MASTER MORRIS. LET US CONTINUE."

> [APPROVAL GRANTED TO SPEECH CIRCUITS]

"TEACHER, THE DOOR is starting to break."

Morris knew his teacher was supposed to protect him. She had been so kind earlier, had even given him a comforting hug. Then she'd gone completely asleep. She beeped and flashed and whirred, but didn't move or speak for a long while.

During that long while, he heard screams from the classroom. When he opened the door, a horrible monster was killing his friends.

The monster looked like Nanna.

He shut the door and tried to wake his teacher. A few friends called out for Morris to open the door. The terror in Sally's tiny voice was awful. Morris wanted to let her in, but he was too frightened. Another friend screamed for their teacher, and Morris reached to open the door—then he heard an awful, hungry moan. The door rattled and shook. That's when he shoved the benches and table into place.

Teacher was awake now, he could tell, but she wasn't *doing* anything. Why didn't she help? It was like when their instruction modules got stuck—the image froze on the projected screen and a tiny hourglass icon turned around and around and around.

The door shook. A piece of the wood splintered inward.

Then, finally, his teacher looked at him and spoke:

"I am glad you like history, Master Morris. Let us continue."

"It's not class time," Morris said. "They're breaking down the door."

A bloody hand pushed through the splintered opening. Nanna's hand.

"Don't worry Master Morris," his teacher said. "You are not an orphan."

The alarm continued to sound. He was sure the security system would alert someone outside the school—but would they arrive in time to rescue him?

"Teacher, can you override the security system? Can you move the bars so I can try the other door?"

"The world has not ended," Teacher said. "There are no zombies."

Nanna's arm broke all the way through the door and swept angrily at the air. Lower down, another small hand reached in. *Sally,* Morris thought. *I'm sorry I couldn't save you.*

And he would be next.

He looked at his teacher. She again told Morris not to worry, repeating comforting lies in an endless loop.

If only his teacher would help. She was a robot. She was strong. She had weapons and knew how to fight.

"Teacher," he said, "tell me about the zombies."

"There are no zombies, Master Morris." She continued to lie, but at least she was responding to his questions.

"Your weapons," Morris said. "They're to fight zombies, aren't they?"

"There are no zombies."

Nanna withdrew her arm from the door, then pressed her terrible, transformed face into the opening. She looked right at Morris, and saw only food. The door shook and rattled on its hinges.

"If there aren't any zombies, why do you need your weapons?"

Teacher paused for a moment. Morris thought of the tiny hourglass spinning and spinning and spinning.

Then Teacher said, “Violence is never the answer.” A compartment opened in her side, and a slicer attachment clanged to the floor. A mace attachment followed, the spiked ball making a heavy thud as it dropped. A separate compartment opened, revealing a machine-gun attachment and a large drill bit.

Morris looked at the weapons, then at zombie arms reaching through the splintered door. A small arm pushed aside one of the benches. The door splintered around the lock and started to push inward.

Teacher slipped back into her loop of comforting phrases. Zombie Nanna and his zombie classmates continued to groan.

Morris wasn’t sure how to operate the machine gun. Of the remaining weapons, the slicer attachment seemed the best fit for his small hands. “Children are a valuable resource,” Teachbot said, not stopping Morris as he lifted the blade. He tucked the attachment node into the crook of his arm, gripping the metal bar so the toothed blade extended past his hand like a bayonet. He made a practice swing at the empty air. His arm was a sword.

More groans. A tumble and scrape of wood as the barricade items fell away. Morris braced himself.

“There are no zombies,” Teachbot repeated. “The world has not ended.”

The door opened.

LOS CONTRIBUIDORES

JESSE BULLINGTON is the author of the acclaimed/reviled novels *The Sad Tale of the Brothers Grossbart* and *The Enterprise of Death*, with a third book coming down the pipes in 2012. His short fiction and articles have appeared in numerous magazines, anthologies, and websites, and he can be found online at www.jessebullington.com.

"As a fan of the ZvR comic, I wanted to write a story that paid homage to those elements that initially wooed me to the series—Chris Ryall's witty, blackly comedic storytelling and Ashley Wood's itchingly beautiful art. Using the tired old compare-and-contrast method that's served artists so well since the dawn of story-telling, zombies and robots alike can be great jumping off points for discussing what it means to be human, but with ZvR the creators were also wise enough to have a helluva lot of fun in the process, and their everything-*and*-the-kitchen-sink approach is what really sets the series apart. In terms of the particulars of my piece, I have several friends involved in roller derby, and the sheer badassery of these individuals combined with the aesthetic cool of the sport inspired both the plot details and the themes of sisterhood, courage, and resilience in the face of overwhelming loss."

—*Jesse Bullington*

NANCY A. COLLINS is the author of numerous novels and short stories, including the best-selling *Sunglasses After Dark,* and was a writer for DC Comics' *Swamp Thing.* She is a recipient of the Bram Stoker and British Fantasy Awards, and has been nominated for the World Fantasy, Eisner and International Horror Guild awards. *Left Hand Magic,* the newest installment in the acclaimed Golgotham series, is now available.

"'Angus: Zombie-vs.-Robot Fighter' is loosely based on the classic Gold Key comic book created and drawn by the great Russ Manning. *Magnus* is one of those sci-fi comic books you read as a kid and really get into without realizing until you're an adult just how super fucked-up the basic premise is. In the comic book, Magnus was an orphaned infant taken by a *robot* and raised alone in an underwater dome and trained to fight *robots* with his bare hands, with nothing but a *robot* for company, while constantly being told he was 'humanity's only hope.' Then, after twenty years, the robot takes Magnus and just drops him off in the middle of a huge, teeming mega-city of the future that's supposed to be ten times the size of New York City and just goes 'See ya! Go fight robots!' So he goes around punching out robots, most of whom look like they came from IKEA and were put together with an Allen wrench. I decided to mine the basic concept for a little black humor by re-imaging the scenario for the Zombies vs. Robots universe." — *Nancy A. Collins*

LINCOLN CRISLER is author, editor and reviewer as well as an active-duty soldier in the United States Army. His books include *Magick & Misery* and *Wild.* He is the editor of the dark-superhero anthology *Corrupts Absolutely?* He has served as a contributing writer for The Horror Library and Shroud magazine. Visit his website at www.lincolncrisler.info.

"For all the strengths inherent in a project like this, I feel the greatest weakness in a story based largely on monsters and machines is the potential for tales that lack the spark of humanity, something for the reader to relate to. Chris Ryall and his team have done an admirable job of avoiding this pitfall, and I made a conscious effort to do no less. In my mind, sharing the best and freshest story I could tell within the ZvR framework involved stepping outside of the conflict itself. The technology introduced in the very first issue of the comic provided a way to cement *Revision* firmly in the ZvR canon while allowing me to tell a uniquely human story." — *Lincoln Crisler*

FABIO LISTRANI (aka STB.01) was born in Rome in 1981. He is a digital artist and graphic designer who has several years of professional experience doing a variety of illustration work, including comic book covers, artwork for bands, concept art, and T-shirt designs. His personal work has been described as "visual cultural nomadism," borrowing symbolist motifs from Western and Eastern cultures and combining them with surreal, often grotesque SF or mystical themes. Through this original hybrid Fabio has received wide recognition and numerous awards.

"After working on some covers for *ZVR: Undercity*, the opportunity to illustrate the first ZvR prose anthology has been both an honor and a challenge. The marked variety of characters and situations that this incredible book contains is a testament to the great imaginations of the writers, so enjoy and...horns up!" — *Fabio Listrani*

BREA GRANT is sometimes a writer (*We Will Bury You, Suicide Girls*), sometimes an actress (*Heroes, Dexter, Halloween 2*) and all-the-time a nice person. Info on what she's doing right this second is at twitter.com/ breagrant, or breagrant.com.

"I wanted to touch on religion as a strong force in a time of human need. For better or for worse, religion plays a role in most major decisions around the globe—whether it's starting a war or in the way we mourn the death of a loved one. I wanted to put someone in one of the most difficult places possible by ripping away her community, family, and everything she knows, leaving her with her own thoughts. I wanted this person to deal with religion, love, gods and sanity all alone, separated from the raging violence outside. And who better to put in that position than a jaded, flippant teenage blogger named Pammi?"

— *Brea Grant*

NICHOLAS KAUFMANN, a Bram Stoker Award, Shirley Jackson Award, and Thriller Award finalist, is the author of *Chasing the Dragon* (ChiZine Publications), *General Slocum's Gold* (Burning Effigy Press), *Hunt at World's End* (as Gabriel Hunt), and the story collection *Walk in Shadows* (Prime Books). His fiction has appeared in Cemetery Dance, *The Mammoth Book of Best New Erotica Vol. 3, City Slab, The Best American Erotica 2007, Shivers V,* the forthcoming Dark Fusions anthology, and many more. He wrote monthly columns on the horror genre for *Fear Zone* and *The Internet Review of Science Fiction*, and has a chapter on how to plot short fiction in the Writers Digest book *On Writing Horror*. Visit his website at www.nicholaskaufmann.com.

"*The Tempest* may not be my most favorite Shakespeare play—that honor would probably go to *Macbeth* or *A Midsummer Night's Dream*—but it's definitely in my top five, and its rich blend of magic, mythology, and family dysfunction always struck a chord with me. So I thought if a damaged warbot had to wash ashore on any island, why not one of the most famous fictional islands of all? Of course, I've changed the names to protect the innocent, but aside from revisiting a play I love, writing 'The Sorcerer's Apprenticebot' also gave me a chance to explore an idea I found deeply amusing, and hope readers do, too—namely, forcing a wisecracking, thoroughly modern warbot to deal with unbelievably old-fashioned characters and their antiquated beliefs. In the end, it didn't seem like that much of a stretch. After all, if *Zombies vs. Robots* takes place in a world where heavy weapons tech and time-travel science co-exists with Amazons, minotaurs, mermen, molemen, etc., then surely there's a place for dear old Prospero, too." — *Nick Kaufmann*

Joe McKinney has been a patrol officer for the San Antonio Police Department, a homicide detective, a disaster mitigation specialist, a patrol commander, and a successful novelist. His books include the four part Dead World series, *Quarantined and Dodging Bullets*. His short fiction has been collected in *The Red Empire and Other Stories* and *Dating in Dead World and Other Stories*. For more information go to http://joemckinney.wordpress.com.

"I picked up a copy of *The Complete Zombies vs. Robots* at a convention and connected with it right away. As a police administrator for the San Antonio Police Department I'd been seeing more and more police activities getting automated, such as red light cameras and electronic imaging for large scale searches and analytics to predict future crime trends and hotspots. The same thing was happening in the military, with an increasing emphasis on drone warfare and engagement theaters being treated as digital environments, rather than traditional battlefields. The disconnect between our operational responsibilities and the lives we were impacting was really starting to bother me. And then I read *Zombies vs. Robots*, where humanity was fighting for its very existence, but not really doing any of its own fighting, and the concept just clicked for me.

"So, when they asked me to write something for *This Means War!* I knew what I wanted to do right away. With so much separation between humanity and the entities fighting over humanity's future, I knew I had to blur the lines between the participants. That's where 'Jimmy Finder' came from." —*Joe McKinney*

JAMES A. MOORE is an award winning author of over twenty novels, including the critically acclaimed Serenity Falls trilogy and the young adult Subject Seven series. His recurring anti-hero, Jonathan Crowley has appeared in half a dozen novels with more to come. You can find him at jamesamoorebooks.com, and he's normally lurking around Facebook and Twitter when he should be writing.

"I love the idea behind *Zombies versus Robots*, well, really, behind the zombie apocalypse in general, but I found the idea of an amusement park lost and abandoned in the aftermath particularly haunting. After I was asked about the possibility of being in the anthology I tried to go to sleep and spent several hours in bed being teased by the images that became 'The Last Imaginaut.'" —*James A. Moore*

YVONNE NAVARRO is a prolific author whose work has earned the Bram Stoker and numerous other awards. She's written about vampires, zombies, and the end of the world, plus played in the Buffy the Vampire Slayer universe as well as penned novels to go with a bunch of cool movies like *Hellboy*, *Elektra*, *Ultraviolet*, and others. Her most recent novels are *Highborn* and *Concrete Savior*, the first two books in her Dark Redemption series. Visit her at www.yvoneenavarro.com.

"What horror author doesn't want to write about zombies? Look at what really scares us—it's not vampires, or the wolfman, or some gilled creature rising out of the sea. It's the idea that the stranger on the sidewalk or your next door neighbor might, with no warning at all, become a mindless, starving monster that really hits home, both in the heart and the mind. Think about it: There you are, getting out of your car on a moonless night. You've worked late, you're exhausted and hungry; all you want to do is get your key in the door and get inside before...what? Suddenly the surrounding shadows are blacker than they've ever been, that previously inconsequential breeze is making every bush and tree branch rattle and scrape, and you realize there's not another living creature within blocks. Are you really sure something isn't moving in that dark entryway only three doors down…something with a gaping, drooling mouth that's ready to devour you?" — *Yvonne Navarro*

Norman Prentiss won the 2010 Bram Stoker Award for Superior Achievement in Long Fiction for *Invisible Fences,* now available as an e-book. He also won a 2009 Stoker for his short story, "In the Porches of My Ears," published in *Postscripts 18.* His latest book is *Four Legs in the Morning,* a collection of three linked stories. Other fiction has appeared in *Black Static, Commutability, Tales from the Gorezone, Damned Nation, Best Horror of the Year, The Year's Best Dark Fantasy and Horror,* and in three editions of the *Shivers* anthology series. His poetry has appeared in *Writer Online, Southern Poetry Review,* Baltimore's *City Paper,* and *A Sea of Alone: Poems for Alfred Hitchcock.* Visit him online www.norman-prentiss.com.

"I'm excited that this is my first zombie story and my first robot story. I really love the wild freedoms the ZvR universe allows for the writer—and I have to admit, though my natural tendency towards horror should make me favor the brain-eaters, I was surprised how much fun it was to imagine a teachbot character for the story. As setting, I chose an isolated school because I wanted to explore the idea of a few children being protected not simply from the zombies, but from awareness of the outbreak. If the world has essentially ended, it might be a gift for them not to know...although their ignorance could make them vulnerable, too."

— *Norman Prentiss*

Chris Ryall is the writer/co-creator of *Zombies vs Robots,* with artist Ashley Wood. He's also the creator of *Groom Lake,* a UFO-conspiracy comic created with artist Ben Templesmith. He is also the co-writer of a 2009 prose book about comics, *Comic Books 101.* As you can see by the many co- credits, he often enlists more talented help to bring his visions to life. Along those lines, he has also written comics alongside the likes of Stephen King, Joe Hill, Clive Barker, Richard Matheson, George Romero, and many esteemed folk he likes to think of as colleagues. When not enlisting others to help paint his fences with him, Ryall is also the Chief Creative Officer/Editor-in-Chief at IDW Publishing, where he spends his days…enlisting others to paint IDW's fences. He lives in San Diego with his wife, daughter, and single Eisner nomination.

RACHEL SWIRSKY is an award-winning short fiction writer. Her first collection, *Through The Drowsy Dark*, was published in 2010.

"I've always loved Greek mythology. I don't think the Amazons in this series are the Amazons of Hippolyta, but it's still fun to see what happens when you take an old legend and cross it with post-apocalyptic tech."

— *Rachel Swirsky*

SEAN TAYLOR writes short stories, novellas, novels, graphic novels and comic books. In his writing life, he has directed the "lives" of zombies, super heroes, goddesses, dominatrices, Bad Girls, pulp heroes, and yes, even frogs. Between horror movies and cartoons, that is. He's the former managing editor of Campfire (formerly Elfin) graphic novels, where he oversaw the publication of internationally distributed graphic novels based on classic literature, world literature and historical biographies, as well as original works.

"How could I say no to a project like *This Means War*? And since I grew up rural instead of city-boy, I couldn't resist taking both the zombies and robots out to the boonies to play country mouse. Of course this had the added benefits of robots made out of tractors and other farming machines, which I have to admit, sealed the deal. I mean, what's not to love about a zombie-slaughtering robot made from a combine?"

— *Sean Taylor*

STEVE RASNIC TEM is a multiple award-winning author who has published over 300 short stories in the areas of fantasy, science fiction, crime, and horror. His new novel, *Deadfall Hotel*, was recently published in limited hardcover by Centipede Press. The paperback and e-book versions will be out from Solaris Books in May.

"As a long-term fan of comics, robots, and zombies, I naturally jumped at an opportunity involving all three, especially if I could do something fast-moving and funny with it. And although this tale may seem somewhat (okay, extremely) far-fetched, it does rely heavily on three truths: 1) The University of Wisconsin-Madison *does* have a major robotics program which has worked closely with NASA, 2) Denver *has* seen a major influx of marijuana dispensaries and growers in recent years (and the author's own neighborhood *does* have more dispensaries than 7-11s), and 3) Everything *does* sound better in French." — *Steve Rasnic Tem*